BRENT LIBRARIES

Please return/renew this item
by the last date shown.
Books may also be renewed by
phone or online.
Tel: 0115 929 3388
On-line www.brent.gov.uk/libraryservice

Baldip Kaur

New Generation P **blishing**

Chapter 1

A pale moon slowly emerged from the shadow of the night and clothed the city of London with its lustrous rays. As it floated in the deep black sky, the round globe shone its sea of silvery moonlight over the city.

"Ishika, you only told me about your sister a few days ago - why haven't I met her till now?" Hetal asked, a frown on his face.

He had a good-looking face with dark hair, a lean athletic body and dark brooding eyes. He was standing near a table and bent down to pick up the rose petals that had fallen under the vase.

Ishika sat on a chair with her chin on her hands, looking pensively out of the window into the garden - her silky brown hair falling over her shoulder, her beige blouse bringing out the brown of her eyes.

She was feeling frustrated because she had not been able to penetrate the secrecy and mystery surrounding Vanita's whereabouts since she left home.

The garden was cloaked in darkness; however, in the glimmer of the moonlight she could see the shapes of the drooping clusters of tiny flower buds.

'They look so frail and defenceless that, as if, by folding their petals tightly around them, they are protecting themselves." she thought. "So much like Vanita."

"Hetal, I don't know." Ishika replied aloud angrily. "You know the state she was in when we bought her from hospital and I haven't seen her for two years - when she was thirteen Vanita ran away from home and does not remember what occurred during the period she was away. She doesn't even remember me – but I know something horrible happened to her. The world can be a

3

cruel place Hetal, and I know that although most of the people are aware of a child's vulnerability and react compassionately to it, so is, God forbid, the urge to exploit and corrupt their helplessness. I mean, come on, everyday there is some story about child abuse, kidnapping and child trafficking."

"Ishika, don't be so dramatic. She appears to be very mature for her age so must have been able to take care of herself, but I must say that for one so young she is very bitter and cynical."

Hetal ran his fingers through his hair, looking perplexed.

"I am not so sure that she was able to, Hetal, for she was so sweet and innocent I don't know how she coped in the outside world. But you are right she is now so cold and mature… I am puzzled and confused by her attitude too for although she is only fifteen years old, in some ways she behaves like an adult and in others like a child. But I am sure that underneath her hard exterior Vanita is still only a vulnerable young girl. And Hetal, please try and ignore her cynicism, for I am sure it is only a shield to cover some deep-rooted fear." Ishika's eyes searched Hetal's face.

"OK Ishika" he said softly. His frown disappeared and he smiled as he dug his hands into both pockets.

Ishika's thought of her sister's present bitter and remote nature for it battled with that of the one she had known and loved.

Vanita had been an innocent and pretty girl with a smooth skin that even at the tender age of thirteen had shown an all blooming potential for beauty. Her cheeks had been full and round, with eyes that twinkled with hidden laughter and shining thick black hair that was sometimes braided in thick plait. However, Ishika had not been able to understand the look of fear that skimmed across her face sometimes and recalled the claustrophobic atmosphere that had bound her family together – an atmosphere that had also threatened to destroy them.

She felt a mixture of emotions towards her sister. Sometimes she felt a pity that was akin to love, at times an aversion and fear that was akin to hate - at other times she felt a mature, parental and almost protective love but most of all she felt unhappy.

"Although we are sisters, she is like is a stranger to me." Ishika remarked unhappily.

Vanita had been passing the room and had overheard their conversation.

She had a sensitively cut nose and determined chin - her eyes were huge and made her heart-shaped face look bony and fragile. The clothes she was wearing emphasised her delicacy and fragility, however, although she looked frail, she had a feisty temper and force of character.

She sighed then went back into her bedroom, feeling tired and exhausted, as if someone had pulled a plug, draining all life from her. It was true what Ishika had said for she did not remember anything about the last couple of years. And just when she thought she might be unconsciously trying to suppress the memories, she had a momentary flashback.

These flashbacks were always shrouded in a thick cloud and she was confused, for blended in the mental confusion were dreams, no not even dreams for dreams one can recall – these were like echo of a dream which consisted of sounds and emotions - only all were so mixed up she could not untangle them. The tears that came into her eyes were more for her lost identity than the confusion she felt. For Vanita there was no 'me' just a past full of secrets - she felt invisible and was sure if she looked into a mirror it would not show her reflection.

However, the only thing Vanita knew for certain was

that the last couple of years had been important and were going to somehow set the pattern for the rest of her life - Life had been fathomless, unchartered and uncertain in its nature- maybe dire in its effects?

Being a sensitive girl she also sensed her sister's mystified affection and Hetal's animosity and even the darkness of the night seemed to be hostile, as if it was filled with invisible enemies ready to strike at her.

. . . .

Chapter 2

At that moment Ishika entered the room, plaiting her hair. Her soft brown eyes looked tender and she smiled warmly.

"Vanita, how are you feeling? Now, tell me, do you remember anything at all? If it helps, I have heard you whisper 'Fanish' in your sleep. Does that jog your memory?" Ishika asked hopefully. "You know everyone remembers something that is important, something that is dear to them?"

"Ishika, I don't remember anything of my time away from home, no Fanish no... nothing!" Vanita replied crossly. "I don't even remember you, although, Ishika, I do get these unfamiliar flashes. I can't make head or tail of them, but I know they must be linked to the missing part of my life somehow." Vanita sighed. "I feel as if I am in a nightmare and that soon I would wake up."

She sat on the bed and threw a cushion across the room.

"Hey steady on Vanita! I'll call Mum and Dad tomorrow; I am sure that Father will come as soon as they know...." Ishika flung her finished plait over her shoulder.

"Nnno, Ishika, No, please you are not to tell him…...!"

Vanita pleaded then looked distraught as she turned to look at Ishika strangely, as if it was she who was her enemy.

"Vanita, why are you so adamant about not notifying father that you are safe?" Ishika asked and shivered for she found Vanita's gaze disturbing.

"I don't know, Ishika, but I don't want you to tell him where I am." Vanita replied nervously.

However, as she turned to look at Ishika, the coldness

in her eyes was replaced by a warm look.

Ishika sighed, then smiled affectionately for she loved her younger sister.

"Vanita, do you need anything?" As Vanita shook her head, she added, kissing Vanita's cold cheek. "Then I'll wish you a good-night. Call me if you need anything."

"Ishika, please don't leave me alone," Vanita whispered, but Ishika had already left the room.

As soon as Ishika was in her room she turned to Hetal.

"Hetal, you know, although I feel I might not be able to accept the truth, I wonder where Vanita was and why she ran away from home?"

"What do you mean that you won't be able to accept the truth? Don't you trust her?"

Hetal pulled the curtains across the windows.

"I do, but although I want to uncover the shadow that has been in her life, I also know that usually when one searches for the truth one finds things more horrible and terrible than imagined."

"Ishika, I am sorry I have been so insensitive. I do realise what you must be going through." Hetal smiled wanly.

"I am sure that is nothing compared to what Vanita is going through." Ishika turned and closed her eyes.

Her eyes filled with tears, spilled out of her closed eyes and trickled down her cheeks as she recalled Vanita's eyes that seemed like two broken windows. The same look of vulnerability, confusion and despair were reflected on her sister's face now as when her parents had treated her unkindly, and once again she felt the familiar stirrings of compassion and guilt for she had not comforted her or made life easy for her.

The image rose before Ishika in mute unendurable reproach, for her silence had only made it easier for her parents to deny her sister a happy childhood.

Meanwhile, although Vanita was pleased and happy to be with her sister, she felt a certain kind of resentment towards her, a feeling that was all the more frustrating because she could not understand its underlying reason. She felt a mixture of confused emotions, but most of all she experienced fear, shame and guilt. At the same time, she felt restless with an unsatisfied need for love that was associated with a strong desire to remain out of sight...but out of sight from who or what? But the feeling that was the most overpowering was one of anger and retribution.

However, she was all the more disturbed and annoyed as this emotion was cloaked in a shroud. She was filled with feelings of distrust, hatred and suspicion - emotions that she realised perhaps stemmed from her childhood, but ones that had somehow intensified during the last few years? If only she could remember...

- - - -

Chapter 3

In Sussex two years earlier, on a magnificent morning in early spring, when the air was woven with the birds of spring and the world was thrilling to the onset of summer, Vanita stared at her father, taken aback by his fury.

"P.p.papa no! Please don't hit me!" Vanita's face showed her fear and confusion.

"Then do as you are told." Devesh, her father yelled, creasing his eyebrows.

There were ridges round his nose and his mouth deepened in anger.

"Don't argue, Vanita, go to your room at once." her father started undoing the belt on his trousers, for he required little cause to demonstrate the stinging power of his belt.

He looked menacingly at Vanita who was cowering against the wall, then buckled his belt and sauntered towards the lounge, whistling. He had two daughters, and although he loved his elder daughter, Ishika and had sent her to a good boarding school, he had resented Vanita from the day she was born. And for no reason that he could explain, the sight of the child infuriated Devesh, and his whole being had revolted against the innocent feel of her small warm fingers when they curled around his hand.

And although she grew to be a chubby little baby, his feelings towards her did not change and he ignored Vanita as much as possible.

However, when she was three years old, Devesh suddenly insisted he put her to bed at night. Esha had been only too grateful for this change of heart for her health had been deteriorating. And later, when Vanita was seven years old, she left all the household chores to her whilst she lay in bed all day long.

"Vanita, I am going out. I will be back in time for dinner with Arun."

Devesh peered through the door then slammed the front door behind him as Esha entered the kitchen.

She was thirteen years old but she was not allowed to go out or see her friends outside school. Vanita was a bright girl, but if she demonstrated any kind of curiosity her parents criticised her for trying to be clever and if she was docile they accused her of being sly. The only time they were happy with her was when she did the housework.

She sighed, and there swept over Vanita an intense loneliness that only a defenceless child feels. She felt hurt, a hurt that was not only caused by fear but the betrayed expectation of rejected love.

"Mum? When is Ishika going to be home?" Vanita ran to her mother.

"Vanita, please don't shout, I have a headache!" Esha replied, massaging her forehead. "And I don't know, I presume when Ishika has her holidays."

"But she is on holiday." Vanita exclaimed. "And why do I have to do all the work in the house?"

"Oh, yes, I forgot, she was going on a tour with her school friends during the holidays. And as for you doing the housework, you know I am weak and ill, and it is your duty to help. Do stop pestering me, child! Ask your father when he comes home."

"Mum, you know that would be a waste of time, he never talks to me for he always ignores me."

What she did not tell her mother was that he would come to her room at night, and that she had come to fear bedtime for her father had started hurting her.

Vanita felt she could not tolerate it anymore and wanted to confide in her mother, but when she realised

11

the depth of her mother's selfishness, her suffering remained unvoiced and unnoticed.

It was at this time that she needed Ishika to talk to, however, when she realised that was unlikely, she returned to the familiar feelings of loneliness, isolation and despair, and soon they became her family and friends.

▪ ▪ ▪ ▪

Chapter 4

The dreary day, the rain, grey sky and gusts of wind blowing through the city shaped Vanita mood.

"Why can't I go to a boarding school like Ishika?" Vanita repeated, tears in her eyes.

"And who do you think will help me? Why are you always so selfish and ungrateful? Vanita, what has come over you today?" Esha answered irritably.

She looked at her daughter angrily for she had been hoping for a quiet afternoon. Maybe Vanita was right, she needed peace and quiet and if Vanita was at boarding school…! She would talk to Devesh about sending her away, but quickly pulled herself together as she realised she would have to do the housework.

"We want you with us, Vanita." she tried to reassure her daughter in a softer tone. "We'd be lonely with both of you away - Now I am going to bed – this headache!"

She pressed her sari in place as she rose from the sofa.

"Vanita, I don't think I will be able to cook any dinner – can you do your homework and see that your father gets his dinner?"

She kissed Vanita on the forehead as she walked past her.

Vanita wiped the tears from her eyes as she looked at her mother's receding figure for the only time she showed her any affection was when she needed something done.

Her mother poked her head from around the corner.

"Oh, I forgot to tell you. Arun Uncle is coming for dinner. I do not know if his wife will be accompanying him, but if she does, can you give me a shout? I do not think it will look nice if I do not come down to dinner."

Esha disappeared into her room as Vanita sighed and walked to her room.

Having completed her homework, Vanita put her books away and prepared to go downstairs to the kitchen. Even under the best of circumstances, adolescents suffer from low self-esteem, feelings of insecurity and inferiority complex that are all a process of maturing. Vanita too was confused at the complexities of life and needed her parent's approval and appreciation, which is every child's entitlement.

'I am only 13 years of age.' she looked out of the kitchen window wistfully.' I would like to go out with my friends...maybe my parents hate me because I am ugly!'

"Hello, I am home!" Vanita heard her father's voice in the living room. "Vanita, where is your mother?" he asked as Vanita came out of the kitchen.

"She has one of her headaches and is lying down." Vanita replied.

"That headache again!" Devesh snorted. "As soon as she knows somebody is coming, it is surprising how the headache appears! Anyway, Vanita, did your Mother tell you that Arun is coming for dinner? Oh, by the way, his wife will come with him."

"Yes, mother knows for she told me." Vanita replied. "But I will let her know about his wife."

"Vanita, after you have given us dinner I want you to go up and go to bed – I will come up and tuck you in."

"Dad, I am not a child anymore, I don't need to be tucked in."

A black weight moved from her forehead and settled in the pit of her stomach making Vanita sick.

"Don't argue with me, Vanita." Devesh snarled.

However, his scowl soon turned into a smile and he rubbed Vanitas's hand.

"You haven't told anybody about our secret, have you? Not even your mother, I hope, for I will get very angry if you do."

"N...no I haven't." Vanita muttered.

The injustice of it all felt like a tight band of frustration around her heart and she felt she needed to make a gesture of rebellion.

"Father, why can't I go away to school like Ishika?"

"You are not going anywhere." Devesh growled at her." You stay with us."

"But Dad I...! I am not doing well in this school; in fact, the teachers want to see you about it."

"Vanita, your problem is that you don't concentrate hard enough. You used to be very good in your studies, what happened? Don't waste my time, Vanita, you better hurry up and finish your work." Devesh raised his voice and stomped out of the room.

Vanita decided she had no choice but to escape, so thought that after serving food, instead of going to bed, she would run away.

'I'll go stay with Fanish, I am sure he will look after me.' Suddenly she smiled.

She trusted him for he had helped her regain her self-esteem and was confident he would help her.

There was a smile on her lips as Vanita went about the kitchen, remembering the day she had first met Fanish.

The green leaves of summer had dried, shrivelled and fallen as she had walked home through the park after school.

Fanish had been strolling in the park with the smooth walk of a predator when he bumped into her.

▪ ▪ ▪ ●

Chapter 5

"Oops sorry! Hi there, I hope I have not hurt you?" Slowly he bent to look at her and smiled. "my name is Fanish".

"No I am fine thank you." Vanita looked up startled, then smiled shyly. "Hi my name is Vanita."

Fanish was wearing a white suit and shoes, white silk shirt, with a bright tie (which Vanita was to later learn was his customary ensemble). His hair was greasy and slicked down, and a huge diamond ring on his finger caught Vanitas's eye as it gleamed in the light.

Following that meeting, Fanish would wait daily outside her school and they would walk home together. It was a time when Vanita would savour the pleasure of the spring air and the sense of freedom it bought. Fanish, with his gentleness and kindness, had been like a seed that was dropped on the soil of Vanitas's oppressive life. He was always so attentive and considerate, that Vanita hoped that this quality would represent hope for her future, a future that was not dominated by fear and betrayal. And as so often happens with neglected children that are made to feel loved and safe, she blossomed in confidence and was sure that this was the beginning of a sincere friendship.

Once Vanita had made up her mind to leave, she finished the house work quickly and was laying out the bowls when Arun walked in the door.

"How is Vanita, my little beauty?" he asked with a wink. "That hair-band suits you!"

He patted Vanita on the behind and she could smell alcohol on his breadth as she cowered against the wall.

"How is Mitali?" Vanita's voice quivered as she tried to change the subject.

Mitali was Arun's daughter and the same age as

Vanita.

However, any pretence at politeness or attempt to control Vanita's resentment was going to be tossed aside by her if Arun continued to behave vulgarly. He was always groping her and she hated it.

"Has she come with you, can I get you anything?"

"No, I don't want anything; I only came to the kitchen because I wanted to be alone with you."

Arun winked again as he walked out of the door with an empty glass and Vanita breathed a sigh of relief.

As soon as Arun had left, her father walked in, a frown on his face.

"What have you been talking to him about?" he snarled.

"N.nothing, Dad!"

"He was in the kitchen too long for a 'nothing' as you say it! But just remember, I do not want you to talk to anybody."

"But he is a friend of yours, Dad. And anyway, we were only talking about Mitali and…"

"Oh, well I don't believe it, you are not even friends with her! Anyway, can you lay out the dinner now?" Devesh slammed the kitchen door as he left.

Vanita sighed knowing that her father's possessive behaviour had nothing to do with love. Moreover, Vanita felt she could never love or be loved, for as Fanish had so often told her, one must first respect and accept and love oneself.

She felt unclean and guilty and that it was only Fanish who was alive whilst everybody else was a shadow in comparison!

Twilight had first trembled on the tip of evening before gradually sinking into the black shadow of night.

▪ ▪ ▪

Chapter 6

Vanita closed the door softly behind her as she tiptoed out of the house whilst her parents, Arun and his wife laughed and talked, oblivious to the fact that she was running away.

As she looked back to wave a silent goodbye, she saw a tree silhouetted against the house, its bear arms reaching the sky.

After getting lost a few times, Vanita finally located Fanish's house. It was covered with stone tiles and the garden was well kept - with a freshly mown lawn, flowers and trees. There was a faint light emanating from beneath the window and the light, to Vanita, looked as if was a firefly caught in cobweb.

Vanita breathed deeply - like a watered plant drawing up food for its strength and vitality. She walked to the bottom of the house and entered through a broken gate, then rang the bell apprehensively.

After some time, Fanish opened the door in his dressing gown. His voice was drowsy and his eyes were bloodshot as he first looked at Vanita then over his shoulder.

"Vanita, what are you doing here!" he exclaimed, running his hand through his tousled hair.

However, seeing Vanita's forlorn and sad face, he put his fingers to his lips and ushered her in to the lounge.

"Who is it, Fanish?" Vanita heard a voice call out sleepily.

"A friend of mine from work – go to sleep Akshita."

"Now, tell me what the matter is, Vanita, what are you doing here at this time of night?"

Fanish moved his hand to his brow and with the

middle finger rubbed his brow as if trying to smooth away the furrows.

Vanita started crying as she stood with her fists pressed tightly together in front of her waist.

"Fanish, I can't stand it anymore, I won't stay at home any longer."

"Hush, hush." Fanish put his arms around Vanita and smoothed her thick hair. "Nothing can be that bad!"

"It is!" exclaimed Vanita. "I cannot and will not go back home! You know my father, I told you about him and...can I stay with you for a while?" Vanita pleaded.

"I don't know...my wife...! However, although you cannot stay here you can stay with a friend of mine – he lives alone and..."

"No, I do not want to stay with anyone else." Vanita's eyes flew open with fright.

So far, all the men she had known had hurt her in one way or another, consequently, apart from Fanish, she felt she could not trust anybody.

"Vanita, you realise you have no choice, unless you want to go back home? Aren't you grateful that I am willing to take responsibility for your welfare?"

Fanish's jaws clenched tightly and his thick brows pulled low over his nose.

"Of course I am, Fanish, but I only feel safe with you, and if you cannot..." Vanita said looking miserable." But you are right, I cannot go back home, my father well. you know, and I have a selfish mother who only thinks of herself. Home should be a place which is warm and comfortable, above all where I would be safe and protected but anyway, you have been kind so yes, I will stay at your friend's place." She nodded her head reluctantly.

"That's my girl! I'll phone Aditya." he patted Vanita on the head.

He picked up a phone, dialled and spoke softly into

the receiver, nothing of which Vanita could make sense of.

After re-placing the receiver, he wrote on a piece of paper and gave her some money.

"This is the address, Vanita, it is not far from here." he said handing them to Vanita. "Take a taxi, and don't worry, Aditya will look after you. And remember, now that you have left home, you have to behave like an adult."

Vanita took the piece of paper together with the money and left. As she walked out, she wondered how she would manage, for all Fanish's confidence in her, she was only a child floundering in the world of adult quicksand.

- - - -

Chapter 7

Aditya looked out of the window impatiently. The rays of the moonlight cast a dim light on the district, making everything look too real for his liking, for the rays were swathing his fantasies with an importance they would not have had in darkness.

He had not been able to understand fully what Fanish had said on the phone, but Fanish had told him about Vanita previously, and how it was only a matter of time before she would run away from home and turn to him for help.

It was strange, thought Aditya, how Fanish had this elusive quality and charm that made all the girls trust him.

'But that just suits me fine." Aditya grinned as he heard the doorbell.

He opened the door and saw a girl who looked younger and prettier than Fanish's description of her.

She was about thirteen years old, had a small waist, boyish hips and long legs. Her thick hair ended at her shoulders and was held in place by a black band. Her face had a honey tint and her features were in perfect place, wide mouth, clean jaw and delicate ears, whilst her eyes had a downward slant that made them look sad.

Aditya was struck by her smile and found it rather beguiling. It was not her childish attire but something else, mysterious and bewitching, that fascinated Aditya. Although she looked confused, she had a quality of assurance, of self-confidence, endearing seduction and at the same time of utter sadness.

"Aditya?" Vanita asked anxiously. When Aditya nodded his head she continued. "My name is Vanita and....."

"Yes, Fanish phoned me that you would be staying

the night. Come in, my dear." Aditya took her arm and ushered her in.

As he looked at her trim figure, his dry lips moved over each other and the light in his eyes darkened as his lids drooped slightly.

"Here, come and sit; can I get you anything to drink?"

The room seemed moon-touched, distorting shapes and images of the room.

"N.no, I am fine." Vanita answered, yawning." Can you show me to my room, please, I would like to go to sleep?"

She was sitting nervously on the sofa twisting her hands, wondering why Aditya was looking at her so strangely.

"In a while, talk to me first. Fanish has told me about you."

"Oh? But thank you for letting me stay, I actually only need somewhere to stay tonight – tomorrow I will look for some work and another place to stay."

"Don't worry, all in good time."

Aditya sat on the sofa beside her and put his arm around her.

"Now tell me, you look terribly sad – Fanish mentioned that you had run away from home?"

"Y. Yes!" Vanita started sobbing.

Aditya moved closer and one of his hands was partly under Vanita's armpit and partly on her heaving young breast.

"There, there, don't worry, a beautiful girl like you? You just have to be nice to me and who knows...?"

His broad powerful wrist with a gold bracelet moved lightly across her breast.

Vanita slapped Aditya and rose, her eyes flashing with anger.

"Y...you bastard! I'll tell Fanish – he won't be happy about this! Where is your phone?"

Aditya gave a chuckle. "Do you really think that Fanish does not know what I plan to do with you? You really are very gullible, you know, that is precisely why he sent you to me."

"That is not true." Vanita was indignant. "Fanish is a nice man who is only helping me out as a friend."

"Of course he is helping you – he is also helping himself!"

"What do you mean?" Vanita's voice trembled.

"Well, we have this understanding, Fanish and me, he sends me a girl and I pay him for it. If you behave yourself he will also give you a cut of the action - see, that way everybody is happy." Aditya looked smug as his eyes narrowed.

"How dare you talk like that about your friend? Fanish will never do that to me, never."

There was fire in Vanita's eyes and her voice was trembling. Behind her look of bewilderment was one of deep dislike.

Aditya looked at her in admiration. His was a turbulent nature, out to conquer and dominate and he felt challenged by Vanita who started crying for she felt betrayed yet again. She ran towards the door but found it locked.

"Let me go!" She cried. "You have made a mistake and…"

She had hoped Aditya to be a kind man but now saw him only as Fanish's instrument - entrusted to abuse her innocence.

"There has been no mistake, darling." Aditya walked towards her. "I have paid the money in advance to Fanish – you can settle your business with him."

He moved his lips one over the other and stared at Vanita with a hard cold look in his eyes.

Vanita drew away from Aditya her face expressing fear and repulsion.

"I want to go to go home!" Vanita repeated again as she cowered against the wall.

"You can go home, but not before I get what I want." Aditya laughed a harsh grating sound.

Vanita marvelled at how quickly his kindness and charm abated when he realised she would not submit to him - so he dragged Vanita screaming and yelling towards the bedroom.

She cursed the day she had met Fanish. He seemed so gentle and understanding and had successfully succeeded in gaining Vanita's trust. Had all his kindness been an act? He had seemed so genuine and sincere, was he planning to exploit her all the while?

Vanita struggled with Aditya in utter and complete terror, frightened as only a girl forced with the unknown would. Vanita recoiled from it and prepared to fight to protect herself.

However, Aditya caught hold of her wrists tightly, but although Vanita tried to wriggle from his grasp, he was too strong for her.

When she finally had no energy to fight back, she had no choice but to close her eyes in pain, and the pain of hurt and betrayal was not only in her body but also in her heart.

- - - -

Chapter 8

The following morning the sun nudged the horizon to let it through, and then gently spilled its crimson colour across the sky, as if it wished to bandage a wound with its glow.

As its rays shone through the window, Vanita lay in bed bruised and crying. Her hair was damp and spread across the pillow, her girl's young body outlined under the sheet.

She lay very still, but as the tears began to roll down her cheeks, she uttered a whimpering sound of utter defeat. She pulled the sheet under her chin and closed her eyes, conscious of Aditya's head at the crook of her neck. She made a feeble attempt to get up but did not have any energy to push him away.

Aditya finally heaved his body from her and she felt as if a mighty weight had been lifted from her delicate young body.

"Good-morning, Vanita! How are you feeling this morning?"

Aditya put his arms around her and smiled for it gave him a sadistic sort of pleasure and power to see the fear in her eyes.

At that moment the door-bell rang, giving Vanita an opportunity to push Aditya away and drag herself to the edge of the bed, one hand covering her face and the other holding the sheet around her, ready to fight back if Aditya dared touch her again.

However, all the dark fiery spirit disappeared as Aditya spoke.

"That must be Fanish; I'll be back, my sweet, just as soon as I get rid of him."

He hurriedly wore his dressing gown and was tying the belt as he opened the bedroom door. As he brushed his hair with his hand, he opened the door to find an impatient Fanish at his doorstep.

"What took you so long?" Fanish asked irritably in a loud voice.

"Fanish," Aditya exclaimed, flustered "Come in, I was hoping it might by you."

Vanita had hurried downstairs seething with anger.

As soon as he saw her he smiled and winked.

" Hello, Vanita," Fanish grinned faintly then turned towards Aditya. "Aditya I trust you had a pleasant evening?"

Fanish's lips moved into a twisted smile as he looked at Aditya for he saw evidence of a struggle. There was a long scratch on Aditya's cheek and his right hand had unmistakable teeth marks on it.

However, as Vanita looked at him she found that he had lost his earlier fascination. Fanish's smile, which like always, was so perfectly in place, was absent in his eyes, which now looked cold and sinister.

"Fanish, how could you do this to me? I had faith in you; I trusted you and you…!"

Vanita started sobbing and she gazed at Fanish like a wild doe in agony. There was bitterness in her voice and accusation in her eyes.

"I what? I helped you – gave you shelter when you needed it …" Fanish answered angrily.

"No Fanish, you did not help me, you helped yourself." Vanita interrupted him. "You sold me to your friend. I never thought you to be that kind of person or I would not have befriended you, for I am not the sort of girl that…"

"Well, now you are, anyway, what kind of girl do you mean? I have helped a friend in need get a job."

Fanish grinned as the rage on his face was taken over

by a fiendish mixture of laughter.

He took out a wad of notes from his pocket and handed them to Vanita.

"You call this a job?" Vanita cried

Nevertheless, she eyed the money keenly, for she realised the injustice and hopelessness of her situation - she could not go back to a father who abused her and a mother who manipulated and blackmailed her emotionally.

Soon her tears stopped and she began to think realistically. Like a spring flower pushing through the hard winter, Vanita began to come alive again, and as she did, she knew the days of patience could be over, as could be the submissiveness that had drained her at home. She did not mind forfeiting the childhood she could not control for an adulthood she could.

She sat down, palms itchy with nervous tension as she willed herself to keep her mind steady.

Suddenly money became important because it involved her livelihood and basic security. She would have no financial problems and afterwards, as soon as possible, she would escape from this sordid life.

Overnight, it seemed she had matured, but her maturity had come at a cost. The affectionate and warm Vanita became cold and cynical, and this detachment was reflected in her eyes.

The expression on her face sent a shiver down Fanish's spine, nevertheless he was pleased that Aditya was happy with her – he had other friends who liked young girls especially the man who they called 'the Ravager'.

■ ■ ■ ■

Chapter 9

Fanish recalled the first time he had seen 'the Ravager'. Subhi, his friend, had insisted he come.
"Fanish, come and with me and see for yourself what kind of monster he is. The only thing is he does not want anybody to see him, in fact you will have to stay back. They went to' The 'Ravager's' meeting place where Fanish saw a bony and slender girl of about twelve, lying unclothed on top of a bed, eyes half closed as if in sleep.

Her face and neck had been deeply scratched and bruised and the angle of her seemed wrong to Fanish. One of her young breasts had been torn off as if by teeth and there was blood on the sheets

"What the…" Fanish had spluttered, turning to Subhi and trying to pull his mask off. "Call the ambulance or something, quick!"

"Shh, Fanish, please keep quiet, he must not know you are here!" Subhi whispered

The 'Ravager' threw a pad of notes at Subhi.. "Forget what you have seen and keep your mouth shut, there will be more if you do as I say."

"But why are you doing this to a young helpless girl"? Subhi asked.

"You know why! And why are you asking me this today?"

Fanish's body had been soaked with perspiration as he saw the 'Ravager' sitting, shaking with spasms of pleasure as he looked at the young girl.

"Girls disgust me; she was beautiful but she had to be punished for her mother's sins." replied the Ravager. "It is only very young girls who are pure of thought.

As they left, Subhi turned to him, "Fanish, my friend, if you send me some of the girls to give to him, I can give you a cut of the money. You saw how generous he is!"

Fanish quickly agreed and the guilt and shame he had initially felt were surpassed by his greed, so he became accustomed to seeing the enjoyment on the 'Ravager's' masked face as he twisted wires into young delicate wrists and ankles and heard them scream.

He was jolted out of his reverie by Vanita's voice.

"Can I have the money?" Vanita muttered under her breadth, stretching out her hand.

But before he handed her the money, Aditya whispered in Fanish's ear.

"Yes, of course you can." Fanish laughed. "Vanita, Aditya would like to spend the night with you again."

The sound of his laughter was too subtly filled with malice to be detected by a stranger, but Vanita was familiar with it by now. She immediately withdrew her hand and cursed Fanish.

There had been a time when she would have done anything for Fanish – but he had only chained her to him with his false sincerity and kindness.

'I'm going to get my revenge somehow." she vowed. "I don't know where or how, but I will.'

Aloud she said. "I will stay some other time but I would like to leave now, I'll check into a hotel for the night or…"

"You are a young girl Vanita, no, you are to stay with Aditya. And I will decide where you are to live." Fanish replied firmly, catching hold of her wrist.

"Why, Fanish, it is not as if you or Aditya love me." Vanita cried, trying to free her wrist. "I might be a young girl but I know that there are many shades of wanting, and as there are shades of love so also there are many forms of control…. I should know!"

Fanish laughed – a sound so harsh and cruel that Vanita winced as if she had beaten by her father's belt.

Vanita shrivelled in her skin as she felt the squeeze of his fingers around her wrist and the brittle tone of his words made her wince with anguish and anger.

"N...no! I don't want to stay with Aditya." Vanita pleaded, running her tongue over her lips for they felt dry and sore.

She glared at Fanish fiercely and looked around her like a trapped animal, but her humiliation had given her courage to voice her anger.

At the moment the doorbell rang again and as Aditya went to answer it, Vanita pleaded again with Fanish.

"Fanish, I thought you at least understood me, I don't want to stay here, I don't like Aditya."

Although her voice trembled with anger, there was a slight look of fear on her face.

Fanish had turned from her indifferently, for now he could be himself and did not have to act to win her trust just so he could take her away from her family. He had successfully taken her down the road that all girls initially said they did not want to go, then were tempted to stay on that very path.

Fanish did not realise that to force a child to become an adult before she was ready was immoral, nor knew the difference between a willingly accepted self and surrender. He expected a complete surrender of a girl before there was a real self to submit.

■ ■ ■ ■

Chapter 10

"Oh, stop crying Vanita!" Fanish growled handing her a handkerchief "that might be one of Aditya's friends!"

Aditya entered the room followed by a young and graceful girl.

"Vanita, this is Gazal – Gazal this is Vanita and of course you know Fanish!" Aditya made the introductions.

"Yes, I know Fanish." Gazal answered in a soft voice and smiled briefly.

However, her eyes narrowed as she looked at Vanita and her eyebrows moved upward from under heavy eyelids that shaded her eyes. Gazal realised she must be the new girl Fanish had been talking about, for although Vanita had been crying she noticed she was pretty, very young and slim.

However, the way Aditya was looking at her made Gazal envious, and an expression of jealousy flickered in her eyes for a moment. However, it was quickly replaced by a friendly look, for she was used to Fanish's girls who entered their organisation then disappeared.

The seasons came and went and each season brought new girls, for sex trafficking was made easier via the internet, corrupt officials, and vulnerable girls, vulnerable as Gazal had once been. Girls that were long legged and lithe, with fresh eager faces and bright faces. However, she always got a feeling of poignant sadness as she saw their youth.

"Gazal, I am glad you have come at this point, we need your help." Fanish smiled as he looked at Gazal.

"Okay, so how can I help?" Gazal asked as she sat on the chair with a sinuous grace of movement.

Gazal sat looking rather like a small elegant black cat, dark, soft voiced, with big dark eyes. Although she sat quietly, Vanita sensed some underlying intense emotion was raging within her.

"Actually you can. We were discussing about where Vanita should stay and I thought it best if she could stay with you for a few days."

"But there is no room, my flat is too small!" Gazal reminded.

Small and graceful, she leaned back in her chair, her eyes occasionally moving from face to face.

"It's all right I will find my own place!" Vanita exclaimed sharply.

"That is absolutely out of the question!" Fanish said firmly. "Now, I must go – Aditya, Gazal see that she stays with one of you!" He strode out of the room.

Vanita realised immediately he was the figure authority so ran after him.

"Fanish, I have decided that I want to go back to my parents!"

"After what you hinted about your father, I can put two and two together." There was a sneer of his face." Would you rather be with him or live on your own – independent and with lots of money, all in exchange for a few favours?"

Gazal had also followed them to the landing and he turned towards her.

"Gazal, explain to her the situation – nobody ever leaves me. And see to it that she has proper clothes and anything else she needs to make her look presentable."

When the position of Fanish was questioned he immediately took control and adopted an attitude of absolute authority.

He opened the door and walked out, slamming it after him, and with him, hope and trust disappeared from Vanita's life. Fanish had abused her faith in him and she could not keep overlook that, not could she forgive him for it.

Planted, nurtured, blossomed, dead – and not a month had passed since she met Fanish. Yesterday she had a friend, today the friendship she had valued most was gone - along with her innocence.

■ ■ ■ ■

Chapter 11

"Ah, here we are," Gazal parked the car outside a flat." "Fanish is right, you know, you are his property now, and he would go to any lengths to stop you from escaping. And I mean any lengths, for many girls have tried and failed."

"Gazal, I have no intention of remaining under his control!"

"I am just warning you, Vanita, we are both Fanish's victims and nothing or no-one can protect us." Gazal was not wary of Vanita anymore, but now felt concerned about her for she had overheard Fanish taunting Vanita about her father.

After having become part of Fanish's organisation, she had seen a slimier side to men, consequently had become cold and heartless. She had changed from an innocent girl to a hard and bitter woman, and each succeeding year had left its mark on her – a settling of hardness, which accumulated like the annual rings on a tree.

By the time she was fifteen, Gazal knew she was irresistible to men, but she only felt contempt and scorn for the men she attracted. However, she had learnt to flaunt her sexual attractions in the most delicate ways with rarely a stir in herself.

Vanita looked around her as they walked towards the house.

"Thanks for your concern, Vanita, I will have to learn to fend for myself."

Although she had felt emotionally confused and revolted at Fanish's suggestion, she began to concentrate on the positive things that her new life could bring about.

She would have her independence, as Fanish had pointed out and with the money, she could buy everything that had been denied her, save and one-day escape from Fanish's clutches.

However, with her new-found maturity, she realised that it could not purchase the one thing she needed the most – Love.

"Would you like me to show you to your room so you can freshen up or would you like a cup of tea first?" Gazal asked, as they entered her flat.

"I'll have a cup of tea first, thank you."

"Coming up, just make yourself comfortable." Gazal went out of the room.

When she returned with a tray of hot tea and some sandwiches, she found Vanita sitting curled on the sofa with her face in her hands

"Feeling better?" Gazal asked, handing her a cup and a plate of sandwich.

Vanita did not answer but ate the sandwich quickly for she had not realised she was hungry. And each sip of the hot, strong and sweet tea seemed to give her new life and strength.

"How did you meet Fanish?" She asked finally, finishing her tea.

"Oh, on my birthday. I did not know then that Fanish constructs lie upon lie like a Chinese basket and that even his smile is masked by a lie." Gazal replied with feeling. "I was neglected by my parents but now I know he only targets vulnerable girls – he normally waits outside the school gates or…."

"Yes I know, that is how we met, but I am sorry I bought up the subject for it seems to have upset you."

"It's all-right, Vanita." Gazal whispered, brushing her hands with the back of her hand as she thought of her parents and how she had been lured and ensnared by Fanish.

■ ■ ■ ■

Chapter 12

Gazal was walking along after school feeling miserable for her parents had forgotten that today was her birthday.

In the morning she had been excited and had rushed downstairs, expecting that at least on this day at least her parents would hug her, give her a birthday present, and even throw her a party. But there had been no change in their routine.

"I'm late, Gazal hurry up!" Nayan, her mother hurriedly brushed her hair then sat on the bed to wear her boots.

"Gazal, hurry up," she said again as she entered the kitchen. "Hurry up or you will be late for school! I am late for a very important meeting and you have not even had your breakfast as yet!"

"Yes, Mum," Her heart sank as Gazal miserably poured herself some milk and buttered some toast." But you know I hate going to school."

"You know you have too, so hurry up; you can eat your toast in the car. Your father's gone to get the car – see that you finish your milk in two minutes."

Nayan disappeared upstairs, leaving Gazal desolate in the kitchen.

"Ah, there you are at last!"

As she heard her father's voice Gazal looked up expectantly.

Sual entered rubbing his hands with the cold.

"Gosh, it is cold out there. Where is Nayan? I thought she wanted to leave immediately? Have you made her late by your dilly-dallying?"

Gazal shook her head. "She has gone upstairs; I think she forgot her bag."

She should have known better than to expect her father to remember so Gazal quietly slung her knapsack

36

over her shoulder.

Gazal was an only child. Her mother held an important position in a firm and her father was a lawyer - and not only were both successful in their careers but led a busy social life. They made her feel she was a hindrance to their ambition so she often wondered why they had bothered to have a child.

Nayan came rushing down the stairs; in one hand she had a mobile whilst with the other she was smoothing her hair.

"Sual, have you brought the car to the front and removed the ice from it?" When Sual nodded, she switched off the mobile and quickly put on her coat and gloves.

"And Gazal, I might be a little late today." she added.

"And so will I" Sual said getting into the car. "Gazal, be sure to lock the door when you come home and do not open the door to anyone. You have the keys, don't you?"

"Yes, Gazal replied in a small voice.

Today was her thirteenth birthday and it was supposed to be an important landmark of her life. All the children in her class had proud parents who celebrated their children's 13th birthday, but she was going to be spending it alone.

"Remember what we told you," Sual reminded her as he sped off.

She had been so miserable that when she walked home from school, she did not notice a man walking beside her.

"And why are you looking so sad?" His round kind face beamed at her.

He was wearing a white suit and his hair was shiny and glossy with gel.

Gazal gave a start but did not answer for she had been told not to speak to any strangers.

"Look," the man persisted with a smile. "I can

understand why you do not want to speak to me, you don't know me. But you look so sad and there's no harm in talking, is there?" He saw the tears in Gazal's eyes. "Let me buy you a cup of coffee, there's a café nearby."

"What is your name?" he asked gently. "My name is Fanish.

"Gazal," Gazal replied in a husky whisper, a catch in her throat. She stood gaping at Fanish, her shining brown eyes deep and soft with gratitude.

However, every nerve in her body tightened with a desire to be silent – but as Fanish gazed at her, she forgot her well-honed instinct to distance herself and remain aloof.

"So, Gazal, what do you say to a cup of coffee?"

Gazal nodded her head, after all it was her birthday and she did not want to go home to an empty house, at least not on this day.

"So would you like to tell a friend what is bothering you?" Fanish asked as they sat at the table waiting for the coffee to be served.

"It's nothing." Gazal muttered.

However, her big eyes filled with tears as she placed both elbows on the table.

"Then how come there are tears in those beautiful eyes?"

Gazal had always considered herself to be plain and ugly, so was surprised when Fanish expressed admiration. The coffee and sandwiches arrived and Gazal discovered with surprise she was hungry, so quickly reached for a sandwich, her unhappiness forgotten.

Fanish watched silently as she ate and as soon as she was finished, looked up guiltily, noticing Fanish had not eaten.

"I'm sorry, Fanish, I think I have eaten all the sandwiches."

Gazal felt ashamed of her manners for she did not want to lose his friendship so quickly. She had come to like him; he was so kind, gentle and considerate.

"I wasn't hungry anyway." Fanish replied. "Tell me, are you still feeling unhappy or was it only the hunger?" He chuckled.

Gazal decided to tell him. "Today is my birthday and …"

Her words were as inaudible as a gentle breeze and her fingers curled around the cup of coffee.

"Happy Birthday! But isn't that an occasion to rejoice?"

"Not for my parents, it is not." Gazal replied bitterly. "They didn't even remember it was my birthday, let alone my thirteenth birthday." Gazal started sobbing.

"There, there!" Fanish handed her his handkerchief. "Parents are like that sometimes. I am sure they love you anyway."

"Love me? Did you say love me?" Gazal was angry. "When will they show their love if not today? It is always like this, day after day. They are too busy in their lives and I am just a burden for them. I wish I could run away, not that that would make any difference to them."

Fanish rose. "Look I have to go, but I will walk home with you, but can I see you tomorrow? Here?"

Gazal got up reluctantly, loath to go home, but happy that she had made a friend.

"Yes, okay." She answered

"And let's keep this between you and me, shall we?" Fanish put a finger under her chin. "It shall be our secret. And don't worry, everything will work out just fine."

Gazal was thrilled as she gazed at him, desperately wanting to hold on to his optimism as if it were a lost wallet filled with money.

He was a mature, distinguished, tall, and handsome man with kind twinkling brown eyes. He seemed to be quite rich too, for she could see a diamond ring gleaming on his finger and was immaculately dressed. She wanted to tell someone, anyone about her new-found friend, but knew he was right, it was better to keep it a secret, especially from her parents.

Her parents had still not come home for dinner so she quickly watched some television, made a sandwich and went to bed.

As she brushed her teeth she looked at her reflection in the mirror. Instead of the ugly girl she saw every day; she looked at herself through Fanish's 'eyes. He was right; she thought happily, she did have beautiful and expressive eyes.

● ● ● ●

Chapter 13

Gazal and Fanish met regularly after school and established a routine of going for coffee to 'their café', as Gazal liked to call it.

Fanish would wait for her outside the gate and always greeted her with a smile, his warm brown eyes twinkling affectionately.

"So how are your parents?" Fanish would ask merrily. "Are they looking after my Gazal?"

And the answer from Gazal was always the same. "No, they are not."

"So they did not give you a present after all? Surely they must have remembered later?" Fanish asked. "Oh, eat up, you are a growing girl!"

They were sitting outside the café in the hazy evening having rolls and coffee. Gazal was sitting with her arms resting wearily on the table and she glanced at Fanish with tears in her eyes

"You are the only person who has shown me affection, is there something I can do to repay your kindness?" she asked tremulously.

"Ah, there is but I will tell you when the time is right." Fanish smiled.

It was a couple of weeks later when Fanish looked at her seriously.

"Gazal, remember you asked me one day if there was something you could do for me? Well, I would like you to meet Aditya, a friend of mine …"

"Not that, Fanish, I do not want to meet anybody else, Fanish." Gazal replied forcefully. "If my parents ever find out about you, let alone somebody else they'll…!"

"They'll what?" Fanish asked sharply "I thought you said they do not care?"

His eyes had hardened and glinted like steel. Gazal

looked at him in surprise for his eyes were usually warm and kind.

Seeing Gazal's expression, Fanish immediately smiled.

"Gazal, I know how lonely you are and Aditya is very depressed. You need friends and he is a nice man, I have told him so much about you that he wants to meet you in person." his eyes twinkled with merriment

"I'm sorry, Fanish, I should have realised you mean well. I am flattered that you would even think about me after you leave, and of course I will meet Aditya if it would help him…. where and when will I meet him?"

Fanish was her only friend – how could she refuse him his small request?

"You let me worry about that." Fanish smiled and Gazal felt better once again. "I'll see you tomorrow, same time, and same place." He waved his hand and left.

Gazal let herself in the house and found to her surprise her mother was home early.

"Gazal, is that you?"

"Yes, Mum," Gazal smiled happily.

She placed her bag on the kitchen table looking forward to spending time with her mother; however, wondered what her mother was doing in her bedroom at this time of day.

After about 15 minutes, Nayan came downstairs drying her hair.

"And how come you are late? Is this the time you come home every day?" she asked.

"I didn't know you knew what time school finished, Mum." Gazal felt a slight thrill of happiness, but her happiness soon turned to disappointment when her mother did not answer.

"Yes, well, anyway, Gazal, I have to go out." She replied after some time. "when your father comes home can you ask him to phone me? I'll leave the number with you."

Nayan saw the expression on her daughter's face and looked at her watch.

"I have to meet some business colleagues who have come from abroad. And Gazal, I am running late, can you bring me some tea in my bedroom? There's a good girl!" she disappeared upstairs.

Gazal felt drained of all emotion but then her parents always had that effect on her. She went into the kitchen, made the tea her and took it to her mother's bedroom.

She sighed, came back to the kitchen and made hot chocolate for herself, glad she had decided to meet Aditya.

▪ ▪ ▪ ▪

Chapter 14

The next day after school, as usual, Fanish was waiting for her. But this time he was not alone for with him was a short stocky man.

They walked across as soon as they saw her.

"And how is my Gazal?" Fanish greeted her in his usual fashion. "Gazal, this is my friend Aditya – Aditya this is Gazal, the girl I was telling you about."

"So at last I get to meet her." Aditya stared at Gazal speculatively, a quirky half-smile curving his lips.

"Gazal, could you take Aditya to our usual place – unfortunately I have to leave but Aditya would like to get to know you better".

For a moment Fanish was touched by Gazal's vulnerability, but the concern soon disappeared when he thought about the money Aditya would pay him - for he was always very generous if a girl satisfied him.

"No I. ...Fanish don't go...." Gazal said, but before she could finish the sentence, Fanish had disappeared.

"Now where is this place? I am thirsty and could do with a nice cup of coffee." Aditya asked with a smile.

However, his smile seemed false and there was a hard and unwavering look on his smooth broad face.

"Eh, it's not far." Gazal replied guardedly.

"You are even more beautiful than what Fanish had described." Aditya remarked as soon as they were seated and had ordered coffee.

As soon as it arrived he sipped his coffee and stared at Gazal, but his cold, clear glittering black eyes made Gazal uneasy.

They sat in silence, and after what seemed an interminably long time to Gazal, Aditya got up to leave.

"I have to go now but I will walk you home." Aditya pushed back his chair and rose.

"No, it's alright, Aditya, I'll go on my own. I'm used to it." Gazal replied quickly. "I have to meet a friend on the way home."

However, her eyes darkened and she hoped Aditya would not sense the aversion she was feeling.

"Oh?" Aditya asked nonchalantly. "I have strict instructions from Fanish that I have to see you home. And I take my responsibilities very seriously – especially this one!" He smiled thinly.

"But…"

"No buts, young girl – you can phone your friend from home and tell her you will not be able to meet her."

Gazal relented, knowing it to be useless to argue and they walked in silence.

The early evening was still cloudy and Gazal could hear the distant hum of the street traffic as they turned into a side street.

"Gazal, I'd like to see you tomorrow." Aditya said abruptly.

"I am busy and…."

The small pulse of life within Gazal seemed to sink simultaneously with the sinking sun.

"Fanish said he was going away for a week and asked me to look after you."

"What! Fanish's gone away? Why didn't he say anything to me?"

Aditya noticed her eyes shining. "Ah, Gazal, that is my fault. He thought he would tell you himself, but I told him I would, and since he was in a hurry, he left it to me."

Without a word, Gazal left Aditya and went into the house, still smarting from hurt and disappointment.

She ran to her room and flung herself on the bed with a sob. She got up after some time and checked the answer phone. Her mother and father, both, as usual, had left a message saying they would be late.

Gazal sighed, got a coke, made a sandwich and went into the lounge to watch television. She was watching her favourite serial when the phone rang. Gazal got up to answer it, convinced it would be her one of her parents, ringing to confirm she had got their message.

As she picked up the receiver, she heard Fanish's voice.

"Gazal, Fanish here." Gazal's heart leapt and she couldn't speak. "Gazal are you there?"

"Yes, yes I am here, just surprised to hear from you because you had said you would not phone unless it was something urgent. Is everything alright?"

"Everything is okay, but, Gazal I have just spoken to Aditya. He says you were upset that I did not tell you my plans?"

"I am…. I began to think that you were just like my parents."

"Sorry, but I'll be back next week. I'll see you then, in the meanwhile you told Aditya you were busy tomorrow after school, how come? I know you always go straight home."

"Yes, but…I don't like him and…."

"Has he done or said anything? Gazal, I am worried about you walking home by yourself. You know I have only your best interest as heart."

Fanish's voice was gentle but at the same time very firm. His concern for Gazal was always expressed with a mixture of tenderness and respect and with a delicacy of tone, voice and manner. "Anyway, Aditya did not like the coffee shop and he wants to take you somewhere better!"

"But..." The thought of spending any more time, anywhere with Aditya revolted Gazal. But strong as her feelings of revulsion were, she did not want to disappoint Fanish.

"Gazal, you won't do me this favour?" Fanish's voice

was gentle.

"Alright, Fanish, if you say so." Gazal said reluctantly.

She did not want to argue if it meant so much to Fanish but the feelings of neglect and isolation had exhausted her so much that she did not suspect she was being victimised or by whom.

· · · ·

Chapter 15

The following day was sunny and windy, and Gazal shivered whilst she waited for Aditya after school.

Every now and then she could see a few clouds travel slowly along the sky and rise up majestically. They would poise in the sky for a moment before the wind blew them away, leaving the sky clear once again.

Gazal did not have to wait long as Aditya drove up and she got in the car.

"Did Fanish phone?" Aditya asked as he prepared to drive away.

"Yes, he did."

"And did he tell you that we won't be going to the café, but I would like to take you somewhere else?"

"Yes, he did," Gazal said vaguely as she looked around her at the passing houses. "Where are we going? I have to be back home as my parents…"

"We won't be long I promise. There is a restaurant I know you will like, but I have to go home first. As usual I have forgotten my wallet." He parked the car in the driveway of a small house.

"Actually, I am hungry; I had been hoping we would go straight to the restaurant." Gazal said in a small voice.

"It won't take long - why don't you come up and wait while I collect my things? You can make yourself some tea and a sandwich whilst I get my wallet."

As they entered, Aditya went straight upstairs, leaving Gazal to find her way around the kitchen. As she made herself a sandwich, she heard Aditya's voice.

"I'm feeling hot; I think I'll quickly have a bath to freshen up."

"But we will be late…."

However, Aditya could not or did not hear her so she took her sandwich and milk to the sitting room and switched on the television.

After some time, Aditya walked in the doorway, a towel around his waist, vigorously drying his hair.

"Is there any tea for me?" he asked sitting next to Gazal on the sofa.

Gazal got up feeling uncomfortable and a heightening colour of red spread first to her neck then to her forehead.

"No, don't worry, I'll make it myself, in fact I'll make you a cup of my delicious tea too" He got up and went into the kitchen.

"Thank you." Gazal sat down again embarrassed at Aditya's attire.

She looked tense and anxious and her hands were nervously clasped on her lap as she moved uneasily in the chair.

"Here you are- my special tea!"

Aditya sat on the sofa beside her and handed her a cup and his hand ran lightly over his face, and for some unknown reason, the gesture of familiarity made her nervous

Gazal sipped her tea then frowned. "I'll have some sugar, please, Aditya."

"Here you are," Aditya said handing her the sugar bowl.

"Thank you," Gazal took the bowl wishing he would get dressed.

She felt embarrassed and wondered whether it was her innocence that made her feel so or if she was becoming aware of her inability to take people lightly so she could feel safe from emotional harm?

Or was it just her fear of either not being accepted or worse still, to be rejected? At any rate, Gazal did not feel strong enough, or curious enough to test the deep waters of the so-called social play.

After some time Gazal felt her lids grow heavy.

"I am so tired!" she thought wearily.

Her eyelids drooped and she fell asleep with her head on Aditya's shoulder.

• • • •

Chapter 16

Gazal woke with a headache and found she was in a strange bed.

"Where am I?" she cried groggily. She was confused for the last thing she recalled was being in Aditya's lounge having a cup of tea.

She tried to get up and the sheet that was covering her body slipped from her shoulders, revealing her naked shoulders.

"Don't worry, you are in my house."

Aditya pulled up a chair and sat down beside the bed, moving his tongue over his lips and bending his head slightly to one side, looking at Gazal intently.

Gazal looked down at her bare shoulders and squirmed under the furtive scrutiny of his glare.

"Why am I not wearing any clothes?" She asked opening her eyes wide.

The modesty in her deep brown eyes proclaimed her embarrassment as loudly as if she was stating her feelings through a megaphone.

"You fell asleep in the sitting room." Aditya tried to explain. "You must have been very tired and you looked so peaceful I did not want to wake you, so carried you to my bedroom, and as your clothes looked tight and uncomfortable, I undressed you."

Aditya spoke with ease and did not have decency to look or feel sorry.

"How dare you touch me! Can I have my clothes? I want to go home. What time is it?"

Gazal was beginning to feel cold, embarrassed and angry.

"You haven't been sleeping for long." Aditya said as he handed Gazal her clothes. "But as it is late, I won't be able to take you to the restaurant like I promised."

"I don't want to go anyway," Gazal muttered as she took the clothes and ran into the bathroom, clutching the sheet tightly around her.

Gazal dressed quickly and could not remember when the chilled cramped feeling was replaced by a throbbing heat and a feverish excitement. Her skin felt dry and her head throbbed.

Gazal felt as if she had somehow changed - as if years had passed, not a couple of hours. She was feeling hot and sticky and wanted to go home as soon as possible to have a long hot bath.

"When is Fanish returning?" Gazal asked, returning to the bedroom.

"Soon," Aditya replied with a smile,

There was a pleased look on Aditya's face as he drove her home. Gazal felt there was something horrible, something fierce and devilish in Aditya's delight when he looked at Gazal, who shrank further in her seat.

"He'll be back on Monday to be exact. So shall I pick you up same time, same place tomorrow?" Aditya asked eagerly.

"No, not tomorrow." Gazal replied.

"But Fanish told me, in fact I believe he also told you that...?"

"Yes, he did, Aditya, but tomorrow I will be staying on at school. I have some extra work I have to finish."

"Please?" Aditya gripped her wrist and looked crestfallen but persisted. "Day after tomorrow then?"

"No, my exams are coming up and I want to study for them."

Gazal opened the door of the car as Aditya stopped the car near her house. However, before she could get out, he put his hand on her arm.

"What about afterwards?" Aditya held her hand tightly.

He began to stroke her hand, his fingertips making

little featherweight brushes on the inside of her wrists. Slowly he bent to look at the back of her hand, fascinated by the fragility of her wrist which he could span easily between with his thumb and forefinger. He turned her wrist upside down and could almost see a pulse beating gently beneath her skin.

Where before his mouth had been a thin mean line, now it curved into a lecherous smile and his eyes seemed to caress warmly and invitingly, as did his fingertips.

"No, please don't" Gazal whispered, not liking the sensations Aditya was arousing in her.

"Gazal, I want to give you this." Aditya gave her a wad of money. "I am feeling guilty for I had promised to take you to a good restaurant and..."

Gazal felt insulted, then remembered the trainers she wanted.

"Oh, all right." She quickly took the money and ran into her house.

She went straight to her bedroom and put the money safely in her drawer then quickly had a shower.

Her body ached and when she inhaled she got a shooting pain below the ribs. For some unknown reason, she felt sad, but could not separate the pain in her heart from the one in her body.

▪ ▪ ▪ ▪

Chapter 17

As soon as she entered the lounge the phone rang.

"Gazal, Hi!" Gazal's heart leapt as she heard Fanish's voice.

"Hello," Gazal smiled into the receiver." When are you coming?"

"Soon, soon but in the meantime, is Aditya looking after you? He said he was taking you out for a meal."

"Yes, he is, and we were supposed to out but instead went to his house for he had to pick up something he had forgotten. And as it got late, we stayed in."

"Anyway, you had a good evening, I trust?"

"No I did not, Fanish" Gazal exclaimed. "I was asleep."

"Oh, how come? Were you very tired?"

"I wasn't and I never sleep during the daytime, but as soon I had a cup of tea that Aditya made for me, I fell asleep and the next thing I knew I woke in his bed...."

"Whoa, hold on, Gazal, what are you trying to tell me?" Fanish's astonishment froze her into a momentary silence.

Suddenly, Gazal was overcome with shyness.

"When are you meeting Aditya again? And did he give you some money. Does he want to see you again?"

"Yes, he does, but I don't know when…"

"Gazal, you didn't refuse him, did you?

"Fanish, I have some work at school and..."

"How long will that take – one hour, two hours?" Fanish persisted.

"I don't know, I ..."

"It could not be more than two hours – you should not study so hard anyway. I will phone Aditya and tell him to pick you up and take you to dinner."

"No, Fanish, really, I…"

"No ifs and buts, Gazal, I know Aditya will like to see you again and you can expect him to be there."

Gazal put down the receiver slowly for she knew it was useless to argue with Fanish.

As she went to the kitchen to get a glass of water, she wished she had told Fanish exactly what Aditya had done. She gulped the water and wiped her hands across her forehead wearily as she went upstairs, feeling groggy and sick.

Her parents had still not come when Gazal went to bed. She felt exhausted, not only physically but also emotionally. She slept badly, not only because of the physical discomfort, but the pain in her soul.

And finally when Gazal did sleep, she had a terrifying nightmare from which she woke in a pool of sweat. The house was dark and cold and her parents still had not come home.

The following day, Aditya was waiting for her and after that day, Aditya and Gazal met regularly and followed the same routine - instead of going out to dinner they would go to his flat.

One day they were sitting in his flat when Aditya turned towards her.

"Gazal, how would you like to meet some of my friends? They are lonely and you are such a sweet girl."

At first Gazal was revolted at the idea, then nodded for she did not want to stay alone in her large empty house.

And soon after, he introduced her to his friends – none of whom she liked, however, they paid her well and after a month Gazal confronted her parents.

▪ ▪ ▪ ▪

Chapter 18

"Mum, Dad, I have something to tell you."

"What is it, Gazal," her mother snapped. "We're going out and don't have time …"

"Is it money you need?" Her father took out his wallet.

"No, Dad, please, I don't need money, can you please listen to what I have to say?"

"Are you in trouble at school?" He glowered at her. "If that is all, there is no need to worry; we'll arrange further tuition for you. Now, Nayan, hurry up or we will be late."

Gazal looked at her parents as Nayan turned towards the door ready to leave.

"Mother, I'm leaving home..."

"What – you're what!" Her father thundered as he took a step towards her.

"What do you mean, Gazal? You are a child; you have a home so why do you want to leave? Where will you go?" Nayan asked impatiently. "Don't be so dramatic, we don't have time for your tantrums, we'll talk again when we get back."

"But you're never home, I am alone all the time, you come late at night."

"You ungrateful girl! Come on Nayan. We'll see how she survives without any money or a roof over head."

However, although Gazal had hoped they would have convinced her to stay, Gazal was a sensible girl and realised that a child is only tied to parents by their need to be loved by them so as soon as they had left, decided to phone Aditya immediately.

"Aditya, listen, I'm leaving home now– can I come and stay with you?"

There was a silence on the other end, so Gazal

quickly explained.

"It's just for tonight, tomorrow I'll start looking for a flat."

Aditya gave a sigh of relief for it would cramp his style to have somebody staying with him, however, it would only be temporary and Fanish would be pleased. And in the meantime he could use Gazal's company and grinned as he thought 'and that will not be all I will be using!"

"Of course you can, Gazal, do you want me to come and pick you up?"

"That will be nice, just give me an hour or so to collect my things."

"I'll see you later." Aditya hung up the receiver.

Gazal was packing her suitcases when the phone rang and rang to answer it, hoping it would be her parents.

"Hello, Mother?" Gazal spoke breathlessly and eagerly.

"Hi, Gazal, it's me Fanish."

Gazal's heart sank and she replied in a quiet voice. "Hello, Fanish."

"Gazal, I have just received a call from Aditya. What is this he tells me?"

"What do you mean?"

"Aditya said you have decided to leave but did not explain further. Where are you going? To go, you're not thinking of leaving town, are you?" He said in a cold voice.

"No, No, I'm just leaving home and moving in with Aditya for the time being." Gazal thought she detected a warning behind his words.
"What do your parents say about the arrangement?"

"They do not know and do not care."

"So how are you going to manage on your own?" Fanish asked.

"I was depending on you, you said that if ever I

needed help...?"

"Yes, of course, but what about your school?"

. "I'll be leaving school – there's nothing in studying anyway. Anyway, can't you come earlier than Monday?"

"I am in London at the moment, I arrived last night. In fact, I might drop in to see Aditya later in the evening. I'll see you there and we can talk again."

Gazal quickly finished her packing and sat down to write a note to her parents. She did not know what to write, so after tearing a few pages, she finally decided to let them know only that she was leaving and not try and find her.

As Gazal licked the envelope and put it on the mantelpiece where it could not be missed, she sat down to wait for Aditya and was nearly asleep with weariness and tension when she heard Aditya's car.

As she closed the door behind her, she knew that one chapter of her life had closed and another was beginning. She wiped the tears as she turned to take one last look at her home before she got into Aditya's car.

- - - -

Chapter 19

And after some time, she realised it was Fanish who had planned everything and that his kindness had only been an act.

His delicacy, politeness, modesty and candour – all were the pretence of a mean, cunning, brutal man, who dropped his guise when his pretence and duplicity gained its end.

And she was not the only one, for apparently this is what Fanish did for a living – he targeted emotionally or physically abused girls and by showing them affection and kindness, lured them into his web of deception.

And it was not long before Gazal realised Fanish was a man who could tame anyone. There was an extraordinary expression on his face and hypnotic power in his eyes. His quite deference, attentiveness and interest coupled with the underlying gentleness in his voice lulled the girls into a sense of security.

But as soon as the girl became dependent on him emotionally, Fanish would strike like a snake and introduce her to Aditya and then gradually to others.

By autumn, the sharp breeze that scattered the dead leaves were like her hopes, to be scattered then whirled away by the wind.

"Vanita, can I get you another cup of tea?" Gazal asked, as she put her past firmly behind her.

Vanita shook her head and laid her head on the sofa wearily.

"Vanita, for what it is worth, I can understand your dilemma, for I have been through it. At some point, you will question yourself and then doubt your ability to make rational judgements in forming any relationships."

Vanita shook her head. "Thanks Gazal, I will manage,"

"As you wish, Vanita, but you will also most certainly face an uncertainty about your own identity, for it is confusing to become physically and socially an adult when you have not have reached the stage emotionally."

Vanita yawned. "Thanks Gazal, but for now I think I'll go to bed."

"I know you will manage, Vanita, just thought I would mention it and let you know that I am here if you need somebody to talk to. Come, I'll show you to your room."

"Thanks, Gazal, just tell me where it is, I'll find my way there" Vanita replied just as tersely as before.

"It's all right, Vanita, I am going up to bed too., the bed has recently been changed., and If there is anything you need, just give me a shout."

As she left, Vanita sat down on the bed for she was not sleepy; she was tired but definitely not sleepy. She had wanted to get away from Gazal and plan to escape from the tangled web Fanish had trapped her in.

She was well aware that Aditya was only the first man that Fanish asked her to be nice to. By leaving home and turning to Fanish for help, she had given him power and control over her.

Vanita felt angry and disillusioned at being betrayed first by her father and now by Fanish, the two people she had loved and trusted.

'I'll never forgive Fanish, never! I'll get him for this one day." she vowed as she drifted off to sleep.

- - - -

Chapter 20

Gazal and Vanita were having breakfast the next morning when the doorbell rang.

"That must be Fanish." Gazal got up to answer the door.

"And how are my two favourite girls?" he asked with a twinkle in his eyes. "Vanita, I hope your anger has subsided by now?"

"No, it has not." Vanita snapped. "I think you are a hypocrite and a snake!"

She looked at Fanish with an expression of bitter contempt, threw down her spoon and rose to leave the room.

"You're not going anywhere unless I say so." Fanish said angrily.

His hand shot out and gripped Vanita's shoulder and his eyes, which Vanita remembered as being kind and warm, were now cold and hard.

"Look, Fanish, I do not have to do what you want all the time. Let me go or…!" Vanita glared at Fanish as she tried to wriggle free.

"Or what?" Fanish whispered his voice soft yet menacing and not relinquishing his tight grip on Vanita's shoulder.

"You used to come crying to me about your parents and I was the only one who listened to you. Now I have provided a home for you and you have the audacity to accuse me?"

"Yes, you have been kind, but you had your selfish reasons. You have deprived me of my childhood innocence by throwing me thoughtlessly in an adult world. I don't think I will ever be able to trust anybody again, you know it took me a long time to trust you."

"Don't blame me Vanita, your anger should be

directed at your father for it was he who betrayed you."

Vanita looked at Fanish tearfully, her lips quivering. "What am I going to do now, I have no money."

"Vanita, I'm sorry, but you have to come to terms with the situation." Fanish said gently. "And as for your financial situation, I have a solution."

Fanish smiled and the warmth diffused cold eyes and erased all the harshness from his face whilst his manner changed to a mixture of firmness and disdain.

A cold and calculating look came in Vanita's eyes. Fanish was right, she would have to make the most of the situation. "But for the moment only!" she thought.

"I have a few friends who…"

"I knew that is what you meant, you mean men like Aditya?" Vanita interrupted.

She tried to keep her voice steady and mask the resentment that had accumulated in her.

"Yes, like Aditya, but some are willing to pay more for your favours, do you know what I mean?"

"Of course," Vanita replied sarcastically, "and we pay you half, I suppose?"

"Whatever," Fanish replied disconcerted by Vanita's reaction. "Gazal, tell her how we operate, I have to leave."

As the door closed behind him Vanita exclaimed angrily: -

"He is a snake! Most probably he has gone to trap another unsuspecting girl." She said bitterly.

"Most likely, but there is nothing we can do about it. I don't know about you, but I had nothing at home to live for. At least here I am independent." Gazal stirred her tea thoughtfully. "I suppose it is a question of counting one's blessing, so to speak."

"I know and neither have I." Vanita replied. "I was actually coming to terms, with it, but what hurts me most is that I trusted him and he betrayed that trust! How can

I ever trust another man?" Vanita murmured miserably as she thought of her father.

"Lesson number one, in this field, it is wise not to, for they are all unpredictable and unreliable." Gazal verified.

"Tell me Gazal, how old are you?" Vanita asked, changing the subject.

"I'll be seventeen in two months' time. What about you?" Gazal answered looking at her nails.

"I'm thirteen. How long have you been with Fanish?"

"I have been with him since I was thirteen too."

"You mean you have been with him for four years?" Vanita was surprised for Gazal looked older. "I am surprised you have not left him for I am sure you do not like living like this? Isn't it illegal?"

"Yes, but Fanish has himself covered. And the girls he targets are vulnerable, so would not implicate him, much as they would like too. They know he is too dangerous. I tried, believe me, I tried and failed. Other girls have also tried and failed. As to living like this – there are positive sides to it – I have my independence and as much money as I could ever have dreamt of and…"

But Vanita sensed the undercurrent unhappiness in Gazal's voice.

"That is not all that is in life, Gazal," remarked Vanita. "I'm going to get out as soon as I can."

"You can try but as I was explaining, it is very difficult to leave Fanish. And yes I do realise there is an emotional vacuum in my life. There always has been and always be that void. But you know, Vanita, you surprise me. You are so young and new to this field, yet you have grasped what it has taken me four years to understand."

Gazal knew now why she had thought Vanita was different; she was wise for one so young, she wanted to escape from Fanish's clutches before it was too late.

However, she also knew Fanish would never willingly let her go; in fact, it was dangerous to try so decided to tell her about Kanan.

"You know Vanita, a girl, her name was Kanan, tried to leave Fanish and…"

"Good for her! How did she manage to escape? Tell me, how did she manage it? I might learn something that might help me break away from Fanish"

"I will …. she was a wild one, was Kanan." Gazal's eyes had a faraway look.

■ ■ ■ ■

Chapter 21

"I am not going to do what Fanish wants, whenever he wants! I am going to escape, Gazal, do you know what happened yesterday?" The words came out in a voice heavy with emotion.

Kanan put her hands over her face then began pacing the room. During the night she had come to a decision – she was going to leave – she was going to leave Aditya, Gazal and most of all Fanish.

Her hands were trembling as she folded her clothes and placed them in a suitcase, each movement precise. She paused and twisted the clothes in her hand backward and forward and started whimpering, then turned toward Gazal.

"I can't imagine, tell me what happened to make you want to leave?" Gazal asked

"No, I can't say, I am too ashamed."

"Gazal, I hate that man! My life had been unbearable before, but it was nothing to my ordeal yesterday, I have just about had enough!" She had learnt to protect herself for some time because one day she thought she could emerge from her self-imposed cocoon when ready.

"I don't know who you are talking about, it cannot be Fanish. Kanan, but tell me in your time." Gazal was watching her quietly.

"No, it was not Fanish but he sent me to this man..." her face was pale, showing up the red weal where a whip had caught her

"That's not unusual, Kanan, but I have a feeling I know which man you are talking about."

"You know about him? He is a monster... h... he...!" Kanan sat on the bed, sobbing.

Her fingers twined together nervously on her lap and her eyes first looked down on the floor than out of the window, and through a blur of tears, saw the flowers gently waving their petals in the light breeze.

"There, there," Gazal put her arms around Kanan, "I'll get you something to drink, if it makes you feel better, all the girls have to go to him."

"You too? You have been to him?"

"Actually, no, I don't why or how, but he is always threatening me he would."

She went to the kitchen to fetch Kanan a glass of water.

"T...t. thank y…you!"

Kanan took the glass gratefully and hiccupped as she gulped the water.

"Anyway, where will you go? And wherever you go you know that Fanish will be sure to find you." Gazal said worriedly. "Look Kanan, I have grown quite fond of you and would not want anything to happen to you."

"I am fond of you too, and I don't know where I will go, but anywhere is good enough as long as it is far away from here."

"Are you sure Fanish does not know that you are planning a runner?"

"Gazal, you're not following me!" Kanan cried in exasperation. "I want to go away from here, not with Fanish's blessing; I will go regardless of what he says."

"You know he will never let you go?" Gazal repeated again.

"Thank you for your support." Kanan remarked sarcastically. "But with your help I know I can escape."

"I'll try to help, believe me, I'll try – but I am afraid for you. I know Fanish has a temper and he is a control freak too."

"So we'll just have to try harder, won't we?"

Gazal finally let herself be convinced that Kanan would escape whilst Gazal distracted him.

"But we have to plan it carefully, so for now you had

best unpack till we come up with a viable plan." Gazal put on a smile of understanding like a fresh coat of lipstick. "I'll see that you go from this place without immediate discovery or pursuit."

Kanan's eyes filled with tears but managed a whispered "Thank you, I will be eternally grateful"

"Don't be silly, you are my friend. I don't' think you should leave immediately but within the next few days, in the meantime, we carry on as normal. Fanish is very observant so please be on your guard."

However, in the following days, Gazal noticed Kanan's nervousness and only hoped that Fanish had not detected it.

■ ■ ■ ■

Chapter 22

"Gazal, what is wrong with Kanan?" Fanish commented idly, crossing his legs as he sat on the sofa.

Gazal gave a start. "Wrong? Nothing is wrong. What makes you say that?"

There was a tremor in her voice, which, she hoped Fanish would either fail to see or ignore.

Even though Fanish glared at her for some time, her eyes did not waver from the probing concentration of his stare.

She knew that if she showed any sign of betrayal, it would be the end of Kanan. Not only would he be ruthless with her, but Gazal too would be resorted to a nightmare existence.

"Oh, I thought she looked nervous, not her usual self at all."

"She's feeling a bit feverish – I think she might be coming down with flu or something!" Gazal smiled, hoping it would successfully mask her lie.

"That may be it, that might be the reason," Fanish replied absent-mindedly.

Gazal breathed a sigh of relief and as soon as the door closed behind Fanish, ran up to Kanan's room.

"Kanan!" she cried, "I think Fanish suspects something."

"Oh no, Gazal, I tried to behave normally, like you suggested, but it has been difficult. I cannot wait to get out of here." Kanan looked at Gazal fearfully.

"Apparently not well enough for he asked if anything was the matter with you. Apparently he noticed you were behaving differently."

"Gosh, he is very observant for I did keep to the same routine."

"You don't know Fanish as well as I do." Gazal said

dryly. "Anyway, I told him you were coming down with flu or something. That might work in our favour in stalling for time. I'll tell him you are resting in your room if he asks again and that you should not be disturbed."

"Anyway, since he suspects something, it would be best if you left tomorrow as Fanish will be busy then. And if and when he finds out, I will decline all knowledge of your whereabouts."

"Thank you, Gazal, but why don't you come with me?" Kanan pleaded.

"No, I can't, anyway, somebody needs to be here to cover for you".

Gazal did not voice her doubts about Kanan's plans to get a job and make a life for herself away from Fanish.

However, that was not the only reason, for Gazal had become accustomed to her affluent lifestyle and was sure she would not be able to maintain it if she left, so was unwilling to relinquish it. It would a hard struggle to get where she was and she did not have the patience or the inclination.

There were tears in Kanan's eyes, for nobody had ever been kind to her.

"How can I ever thank you?" There was a catch in her throat.

She cleared her throat and with trembling fingers wiped the tears that had started trickling down her cheeks.

"Don't be silly, what are friends for?"

"I have never had a friend before." Kanan said in a little voice.

Gazal raised her eyebrows. "A nice affectionate girl like you? You know, Kanan, you never told me about your life before you met Fanish." Gazal remarked. "Oh, I'm sorry, I don't mean to pry."

"No, no, it's alright, it's just that there is, no was, nothing to tell really. I am an orphan and was put in an orphanage ever since – ever since I can remember. In fact, that is the only life I have known and I have very bad memories of it for the owner and carers were cruel people."

"Surely you must have made friends? How come you were not adopted?"

"No, I did not make any friends for most of the children were mostly coming into or leaving the institution and somehow nobody wanted to adopt me. Anyway, that is where I met Fanish for he was a friend of the owner and now when I think back, I am sure they arranged for me not to be adopted. And soon after, when I was miserable seeing the other children go to good families, was the time Fanish introduced himself and told me about this dream family who wanted a daughter just like me."

"So that is how he trapped you." Gazal remarked. "However, I would have thought the care institution had a responsibility to look after you?" Her voice and expression both reflected her shock and repulsion.

"They do, but there are so many children that…anyway, at every opportunity I was sent to the head's office where I was beaten with a belt, usually for no reason at all." When Gazal looked sceptical she pulled up her blouse. "I still have the scars; here, look for yourself."

Gazal gave a gasp as she saw her red back, the scars of the lashes on her back and fresh ones.

"Oh Kanan, I am so sorry, I had no idea." Gazal exclaimed, horrified.

" In the orphanage I lived in fear always, so much so that I did not trust myself or the world. That is other than Fanish, for somehow, he always seemed to be there to console me after I had been whipped."

"Didn't you say anything to anybody?" Gazal asked, appalled.

"I was so frightened that I could not voice or express

my fears to anybody, I did not know who to trust anyway, so each day was a nightmare."

"Now I can see why you turned to Fanish, after experiencing all that he must have appeared a wonderful man." Gazal whispered.

"Yes, but now I see that between them that is what Fanish and the head planned all along – I was whipped to ensure that I would turn to Fanish for help."

"Kanan, don't you think after all you have been through you should stay? Apart from yesterday, and what you have told me, it seems a fairly comfortable life."

"How can you even suggest such a thing?" Kanan asked in a surprised tone.

"I don't mean to sound callous, but it seems to me you have endured so much for so long, and here at least you have independence and security."

"Only as long as I do want Fanish wants. But you know, Gazal, you are right for I know it won't be easy alone in the world. I have no skills and no training, but if I stay here I …"

Gazal was confused. "What are you afraid of, Kanan? What is the worst that can happen to you?"

"Gazal, it's that man I was telling you about, the man Fanish sent me to."

"What did he do that was so terrible as to make you decide to run away?" Gazal asked.

- - - -

Chapter 23

"Well, not him, but it was one of Fanish's friend, Subhi, who took me to this other man who ..." Kanan shuddered. "who, Gazal, is a pervert. He wore a mask, tied me and beat me and..."

In a voice devoid of emotion Kanan told her about her visit to man call the 'Ravager'.

"Gazal, my back was already sore from the beatings I had received in the orphanage." There were tears in her eyes. "Although my hands were tied, I begged him to stop, but the more I begged, the harsher he became."

"Oh, you poor girl," Gazal cried, horrified. "If you were taken to him by Subhi, it may be possible Fanish does know about this pervert...."

"You know as well as I do that that is not possible.. The man they call 'the Ravager' pays well, and Fanish is only concerned with money." Kanan's lips trembled and she swallowed.

"No, don't say that, Fanish would not sink that low, well he would!" Gazal said. "You should try and talk to him, maybe he will understand."

"Gazal, do you know what that man said to me as he left? I was screaming that I hoped I would never see him again, but he looked smug. And through his mask I felt he was sneering at me."

'Oh, you will, my dear, be sure of that, you will! 'he said.

"I screamed, but he only laughed cruelly, Gazal, I will never forget that laugh as long as I live."

Kanan's large eyes, which had become intense with fear and hatred filled with sorrow.

"Anything is better than going to that pervert!"

Kanan put her head in her hands and sobbed uncontrollably.

Gazal was shocked and appalled, nonetheless she

tried to calm her friend.

"Kanan you know I will do anything to help you and more so now that I know why you are escaping – I only hope you can manage it without Fanish finding out."

The following day, Gazal went to the bus station with her, and when Kanan was sitting in the bus, spoke to her through the window.

"Kanan please do not write to me for Fanish sometimes looks through my mail. And good luck, Kanan." she whispered as the bus drove out of the station.

Before returning to her flat Gazal went to the mall and spent a couple of hours walking aimlessly in the shops, then finally returned to her flat desolately, for she would miss Kanan.

As she entered the hall and switched on the light, a hand suddenly got hold of her wrist. Gazal gave a start as she saw Fanish looked at her furiously.

"How did you get in?" Gazal asked angrily.

"Never mind that! Where have you been?" Fanish snarled.

"I have been out shopping." Gazal was trembling with fear at the look on Fanish's face.

"Oh, have you? And where is Kanan?"

"I don't know; she must be in her room upstairs. She hasn't been feeling too well and…"

Gazal started sweating but she tried to keep her eyes steady as she looked straight at Fanish.

Fanish glared at her, his eyes black as coal, then brought his hand up across Gazal's cheek with such force that Gazal staggered and fell against the wall, trembling and terrified.

"Don't lie to me, you bitch! I've checked her room!"

Fanish glared at her and the hardness of his eyes showed his loathing.

"Fanish, I don't know, she must have gone out, I am

not responsible for her whereabouts."

He looked at her and smiled cruelly.

"Well, then I'm sure you won't mind if I make myself at home and wait for her?"

Fanish became solemn and looked almost dignified as he held up his hand, staring at Gazal with an unpleasantly penetrating look that seemed to look right through her.

Gazal's heart sank as Fanish switched on the television and sat on the sofa.

"Fanish, you don't need to wait. We don't know how long she will be, but I will phone you as soon as she comes." She tried to reason with him.

She looked at the watch and saw that by now Kanan's coach would have taken her to her destination.

"Gazal, why are you looking at your watch? Do you have to go out or is there any other reason? You don't have something you should tell me, is there?"

He tilted his chair back and a cunning smile came to his lips.

"Of course not, Fanish, what would I have to tell?"

Gazal shook her head and ran upstairs into the bathroom to splash some cold water on her face. She cupped her hands under the faucet and gulped the water, hoping for some relief from a nervousness and fear that was making her sick.

Gazal, where are you?" Fanish called loudly and angrily. "Come down at once or else I'll come and drag you down!"

"I'll be down in a minute, Fanish. I am just freshening up"

As Gazal walked down the stairs, she tried to think of ways she could defer from talking to Fanish, for she gathered from his behaviour that he knew something about Kanan's escape.

Fanish was going into the kitchen, but as soon as she

entered, he stepped back into the room with a stealthily.

"Sit down Gazal. I want to tell you a story." His voice had the silky softness of a snake about to strike.

He pushed her into a chair and towered over her threateningly.

"One day a girl of mine thought she could escape from me – but to cut a long story short – do you know what happened?" His eyes glittered with malice and triumph.

Gazal looked at him with an expression of furtive uneasiness and her heart started thudding. What was Fanish trying to tell her? She gripped the arms of her chair till the knuckles were white.

"No, and I don't want to know, Anyway, it has nothing to do with me, I'm here, aren't I?"

"I have given you every opportunity to tell me where Kanan is. Anyway, I will complete my story; do you know what happened to the girl who helped her?"

Fanish sat down, a mockery of a smile hovering on his cruel lips.

"No" she whispered.

A light of hatred lurked deep in Gazal's eyes and a fearful dread overtook her body and soul.

"Fanish, I don't know what you are talking about." Gazal's felt dizzy and the room started spinning.

Her eyes fixed on Fanish's face and her heart somersaulted at the grim expression on his face. His eyes glittered and seemed to pierce her innermost soul.

Fanish put his hand into his trouser pocket, took out something that shone, opened his palm and said with detestable composure.

"Maybe this will help you remember?"

Gazal gasped as she saw the gleaming necklace in Fanish's hand. Her face paled with shock and her eyes flashed with disbelief, for it was Kanan's necklace, and one she was wearing when she left.

Gazal remembered it well, for not only was it one of a kind, but she had given it to her as a going away present. After Kanan had tied the necklace around her neck she had turned towards her emotionally.

"Gazal, it was very sweet of you to get me this lovely necklace. I am never going to take it off, for it will remind me of you, a wonderful friend, always."

Kanan had hugged Gazal with tears in eyes.

▪ ▪ ▪ ▪

Chapter 24

What did it all mean? Why and how was it in Fanish's possession? Gazal trembled at the sinister and underlying indication, and the expression on her face turned from understanding to astonishment and finally to horror

"That is Kanan's!" There was a catch in Gazal's voice. "Where is Kanan? That means she is back. Where was she all the time? Did you tell her how worried we were?"

She tried to get up but Fanish towered over her and slapped her again.

"Stop lying to me, you bitch!"

Fanish's thick eyebrows were raised as his chest heaved with anger.

As Gazal realised that Fanish knew about Kanan and her escape, she felt the colour drain from her face - but he was keeping her in suspense about Kanan's fate till she admitted her part in helping her.

Suddenly she was angry.

"Alright, alright, I helped her to run away - however, I only helped her escape from you because you were going to sell her to that horrible man who, who…! Kanan showed me the scars he inflicted on her. Anyway, now that you have made me confess, can you tell me where she is and if she is safe?"

Gazal's eyes moved uneasily from object to object in the room.

"No, I will not tell you where she is. That will be part of your punishment. You can wonder all the time where she is and how she is." Fanish grinned maliciously.

"Fanish how did you know? We were so careful."

Gazal lowered her eyes in an expression of gentle remorse.

"You didn't think I trusted you, did you? Here let me show you something."

Fanish's eyes glittered then looked through the open door and fixed on a painting hanging on the wall. He moved towards the painting and lifted it down on the floor.

He took out a small stone from the frame but as Gazal looked closely she saw it was not a stone.

"What is it?" she asked confused.

"It's what is called a bug. I have installed one in each room. You can't deceive me for I know that you know more than you are telling me. I know every little secret of yours, all your gloating and whisperings.".

Her slim hands, which were usually steady, trembled violently as she realised that Fanish had known all along what they had been planning.

"Now, I think I have given you enough to think about." Fanish opened the door to leave, and then looked over his shoulder. "Oh, let me tell you what the other part of your punishment will be – you will go to the same gentleman that Kanan was escaping from."

"N.no..!" Gazal screamed.

Fanish stepped back into the room and grabbed her arm.

"You will do as I say or…!"

He snarled as he put his face close to her face and ran his fingers down her cheek.

"You don't want anything to happen to that beautiful face of yours, do you?" He said softly.

He pushed her backwards into the room and slammed the door after him.

Gazal put her hand on her pounding heart and gasped. Her teeth were chattering and her palms felt wet.

She sat down on the table and rested her arms wearily on it, then hid her face in her arms in fear. But then as the pang of fear passed, she hoped that it was an idle threat only made in the heat of the moment, however, Fanish kept his promise.

He told Subhi to take her to 'The Ravager's and Gazal found him to be every bit as perverse as Kanan had said – a depraved and sadistic animal in human camouflage who seemed to get his pleasure by beating young girls.

He had beaten her repeatedly and by the time he was done with her, she was bruised and bleeding and like Kanan, had scars and lashes on her body.

When Gazal had screamed at Fanish later he had remarked casually.

"He's letting you off lightly, now you'll think twice again before you help anybody to escape from me."

And the Ravager was Fanish's weapon. Every time he thought any one of his girls was either rebelling or thinking about it, he would send her to him.

To this day, Gazal had still not heard from Kanan, and wondered what fate had befallen her. She hoped she was safe, but knew that was unlikely, for if Fanish had got to her before she reached safety ... and every-time she tried to bring up the subject with Fanish, he always replied.

"Gazal. You do not want to know, believe me!"

And after that Fanish, if he felt Gazal did not agree with him, would quickly remind her of Kanan.

"And I still don't know what became her." Gazal said sadly. "Maybe if I had not encouraged to escape she would be safe."

- - - -

Chapter 25

Gazal opened the front door a couple of months later and noticed in astonishment that the house was in darkness.

She switched on the light and saw Vanita in the dark crying uncontrollably.

"Vanita, what is the matter?" Gazal asked then recoiled in surprise as she saw Vanita.

There was a streak of blood across her face and she stood with joined fists pressed in front of her waist. Vanita's face was swollen and she had a black eye, which was swelling to surprising proportions. As Vanita's body stopped its rocking, Gazal saw the terror in her eyes.

Gazal knew immediately who was responsible - but why so soon? May be Fanish had heard Vanita was going to try and escape - and suddenly she remembered the bug he had installed in each room to ensure he knew everything about his girls.

"Vanita, Fanish must have felt threatened by your strength and determination, so decided to break you as soon as possible. Here, I'll get some warm water and tea for you."

She hurried into the kitchen and came back with a mug and a bowl of hot water.

"Here, drink this." She said handing the tea to Vanita.

"That man is depraved, what he did to me." Vanita cried." Fanish is evil but this gentleman is a monster."

She took a sip from the glass, choked on it and had to bend forward, hand on her mouth as the water sprang from her eyes, mixing with her tears.

She daubed her face with a wet towel that Gazal handed her, then sat gasping and twisting it.

As she held the cup in her trembling hands she felt as

if her body had been put through a washing machine and wrung dry. In addition, she had an excruciating headache which seemed to be getting worse.

"Tell me, Gazal, have you ever been to this monster?" Vanita asked in a tremulous voice, her hand on her brow.

Her voice held a hint of anger at the list of misfortunes that fate had so cruelly dealt to her.

"I have, we all have." Gazal wiped her face as she recalled the awful day.

"Tell me all about him, about Fanish about everybody." Vanita calmly asked, as she looked at Gazal through puffed lids.

A storm of such vindictive brutality was churning within her that she started stalking the room, painfully clutching her bruised body, like a caged animal.

Gazal was surprised at Vanita. She was beaten and bruised and had been crying hysterically. Now she looked so calm and composed and the sudden inflection of tone in her calm voice made Gazal think that maybe her present state of suppression was concealing something dangerous in her nature?

Her eyes looked so cold that they sent a shiver down Gazal's spine. It seemed as if something within Vanita had snapped and was replaced with something so dangerous and oh, what was she thinking of?

Then suddenly Vanita's eyes dilated and looked like the eyes of a wild frightened deer that has been trapped. Gazal wondered again if Fanish had somehow found out that Vanita had been planning to escape. She did not want her to suffer the same fate as Kanan; for by now she was sure Fanish had killed her.

She decided to remind her about Kanan.

"Vanita I told you what happened to Kanan didn't I?"

"Yes but you still don't know what happened to her? Fanish did not sell her to that, that…"

Vanita could not bring herself to say his name, which

nobody knew anyway. Everybody had originally called him 'the gentleman' but after being with him they changed 'the gentleman' to 'the Ravager'.

"No, I think not. For then he would not need us, would he?"

"I suppose not, but then anything is possible with Fanish, that bastard!" Vanita's anger and hurt fuelled into bitchy meanness.

She rubbed some cream on her arms gingerly then flinched and a thoughtful look become visible on her face.

"Gazal I was thinking of…"

Gazal realised she was going to tell her something of importance which could be dangerous for both if Fanish found out.

She quickly put her fingers to her lips, took a piece of paper and reminded her about the bugs in the house.

Vanita read the note looked surprised but nodded her understanding. She decided to say something for Fanish's benefit.

"So you don't know what happened to Kanan? Do you think Fanish hurt her?" She brought a note of terror in her voice.

"Yes, I think he did." Gazal nodded her head in approval, "Now you must be careful not do anything rash."

"To be honest, I was planning to escape, but after what you told me, no way!"

Vanita jerked her head up, and then flinched, for the movement was painful. The muscles of her face were twitching and she her lips were trembling.

Gazal had seen the look of pain. "Look, Vanita, do you want me to call the doctor?"

"And how do you think I will explain all these bruises and welts!" Vanita moved her body gingerly then winced in pain. "Ouch! I am sure I have a few broken ribs as well!"

She grabbed herself around the midriff, so acute was the pain that shot through her. She felt the blood pounding in her head, and its thunderous beating hurt so much she winced.

"Here don't move. Sit down and be still."

Gazal took a couple of cushions and handed them to Vanita. When she saw her having difficulty she gently placed them behind her head.

"There is that any better? And don't worry about the doctor, Fanish has one who he trusts and does not ask unnecessary questions."

"Of course, I should have known." Vanita remarked bitterly. "Don't worry, I'll manage, all I need is a good night's sleep."

"You might need an x-ray or something. You seem in a bad state."

Vanita was tired of Gazal's fussing. "Don't fuss, Gazal, I am going to sleep here on the couch." she said and her eyes took on a blank dead look.

Gazal was surprised at the sudden change in Vanita's voice and shivered when she heard the coldness in it. When she looked into Vanita's eyes, they, like her voice, were cold and distant and a look of hatred came into them when she looked at Gazal, as if she was blaming her for everything.

"OK, but let me know if you need anything."

As Gazal left the room, Vanita massaged her brow with the palm of her hand. She had a splitting headache and her body was aching, but more than the physical discomfort Vanita was angry.

Vanita lay awake that night for not only was she in pain but she was also trying to find a solution, to her dilemma - for she knew that if she stayed she might be sold to the 'Ravager.'

Her last thoughts before drifting off to a restless sleep

were

"One way or another I'll get Fanish! He will have to pay for he what he has done to me, what he has taken from me, from us."

Even her sleep was restless, for she was terrified by a nightmare which haunted Vanita at intervals and filled her mind with foreboding.

• • • •

Chapter 26

Gazal entered her room the following morning with a cheerful 'good-morning, did you have a good night?" and pulled back the curtains.

The glare of the emerging sun gave the furniture a faded splendour and picked out specks of dust that coated and sparkled.

She saw Vanita lying on the couch, her face contorted with pain. Where before her eyes, had been swollen and discoloured; now they were blue green and purple.

"Vanita, are you alright, shall I call Dilawar?"

"No, Gazal, I am not all right! But do stop fussing, I don't need a doctor." Vanita replied.

She flinched as she put her hand to her head, for a stabbing pain shot through the back of her head. The pain made her sick and she clutched her head and moaned.

Gazal felt hurt, thinking she did not warrant such rudeness. She had tolerated it yesterday when she thought Vanita was in pain and had controlled her rising irritation, but not again.

"Look here, Vanita," She said in a firm voice. "I have tried to do everything possible to make you comfortable. I don't think you should be so rude."

The pain in Vanita's head subsided and her expression changed from slyness to one of meekness.

She lay back silently and looked at Gazal quietly, her submissiveness being familiar to that of a faithful dog.

"I am sorry, Gazal, you're right. I think I do need to see a doctor. If anything I am feeling worse, there's this lump on my head which was not there before."

A stabbing pain seared through Vanita's head again and Gazal's face blurred whilst everything in the room merged and swam before her eyes.

Gazal looked at her in alarm but at the moment the

doorbell rang and she went to answer it. When she came back Fanish was with her.

"Ah, Vanita, how are you?" he asked genially.

Fanish's voice was delightfully hearty and unaffected, his face all aglow with his own amiability. However, he was shocked to see Vanita for her face was so swollen that he could barely see her features.

"You know how I am!" Vanita retorted angrily.

She glared at Fanish through her swollen eyes and gazed at the depths of Fanish's eyes that had, till recently, reflected nothing but devotion and kindness.

"I presume you are referring to yesterday? Oh, by the way Subhi asked me to give you this." he sneered and opened a small box. Vanita could see something glittering. "And this!"

Fanish threw her a wad of notes and took a deep breath, his sneer contemptuous as his eyes darted from Vanita to Gazal. "Yes, you were saying?"

Vanita threw the money and box away from her. "You cannot buy me, not this time, you scoundrel!"

She had risen from the bed slightly to throw the money but fell back on the couch with weakness. As she gazed at Fanish, his form was lost to her vision behind the tears that stung her eyes.

Vanita felt herself disappearing into shadows.

"I already have." Fanish replied as his lips curled slightly. "Now do you need anything?" He turned towards Gazal who was standing quietly.

"Vanita says she is feeling worse so might need to see a doctor." Gazal said, looking worried. "Vanita?"

Vanita did not reply and lay with her eyes closed and looked so still that Gazal was uneasy.

"Vanita, speak to me!"

When Vanita did not reply, Gazal went up to her and shook her, but Vanita lay as still as a statue.

"Fanish, I think she has fainted, quick, I think we

better call the doctor."

"I have already phoned Dilawar." Fanish said calmly. "She'll be alright. Give her this when she wakes." He gave the jewellery box and money to Gazal.

Gazal felt a pang of jealousy as she saw the all the jewellery and the money, wondering why she was not getting any clients, so decided to confront Fanish about it.

"Fanish, why don't you send me to somebody? I am free tonight and I thought..." She looked at Fanish with an odd expression in her eyes.

"Yes, yes. I'll let you know if I hear something. In the meanwhile, look after Vanita... she is valuable property, though at the moment she looks...." Fanish said harshly.

"Look here, Fanish, I am neither a baby-minder nor a nurse." Gazal retorted, suddenly resenting Vanita, her youth and fragile beauty.

She crossed her arms on her chest and glared at Fanish, her gaze steady. However, her tamed and disciplined anger, as always expressed itself only in her tone and manner, for till Vanita came on the scene, she had been made to feel special.

"Of course, of course, I realise that." Fanish replied hurriedly, however he felt her beauty, together with her tenderness and youth, had faded.

"And anyway, Fanish, you do not seem to realise how badly hurt Vanita is. I don't know what the 'Ravager' did to her but she has changed and matured. Her face is wasted piteously and when it is not swollen, there is pain, grief, and fear written on it like a band. Her eyes, which were beautiful, are now like a wild animal's. Sometimes when she looks at me, I see a strange terror in them."

Gazal spoke the words quickly, fiercely and vindictively, though she knew it was cruel to think of anything but the necessity and humanity of restoring Vanita's health.

"And she got paid for it, didn't she? And you too have got your commission out of it, so I do not know why you are grumbling, Gazal. Anyway, Dilawar will look after her."

"It appears she might have broken her facial bones and be disfigured. You should tell the 'Ravager' to be more careful."

"You've got a point there." Fanish replied. "My main motive was to frighten her."

"You certainly succeeded, Fanish"

"I did, Gazal, but you did not, for I told you to tell her about Kanan."

Although he was angry Gazal could feel the calm cold eyes of Fanish.

"I did, Fanish, I did, but she is stronger than I thought."

"Anyway, she is not planning to do anything silly, like Kanan, is she?" Fanish asked.

"I don't think so…" Gazal replied but her voice sounded unconfident." But you have got your bugs to track our every move, haven't you??

"Of course I have!" Fanish laughed heartily. "Why I have even bugged my own house!"

Actually Fanish was worried, for Vanita, at the moment, was his main livelihood. He had not been able to find any other girl as young and pretty, and Gazal was getting too old for his clients.

However, that was not the only reason, for there were plenty of girls who were vulnerable and could be taken advantage of, he just did not seem to have the time to reach out to them. He had recently got married, and it was his wife, Akshita, who was the problem. He was afraid that her clever and suspicious mind would penetrate, creating a chink in the wall of delusion that

Fanish had striven so hard to erect around her.

She was beginning to ask questions about his work, his disappearance and the phone calls from girls. Nor did she like Aditya or any of his friends.

Fanish had thought Akshita to be gullible and naïve and been confident he would make her believe his lies. However, he soon came to realise that she was in fact a headstrong and stubborn woman.

Furthermore, he had not been aware that her father, Aakar, was an inspector in the police force. Fanish was scared that if he ever found out about his illegal and immoral businesses, he could make things very difficult for them.

Therefore, Fanish felt he did not have the liberty and freedom to move about and nurture his business as he once had, and so had begun to depend on Gazal and Aditya. Till now everything had been running smoothly and she had never given him any problems - the last thing he needed at the moment was trouble between Vanita and Gazal.

"Yes but that is only when you girls are in the house, Gazal, if there is anything you are not telling me about Vanita, please tell me now… Akshita will be waiting."

A fresh pang of jealousy shot through Gazal, she had sacrificed so much for Fanish and he only seemed concerned about Vanita.

"Gazal, is anything the matter?" As Fanish opened the front door, he noticed anxiously the expression on Gazal's face.

"No, nothing at all, nothing is the matter." Gazal said with a heavy heart. "You said you have already sent for Dilawar to have a look at her. If anything else comes up I will let you know."

As she spoke, Fanish saw the lost tenderness and youth tremble back into her face for a moment.

"Is that all?" Fanish said in exasperation. "So why are

you so angry?!"

His lack of understanding was evident on the furrow of thick eyebrows, sharp concentration of his eyes and the tightening of his lips. He gave a snort of contempt as he walked out of the door.

As Fanish got into the car he thought he would phone Dilawar as soon as he got home, for he had lied when he said he had already phoned him.

Fanish had begun to depend more on more on Dilawar, for the last couple of months he had to be called to treat his girls for similar bruises and wounds.

He was running late and Akshita would... Women!" he cursed as he drove fast.

• • • •

Chapter 27

As Fanish drove home, he looked up briefly and saw that the clouds that had been poised in the blue sky in the morning were gone, leaving an empty sky.

He parked his car, opened the door of his house and entered quietly, surprised to find the house quiet and in darkness. He was angry with Akshita for he had specifically told her he would be coming home early.

As he deposited his keys on the table he noticed a white envelope on the mantelpiece. He picked it up, then, with a smirk, threw in on the table, unopened.

He picked up the phone to ring Dilawar again; glad now that Akshita was out, for he did not like talking about the girls in her presence. He dialled his number, hoping he would be home.

"Hello." Dilawar answered.

"Hi, Dilawar, it is Fanish. How are you?"

"Ah, hello Fanish, sorry I can't talk for long…." Dilawar answered. He did not waste any time on preliminarie with Fanish. He knew the only reason Fanish phoned anyway was because there was another young girl who was in trouble.

"What do you want me to do?" he asked abruptly for Ena would be coming home at any time.

"I want you to attend to a young girl called Vanita."

"Is she at the usual place?" Dilawar asked.

"Yes, she is with Gazal."

"And what is the problem?" Dilawar did not know why he asked for he already knew the answer.

"Err, the usual."

"By the same…?" Dilawar could not bring himself to say man for to him he was a perverted monster.

"Yes, but this time he has been more severe with Vanita." Fanish replied.

"If that is possible." remarked Dilawar, remembering the state of the girls he had attended. "You mean he has been crueller, Fanish, why don't you stop sending poor young and vulnerable girls who trust you to him? That man is a monster!".

Dilawar did not like Fanish and only treated the girls because he knew about his affair with his secretary, Sai, and was blackmailing him.

He loved his wife and knew the information would break her heart. He thought of Ena, his wife's beautiful face, with a pang, and how deeply he loved her.

Ena's steady warm love sustained him and the painful thrill of being in love with Sai now was pressed between sadness and joy that only made him aware of the value and difference of the two different states of love.

He had reluctantly agreed to look after Fanish's girls whilst loathing himself for being a gullible naïve fool.

But he was in Fanish's clutches – Fanish, a clever man who knew that people's vulnerabilities, from need to greed, enabled them to commit a variety of sins and then camouflage their weaknesses in a variety of ways.

It was this understanding and distinguishing their weak points, then knowing which of their buttons to push and when, that enabled Fanish to get what he wanted, as well as to sustain a wide and varied circle of friends.

Dilawar shivered as he remembered the first girl he had treated.

She had been badly beaten, her face distorted by marks of fists and her eyes black and swollen. There were cuts on her arms and shoulders, and lacerations on her abdomen. There was a small red streak of blood flowing slowly from a cut on the side of her head.

The feeling that he got when he was called out to treat the girls was always the same too. A chill would spread through his body and he would feel goose-pimples rising on his arms as he looked at the frail and broken girls.

The conversation between Fanish and himself was always the same too.

"Fanish, how can you let this happen to your girls! Should we call her family?" he would ask, bandaging her.

"No, she does not have anyone." Fanish would reply curtly.

Dilawar was quiet as he did his best to treat the girls. He had had heard of accounts of abused young girls, of tales about girls who vanished from their homes, of unsuspecting girls in movie theatre who had needles stuck in their arms and disappeared. Is this where they came to?

"How does this happen?" Dilawar cried." These girls have been raped and beaten."

"Dilawar, don't ask questions"

As Dilawar silently bandaged the girl, he would be angry and hoped that whoever had mutilated the girls would, at the very least, be imprisoned for life.

Subsequently, he discovered, to his horror that not only was Fanish a sex trafficker and dealt in drugs, but that he also made a fortune by selling babies.

He employed a gang of child –stealers in the third world countries and sold them to foreign couples looking for babies to adopt. Fanish would first send Aditya to 'scout' and obtain a child, sometimes even by kidnapping, then take the child to some corrupt official to register the baby as his own so he could sign it away to a couple.

One day Dilawar had decided to confront Fanish.

"Fanish, you exploit people and their need to have children. And you not only exploit the adults, who can defend themselves, but children, and that is unforgivable!"

Fanish laughed unpleasantly.

"I do not consider it to be inhuman at all, like you are implying, my friend, I am merely doing a social service by placing abandoned minors with excellent families. If I leave them where they are they might die, and the children and babies you speak of are mostly neglected babies of prostitutes and junkies who are either unable or unwilling to look after them."

"Fanish, if all you think of is their welfare, why are you concerned about the money that you take from the couples? You don't even check what kind of people you are giving the babies to! Did you know the police found 5 boxes of child pornography in one couple's house and another so called 'father' who had served sentence for molestation?"

Fanish shrugged his shoulders. "So what? And why shouldn't I be paid for my troubles? If the international market in selling children is unchecked, unregulated and morally unconcerned, why should I or you for that matter, worry? My business is flourishing not only in that field but also in that of drugs."

"How can you live with the fact that girls become addicted and then…."

"Dilawar, I encourage my girls to take drugs for it provides them with a much needed endurance and numbness for the brutal and traumatic effects of their jobs. I looking after their welfare by encouraging the use of drugs - for it has an anaesthetic effect that shields them from the pain inflicted on their frail bodies."

"Fanish, I do not want to take part in your dirty schemes."

Dilawar had objected many times. However, he was reminded by Fanish that he was now an accessory, so Dilawar had finally given up voicing his objections, which to Fanish, were like vehicles spinning their wheels in sand anyway.

"If that is possible." remarked Dilawar, remembering

the state of the girls he had attended. "You mean he has been crueller, Fanish, why don't you stop sending poor young and vulnerable girls who trust you to him? That man is a monster!"

"I only send the girls to my friend abroad!" Fanish expostulated, then added. "And give up all the money people pay for them? No way! Anytime I want, a girl of mine has to go wherever I send her!" Fanish made a deep laughing sound in his throat.

" Y...you beast!" Fanish turned around as he heard Akshita's voice

"I'll call you later." Fanish said quickly to Dilawar.

He turned around with the receiver still in his hand, his heart thudding, and saw with dismay that Akshita was looking at it as if it was a venomous snake in Fanish's hand.

▪ ▪ ▪ ▪

Chapter 28

"Y...you beast!" Akshita repeated. "you are a monster!"

Fanish saw that standing next to his wife was his father-in-law, and both were staring at him in repulsion.

"Hello, Akshita, I thought you had gone out?" he remarked, wondering just how much of his conversation with Dilawar they had heard, and judging from their expressions, it was enough.

Fanish's hands were trembling and he moved uneasily from one foot to the other. The muscles on his face seemed to first drop then contract suddenly.

"Yes, I had, I only came to get my bag, which I had forgotten, other-wise I would not have overheard your conversation. So that's what you do for a living -you send innocent girls to men and get money for it, you are a monster!"

The tears that flowed down Akshita's cheeks were of anger and shame. Part of her hoped it was another of his lies, but in her heart was convinced what she had heard was true and it was not just another lie, lies that gave credence to his life.

She brushed the tears with the palm of her hands and saw the envelope containing her note carelessly thrown on the table, unopened. She had loved Fanish so much and he hadn't even bothered to read what she had to say.

She had planned to spend some time with her parents and had only returned to the house to collect her bag, which she had forgotten.

Her heart pumped hard as wave after wave of conflicting emotions stormed over her, but most of all she was angry that the man she had loved and married had turned out to be such a criminal and a monster.

"Err, I was only talking to this friend of mine who..."

Fanish ignored his father-in-law and focused his eyes

on Akshita, his twisted and narrow smile reflecting the growing unease between them.

"That you send a young girl to a strange place? No, you sell young girls! How can you do such a thing? Who have I married?" Akshita was sobbing hysterically.

Aakar, Akshita's father put his arms around his daughter and tried to calm her.

He was a tall-dignified man with sharp handsome features and had grey hair that was flecked with black.

Aakar did not like Fanish and had always thought that there was something artificial about him, and his judgement of Fanish was proving right, though it was a pity his daughter had not recognised it earlier. And being in the Police he should have had him investigated, but that would have only opened Pandora's box and he had trusted his daughter's judgement. But was he going to have to sacrifice his daughter's happiness now and more importantly, could he?

"You bastard, how can you do such cruel things?" Aakar looked at Fanish scathingly, as he tried to control his rising temper.

"The money is good, father-in-law." Fanish looked at him disdainfully and shrugged his shoulders, however he was scared.

Aakar could not contain his temper. He moved quickly and caught Fanish by the throat, his face suddenly dark with rage. The silence was only broken by Akshita's sobs and a sickening crunch of splintering bones as Aakar hit Fanish on the nose.

Caught by surprise, Fanish slumped against the wall, blood pumping through his fingers and from his mouth.

"Stop it, Dad!" Akshita shrieked.

She covered her eyes with her hands then gently lowered them and soundlessly wept.

"No, you have misunderstood...Akshita?" Fanish was cowering against the wall.

"I think the only misunderstanding has been on my part." Akshita jerked her head up and looked angrily at Fanish through her tears. "I trusted you, however, everything fits, all those mysterious calls– all those young girls who you said were daughters of your friends and all those times you went away. My, how gullible and naïve I was to have ever believed your lies? How could I ever have thought that I loved you? Do you know how much I stood up for you with my parents?"

Akshita stood still and held her breath willing herself to feel nothing, think nothing, and do nothing. She found she was talking but felt removed from it all. For a few blissful minutes, Akshita had detached herself from everything, including her sorrow.

"Akshita, don't waste your time and words on him - he is not worth it. Let's go, and this time you are not coming back." Aakar took Akshita by the arm.

"Don't worry, Dad, I don't want to." Akshita said fervently.

As she looked into Fanish's eyes, she detected a subtle change in them which convinced her that he had always put on an act for her benefit.

"Akshita, listen to me, give me a chance to explain." Fanish pleaded.

Fanish's attention was so focused and so magnetic that Akshita felt she might be danger of being lured into his charm again.

"I don't want to talk to you. Akshita turned in disgust.

As the door closed behind them, Fanish did not know whether to be glad or sorry. He loved Akshita in his own way and would miss her, but in a way he was glad too, for was tired of the lies and deception. However, he was frightened of Aakar, the power he possessed and how he would use it in light of the latest information.

He flung himself on a chair with a handkerchief over his face to try and stem the bleeding from his nose. He knew he would have to be careful now; he always was, but now more than ever, for without Akshita, Fanish realised he was at the mercy of his father-in-law.

Fanish had to ensure his sins against exposure, and to that end, would leave no stone unturned and no form of treachery untried to try and conceal them.

Therefore, it was not long before an idea formed in his devious and cunning brain – one which he was sure would solve his dilemma.

· · · ·

Chapter 29

"I told you not to marry him!" Aakar was driving furiously as he glanced angrily at his daughter.

The lights were being lit in the houses as dusk fell like a shroud around them.

"D... Dad, how can you say that?" How was I to know what he really was like? He was always so kind, gentle and caring."

"Ha!" Aakar snorted "So caring that he is into child trafficking? I'll have him for this, I'll send him to jail, I'll…!"

"Dad, Dad, you'll do nothing of the sort."

"Akshita, are you out of your mind? What do you mean do nothing?"

Aakar looked at Akshita in amazement and saw on her face a loyalty that was powerful enough to smother intelligence.

"Leave him alone, Father, please. Although I am horrified and repulsed at what he does I love him, or at least loved him."

Akshita scanned her data screen of memories and isolated the times she knew could not be forgotten.

"You don't really mean that, do you? You know, Akshita, you were born into the best social structure, given the best opportunities, the best money could buy, and you wasted it all by mixing with misfits like Fanish and his friends. You are gullible, you trust people, believe what they say, when all the time you were being used." Aakar parked his car outside their home. "You have never appreciated what was done for you and even now, when you know what Fanish is like, you are defending him."

Akshita gave a little sob as she got out of the car and saw the look of triumph on her father's face and something else – was it mockery at Akshita for not admitting and accepting the degree of Fanish's wickedness?

They walked down the pathway that was shrouded by laurels towards Dakar's house. They could hear muffled noised from neighbouring house, children playing, doors slamming, dog barking in the distance.

"I hope Aninditi is home." Aakar remarked as he opened the door. Aninditi, we are home - Look who has come with me."

Aninditi came out of the kitchen, rubbing her hands on her apron.

"Akshita, what a lovely surprise, but you have come without Fanish, is he too busy to meet his mother-in-law?"

She smiled tenderly and hugged Akshita, who at the warm reception and the mention of Fanish started crying.

"Akshita, what is the matter?" Aninditi looked enquiringly at her husband. "Aakar, what is the matter with my daughter? Is Fanish alright?" They were still standing in the landing. "Here, come to the sitting room and tell me all about it. I am sure it can't be all that bad. Aakar, can you make us some tea?"

Aninditi led Akshita to the lounge whilst Aakar gratefully disappeared into the kitchen, for he could not deal with hysterical women.

As soon as Akshita and her mother were seated, Aakar came to the room with a glass of water.

"Here, have this first." he said, handing Akshita the glass.

"Aakar, she doesn't need water but hot, strong and sweet tea." Aninditi said indignantly.

"Coming up!" he said disappearing into the kitchen again.

As soon as Aninditi saw that her daughter had calmed somewhat she questioned her again.

"Now tell me what the matter is, what has made you cry, is it Fanish?" Aninditi affectionately patted Akshita's head.

"Mum, how can I tell you? I feel so…so ashamed, dirty and used." Akshita blurted

She kept reliving the conversation she had overheard. How could Fanish taint and despoil innocent young girls? She did not want to tell her mother, but knew if she did not her father would.

"Mother, I, no we have found out something horrible about Fanish and…" Akshita fidgeted in her chair.

"Nobody is perfect, beti." Aninditi tried to reassure her daughter. "In marriage one needs a great deal of tolerance, and nothing can be so bad as to walk out on your husband. Don't worry, you'll feel better in the morning. Ah, here comes Aakar with the tea."

"Aninditi, do you know what your Fanish has been up to?" Aakar asked as he put the tray on the table with a grimace.

He had only offered to make the tea so that mother and daughter could have a chat- however; it seemed to him that it was Aninditi who was doing the talking.

Aninditi interrupted flourishing her hand.

"I don't know has happened between them but why are you supporting Akshita? You have never liked Fanish, but I have just been telling her that these things happen in marriage, and it is up to both of the partners to make it work by enduring each other's faults."

She glared at Aakar whilst she poured the tea and handed Akshita a cup.

"Mother, he is right."

Akshita felt better after meeting her mum, but her heart was full of hurt and disillusionment as she gulped the hot liquid quickly.

"Will one of you tell me what he has supposed to have done?" Aninditi said sharply.

"H. he.." Aakar was so angry that his hands trembled and the cup in his hand started rattling.

"Dad, let me tell her." Akshita hiccupped.

As Akshita sipped her tea, she told her mother about the conversation they had overheard with an occasional muttered "Hey Ram, Hey Ram." From Aninditi.

"So now you know why I am here." Akshita said with a catch in her throat.

"Is there no way you could be mistaken? Maybe he was talking about a daughter of a friend of his who was being naughty...!"Aninditi asked anxiously.

"For goodness sake, Aninditi!" Aakar retorted angrily. "You're just as gullible and naïve as your daughter!"

Tall and dignified, he leant against the wall, lighting his pipe and gazing thoughtfully at his wife.

"No, but I was hoping that...anyway, Akshita will stay here." Aninditi put her arm around Akshita protectively.

"Mum, where is Urvi? She is not back from school as yet?" Akshita asked.

Urvi was her younger sister. More than her parents, Akshita missed her young sister, Urvi, with her clear and steady eyes gazing up at her from under a shock of fiery curls, curls which gave her otherwise plain face a hint of suppressed excitement that threatened to erupt at any moment.

"She should be back at any moment...." Aninditi replied absent-mindedly looking at her watch. "But she is late today."

Aninditi marvelled at her eldest daughter's coolness for her initial hysteria had subsided and she appeared calm.

"Aninditi, what is for dinner?" Aakar asked.

"It's nearly ready. Akshita, you go up to your room and freshen up."

"I presume my old room? Mum can you find out why Urvi is late?" Akshita asked again.

"Yes, your old room and I will ring her school and friends. Now go!" Aninditi smiled and gestured towards the stairs.

"Great, mum, I am glad you have not changed my room…" Akshita gave a cry of delight and hugged Aninditi.

As long as she could remember she had felt that her little room had wrapped itself around her like a protective shell, holding her as she slept through the night.

"… and don't worry, Urvi will be back any minute, I will call you as soon as she does, for I know how close you two are."

Aninditi embraced her daughter and kissed her on the cheek. She had always protected her daughter from the harsh realities of the world but when she looked into Akshita's eyes and saw reflected there the pain of betrayal and disillusion, wished there was some way she could take away her daughter's sorrow.

As Akshita went up to her room, Aninditi turned to her husband.

"Now, Aakar, tell me again what you heard."

Aakar repeated the conversation they had overheard.

"My god, what an awful man Fanish turned out to be, Akshita is not going back. Sounds like what he is doing is illegal, is there anything you can do about it?"

"Unfortunately no, we have no evidence except what we overheard. Ani, I am starving!"

- - - -

Chapter 30

Akshita had still not finished freshening up when Aniniti called up from the dining room where she was laying the table.

"Akshita, dinner is ready!" Aniniti called, setting out the plates and cutlery on the table.

When there was no answer, Aakar got worried.

"Hadn't you better go up and see everything is alright?" Aakar frowned at his wife. "You, know, the discovery about Fanish might have hit her harder than we think."

"I'm coming, Mother." Akshita called, and appeared soon after.

"Thank God!" murmured Aakar, for he was extremely fond of his daughter. "And that must be Urvi." he remarked as he heard the doorbell.

"Aakar, you're hungry, carry on with your dinner while I get the door." Aniniti rose from the table.

"No, Mum, I'll go, I'm dying to meet Urvi." Akshita ran out of the room.

Aakar had placed some food on his plate and was just going to tuck in when he heard the front door slam.

"Why are the girls talking for so long?" he asked impatiently.

"They have a lot to catch up on. It is good for Akshita to have someone to talk to." She'll…why what is the matter, Akshita?"

Akshita, her face white, had entered the room and was standing quietly, holding an empty envelope in one hand, whilst in the other she held a piece of paper.

Her hands had turned sticky with the clammy

perspiration running down her fingers.

"Where's Urvi?" Aakar was getting impatient. "Aren't you girls' hungry?"

"Father, that was not Urvi but a man sent by Fanish." Akshita glanced down at the paper in her trembling hands.

"Akshita, what are you talking about?" Aakar snapped." What did he want?"

"He came to give us this." She held out the piece of paper clenched in her hand.

"Come on, Akshita, what does it say?" Aakar barked.

Akshita gazed at her father unbelievingly, then, she began to read aloud in a voice as flat and grey as an endless stretch of motorway.

"Here, give me that!"

Aakar snatched the letter from her and read the contents of the paper.

"Oh, my God, no!"

"What is the matter? Akshita, Aakar, where is Urvi?" Aninditi looked at her husband, her daughter then at the empty doorway.

"Damn him! He says he has got Urvi with him and has a few demands…the cheek of him! Firstly, he wants Akshita to go back to him, secondly, that I don't take any kind of action against him, else, he will hold Urvi hostage and we know what that would mean. The bastard!" Aakar banged his fist on the table.

Aninditi snatched the letter from Aakar and her face paled as she read it.

"Urvi, my Urvi, no!" Aninditi got up restlessly.

"Don't worry, we'll get her back." Aakar tried to reassure a distraught Aninditi.

Aninditi began pacing the room, looking strangely pale and quiet. She felt dizzy and put her hands on the table to support herself.

"I should have realised that Fanish will not let go of

you easily." Aakar retorted.

He went towards the telephone and dialled Fanish's number, drumming his fingers impatiently on the table as he waited for Fanish to pick up the phone.

"Ah father dear." Fanish answered his voice silkily smooth as a snake ready to strike.

His voice was smug and dropped low in his throat as he gave a mirthless and derisive laugh.

Aakar shuddered as he imagined Fanish's sly beady eyes, the expression on his face and his flesh crawled with revulsion.

"Where is my daughter, you bastard?"

"Yes, yes Urvi is with me, she waiting for Akshita. What time shall I say she is coming?"

"Fanish, you.... you...!"

"Yes, yes of course, Urvi will wait for Akshita till she comes home. What did you say?"

"Akshita will not come back to you! And even if she does I can take action later after Urvi is back with us."

Aakar knew Fanish's conversation was for the benefit of Urvi, who must be nearby.

"Oh, Urvi wants to say hello. She is insisting she wants to talk to you!"

"Hi, Dad," Urvi's voice was breathless.

"What are you doing there, Urvi? Why didn't you come straight home like we told you? Come home and leave that house immediately!" Aakar's voice was insistent without trying to alarm Urvi.

"Dad, I am waiting for Akshita, Fanish told me she wanted to see me about something, and we are having fun here. Aditya uncle is here and...."

"Did you say that Fanish told you that Akshita wanted to see you? And who's there with you? Did you say Aditya? Don't stay because...!"

Before he could complete his sentence Fanish was back on the line.

"Of course, Dad. There is no need to worry. Urvi will stay here till Akshita comes home. She is having a great time with Aditya." Fanish replaced the receiver with a satisfied grin.

"Damn him!" Aakar slammed the receiver. "I'll take action..."I'll..."

"You'll do nothing, Dad, for I'll do what Fanish wants, we have to see that Urvi is safe." Akshita put on her coat and gloves. "Dad, can you drive me back, please?"

Although Akshita's helplessness was mixed with fear, she somehow managed to feign a calmness that belied the turmoil in her. The safety of her sister paramount in her mind.

"Akshita, you can't go, he'll..." Aakar did not know what to do.

"Fanish won't do anything to me" she said calmly.

"Akshita, wait a minute, let's talk it through We might arrive at another solution." Aakar held her arm.

"We do not have time, Dad," Akshita said impatiently. "Don't you realise what Fanish was trying to tell us? His friend Aditya is there and I don't trust him with Urvi. God alone knows what his devious mind is planning."

"She's right." Aninditi whispered.

She had been sitting quietly, wringing her hands, her face pale as she listened to the conversation between Akshita and her husband. As Aakar looked at her in amazement she explained.

"I don't want Akshita to go either but she is older and will know what to do. It does not have to be permanent but whilst Akshita is there, we can stall for time."

"You're right, very sensible, Aninditi." Aakar commented as he too put on his coat, impatient to be on his way. "Hurry up, let's go."

He drove fast and as there was no traffic, reached

Fanish's house within fifteen minutes.

Fanish opened the door as Akshita rang the doorbell, for she had flung her keys at Fanish when she had stormed out.

"Where is Urvi? Is she alright?" She asked angrily as she stormed into the house.

Akshita went into the lounge and found Urvi sitting with her legs tucked up on the sofa, howling with laughter and tears streaming from her eyes.

As soon as she saw Akshita, Urvi got up and hugged her, her eyes dancing with mischief.

"Akshita, Dad, I am glad to see you. You know, Aditya and Fanish were telling me about some funny incidents that happened to young girl's abroad. He was telling me how lucky I was for one eight-year-old girl was put in jail for no offence, and in many places they don't go to school but have to work so they can eat. Actually that is not funny, isn't that awful?" She shuddered and her face became serious. "My, I am glad to be here with you!"

The blood drained from Akshita's cheeks and she looked alarmed when Aditya put his arm around Urvi in an intimate gesture.

"How are you, Bhabhi?" Aditya said. "You have a charming and beautiful sister …"

"Urvi, come here! Are you alright?" Akshita and Aakar both asked simultaneously.

"Of course I am. Why what is the matter?" Urvi replied as she looked from her sister to her father, confused.

"Come here, Urvi, let's go home, your mother is waiting for you." Aakar said, grabbing Urvi 's hand.

"Dad, I am not coming with you, I want to stay with Akshita. She wants to talk to me." Urvi exclaimed.

"Why don't you let her stay?" Aditya remarked slyly. "We were having such a good time."

"No, Urvi, go with Dad, I'll talk to you some other time, it was nothing urgent." Akshita said quickly.

"But Fanish said .... Anyway, I am hungry, Akshita makes my favourite food. "Urvi replied, more baffled than ever.

"He misunderstood, and you can eat at home. Mother is waiting for you and Urvi, don't argue. Go with Father!"

"Urvi, wait outside, I want to talk to Fanish". Aakar said through clenched teeth.

As soon as Urvi had put on her coat, grumbling all the while, she opened the door and left.

As soon as she had left, Aakar grabbed Fanish by the throat. His fists were clenched as he snarled at him.

"I'm warning you, you snivelling rat! Don't you dare harm any one of my daughter's or else...."

Aakar spat the words in Fanish's face, who nearly stumbled and fell.

"We'll see about that… it all depends on you, doesn't it?" Fanish hissed as he recovered his balance. "Don't forget I am holding Akshita hostage and kidnapping Urvi was just to let you know that I can get her anytime I want to."

His eyes first flicked over Akshita, then out of the window at Urvi as he licked his lips. Fanish leant against the wall with a smug grin.

"Now you know that Aditya likes Urvi, I think he even likes Akshita. And even after Akshita is back with me and you decide to investigate me and I am jailed, Aditya will take my place – in all respects!" Fanish said nastily.

■ ■ ■ ■

110

Chapter 31

"Dad, I don't want to go home! I want to stay with Akshita!" Urvi yelled.

"No you are not, young lady!" Aakar replied brusquely

Aakar dragged Urvi to the car, holding her arm whilst his fingers dug into them.

As soon as they were in the car, she asked.

"Dad, what was Fanish talking about? What is happening?"

"Nothing, Urvi, nothing is the matter, but in future you are not to talk to either Fanish or Aditya, even if they say it is Akshita who wants to see you. Understand? That is why we have given you the mobile, check with her before."

Meanwhile, as soon as Fanish closed the door behind them, he stood in the landing and glowered at Akshita, who instinctively cowered against the wall, terrified of Fanish's new dark nature.

He had always, till now, shown only kindness and consideration, although there had always been something elusive and mysterious about him.

Now, Fanish was making it clear to Akshita that he was the one who was not happy with her. To Fanish, Akshita became another conquest, somebody to use only when it suited him. Akshita wished she had not discovered the truth about Fanish, for not only did it put her in a dangerous position; it also put her family at risk. Urvi especially, as Fanish had so rightly taken pains to let them know. Her father was head of police, but even that could not help any of them now.

Aditya re-entered the lounge and made himself comfortable, treating it as if it was his own home.

"Come in, sister-in-law and make yourself comfortable!" His laughter was harsh and made a grating sound.

Akshita followed him angrily.

"This is my house and I want you out!"

"No, you won't. Fanish's eyes glittered maliciously.

"You're forgetting something, Akshita This is my house and you have no say in who comes or goes in this house – especially my friends."

The cruel and careless truth was delivered with authority and through narrowed eyes he saw with relish the horror on Akshita's face.

The sharpness of Fanish's tone and the unexpected coldness was as effective as a slap, and Akshita instinctively put her hand on her cheek.

■ ■ ■ ■

Chapter 32

Akshita felt humiliated and was silent, for to answer back in the presence of Aditya would only result in Fanish demeaning her further.

"Fanish, my friend, have you had dinner? I am starving." Aditya got up to switch on the television." Shall I order something?"

"No, Akshita will make us her speciality. Did I tell you she is a great cook?"

"No – yes, Urvi did mention it and I will look forward to enjoying it."

"That settles that then, Akshita, Aditya will stay for dinner."

As Akshita disappeared into the kitchen, inwardly seething, she heard Aditya.

"Fanish, have you heard from Dilawar? You did remember to phone him, didn't you?"

"Yes, I did, and that is how the trouble started.." Fanish threw himself into an armchair and stretched his legs. " If it had not been for that call....!"

"What do you mean?" Aditya asked, raising his eyebrows. "I cannot ever imagine you to be in any kind of trouble. Now, tell me what happened for I received a call from you asking me to come here immediately. I didn't ask any questions then, but, to be honest, I am very curious." Aditya remarked taking out a cigarette packet from his pocket and lighting a cigarette.

He listened in astonishment as Fanish briefly recounted what had consequently transpired between Akshita and her father.

"So what are you going to do now? Fanish, I am nervous at this development for I am implicated as well. Why did you have to marry the daughter of a someone from the police profession? An inspector, no less!

Fanish, I know you well, I don't think it was love but a challenge that you could not resist."

"No Aditya I loved Akshita and did not know anything about her background, but I have sorted it out …. I can say with certainty we are now safe. In fact, more so now for I have the upper hand. And even if I do say so myself, I think calling you here was a stroke of genius on my part." Fanish said complacently.

"Fanish I am puzzled, what have I missed?" Aditya looked confused.

"Don't you see?" Fanish cried in exasperation. "Aakar now knows that I can get hold of Urvi anytime I want if he says or does anything that is the least bit threatening to us."

"So why is Akshita here? I thought you wanted to get rid of her? You haven't found out that you really love her?" Fanish's devious plan dawned on Aditya and he smiled.

"No, of course not, not now." Fanish snorted contemptuously. "However, she too is our meal ticket and security!"

Everybody in Fanish's life had a function, and it was slowly becoming clear to Aditya what it was. Fanish usually took what he needed from people and left the rest lying around, and it seemed his wife was to be no exception. Fanish did not wait to be offered what they wanted to give – he made his own selection.

"Fanish, I have never told you before, but I think she is beautiful, although I prefer them young. You know what I mean?" Aditya ran his lips over his thick lips.

"I am glad you think so, Aditya, but not as yet." Fanish grinned.

Aditya walked over to Akshita as she laid the table.

"Err, Akshita, I am so glad that you have been kind enough to ask me to stay for dinner." He looked at her lecherously as Akshita glared at him.

"You are forgetting something, I did not invite you, you invited yourself." Akshita drew her sari around her, her eyes fiery.

He smelled of sickly after-shave that made Akshita's skin crawl.

Aditya took her chin in the palm of his hand and caught Akshita's wrist as it came up to slap him.

"Don't you dare touch me!" she hissed.

Fanish laughed heartily.

Akshita glared at Fanish and Aditya in disgust and turned to leave the room when Fanish stopped in front of her.

"Where are you going?" he asked.

"I am not hungry and…"

"You are to have your dinner with us." Fanish said, softly but firmly and as soon as they were seated, remarked. "After dinner, I think I will ring up Gazal and find out how Vanita is. No, I won't have the time, Akshita; will you do it for me?"

"No, I don't want anything to do with your disgraceful and shady business."

Akshita flung her napkin on the table and stormed out of the room with a sob, followed by Fanish's and Aditya's laughter.

"That was not very nice of you." Aditya helped himself to hot lentils and vegetables. "No, seriously, I approve, but you will have to phone Dilawar soon you know."

"Oh thanks for reminding me. He left a message with Akshita, but I am sure Vanita is fine." Gazal was just making a fuss, as usual!"

"I don't know about that." Aditya remarked doubtfully. "Do you remember Kanan and the problem she caused? We don't want Vanita to do the same."

"Who? Kanan? Of course I remember her! That is why she was sent to …. But maybe you're right; Vanita can land us in a different kind of trouble if we are not careful, we'll to Gazal and see how Vanita is, Dilawar should be there by now."

Aditya nodded curious to know how things were panning out.

"What about Akshita? How do you know she won't go the police?"

. "Aditya, you seem to have forgotten my plan…. Fanish looked at his friend in astonishment. "She knows that Urvi can be taken anytime and neither she nor her family will risk that. And as a precaution, don't forget I am known by another name in our organisation and by the girls, except Vanita and Gazal, of course."

"True, but what if she runs away and goes back to her parents?"

"Man, you are a pessimist! However, I'll just have to have a little talk to her before and remind her how interested you were in her sister - she'll do anything to protect her."

Fanish had no qualms about the treachery he was carrying out and Aditya suspected that even in his dreams Fanish plotted ways to control people.

• • • •

Chapter 33

Dilawar drove through quiet streets for the shops had closed for the day.

He had a rather soft and effeminate face and wore his hair parted on the left side. His eyebrows and lips were thin, giving an overall impression of a weak personality.

As he drove he watched the rain fall like a grey striped curtain and trickle down the windscreen of his car.

Gazal opened the door and gave a sigh of relief as she saw him.

"Dilawar, thank God you are here." Gazal looked at him with worried doe-like eyes." Come I will take you to Vanita, I think something is very wrong"

Vanita's face had swollen even more during the night and as Dilawar examined her, he discovered she had broken ribs, her skin was red and blotched, had red welts running down the whole of her body which had been either been bruised or broken.

'That man is an animal, absolute animal. How can anyone do something like this, especially to a delicate young girl?" Dilawar exclaimed in horror.

He took a tiny flashlight from his bag and tried to peer into Vanita's swollen eyes.

"I don't know what to do…" Gazal whispered wringing her hands.

"There is this lump on my head which is paining and…". Vanita whispered running her tongue over her lips for they that felt dry.

Her words were slurred as she tried to speak through swollen lips and she felt sick.

"You'll have to go into hospital." Dilawar remarked putting his stethoscope away." I don't like the bump on your head."

"You know that is not possible, Dilawar, Fanish would not like that. Do what you can for me here!" Vanita said.

However, she realised through the searing pain that coursed through her, that nothing she said or did anymore would make any difference. She was oblivious to everything but the pain as another stabbing pain shot through the back of her head and she clutched her face and screamed.

Gazal was standing watching as Vanita nearly fainted from pain.

"She is right. You know what would happen if she went into hospital? Fanish said she is to be treated here" Gazal repeated.

"Yes, and I also know what would happen if she does not." Dilawar snapped. "I can't do anything for her here, I don't have the equipment." Dilawar looked in astonishment at Gazal's cold and inscrutable face. "Look, I can give her some temporary medication to help alleviate the pain. I will talk to Fanish as soon as I go home."

As Dilawar drove home he felt sick to his stomach that he was part of something so evil and sinister. Vanita's face appeared before him as he had seen her once before.

She had been beautiful and her eyes, which had been full of youth and energy, now seemed tired and grey, reflecting the dullness of the river that flowed nearby.

As soon as he reached home he rang Fanish and left a message with Akshita for him to contact him as soon as possible.

Dilawar sat down and wiped his brow for the images of Kanan and Vanita – young and innocent faces -

floated in his mind whilst their screams resounded in his ears

"Dilawar, you look terrible," His wife, Ena exclaimed, handing him a cup. "Whatever is the matter?"

"I feel terrible!" However, Dilawar smiled feebly as took the cup. " Look, there is something I want to talk to you about but…"

Dilawar loved Ena, on whom he depended and the thought of what she might do if she ever found out about him and Sai terrified him. Worse than that was the thought she might hate and leave him. For how could she love someone who was too weak to stand up to Fanish and tolerate what he did to innocent girls?

He had always thought himself to be a man who could distinguish the truth from a pack of lies, but since his dealings with Fanish, his mistrust of that self-proclaimed ability haunted him. Time and time again he thought of quitting, but was too deeply implicated and the longer he left it the deeper he was embroiled.

Ena sat silently, hands folded on her lap.

"Dilawar, tell me what is bothering you." she asked again.

Before he could answer the telephone rang and Dilawar got up hurriedly.

"Hello, Dilawar." It was Fanish. "I believe you wanted to talk to me?"

"Yes, I wanted to talk to you about Vanita …"

"I am with them at the moment, with Aditya, but did you tell Gazal?"

"Just that Vanita should be taken to hospital as soon as possible."

"Why did you say that, what the hell do I pay you for?" Fanish barked.

"There is nothing I can do for she needs the hospital and…." Dilawar spluttered.

"You said the same about Kanan." Fanish expostulated.

"Yes, and look what happened to her." Dilawar retorted.

"Dilawar, you have no idea what happened to Kanan and why. Now, I want you to come back immediately and treat Vanita, and bring any medicines you think she might need."

"Fanish, Vanita is in a coma and there is nothing I can do for her, the only thing she needs at the moment s to be into hospital. All this is your fault for sending her to that pervert. I don't want anything to do with your illegal businesses and...."

"Hey, steady on, do you want me to talk to your wife?" Fanish asked maliciously.

"I'll talk to her myself – I will also talk to the police too. Look, I've got to go – I'll talk to you tomorrow, better still, I'll see you tomorrow!"

Dilawar slammed the receiver and swung around to see Ena standing quietly in the doorway.

She looked thoughtfully at Dilawar,

"I heard you talking to Fanish, what were you going to tell me?" she asked softly. "You know, Dilawar, I don't like Fanish; I think he is a fishy and devious character. You were talking about the police, what has he done to implicate you?"

"Yes, it was Fanish, and yes, he has implicated me." Dilawar nodded his head. "It's a long story and one that I am sure you will not like."

As soon as Ena sat down, she crossed her hands on her laps. The rain hammered on the rooftop and Ena could hear it overflowing along the gutter, sounding like an endless river.

As Dilawar drank the hot liquid, he revealed everything about Fanish to his wife, but his voice was so soft and low that Ena had to strain forward to hear him.

With her legs tucked under her, her chin under her face, face shiny and damp, Ena listened to her husband quietly as she sat on the sofa.

Ena felt disillusioned; as if a chill wind had enveloped her and that she was being slowly blown away from him, for he was revealing a new side to his character.

She held her breath whilst Dilawar was talking, and his voice had a definite strange effect on her, as though he were speaking to her from another world. It appeared to Ena that everybody she trusted and loved was playing one role or another, so was confused as to what was true and what was real

"Dilawar, I don't think you are telling me everything."

She clenched her fists and held them firmly at her side, her entire body stiff and poised.

- - - -

Chapter 34

"My god, what is Dilawar thinking of?" Fanish cried as he put down the receiver.

Just when he had straightened out one problem, another rose and Fanish felt as if a net was closing round him.

"Why, what did he say?" Aditya asked anxiously.

"Would you believe it; he is threatening to go to the police."

Fanish rubbed his fingers across his forehead in perplexity. He usually showed some kind of control and this ability to stay cool gave him an advantage over people.

"He can't do that." exclaimed Gazal. "Did you remind him you would tell his wife?"

"That threat, my dear, did not work today for he said he is going to tell her himself."

"So what are you going to do?" Gazal asked worriedly.

"I don't know. At this stage we can only hope that Ena will persuade Dilawar not to go to the police, for he too deeply implicated, and is an accessory after all."

"Fanish, everything is getting too complicated and I think out of your control now." Aditya declared.

"Now you know why it is a good idea I stay married to Akshita, Aditya. If worse comes to worse, we can always rely on good old father in law!" Fanish laughed heartily." And don't forget, I am known by another name."

"You're a genius!" Aditya clapped Fanish on the shoulder. "Akshita is so…"

"She is beautiful, you know!" Fanish remarked.

"I thought you said…" Aditya looked confused.

"Leave everything to me, Aditya, I will sort it out and

if need me I will ask for your help."

"But for now what are you going to do about Vanita, Fanish she is lying so cold and still that I am frightened." Gazal looked at Fanish imploringly.

"The best thing would be for both of you to take her to hospital." Fanish suggested "Yes, I think that is the best thing to do at this stage. That could work in our favour, for if anything should happen to her and the police know about it – which is what Dilawar is going to do – we can at least say that we tried everything possible to help her."

"Fanish, I think you are wrong, the hospital is going to ask questions about her injuries. How they happened, who was responsible etc.?" Aditya looked frightened.

"Are you questioning my decision? Say that she is your niece and that she fell down some stairs or something."

"You don't really think they'll believe that, do you?" Gazal asked. " Have you seen her - her bruises, swelling and the lacerations on her body!"

"Yes, I can see how that can be a problem. Gazal, maybe you should go alone, and then you can explain that she interrupted a burglar who then attacked her."

"Yes, but again that will involve the police."

"I don't think we can avoid that now. Not if Dilawar is going to talk, which I think he will."

"Should I call the ambulance?" Gazal asked.

"Let's get our stories straight first, for we will have to tell the hospital something."

Fanish was giving directions hastily whilst he walked about the room. His face had turned pale and there were beads of perspiration on his forehead.

"I'll go and make some coffee, I think we need some, it seems it is going to be a long night."

"Yes, thank you Gazal that would be nice."

Fanish and Aditya made themselves comfortable

whilst Gazal went into the kitchen to make a pot of coffee. Soon she re-entered the room with a tray in her hand.

As soon as they had their coffee and got their stories straight, Vanita was taken to hospital by Gazal and Fanish and whisked away in a wheelchair to X-ray.

▪ ▪ ▪ ▪

Chapter 35

When Vanita opened her eyes she found she was lying in bed with a searing headache whilst her body ached every time she tried to move.

Suddenly, she trembled as she remembered a monstrous face staring at her then whipping her. She had screamed with terror, fighting desperately to fight free whilst her body jerked in spasms of pain, but he had been too strong. Through her tears Vanita had seen another gentleman wearing a mask sitting quietly at the back of the room, enjoying Vanita's pain

After some time, he strolled over to her and with a key, opened her handcuffs.

Her eyes dilated with terror as she tried to claw at his face, but strong hands gripped hers. She screamed but was slapped hard and thrown back on the bed, but not before she had pulled off his mask

"Are you awake?"

Vanita heard a voice nearby, and as her eyes adjusted to the light, saw was she was in a hospital cubicle.

A nurse was peering over her, but the face was blurred and everything in the room merged and swam before her.

Her faintness gradually disappeared, but although the nurse was looking at her with warm twinkling eyes, she shrank back in terror.

"Who are you? Don't come near me! Where am I?"

Vanita's voice sounded unrecognisable to herself and a scream burst from her again as she recalled her ordeal.

"It's alright, luv, don't worry, you're in hospital. Your cousin brought you here a couple of days ago."

"Why? What's wrong with me?" Vanita touched her face gingerly.

"Apparently you caught a burglar in the act of

stealing from you house and he violently attacked you. Don't you remember?"

"Oh my God! No, I don't remember anything." Vanita replied.

Gazal entered the ward at the moment and seemed glad to see Vanita. There was an I.V leading into Vanita's arm and there was a hollow glass tube to indicate the amount of medicine being administered.

"Now, now don't tire her!" Jane scurried off.

"I'm glad to see you are awake, Vanita. You had us all worried, you know!"

Gazal immediately saw the change in Vanita; and the transformation was not only physical but mental.

"What do you mean you all? I have this dreadful feeling that nobody really cares." Vanita was shaking with fright.

"You are wrong, Vanita, we..."

"No, you don't, at one time I thought you did but not now." Vanita replied strangely with a weary calmness and coldness. "What have you told the hospital? That I am your cousin and I interrupted a burglar who violently attacked me? Why didn't you tell them the truth? If you really are such a good friend of mine, as you claim to be, why didn't you tell them about Fanish and his...? And anyway what would happen if I had told them the truth? I may still do so." Vanita leant back on her pillow wearily.

Jane came back to check on Vanita, but when she saw how pale and tired she looked, scolded Gazal

"I told you not to tire my patient!" Jane unscrewed the narrow tube and was going to place the needle of her syringe into the burette when she stopped by Gazal.

"No, Nurse, just give me a few minutes more, and then I'll be off" Gazal replied with a frown.

"Now, just a few minutes more. You realise she has not woken up and needs to rest." She took the syringe back. "I will be back soon to give her medication. "Jane hurried off like a pony express between patients, taking the pulse and blood pressure of the other patients on the ward.

"Now, Vanita, you were saying?"

"Nothing, however, I think I should let you know that I have told the nurse I cannot remember anything about the incident. That should keep you safe for the moment, but don't forget, I might change my mind for I remember everything…." Vanita's voice was low.

"I'm not trying to change your mind, but let me know what you plan to do" Gazal asked. "But before you decide, do keep in mind that Fanish is a ruthless man and would do anything to protect himself and his businesses."

"Are you threatening me, Gazal?" Vanita gave a gesture of disgust. "Remember, I was the one who was beaten, and the same thing will happen again to another girl, and she might not be as lucky as me. And you never did tell me what happened to Kanan?. Oh, my head hurts and I think I can feel a lump….!"

"Vanita, don't tire yourself, but think before you say or admit anything. As for Kanan, I really don't know what happened to her, but whatever it was must have been terrible, that much I am sure of. I, too, do not want the same thing to happen to you or anyone else. But I am afraid of Fanish and touched by your concern for us."

"Really?" Vanita replied sarcastically, for she did not trust Gazal's- for although she was trying to calm her, Vanita could not shut out the feeling of hostility emitting from her. "Oh, by the way, in the struggle I managed to pull of 'The Ravager's' mask. I saw his face and…"

Gazal thought her to be hallucinating so made light of it as she remembered her last conversation with Fanish.

"Gazal, when Vanita wakes up she will nurse feelings

of revenge and hatred. You know I always give you some commission if you persuade the girl to stay, if you can persuade Vanita to remain quiet, I will double it."

"No, Fanish, I will not do so, she has suffered enough!"

"All-right, Gazal, if money does not tempt you, I will tell you stories of my girls who were shipped abroad if they disobeyed me, or became too old. Why, one girl ended up by hanging herself in a Mexican house."

Gazal thought she detected a warning in his voice, so what else could she do but keep quiet and agree with him?

Vanita looked tired and sleepy and before Gazal left, reminded her not to talk to anybody.

"Wait until tomorrow." Gazal whispered. " Promise?"

"Promise." Vanita answered sleepily.

Gazal caught sight of Jane and went up to her.

"Nurse, can I talk to you for a few minutes? What has Vanita said and what is the diagnosis of the doctor?"

"Vanita is very badly hurt, but when she was admitted to hospital was in an even worse condition. She cannot tell us how she was injured- though at times she mentions a burglar. Even though we can treat her physically, we do not know how far the trauma has affected her. She does not remember everything, but apparently she recognised you. These flashes of memory will come and go, so she will have a difficult time ahead. So now mostly what she needs is rest and care and…anyway, we have informed the police and they will investigate further."

"The care I can give at home, but considering her trauma, we would not want to prosecute, should the burglars be found. We do not want to waste police time." Gazal interrupted hurriedly.

"I don't think that will be for some time yet." Jane

replied. "Anyway, on your next visit, the doctor will explain to you in detail."

She raced off patting her cap in place as a matron called to her as Gazal walked thoughtfully down the hospital corridor.

■ ■ ■ ■

Chapter 36

"Fanish, who is Dilawar?" Akshita asked." He is the doctor we overheard you talking to, isn't it?"

She stood at the window, her hair pinned back. Her stance emphasised the smooth lines of her neck, sharp sculptured curve of her chin and jaw and brought out the depth of her hazel brown eyes.

She was trying to look out of the window past the drizzle of the rain, which had become a dirty curtain on the window.

"Yes, he is the one, why?" Fanish answered irritably. "Akshita, don't disturb me, and why are you asking so many questions anyway? You know what will happen if…" he snarled.

He had been sitting so still with his hands on his knees that Akshita thought he looked like a wax figure. Fanish looked troubled because nothing was going right and he felt he had to think so he could mark the places at which obstacles were occurring so he could address them when making his plans.

He struck his forehead from time to time with the back of his hand

"I know you are running a business that involves young girls, a business that corrupts young girls. Dilawar seemed terribly worried when he phoned, I think it was about a girl, is she OK?" Akshita asked. "and where is Aditya, I haven't seen him for a while."

"No, she is not." Fanish answered tersely. "Akshita, I am trying to think! No, listen, do you want to hear about my problems? Do you want to know about my business, a business that clothes you and puts food in your mouth?"

"Alright, Akshita, I will tell you everything. Maybe that will stop your questioning and at the time scare you too. As for Aditya, he has gone abroad, not for a holiday, as he said, but most probably is afraid of any kind of involvement if something goes wrong."

Slowly, with a cruel smile on his face, he told her told about Gazal, Kanan, and Vanita. He was going to tell her about his baby-selling business when Akshita put her hands over her ears.

"No, Stop! Fanish, I don't want to know anymore. You are a criminal – a child trafficker and I am sure you deal in drugs too." Akshita felt a stab of guilt, shame and sorrow. "What kind of monster have I married? Anyway, why are you telling me all this? You know my father is just looking for something like this to put you away. I will see to it that he gets all the evidence he needs." Akshita walked towards the phone.

"My dear wife, you were the one who asked and I know your father will not take any action because you are my hostage, and Urvi too if need be."

"You don't have me hostage." Akshita shouted. "I am going to phone him this very minute."

"Before you do anything, Akshita, just remember that Aditya likes Urvi. He also thinks you are a very beautiful woman, and you know I am a very obliging man."

Akshita went up to Fanish and slapped him, then began scratching his face with her fingers.

"You'll regret this, you bitch!" Fanish roared as he put his hand on his cheek.

Akshita lunged at Fanish again, but this time he was prepared and caught her wrist tightly looking into her eyes.

"If you know what is good for you and Urvi, you will keep quite." he hissed his head and neck strained forward.

"Fanish, whatever you do with me, please leave Urvi alone." Akshita pleaded.

She now realised him to be capable of carrying out his threat ruthlessly. It seemed there was not limit to his cruelty, for just when Akshita thought she knew him; he would show her a darker side of his character.

"That is easily done, Akshita, just tell your father to keep well away from my affairs."

"But somebody has to save those girls from you…"

"And who is going to do it? You?" Fanish growled. "Just remember, either it's them or Urvi. And if anything should happen to me," Fanish continued "or if I am jailed, just remember that I have a lot of friends who owe me a favour and would only be too willing to do anything I ask."

"You bastard, you are a sick and evil man - I wish I had never married you."

Akshita sat on the sofa and started crying at her helplessness.

At that moment Fanish's phone rang and he chuckled as he left the room to answer it.

Fanish was waiting to hear from Gazal, but it was Dilawar.

"What do you want now? Did you tell your wife and has she left you? Or do you want to continue to work with me, earn a lot of money to make her happy so she stays?" Fanish asked sarcastically.

"Fanish, she does not care about money. I have rung to warn you."

"Oh, you, warn me? About what? What are you talking about? You told me you were going to the police?"

"Yes I spoke to Ena and explained everything and…" Dilawar spluttered.

"Are you sure?" Fanish interrupted. "You did not miss any small details as how great a part you took in looking after the girls?"

"I have told her everything, from beginning to end and my role in it. Surprisingly, though I do not deserve it, she is very understanding, and we have agreed to go to the police. I thought I would ask you to accompany us." Dilawar thought of Ena and sighed.

She had looked so miserable and he knew it was all because of him, his fault. He was the one who had hurt her and was causing her pain. For all Dilawar's intelligence and professional achievements, he just did not have an insight when it came to dealing with people, especially loved ones.

"You want me to accompany you?" Fanish repeated. "Hah! Go and tell the police everything, I thought you already had for that I am sure Ena does not know how implicated you are and that you will go down with me. Or maybe, Dilawar, think about this, maybe she is taking her revenge by sending you to jail? Maybe she has got somebody else she would rather spend her life with." Fanish said nastily.

"Shut up, you bastard!" Dilawar raised his voice. "I thought by giving you a chance to come with me, the police would be lenient with us but it seems you are not interested."

"Goodbye, Dilawar, I am expecting another call."

Fanish slammed the phone and wiped his forehead, but as soon as he had, it rang again and he heard Gazal's agitated voice.

"Fanish, what are we going to do? Vanita is adamant she is going to the police... in her struggle she took off the mask of the 'Ravager' ...."

- - - -

Chapter 37

"What! Why didn't you tell me before? Did she see who it was?" Fanish asked uneasily

"Yes, no, I don't know, actually I thought she was inventing stuff…you know, the after effect of the head injury."

"Yes maybe, I knew I could depend on you, now leave everything to me." Fanish heaved a sigh of relief, maybe he could blackmail him?

Nobody knew who 'the Ravager' was for he always took care to wear a mask and the fact had always angered him.

Fanish liked to be in control of any given situation and had even tried to conceal himself in 'the Ravager's room so as to see his identity when he when he took off his mask, however, 'the Ravager'. His hand was on the light switch when he had sensed had sensed his presence.
"Who is there? What are you doing in my room?" he had snarled taking a gun from his pocket. "That is as far as you come, my friend! Get out!" he growled huskily and Fanish knew that his voice was also disguised.

Fanish had left the room hurriedly and after that incident, Fanish realised 'the Ravager' would do anything, even kill, to protect his identity, and for the first time, Fanish tasted defeat and did not like it.

"Fanish, you do not understand, she is threatening to go the police and tell the hospital everything, but I have managed to calm her somewhat."

"She hasn't spoken to anybody as yet, has she?"

"No, I have told her to leave it till the morning. However, she was acting strangely. Fanish, I am afraid."

"Now I will talk to Vanita tomorrow, you are not to

phone the hospital or get in touch with Vanita."

A plan was beginning to form in Fanish's devious mind, and as soon as he finished talking to Gazal, rang up Dilawar again.

"What is it?" Dilawar's voice was curt. "We are just leaving to go to the police station."

"Dilawar, I have been thinking about what you were saying, and I think you are right. Can I come over now and talk about it?"

"Of course, you'll come to the station with us? What made you change your mind?"

"I will tell you when we meet. Is Ena at home with you? Anyway, we'll see you in about half an hour."

"Of course she is, why…?" Before Dilawar could finish the sentence Fanish hung up.

"Was that Dilawar?" Akshita asked as she came into the room.

As he heard Akshita soft voice Fanish thought it about time he executed his cunning plan.

"Akshita, I am going out and I would like you to come with me."

"I don't want to go with you to meet your seedy friends!" Akshita blurted indignantly.

"Hear me out, Akshita that was Dilawar on the phone. I am going over to meet him and his wife." Fanish replied irritably.

"So why do you all of a sudden want me to come along with you?" Akshita asked. "You have never asked me to go out with you before."

"Well, actually, I wanted a favour from you."

"I thought so." Akshita exclaimed. "No, no, and a thousand times no! I don't want to get involved in your seedy businesses!"

"Aren't you forgetting something? What about Urvi?" Fanish asked softly.

A cruel smile turned his mouth into a curve. His

135

hands folded into fists and his shoulders rose in anger.

"All-right, I'm sorry." Akshita tugged her gaze from the hard ugly slash of Fanish's mouth and her voice trembled. "What do you want me to do?"

"We will leave in about half an hour. I have things to do so I will explain in the car."

As they got into the car, Akshita trembled with fear as she thought that this was how the rest of her life was going to be – Fanish would always be there, laughing over her shoulder like a fiend relishing in her misery.

"It's nothing unpleasant, contrary to what you think. I merely want you to befriend Ena, Dilawar's wife. That should not be too difficult for you too need company. I would like you to invite her to come and stay with us. Dilawar said she was upset with him and I think she would welcome a break from him." Fanish explained quietly.

Fanish's ability and confidence to draw her into his own enterprises was evident as he spoke.

"Fanish, I don't believe you to be a kind man, so what are you up to? And why are you driving so fast?" Akshita clutched the car handle.

"Akshita, I just want to see my friend who seems to be in trouble. Why don't you believe me?"

Fanish replied with a surprising gentleness which seemed to address itself more to Akshita's forlorn situation instead of himself.

"They had a disagreement and also I need to talk to Dilawar alone. So just make an excuse, leave us alone and persuade Ena to come home to us."

"What if she doesn't come?" Akshita sounded doubtful.

"Leave that to me." Fanish said as he parked the car outside Dialler's house.

- - - -

136

Chapter 38

Dilawar waited nervously for Fanish, and the nervousness showed in the set of his jaw and his posture was more stone-like then ever. However, his formal ways were only disguises, disguises Dilawar depended on because it was always difficult for him to show emotion.

He was born in India, was an orphan who had been brought up in an orphanage till the age of eleven, where he had often been beaten for showing any emotion, be it fear or hunger.

He often recalled the building which had been in a state of dereliction, for the roof of the building leaked and there were no proper doors and windows – just holes and broken floorboards. The food provided was of poor quality and the water was unhygienic.

Dilawar recalled how one of his friends had had his leg unnecessarily amputated. Medical care had been so inadequate that his friend had died soon after, and from that day on Dilawar vowed to himself that if ever got the chance he would become a doctor.

He had, like the other children often run away from the home, and since the staff were not strict, and if they noticed their absence, were only too glad to get them out of the way. He liked the time away, for then he would roam the streets, station himself at a traffic light, sleep on pavements and dash around amongst the traffic begging for money.

He was not lucky with foster homes either, for although he was placed with different families, he encountered problems there too. In the first foster home the father ran away with another woman and in another the mother had a nervous breakdown so he had to be returned to the orphanage.

However, at the age of twelve, just when he had given up hope of ever being fostered, he was adopted by a loving couple who later moved to England.

They gave him the love and nurturing that he had been deprived of, and with their love and support became a doctor. However, the years in the home had left their mark and the thought that he was helping vulnerable children to be exploited kept him awake at nights.

As he looked at Ena, he thought how much he prized their love – which is why he had strived so hard to keep the truth about Sai from her.

Ena had listened to Dilawar come clean about Fanish and his businesses', all the while wringing her hands on her lap nervously, but the silence around her was filled with her unspoken anger. She was devastated, shocked, surprised, but most of all she was disappointed in her husband, for she had thought him to be a man of a strong and good character.

However, it seemed as if weakness was as much a part of Dilawar's nature as was his gentleness. Ena recalled his words, over and over again as if by doing so she could omit or exonerate her husband's behaviour.

"I did it for you!"

Dilawar had squatted in front of Ena's chair, clasped her hands and stared at her pleadingly, murmuring over and over again.

"What else could I do? What can I do now to make up for it? He always said he would take it out on you if I did not do what he wanted."

"How can you say you have been doing it for me?" Ena swallowed to disguise the tremor in her voice. "All those girls – Fanish – I have never liked him and whose actions you tried to cover. And you say you did it for me? You have been lying all this time and now you are trying to justify your actions by putting the blame on me? He is coming over, after all that he has done; you are still willing to listen to him?" She turned away in disgust.

"I am sorry, Ena, but I want to make up for all the mistakes I have made. I thought if he could come to the police station with us…." Dilawar whispered as he put an arm around her to comfort Ena.

Dilawar suddenly felt alone and hurt, but the real pain came from the belief and confirmation that he was low and weak. He had always wanted to be in control, had thought he was, but now knew he never had been.

"Ena, why don't you see, I had no choice. I could not take the chance of losing you."

Dilawar kissed his wife tenderly on the forehead, fearing anything more passionate might destroy the now frayed and slender thread that bound them still, hoping that his self-respect, which had been bruised by Fanish, would be restored.

"If I didn't do what he wanted, he threatened to tell you everything - and he would have surely exaggerated. And I didn't want to lose you." He repeated.

Dilawar held Ena so that her face pressed so tightly against his shirt that she could hardly breathe.

Ena pulled herself out of his embrace.

"Isn't that what you have done now? How long do you think you could have gone on without my knowing? Anyway, what hold does Fanish have over you, for somehow, I do not think you are capable of doing all those awful things you have told me about. What is that you are so scared I will find out?"

"Your right there is, but please before I tell you, please remember that I have, and always will love you and only you."

Dilawar finally reluctantly told her about Sai.

Ena put her hand over her mouth in astonishment. As she turned her incredulous eyes on Dilawar, her mouth opened to form a denial and she slumped against the sofa. She felt she could have forgiven Dilawar almost anything; accept for Dilawar being with another woman. Her face became red and she bit down on her lip then finally exclaimed.

"No! Dilawar I never thought you to be the kind of man who would cheat on me. Oh God!" Ena said in anguish. "Why are you doing this to me?"

"I am sorry, Ena, believe me I am not proud of it. I did not mean to hurt you and it lasted only for a brief period. Unfortunately, Fanish found out about it, and since then, has always managed to manipulate me through my sense of guilt and shame. He bullied me into accepting his terms; otherwise I would never willingly have done what I did. He threatened to tell you. Ena, you must understand, I love you, and I did not want to lose you."

A constraint of silence fell over them and Ena felt the warm tears running down her cheeks. Finally, she blurted.

"Dilawar, it would have come out at some point. Anyways I do not think I can stay here any longer. I am going to my parents"

As Ena pushed back a wisp of hair from her forehead, she felt defeated and helpless. She thought they had a good marriage for they communicated and shared and made what she thought was a good team. She thought Dilawar told her in a thousand silent ways that he loved her but obviously she had misread the signs.

"Ena, I thought you were coming to the Police station. I am waiting for Fanish; he should be here soon." Dilawar pleaded.

"Why can't you do anything on your own?"

Ena now saw that the weakness in Dilawar manifested itself in physical ways – the way his shoulders drooped and his face that looked haggard and wane.

She ran past him to her room and collapsed on the bed sobbing. Marriage for Ena had been a gift given to her on a fragile plate, a plate that had now broken and shattered into a thousand pieces.

She had always believed Dilawar to be honest and upright, a man with integrity. That belief moulded solidly in his form, so much so that she had been sure that the slightest change would crack and shatter him. How wrong she had been.

After some time, as though in a dream, she moved to the dressing table, combed back her hair and made up her face to a becoming pallor then threw some of her clothes in a suitcase.

Dilawar was sitting with his head in his hands when the doorbell rang. He got up to open the door.

"Come in, Fanish" Dilawar said wearily. "Have you come to add to the mess I already am in, all thanks to you?"

Fanish burst into the room, bringing with him his own particular atmosphere of intense energy.

• • • •

Chapter 39

"What are you talking about, Dilawar? I thought you were going to the police? Oh, Dilawar, I don't think you have met my wife Akshita." Fanish said as he entered, followed by Akshita.

Still standing in the landing, he made the introductions and as he looked up, saw Ena came slowly down the stairs, carrying her suitcase.

"Dilawar, I am leaving because I do not know what to do. I can't live with the knowledge about…"

Fanish could see the determination and sadness reflected on her face, for although her lips were trembling, her voice was calm and controlled.

Ena's hands flew out in a despairing gesture and Fanish thought how very lovely and sensitive her hands were.

Dilawar looked at her in dismay.

"I am sure everything will be alright, just give Dilawar some time, Ena."

Fanish's voice was warm, resonant and charmed the ear whilst the magnetism of his personality was felt by everybody in the room except Ena as he tried to take charge.

"I am not staying in this house a moment longer – especially now that you are here." Ena's eyes darkened with bitterness, anger and frustration.

However, Ena in her heart was hoping Dilawar would urge her to stay.

But, as Dilawar was silent, she sighed and thought it to be for the best as the ghost of Sai and the innocent young girls who had suffered would always be between them. Better banishment, better loneliness, and better a drab of winters alone then life of sin and betrayal.

Until now, she had not known her capacity for

jealousy and Ena did not want to live at close quarters with a man whose mind and heart she thought held Sai as a permanent guest. For although Dilawar had tried to convince her otherwise, Ena felt he still loved Sai.

Dilawar was sitting on the sofa running his hands through his hair.

"Ena, I see you have found out about Dilawar. Akshita, why don't you talk to Ena in the other room, woman-to-woman, whilst I talk to Dilawar?" Fanish asked quietly

"Come Ena, come with me." Akshita took Ena's arm and led her to the next room.

"Ena, Dilawar is not so much at fault as Fanish. I take it you have found out about Fanish and his business – ess? I can understand how you feel for ever since I found out; I cannot find it in my heart to forgive Fanish either."

"Yes, he told me."

Akshita's eyelids flickered and there was a moment's hesitation before she said with a sigh.

"Ena, sometimes the truth, however bitter, can be accepted and woven into a design and adapted into a normal life. I suggest you do not make any rash decision."

"I have made a choice - which I don't call rash for I cannot and will not stay in the same house as Dilawar. I don't how you are so calm, are you sure Fanish told you everything about him?"

"Yes he has, but Ena, I hate it every much as you do. But I…. anyway, I know what, why don't you come for a drive with me? I'll drop you wherever you want, afterwards." When Ena nodded, Akshita called out to Fanish.

"Fanish, I am taking Ena for a drive and coffee. We'll be back soon."

"That is a good idea, Akshita. Dilawar and I have something we need to talk about privately anyway."

Dilawar looked alarmed but quickly assured himself that Ena would be back so smiled with relief.

As Akshita and Ena left, Fanish tilted his chair back and a cunning smile came to his lips.

"Now, what is all this about the police?" he asked gently.

The smile on his face masked his lie and his voice was chillingly soft as his voice shattered the tense silence.

"As soon as Ena is a bit calmer, I plan to go to them, anyway, how is Vanita? Did Gazal take her to hospital?"

Vanita's face had been haunting him, which in turn induced him into suffering incessant nightmares of evil and deceit.

"Yes she did and Vanita is fine. All this fuss, for nothing." Arrogant as ever, Fanish showed no remorse, no guilt no shame.

"That is a surprise" Dilawar remarked. "She is lucky, for with her injuries, I was sure she was going to die."

"I was asking about your going to the police, Dilawar. Or was it just an idle threat, for you know you are implicated as well?"

Fanish's voice was weighted with sarcasm and the smile on his face showed he could not be intimidated.

"Listen, Fanish, if you have come to talk me out of going to the police, you can forget it for I have made up my mind. I should have known better than to believe you when you said you would come with me. Now, if you will excuse me…"

"Before you leave, Dilawar, I have something to ask you. Do you love your wife?" .

"What kind of question is that? You know I do and that is the only reason I did what you asked."

"And where is Ena now? She is with Akshita and Akshita is my wife. I am sure you can put two and two together."

Fanish smiled a cold wry smile that left a layer of ice on Dilawar's heart.

· · · ·

Chapter 40

Suddenly Dilawar sat up straight for the tone in Fanish's voice sent a shiver down his spine. He was suddenly afraid, for he understood Fanish only too well, he was like an iceberg – most of him was concealed under the surface and only surfaced to destroy the people who crossed his path.

His face became pale, registering a kaleidoscope of changing expressions of which fear was the most obvious.

"Fanish, what are you implying?!" he whispered.

"I think you know, Dilawar. Ena is with Akshita who is my wife." Fanish repeated slowly.

"Yes, but Akshita would not harm Ena – she seems a good woman and you are here, Aditya is away, so how is she in danger, for that is what you are implying, isn't it??"

"I have instructed Akshita to take Ena to my home where she will stay with us. Dilawar, Ena looked beautiful in that blue sari. Do you know the way she ties the sari shows her figure and lovely curves to perfection and who knows whilst she is with us…?"

Fanish smiled and smacked his lips. There was a smug expression on his face, the expression he usually took on when he had gotten the better of someone.

"Don't you dare talk like that about my wife. If you ever lay a finger on her, I'll kill you! Anyway, Ena would never stay with you."

Dilawar rushed out of his chair and grabbed Fanish by the throat.

"Your right, she will not stay with me but she will with my wife; I have made sure of that. As for your harming me why, you wouldn't have the guts." Fanish said with a sneer.

146

He flicked his hand over his coat idly looking as calm and calculated as ever.

"Don't be too sure!"

Dilawar rose to face Fanish. His anger had increased and revealed itself in his complexion, his bulging eyes and his clenched fists that were held tightly against his thighs.

"Dilawar, don't worry about Ena, she'll be fine. That is as long as you do not go to the police." Fanish looked indifferent.

As usual, Fanish had put all events and obstacles into perspective and organised them in such a way that permitted him to deal with them efficiently and ruthlessly.

"You bastard!" Dilawar put his head in his hands and groaned.

Fanish got up, smiled warmly and put on his coat.

"So you see, it is really up to you. She was leaving you anyway, at least with me you know where she is."

"You win, Fanish." Dilawar said in exasperation. "I won't go to the police. Is that what you wanted to hear? Now, will you please ring up Akshita and tell her to drop Ena back home, or shall I come and collect her?"

"Not so fast, my friend. How do I know that you won't go to the police as soon as she is with you? No, Ena stays with me while you stay here alone and think about your wife with me. Oh, and there is another favour I have to ask of you."

Fanish's voice was cold and his brown eyes, although no longer bright and warm, were fixed on Dilawar.

"Ok, Fanish what do you want?" Dilawar answered wearily.

He felt depleted of all emotion as he realised that Fanish controlled the strings of his happiness - again.

"It's about Vanita. Do you know the hospital she is in?"

"Yes, of course."

"Do you know any Doctors in that hospital?" Fanish asked.

"Yes, as a matter of fact I do, why?"

"That is all I wanted to know for the present."

"But I thought you said …?"

"I'll tell you when the time is right." Fanish said as he opened the door.

"What about Ena? What are you going to do with her?" Dilawar asked.

"Like I said, nothing at present, and she will be safe, - as long as you do what I say that is." Fanish's voice cut sharply through the chill of air before he left.

Dilawar was left alone in the shadows and darkness of the night and he felt the silence around him suffocating him. He missed Ena and needed her warmth, stability, companionship, laughter and love.

She had not given him time to convince her that Sai was now only a projection from the past and had nothing to do with his present.

• • • •

Chapter 41

The sun had gradually receded from the sky, making room for the gentle rays of early evening that bathed the lawn and the flowerbeds of the houses.

"Ena, you look miserable, why don't we go to my place? We can talk and you can tell me everything over coffee. In fact, you are welcome to stay with me for now."

When Ena nodded her head, Akshita drove to her house and parked the car.

"Thank you, Akshita, that is kind of you, it sounds tempting, I need a friend to talk to at this time. I know today's the first time we met, but I like you. I will take you up on your offer, thank you, but I don't have my clothes, I left my suitcase."

"That's settled then, and don't worry, I will ring up Fanish to bring it with him."

"Thank you," Ena whispered.

As she followed Akshita into the house, she felt that her dreams had been trampled upon again. Her childhood had been lonely, and she only remembered a few happy instances' from it, which she treasured.

However, when she had felt the warmth of Dilawar's lips on hers, his affection and love had warmed the cold desert of her heart .

But the affection, honesty and truth that she had believed in Dilawar were alien to her once again.

"Akshita, although I don't trust Fanish, I would like to confide and seek your advice, for I cannot return to Dilawar nor can I go to my parents."

"Don't make any rash decision, let us have some first."

As Akshita went to the kitchen, Ena first sat gingerly on the edge of the armchair, and then slowly sank deeper in the chair.

However, she felt restless, so leapt to her feet, walked to the window and stood looking out. A small sigh escaped her as she leant her head against the pane of glass

"You will feel better after some coffee, Ena." Akshita said placing a tray on the coffee table.

"Thank you, Akshita, you are very kind." Ena smiled weakly as she walked back into the room.

"Can you pour some whilst it is hot, Ena, I have to make a call to Fanish to ask him to bring your suitcase.

She came back, a smile on her face. "He said that would not be a problem."

She took a cup that Ena handed and sat on the sofa.

"Thank you, now we can talk."

"Thanks again, but tell me, Akshita, are you sure you know everything about Dilawar, Fanish and Aditya?" Ena repeated her question she had put to Akshita earlier.

"You mean about their so called 'businesses? Yes!" Akshita answered patiently.

"What was your reaction?"

"The same as yours – I was first shocked, then disgusted. Being a woman, how can I but hate what they do? My father told me the other day how crime has increased, and it is but obvious that Fanish and people like him are the reason."

"What are you going to do? Don't tell me you are going to stay with him now?" Ena asked, stirring her coffee with a spoon. "Anyway, thank you for inviting me to stay; I cannot go back to Dilawar under the circumstances."

Akshita felt guilty as she sipped her tea. Wasn't what she doing similar to Fanish? She shuddered. But she was doing it to protect Urvi whereas Fanish liked to exploit girls and profited from their vulnerability.

She liked Ena who she thought was a very nice woman and thought she would tell her the truth, when the laughing face of Urvi swam before her, then thought of her with Fanish and Aditya - and the vision filled Akshita's heart with terror.

'At the moment Fanish is using Urvi to blackmail me – swinging her fate about in a way he would swing a whip against my back - extracting some awful satisfaction from each blow – but beware Fanish, you will pay for this one day." Akshita swore under her breath.

"Akshita, are you all right? You were saying...?"

"No, I am fine, I was just thinking that I should go up and get your room ready." Akshita smiled.

But her heart was heavy, for she too was in Fanish's clutches, how could she help Ena?

At that moment, Akshita heard the door slam and Fanish entered the room, a faintly triumphant smile curving his lips.

"Your suitcase, Ena." He said, placing it on the floor, a strange look burning in his eyes. "You cannot travel alone at this time of night."

The expression momentarily distorted his features and an icy cold shiver ran down Akshita's spine. One moment he was gentle and sensitive, the next he was cruel and vindictive, and the transformations were making Akshita frantic.

Ena too looked puzzled.

"She is not going to, Fanish, I have persuaded Ena to stay here before she makes any rash decision which she might regret later." Akshita rose from the sofa.

"Good! That is the least we can do. Have you made any dinner for our guest?" Fanish smiled and kissed her affectionately on the cheek.

"N.no." Akshita replied, surprised at Fanish's show of affection.

Fanish was a man of bright flashing colours that kept changing from one moment to the next, reminding her of

151

a chameleon.

• • • •

Chapter 42

"Sorry about that, Ena, would you like something to eat?" Akshita asked.

"No, please don't worry, I'm not hungry." Ena quickly intervened, for Fanish was glaring at Akshita.

"Don't worry, I have eaten, I was only thinking of Ena." Fanish said genially then yawned. "It's been a long day, Akshita, I'm going to sleep. By the way, there wasn't any message from Dilawar, was there?"

Ena's lips begin to quiver as she brought her hands to her face. She looked distressed at the mention of Dilawar and Fanish took pleasure from her distress.

"No, he did not call." Akshita replied tersely hating Fanish's calculating smile.

"No matter, it can wait."

Fanish's eyes were like inquisitive probing scalpels with which he sought to slice out a hint, a clue, and a sign of Ena's distress. He laughed derisively then left the room, his footsteps echoing down the hallway.

Ena's face had blanched as she bit on her lower lip and Akshita could see the disquiet in her eyes.

"I apologise for Fanish." Akshita put her arm around Ena who broke into tears.

"It's not what he said, Akshita, it's just the way he said it." Ena shivered as she recalled Fanish's cold eyes. "I am only here for a couple of days, thank God. Well, not that long even, tomorrow I'll go to my parents and..."

"No, no, Ena, you are welcome to stay here as long as you want. I will talk to Fanish about his insensitivity, don't worry it will not happen again." Akshita hastily interrupted. "In fact I would like you to stay for I too have just found out what kind of man Fanish really is and do not want to be alone with him."

"Are you sure?" Ena asked, "Are you sure Fanish

would not mind? I mean, he won't be angry with you?"

"No, to be honest, I think he will be only too glad to get me out of his way for Fanish and Dilawar have some matters to sort out, I think."

"Now, I wonder what problems they have to talk about? Oh yes, I know, which young girl should they send abroad?" Ena remarked sarcastically. She put her palm on her forehead. "Gosh, I have a headache!"

"Oh Ena, that is awful! Here, I'll make us something to eat." Akshita got up hurriedly. "We have been talking and I didn't realise the time."

"Akshita, don't cook anything for me, I'm not hungry."

"Your headache may be due to hunger and tension."

"No, I don't think so." Ena said tearfully, for in her life, only Dilawar had been kind and considerate.

"Akshita, what am I going to do?" She cried her hands on her face.

"Nothing, at least for the moment." Akshita replied. "Forget your problems. Now I am hungry, and as I am not really in the mood for cooking I'll order some take away."

As she picked up the receiver, she heard Fanish on the line.

"Akshita, what are you doing?" He yelled, "Can't you see I am using the phone? Kindly have the courtesy to wait till I finish."

"I was just going to order some food and..." Akshita's hands started trembling and she hurriedly put the receiver down.

"Any problems?" Ena was massaging her head.

"No, no problems, at least nothing major. Fanish was on the phone."

"Akshita, I have ordered food for you two." Fanish looked down from the stairs.

"But you don't know what we would like...?" Akshita

remarked, but Fanish's face had already disappeared.

The food was delivered within ten minutes and as soon as they had eaten Ena yawned.

"You were right, Akshita, I am feeling much better Do you mind if I go to bed now?"

"No, not at all. We'll talk some more in the morning."

As Ena unpacked the few clothes she had hastily packed, glad she had made a friend - and the knowledge itself was a healing experience.

Akshita however, started crying as soon as Ena left the room. She wept first for the horrible things Fanish was involved in, and then for the ugliness and the underlying violence and cruelty she was being made to witness. Most of all, she was frustrated at not being able to control the situation that she was and trapped in. She did not know who she felt sorry for the most, Urvi or for the innocent girls who Fanish was exploiting.

She wept too for the waste of her love, a love that had craved to discover everything about her husband, then cherish any secret of his. Hers had been a selfless love that would have endured the endless journey of discovering a person and his flaws over a period of time and loving him for it. Because this mixture of emotions confused her, she was angry, and this fury was not only directed at Fanish but also at herself for falling in love with Fanish without truly understanding his character.

But he had been considerate and kind in the early days of their romance. He had showered her with gifts which had become dearer and more expensive, till finally he had brought her a diamond engagement ring. But as her parents had not agreed to the marriage, they had thought the only solution was to run away to get married. And it was Akshita who had been adamant to do so for she loved him and felt she could not live without him.

However, the present Fanish made an ugly distorted

image of kindness and decency, the two qualities she had loved about him. She realised now that her elopement was only an act of bravado and a response to her parent's anger that had backfired, leaving her feeling empty and lonely. What she had thought was going to be a lifetime of wonderful experiences with Fanish had proved nothing but a horrible mistake.

She knew she was caught tight in Fanish's web but could not expose him. How would she live a life of charade with a husband who had begun treating her worse than a stranger?

She wanted to put Ena in the picture, but knew that the knowledge that her new-found-friend, who had divulged her innermost secrets to her, was betraying her, even if only by coercion, would destroy her.

Akshita regained her calm, then rose and wiped the tears flowing down her cheeks. She steadied herself by resting her trembling hand on the table.

"I have to find a solution, for Urvi's sake! But the only way I can think of is by not looking too far ahead. Maybe if can I manage to get through today, tomorrow will take care of itself?"

- - - -

Chapter 43

Vanita woke in the morning with a throbbing headache and saw Jane standing beside her bed.

"How are you this morning, Luv?"

Jane's eyes were warm and she had a glass of water with some tablets in the palm of her hand.

"Where am I? I have a splitting headache!" Vanita said grumpily as she looked at Jane with distrust.

"Here, take this you will feel better." Jane said handing her the glass of water and tablets.

Vanita tried to get up and flinched. She put her hand at the back of her head and felt a lump.

"My God, the lump has grown bigger! What's happened to me?"

"The burglar hit you on the head and threw you down a flight of stairs." The nurse repeated calmly.

"Burglar, what burglar?" Vanita was confused.

"The one your cousin said attacked you. Apparently, you disturbed him when you interrupted him in the act of trying to rob your home."

"What cousin?" Vanita asked a frown on her face.

"Gazal, the girl who came yesterday. Vanita, you spoke to her when you woke up!"

"Why did you call me Vanita?" Vanita looked at Jane sharply.

"You mean you still don't remember...?"

"Who am I?" Vanita voice was frightened, almost panic-stricken. She thought she was in a nightmare, a bad dream from which she hoped to awake soon. "I think you should call the police. I am frightened!"

"Keep calm, Vanita, you are safe here. It is important

that you do not panic. Sometimes after a trauma there is usually a loss of memory."

"What if I never remember?"

"I doubt it, here, take these tablets, they will calm you in and in the meantime I will contact the doctor." Jane hurriedly left the ward.

The nurse on duty was on the phone and as soon as she saw Jane waved to her, and putting one hand over the receiver whispered.

"It is your patient Vanita's cousin asking about her. Do you want to talk to her?"

"Yes, I'll talk to her." She tried to explain to Vanita's cousin. "Vanita woke up this morning with a slight case of amnesia but was insisting we call the police."

"Why the police? I spoke to her yesterday and she seemed to be recovering."

"Her amnesia might either be a delayed reaction to the trauma or due to the lump she has been complaining about. Obviously the doctor will be able to diagnose it, but there is no need to worry. Amnesia happens sometimes with any kind of brain injury."

"Can I help in any way? I'd like to come and visit her."

"She is not allowed visitors for that could trigger stress which in turn would hinder her recovery. I am sure you understand."

"Of course, nurse, and thank you for your help, I'll ring later to find out how she is."

After she had hung up, Gazal sat staring at the telephone for a few minutes, a frown on her face, then decided to phone Fanish.

- - - -

Chapter 44

"What is it, Gazal?" Fanish asked impatiently.

"It's about Vanita. I think we need to talk for she is threatening to go the police and…"

"I'll be there immediately." Fanish slammed the receiver.

Fanish drove to Vanita's house anxiously for he had been sure he had managed the crisis with Dilawar satisfactorily.

"What is you wanted to see me about?" Fanish stepped into the house with a quiet cat-like step.

"I just spoke to the sister in hospital regarding Vanita." Gazal followed Fanish into the lounge with a frown on her face.

"What did they say? How is she? Did you speak to her?"

"Yesterday when Vanita spoke to me she threatened to go to the police because she has some information. This morning the nurse told me that she has got Amnesia. Vanita told her she can't remember a thing, not even my name."

Fanish's eyes had grown small and although his gaze was intense he looked confused.

"I am confused." he blurted finally. "Is she or isn't she suffering from amnesia?"

"Well, I don't really know for sure, our problems may be solved, but only temporarily."

"What do you mean?" Fanish asked. "I thought you said the nurse said Vanita did not remember you?"

"She did, but I too have no idea, but I think we have to believe what she told me yesterday…. that she was faking amnesia"

"We'll have to make sure that Vanita comes to us as

soon as possible."

"That will be difficult to manage as the hospital does not even want her to have any visitors."

"I'll deal with it". Fanish looked at Gazal impatiently, his voice firm and authoritative. "I'll talk to Dilawar."

Fanish was a ruthless man, even with himself, and did not permit himself the luxury of wavering indecision. The misfortunes of others were a distraction for him and his selfishness permitted nobody else but the demons of his heart and soul to hide in the shadow of his heart, waiting for an opportunity to act.

"What about Dilawar? Is he going to the police?

"Err, nooooo, but his wife is staying with me." Fanish looked at Gazal and winked.

"You mean you have …?"

"She is with me, safe unless Dilawar changes his mind and decides to go to the police."

Each move of Fanish's was made shrewdly with cool calculating intelligence and after considering every possibility.

"Does Dilawar know that Ena is with you?" asked Gazal.

"Yes, he does, that is the whole point." Fanish chuckled.

"However did you manage it?"

"You will never believe it; it was Akshita who helped."

"Did you say Akshita? You mean your wife Akshita? I thought you said she was against everything you did? And what about her father?"

"They're all under my control!" Fanish said smugly. "I have threatened Akshita that I will kidnap Urvi, her sister, so that has taken care of her. She and her father will now do what I say. As for Dilawar, I have Ena."

"Those were clever moves, Fanish, not honest and decent, but clever. So I take it we carry on as before?"

"Yes, we do." Fanish grinned. "In fact, I think things are better than before, now the only think endangering our safety is Vanita.

"I hope that is taken care of too, Fanish, for I have no wish to go to prison."

Fanish got up to leave. "Let me know if the hospital calls about Vanita."

"I will, but Fanish I was wondering about Vanita's background?"

"I thought you two would have got to know each other by now."

"Not really, that is apart for the bit about her father, Vanita is a very reserved girl. If I know more about her it might help jolt her memory, if she really has amnesia that is."

'Any information will be useful and might help her escape, for I cannot.' She thought to herself. 'I am deep in Fanish's jungle, so deeply entangled that I cannot find a way out even if I tried!"

"Gazal, there is no need for you to know anything else about her, in fact I don't know much about her either." Fanish opened the door and left.

■ ■ ■ ■

Chapter 45

Vanita woke the following morning after a night of a troubled sleep to find a faint light of sunshine gleaming through the windows.

She trembled with fear as she recalled her recurring nightmare of twisted fingers around her throat trying to strangle her.

A cheerful nurse, all dimples and smiles, with a white starched cap on her head, stood by her bedside.

"Good-morning." she buzzed. "How are we this morning? Do we remember our name? Oh dear, we are looking distressed, did you have the same nightmare that you had yesterday?

"Yes, look, nurse, I am frightened, I seem to remember, then suddenly, I don't even know who I am"

"Well, if it will make you feel any better, your cousin phoned." Jane said tucking the bed sheets.

"Which cousin, I don't have any cousin? No, I don't mean that, for she can tell me about my life and who I am - when is she coming to visit?"

"Oh dear! I am afraid that she cannot visit for she had to leave town urgently."

"Oh!" Vanita's face, what could be seen of it, fell and Jane fell sorry for the young girl.

"Just try and relax, your memory will be back when you least expect it. Now, how are you feeling otherwise?"

"Terribly stiff and bruised, I can't move and…do you want me to go on?" Vanita answered

Her head was bandaged, her arm was in a sling and her face was swollen and purple.

"Sorry, Vanita, I know you are feeling lousy, but I can give some painkillers that will away the pain."

"No!" Vanita's melancholy expression deepened and

she was silent.

"Well, at least that is a good sign!" Jane said cheerily and left.

She touched her face gingerly. Jane had not let her see a mirror, but Vanita had seen her reflection in the window glass and most of all she saw herself in the eyes of others, through the eyes of the visitors who passed her bed. And they all gave her one look, first one of horror and then of pity.

She started crying - when she was well enough - where would she go? Jane had told her not to try too hard to remember, but she felt intuitively that not only had somebody been kind to her but a wrong had been done her, as well. But by who and why?

■ ■ ■ ■

Chapter 46

Dilawar had not slept the whole night, amazed how easily and deviously Fanish had managed to manipulate the whole situation to his advantage.

He rose in the middle of the night to make a cup of tea and as he waited in the kitchen for the kettle to boil, wondered how stupid he had been in underestimating Fanish.

The next morning just as he was to leave for work the phone rang.

"Dilawar, remember I said I wanted you to do me a favour?" Fanish asked.

"Yes I do, but first tell me how is Ena?" Dilawar asked.

"She is fine for now, Dilawar but her future lies in your hands, Anyway the reason I called was because you had mentioned you had some contacts in the hospital Vanita is in, well, I would like you to find out how she is."

"Please, at least me talk to her ...." but before he could complete his sentence, Fanish had disconnected the call.

He phoned the hospital to let them know he would be coming in then decided to meet Parul, his friend, who worked in the same hospital that Vanita was admitted in.

As he walked down the busy corridor of the hospital, he passed people walking with quiet brisk footsteps and wondered how he was going to explain his interest in Vanita without arousing suspicion.

As he entered Parul's office, he saw that there were papers strewn on the desk and on filing cabinets around the room whilst Parul was standing with a pile of papers in one hand and running his fingers thorough his hair with the other.

He was glancing through some papers without paying much attention, which Dilawar knew, was normal for him, for paper work had never been his strong point. Parul had been in the midst of clipping some papers together when he saw Dilawar.

"Dilawar! How nice to see you!" he gave an exclamation of delight as he shook Dialler's hand vigorously. "What brings you to this part of the world?"

"I had not seen you for some time, and as I was passing this way thought I would say hello. You are not too busy for a cup of coffee, are you?

"Of course not, Dilawar, it will give us a chance to catch up." Parul answered genially.

He ushered him out of his office to the canteen only too glad to postpone his paperwork.

He was a handsome, arrogant yet uncomplicated man – a person with a great sense of humour and had it not been for him - Dilawar often thought he would not have got through Medical College.

He remembered the deprivations all the students had suffered, for all in all they only had a dozen night's sleep and lost the springtime of their lives in studying to acquire skills to benefit their fellow men.

Yet, often, many doctors were often accused of callousness, disregarding the fact that many of them sacrificed their marriages and lost the unique opportunities of seeing their children grow.

Parul, along with some of their fellow students, would often argue that the world owed them some of sort of appreciation in the form of wealth, respect or social status and Dilawar felt their demands were not entirely without cause, for he was convinced that whilst broken bones can be mended, no-one can repair a broken marriage or re-establish children that have been damaged by a father's neglect.

As soon as they were sitting with the hot steaming cups on the table, Parul asked with concern.

"Dilawar, you are looking pale. Is everything alright?"

"Yes, everything is fine, Parul," Dilawar replied vaguely as he sipped his coffee.

After they had reminisced for some time, Dilawar finally blurted.

"Actually, Parul, I would like to ask a favour."

"Anything, my friend, now what can I do for you?"

"The daughter of a friend of mine by the name of Vanita was admitted to the hospital a few days ago and I would like to find out how she is."

"Really, her father is a friend of yours? A colleague is looking after her, in fact you can be of help, for James was concerned about her and the hospital is trying to locate her family."

Dilawar looked uncomfortable. "No actually Vanita's his cousin but anyway, how is she?"

"I can't say much, but according to James, Vanita is suffering from amnesia due to the violent assault she received at the hands of some burglar. We will only be able to salvage some of her lost beauty."

Dilawar felt guilty for not being firm in sending Vanita to hospital earlier.

"Dilawar, are you feeling alright?" Dilawar heard his friend's voice as if from a distance.

"Yes, I am." Dilawar took another sip from his cup. "It is such a pity…a young girl."

Parul's pager started bleeping and he quickly pushed his chair and rose.

"I know you will understand, Dilawar, I have to cut this meeting short as I have to attend to some emergency. I don't know if I have been of any help, but please, if Vanita's father or her cousin can contact us? And we must meet again soon." He quickly ran out of the door.

Dilawar finished his coffee and went home to phone Fanish.

"Yes, yes I know." Fanish answered curtly.

"If you knew, why did you tell me to…?' Dilawar asked in an exasperated tone. "And when is Ena coming home?"

"Dilawar, do not talk to me in that tone, she does not want to come to you."

Dilawar's heart sank. "I am sure that is not true, Fanish, you have nothing to worry about. I have checked with the hospital and Vanita has amnesia so won't remember anything and you have my word that I won't either so now can I talk to Ena?"

"I doubt she will talk to you but you can try… Ena?"

Fanish's voice became faint as he went to call her. After about a minute he was back on the line.

"Dilawar, she does not want to talk to you. And don't blame me." he exclaimed in an angry voice. "It is because of your actions she won't talk to you."

After his conversation with Fanish and Parul, Dilawar felt even more despondent than he had been was in the morning - and as the soft firelight glowed in the living room he sat in the armchair whilst the wind clawed at the windows.

- - - -

Chapter 47

The sun was lured to the west and its brightness was fading, the light was losing its intensity and turning gold, which in turn brought out the deeper shades of green of the leaves on the trees with glowing effect.

Aakar pressed his foot on the accelerator and drove fast whilst Urvi sat quietly squirming in the seat next to him. He felt torn in two, for whilst he was glad that his youngest daughter was safe and unharmed, he felt afraid for his eldest daughter.

"Dad, what is going on?" Urvi asked turning her head.

However, as her father looked worried she did not press him further, but as soon as they reached home, ran upstairs to her room not acknowledging her mother, who followed her.

"Urvi, what is the matter?" Aninditi asked with a frown. "Your dinner is ready and…"

"Mum, I'm not hungry!" Urvi exclaimed in exasperation. "Why is everybody so concerned about my health all of a sudden? Is something wrong?"

"We were worried because you did not come home …" Aninditi looked at her with eyes that had filled with tears.

"I went to my sister's house. Is that such a crime?"

"No it is not, but you should have told us and saved us unnecessary worry."

"I thought Fanish Bahia had told you." Urvi muttered. "Mum, can I go to sleep, please?"

"Of course you can." Aninditi replied tenderly switching off the light. "Good-night."

"Good-night." Urvi was already asleep when Aninditi closed the door softly and went downstairs.

"How is she?" Aakar asked running his fingers

through his hair.

"She's fine and is sleeping., Aakar, I was so scared! Thank God she is ok." Aninditi sat wringing her hands whilst Aakar paced the floor.

"Well, in future, don't let her out of your sight!" Aakar stopped pacing the room and sat down beside his wife.

"I don't know how that is going to be possible. Did you tell her about Fanish?"

"How could I? She thinks of him as her brother but I forbade her to talk to Fanish or any of his friends unless Akshita was present, but of course, as is to be expected, that is confusing for her." Aakar ran his fingers through his wavy grey hair again. "But she is an intelligent girl and knows something strange is going on."

"Yes, she was asking me too. She wanted to stay with Akshita and cannot understand why we did not let her."

"Maybe we should tell her about Fanish. She is old enough and will be better able to take care of herself."

"Or it might scare her. In fact, I am sure it will. Akshita and Urvi are very close and fond of each other. She will constantly worry about her and the doctor has told us that is one thing she should not do."

Urvi was a delicate child – both Aninditi and Aakar always attributed it to the fact that she had been born prematurely. However, a couple of months ago, after some tests, they found she had a hole in the heart.

"However, what are we going to do about Akshita? It seems we cannot have the satisfaction that comes from having healthy and well-settled daughters." Aninditi wiped the tears from her eyes.

"Ani, don't cry." Aakar said uncomfortably, his heart wrenched seeing his wife crying. "We won't mention anything to Urvi."

"But what about Akshita?" Aninditi repeated. "She is with Fanish who is capable of anything."

"No he won't," Aakar replied. "He won't harm her."

"How can you be so sure?"

"I know because Fanish is too clever. He realises that if anything happens to Akshita, I will do everything in my power to destroy him."

"But Akshita will be unhappy and..." Aninditi started crying again.

"Fanish has not said we cannot talk to her. In fact, now is the time she needs us so the least we can do is show her we are there for her."

"Urvi, I thought you were asleep." Aninditi rose from her sofa. She had just spotted Urvi walking down the stairs rubbing her eyes.

Urvi looked alarmed as soon as she saw her parent's faces.

"Mum, Dad, what is the matter?" She asked worriedly.

"Nothing is the matter, Urvi." Aninditi and Aakar answered at simultaneously.

"What are you doing downstairs? I thought I had tucked you safely in bed?" Aninditi asked crossly.

"I could not sleep. Anyway, Dad, don't treat me like a child. I am sure something is wrong, and I also know it has something to do with Akshita and Fanish."

"You're right." Aakar said quietly.

"And....?" Urvi asked whilst Aninditi looked in surprise at her husband.

"Well, it is complicated, they had a bad fight and it blew out of hand."

"That is the reason she wanted talk to you." Aninditi added, breathing a sigh of relief. "She must have mentioned it to Fanish, and he thought by taking you home, he would surprise Akshita and that she would be so glad of the kind gesture, she would forgive him."

"So is everything alright now? Maybe I should go and stay with Akshi for a few days as I have holidays at school and…" Urvi said looking perplexed.

No!" Again both Aninditi said simultaneously. "No Urvi, there is no need to go now. In fact, it is best they are left alone. In future, even if Fanish says that Akshita wants to talk to you, just come and tell us and we will sort it out. Anyway, your mother is not feeling too well and needs you here."

"OK, as long as Akshita is okay. Mum, what is the matter?"

"It's just the tension between Fanish and Akshita." Aninditi replied. "It is very worrying,

"Can I phone her to find out how she is?" Urvi asked.

"There is nothing to worry about, Urvi, go back to bed." Aakar looked tenderly at his daughter.

"As long as she is okay," Urvi muttered and both Aakar and Aninditi gave a sigh of relief as she left the room.

• • • •

Chapter 48

Ena and Akshita were having a cup of tea when the doorbell rang.

Akshita answered the door apprehensively, and to her surprise saw Dilawar standing in the doorway, a bouquet of flowers in one hand and a dripping umbrella in the other.

"Dilawar! What a surprise!" Akshita looked flustered.

"Akshita, what is the matter?" Ena had followed Akshita and gave a gasp when she saw Dilawar.

"Ena, can I come in and talk to you?" Dilawar gave her the flowers.

"There is nothing to talk about! Dilawar, leave me alone."

"Ena, at least hear me out. I realise you are angry with me and it will take some time for you to forgive me, but at least go and stay with and your parents. On no account must you stay here, especially after what I told you!"

"Why are you so worried where I stay?" Ena asked indignantly. "And I am sure you were exaggerating!"

"She is perfectly comfortable here." Fanish's voice interrupted them.

Dilawar swung around in surprise to find Fanish had been out and had quietly come up behind him and been listening to their conversation.

"I was just saying she should…"

"Ena, do you want to go with Dilawar?" Fanish enquired.

Akshita had made her feel so welcome and comfortable that he was fairly sure of the answer.

Ena looked at Fanish pleadingly. "If it is alright with Akshita, I would like to stay here a couple of days more before I decide my next move?"

"Of course!" Fanish exclaimed triumphantly. "You

can stay as long as you like."

Dilawar marvelled at Ena's foolishness, for it had blinded her to Fanish's ruthlessness. However, he knew that Ena's judgement was based on her fondness for Akshita.

"Ena, please, I am begging you, don't stay here, you don't know what…"

"Dilawar, why don't you give up?" Fanish said angrily. "Ena does not want to come home to you, the sooner you accept that the better it will be for you."

"Leave her out of this, Fanish, it is me that you are after, and I have given my word to you."

"Dilawar, I am getting fed up of having the same conversation over and over. I have left 'her alone' as you say, and she is welcome to leave anytime she wants, as I just proved to you."

Dilawar knew it was useless to get Fanish to change his mind so content himself by giving him a nasty look as he turned around.

It was dusk as he opened the car door and drove home, watching the sun drop in the sky taking and taking with it the mild heat of the day, leaving the air cool and thin.

- - - -

Chapter 49

Parul walked back down the corridor of the hospital, a frown on his face. He decided to check on Vanita after he had seen to his emergency patient, for he knew James would not mind.

"Good-morning, Doctor," Jane smiled cheerfully as he walked into the ward. "Have you been called to see one of patients? I didn't know that…. oh my I hope none of my nurses have made a mistake …"

Jane was flustered for she knew that the doctors were quick to find fault with them, sometimes without any cause.

"Good-morning, Jane." Parul grinned and tried to put her at ease, for it was rarely that two doctors came to see the same patient. "Jane, how is our patient Vanita? I believe James came in to see her morning? Has there been any improvement?"

"No, she is still the same." Jane replied.

"Has she had any visitors?"

"No, her cousin phoned yesterday saying that she had to leave town urgently."

"So who brought her in?" Parul enquired.

"Vanita's cousin."

"Anybody else?" As Jane shook her head, Parul continued. "We need to know her identity so we can inform them. At least did you hear her talk about anybody?"

"Now that you mention it, Doctor, the cousin made a phone call and I overheard the name 'Fanish'. I remember thinking what an unusual name it was. 'Fanish', yes that is what she called him."

"That is not good enough, we can only hope the amnesia lifts so she can shed light on the matter, I would like to see Vanita though."

174

As Parul walked up to her bed, he saw a frail and delicate girl in bed. Vanita was looking confused and lost.

"Hello, Vanita, I am Dr. Parul." Parul said introducing himself.

"More tests?" Vanita asked looking at Parul dispassionately.

Parul looked into her eyes and shivered, for a second he saw an expression in them that was cold and distant however, the gaze was so fleeting that he thought he had imagined it. But he understood Dilawar's concern, for although Vanita's face was bruised and swollen, he could detect an underlying fragile beauty.

"Parul, she looks so vulnerable, just like a torn butterfly!" James had told him.

James had told him Vanita was a young girl of thirteen, but somehow Paul had expected a grown up thirteen. His heart went out to Vanita, who looked so pitiful and vulnerable.

"No more tests, young lady. How are you feeling?"

"The same, doctor, I do not remember anything."

"Does the name Fanish mean anything to you?" Parul asked as he checked her pulse.

Vanita shook her head slowly,

"The name does seem familiar but I can't say…. Oh, it is so frustrating!" she put her hand on her throbbing head.

"Be sure to tell Jane immediately if anything comes to mind." He turned and left the ward, followed by Jane.

"Well, doctor, what do you think?"

"Poor thing, she does seem to be in a bad state. What kind of sick person would do that to a young girl? Was it a burglar and have the police been informed?"

"We don't know how it happened and of course the police have been informed…we are required to do so by law but since she has amnesia she is not going to be of much help to them. And anyway, strangely, the cousin does not want to prosecute even if the burglar is found, so the police have dropped the case."

"You are right, Jane, that is odd, I would imagine they would want to catch the guy who did this. There is something fishy about this case!" Parul exclaimed. "Jane, can you page me if anything, anything at all changes?"

"Sure doctor, I will do that, in fact I will note it in her sheets so that the nurse who is looking after her after my shift finishes knows about it."

However, Vanita's face haunted him all day and by evening he was feeling depressed. He decided to phone Sai. Maybe if she was free they could see a movie and grab something to eat?

He phoned her as soon as he reached home and they decided to meet for dinner, so after Parul had quickly changed into freshly laundered clothes, he drove to Sai's house.

She was waiting for him outside her house, and as she got into the car, Parul thought what a lucky man he was for Sai was a beautiful woman.

She was a slender girl with long hair that reached her waist, beautiful features with big black-almond eyes that seemed even larger in her childlike face. Everything about her was delicate, almost dainty, and Parul thought her to be enchanting.

"His Sai, hop in, it is freezing out there." Parul said opening the door for her.

"Hi." Sai said smiled as she got into the car showing perfect white teeth.

She liked Parul for he was so strong and dependable, and Sai was exhausted and defeated by her affair with Dilawar.

"Where are we going?" Sai asked.

"First I thought we'd see a film then I have booked a

table at your favourite restaurant dinner. There is something I want to talk to you about."

"Why, what's happened?" Sai glanced at Parul's profile.

"I was thinking that everything between us has happened so quickly and…"

"Yes, I know." Sai sighed, hoping Parul was not going to ask her about her past.

After the film they sat in the restaurant in a companionable silence.

"Sai, you know I like you very much don't you? You do feel the same about me, I hope?"

Parul looked at Sai's beautiful face and suddenly asked, "Will you marry me?"

Sai was surprised, but pleased for she too was in love with Parul. He was not an arrogant man and there was no air of superiority about him. He had the ability to get along with people of all social backgrounds, was natural and spontaneous and there was a freshness about him that made her comfortable in his presence.

However, she had at one time thought she was in love with Dilawar too and for a moment was scared as she recalled the heartache that had involved.

■ ■ ■

Chapter 50

Sai had only worked for Dilawar for a short while, but in the short space of time had come to admire him. Dilawar too had been impressed and fascinated by Sai, for she was enthusiastic about her job, asking him endless questions and thinking up ways of streamlining office routine.

Sai, to Dilawar was not only a very capable woman but also very elegant and beautiful, and it was not long before they became more than friends.

"I'm going to fall in love with you!" Dilawar had laughed jokingly, "But don't let that interfere with your work."

Sai had not expected to feel so much so soon, but she warmed to Dilawar. He was not only gentle, sympathetic and vulnerable, but also a very decent man.

Whenever she saw his face, she was filled with tenderness, but was also alarmed at such emotions since Dilawar was a married man.

But Sai was lonely, and Dilawar was a good companion. They would talk over dinner and coffee, making each other laugh, discussing books and authors, there hobbies and interests. Sai told herself in the beginning that their relationship was beautiful and harmless, but realised soon that her feelings were much deeper.

However, although they did end up having an affair, it was not long before it became apparent to Sai that Dilawar only loved his wife. Sometimes when his guilt was strong, he would shy away, and Sai felt that although he was near, he was not near enough.

Soon, she began to grasp the limitations on their relationship, for they could not phone freely, he was always concerned who would see them together, she could not send him cards, give birthday presents or even mention him to friends.

And when the first stage of the relationship was over, and they had either to embark on the second stage or part, Sai began to realise that their relationship, if it could be called that, had a finality about it that could lead nowhere. She was moved by an odd sort of desperation arising from nothing she could not pinpoint, and which was nothing more tangible than the general atmosphere when Dilawar was around.

One evening she decided to confront Dilawar.

"You only love your wife and reputation, Dilawar. Me, I only love you, but that means nothing to you. All the stolen hours, the secrecy, isolation and deceiving people, I feel so shabby so cheap."

The long lace curtains fluttered as a slight breeze fluttered in through the half-open window of the motel.

There was a look of resigned disillusionment on Sai's face, for she felt they had reached the end of a journey; however, she felt relieved after voicing her concern.

She went up to Dilawar and held his hand, not wanting his arm around her, not because she did not love him, but because she had never felt so alone, as all feeling of security had gradually flowed away.

Dilawar hand fluttered helplessly as if he had been taken unawares. Something drained out of him, some bright glowing hope of being distracted and amused by Sai. However, Dilawar was a decent man, one who respected women, and did not regard his brief relationship with Sai as a conquest. He was angry with himself for letting it get so far, for he had known all along that the relationship would lead nowhere and would only ruin a professional relationship.

"I think you are right, Sai, it was my fault for letting it get so far knowing that I could not...Sai?" Dialler's hand fell helplessly to his side as Sai rushed from the room.

Nevertheless, Dilawar's need of her had been distant from his want of her. It was the same sensation he got when he saw a picture or furniture that would be ideal for him, only the sensation was wildly intensified, out of all proportion, and an authentic feeling of insanity would sweep over him. He justified the thought by thinking that the situation was predestined and right and had complete trust in the madness of it all.

The slight warmth of the day had disappeared with the setting of the sun.

As Sai drove home that day the streets seemed deserted and the few people who were lingering in the streets looked as if they either had no reason or no home to go to. Most of the stores she passed were closed and the single light in their window seemed blank and stark.

As Sai listened to the silence around her, she wished it would be in her heart also. She wiped the tears from her eyes as she realised that love alone was not enough to sustain a relationship and she had been right in being strong to end it.

She looked at Parul and smiled faintly as she thought:

'Perhaps there is something wrong with me for I always seem to want the people who are not the people I need! They are too much like me; and together we just drown in a terrifying swamp of emotions! Perhaps what I am only looking for is security, not love? Or are they the same things and the rest just human weaknesses?' Maybe I am not ready for any deep relationship?' But I do love Parul and...'

"Hello, Sai, come back from wherever you are!"

There was a new look in Parul's eyes, a cross between anger and hurt as he saw that his proposal had sparked an unpleasant memory.

The dark expression which had been clouding Sai's

lovely eyes disappeared, and she smiled at Parul, sure that she only wanted Parul to be in her future, a future in which she would not permit any shadows of the past to hang over them.

She needed to be free of Dilawar with no encumbrances from the past, to firmly close that chapter of her life. It was not that she harboured any emotional feelings for him, those had been well and truly killed some time ago, but she certainly had no desire whatsoever to be haunted by the spectre of him.

With his usual sensitivity, Parul realised that Sai had loved and been hurt in the past, and wondered if it was impossible on his part in believing that he could fashion the future from a scrap of the past?

"I would love to marry you, Parul, but don't you think we should get to know each other longer before we make any plans?" Sai said asked.

"I feel I have known you all my life." Parul exclaimed. "I met my friend Dilawar this morning, and you don't know how difficult it was not to mention you to him. We are childhood friends and have no secrets from each other."

"You mean Dr. Dilawar of ...?" Sai looked alarmed.

She was just beginning to come to terms with her past, ready to put it behind her when Parul told her Dilawar was his childhood friend, one that would no doubt would be a part of in their lives.

"Yes, do you know him?"

"I once worked for him for a short while. He is a brilliant doctor."

"He is." Parul remarked proudly. "And an even better friend."

It seemed to Sai that she would have to break off and end this relationship also. He was such a close and dear friend of Parul, how could they carry off the deception, for it would be complicated for Dilawar too, for both were too honest and decent to suppress uncomfortable emotions

"Parul, as I was saying, I think we should take things slowly and see how things develop."

"Alright, whatever you say, I am willing to wait for as long as it takes. Look, are you feeling alright, you are looking pale?" He gestured to the waiter for their bill.

Sai was quiet on the journey home, and Parul thought she looked as if she had a lot on her mind for a woman who had just been proposed to.

"A penny for your thoughts?" he asked as he stopped the car outside Sai's flat.

"Huh? Are we home?" Sai gave a start. "Nothing, nothing is the matter."

Parul looked at Sai as she got out of the car thoughtfully, convinced that something was bothering her, and then waved his hand as he drove off.

As soon as Sai entered, Sai threw herself into a chair and started crying. She switched on the wireless to cheer herself up as she thought of Dilawar and their brief but passionate affair, the stolen hours, the secrecy, and isolation.

She closed her eyes, trying to concentrate on the present. Parul had become very important to her in the last couple of months and had represented a new beginning for her. She laughed at the irony of it, for now that they had a future together, it turned out he was a friend of Dilawar. A worried crease wrinkled her brow as she sat brooding.

She got up to draw the curtains, and as she looked out of the window, noticed that the street-lights were clear and bright, scattering patterns of shadows across the road.

Chapter 51

The morning brought cooler air with cotton like clouds drifting across the sky. As Vanita walked back to her bed she noticed that the clouds were translucent and filmy with not a hint of moisture.

Although she was getting stronger day by day, so was her restlessness.

"Jane, when can I go home?" But as soon as she spoke, she had tears in her eyes.

"Soon, Vanita." Jane looked thoughtfully at the face of the young girl looking up at her earnestly.

"I don't know why I am asking; I don't want to leave hospital for I have nowhere to go anyway."

"The doctors were talking about you this morning. They had to involve the police."

"But I have done nothing wrong." Vanita sat up in alarm.

"Oh don't worry, my dear, I did not mean to scare you." Jane smiled reassuringly. "They will advertise your photo or whatever and hopefully someone will come forward."

A doctor on the spot had overheard the conversation.

"That has already been done successfully and you are being discharged tomorrow for a woman named Ishika phoned the hospital claiming she was your sister. She is coming to visit you this afternoon.... does the name ring a bell?"

As Vanita shook her head in bewilderment, the doctor left to finish his rounds.

"There you see." Jane said triumphantly, fluffing Vanita's bed.

"But I don't remember if..."

"There is no need to worry. Just wait till you meet her."

As visiting time approached, Vanita got more excited and apprehensive and expressed her worries to Jane.

"Jane, what am I going to say to this woman, Ishika? I was thinking, how could she recognise me like this, for my face has been disfigured?"

"The photo that was advertises was not in your present condition, but what you looked like before."

"I myself do not know how I looked so how could anyone else?"

"Police artists can do wonders."

"What about my cousin? The one who brought me to hospital?"

"Sorry, Vanita, she has not phoned again."

"Then she could not have been my cousin. She knew the state I was in and would surely have phoned or visited."

Jane was quite as she tucked the sheets of Vanita's bed, for that is what all the staff thought. Vanita had become a mysterious figure for them and all the nurses were weaving different stories around her, her cousin and now her sister.

"Ah, that must be your sister." Jane whispered as she saw a woman looking around her.

Ishika was wearing a soft blue sari and her fine brown hair cascaded down to her waist. Her eyes were soft brown and warm as she searched the ward.

Jane quickly left Vanita's bedside and went up to her.

"Excuse me are you looking for Vanita?"

"Yes, my name is Ishika and I am her sister. The police said that…"

"Yes she is here come with me." Jane took her into the ward. "You must be prepared for a shock, but do not be alarmed. She has been raped, beaten terribly and you will find she is changed, but most of her injuries are superficial and will heal. She is suffering from Amnesia and will not know who you are. Something terrible

184

happened to her, something she wants to block out from her mind."

There were four beds in the ward and Vanita lay in one of them, her face bruised and one eye was swollen.

"You will need to be calm and have a lot of patience with her." Jane said quietly as they approached the bed.

Ishika nodded her head silently.

"I will be patient for as long as it takes. I am only thankful she has been found."

"Look who's come to see you!" Jane said cheerfully as they neared Vanita's bed." Your sister is here."

■ ■ ■ ■

Chapter 52

Although she had been warned to expect the worst, Ishika was shocked to see Vanita, for she had never seen anyone's face in such a condition except perhaps the wrestlers on television. She had meant to kiss Vanita on the cheek, but the sight of Vanita's swollen face, techno-coloured bruises and half closed eye repelled her.

Ishika felt herself trembling at the sight of her sister, and then felt guilty about how sad that would make Vanita feel if she knew.

"Vanita?" Ishika asked tentatively as she moved closer to the bed.

"Yes, I believe you are my sister?" Vanita raised her eyes and looked at Ishika through her swollen face.

At that moment, Ishika recognised her sister for her eyes had not changed- though the expression in them had....they were now sad, cold and detached. No longer was Vanita the young and innocent sister she knew, but a sad young girl.

Ishika found herself searching for signs of Vanita's innocence enthusiasm and the spontaneity that her parents had tried to suppress.

"Vanita, yes, I'm your sister, Ishika." She said with a lump in her throat. "I'll be taking you home with me."

"I am sorry, but I do not recognise you...?" Vanita asked in a pitiful voice.

"Never mind, your memory will return in time, in the meantime I will look after you!!" Ishika went up to Vanita 'bed and hugged her.

In reaching out to comfort Vanita, Ishika felt conscious of a shift in their relationship, for it had been Vanita, who, since childhood, had been the carer of their family, whereas Ishika had stood back and been content to let her take charge.

Vanita held Ishika's hand, and the moment of closeness took Ishika back before everything was so complicated, when they were both young and innocent.

"I do not remember anything, anything at all." Vanita replied. "I look terrible, scary even, are you sure you want me to come with you?"

Tears oozed out, trickling down her swollen cheeks.

"Don't' worry, Vanita, everything will come back to you gradually. All you need is rest, and I can look after you at home."

"So tell me about yourself, Ishika, maybe something will jog my memory?"

"Ok, but where shall I begin? I got married a couple of years ago to a wonderful man called Hetal who is quiet, kind and sensible and we have a daughter called Ekta."

Ishika did not tell her that despite his compassion and understanding, he had been upset when she told him about Vanita.

"She is your sister why aren't your parents taking the responsibility of looking after her?"

"Hetal, why are you being so difficult? You know my mother is not well and…"

"Don't say that, Ishika. You know jolly well that there is nothing wrong with her. When things get difficult, or even if they don't, she panics and tries to shun any kind of responsibility!"

Ishika knew that Hetal was right but was not willing to admit it.

"Whatever the reason, Hetal, I want Vanita to stay with me till she is well enough. I feel guilty for letting her take on so much responsibility at such a young age. She was the one who looked after mother whilst I was away at the boarding school."

Now looking at Vanita's fragile person, then at her detached eyes, she wondered for a moment if Hetal was right, for there seemed no way to bridge the worlds that separated them.

Vanita and Ishika had travelled so far from each other that there was no road back. But then she shrugged away her doubt for there was still that bond of kinship.

"So tell me Vanita, when are they discharging you from hospital?" Ishika held Vanita's hand tenderly.

"It would have been sooner, but as I didn't have anywhere to go….anyway, now I think they will discharge me soon. Well, I am sure they will only be too pleased to see me go for they need the bed."

Jane had overheard their conversation as she passed Vanita's bed.

"You are right, Vanita, I spoke to the doctor and you will be discharged tomorrow. You could have gone today but we have to go through a lot of paperwork before you are finally discharged, so I would say about eleven .a.m?".

"That is settled then, I'll be here at eleven." Ishika looked around her uncertainly. "Is visiting time over?"

"No, there is still half an hour to go." Jane replied as she hurried off

"Oh good, Ishika, now you can tell me about myself and our family." Vanita asked.

Ishika relaxed and told Vanita about their parents, where she had lived, all the time watching Vanita's face for something that might trigger her memory, but there was no sign of recognition on Vanita's face.

Vanita had been listening eagerly, but instead of a feeling of familiarity, when Ishika spoke of her father, a strange feeling seized Vanita and she trembled.

As soon as visiting time was over, Ishika reminded Vanita to be ready the following morning.

Vanita sank back into her pillows and Jane came appeared at her bedside.

"Vanita, do you need anything? What did you think

of your sister? Do you remember anything?"

"No not a thing! She seems such a nice and warm person but I did not even remember her." Vanita exclaimed exasperatedly.

Jane looked at her oddly. "I think your sister's visit has tired you now but do not worry. Just go to sleep and I am sure you will feel better in the morning."

Vanita took a deep breath, feeling physically and mentally drained as she willed herself to remember

She turned slowly to her side, and as she drifted off to sleep, something stirred, took root and spread till she felt angry. Then a haunting sense of guilt awakened her – she felt there was something that was eluding her, followed by certainty that she had left something unfinished.

• • • •

Chapter 53

Whilst Vanita had been in hospital, she had seen many patients being discharged, and all had grumbled at the long procedure, so morning was well under way when everything was finally completed

Whilst waiting in the reception for Ishika, she felt peculiar, for she was going with a stranger to an unknown place.

The waiting room was near the casualty department and Vanita could see the new arrivals, some people who had injured themselves, others who had brought the injured party.

She was getting impatient and tired when she saw Ishika walking towards her with a young man with dark hair in casual attire.

"Vanita, how are you today? This is my husband Hetal." Ishika hugged Vanita.

"Hello, Vanita," Hetal smiled as he ran his hair through his hair.

Vinita's bandages had been taken off; however, he was startled to see the queer look in her eyes and shuddered.

"Let's go." Ishika said as she led the way and Vanita followed bewildered, sensing Hetal's uneasiness.

It was a nice day, with the clouds sweeping over a pale blue sky and the sun shining between them. Everything was a varying shade of green, from dark brown to blue green.

As Vanita looked out of the car window, she was fascinated at the patterns made by the clouds as they were chased by the wind. They were blown across the sky, where they tried to encircle the sun, diffusing its light and scattering shadows in its wake. The wind was also constantly altering the light, colour and movements of the trees and shrubs.

After driving for about fifteen minutes, Ishika parked outside a house with a well-kept garden.

"Here we are – home!" Ishika said as she got out of the car and opened Vanita's door. "Hetal, can you please collect Ekta from the Anushka? Thanks." She opened the door with her key and dropped the suitcase with Vanita's few clothes on the floor. "Whew! Come in, Vanita. Make yourself comfortable whilst I get some tea. I am sure you must be tired." Ishika went into the kitchen.

Although Vanita was feeling tired, she paced the room restlessly and was looking at a group photo of a family when Ishika entered the room carrying a tray.

"Ishika, who is this?" Vanita asked.

"That is a photo of our parents." Ishika said as she poured the tea into a cup and handed it to Vanita.

"Thanks," Vanita said taking the cup. She took a sip then asked. "And these two girls are…?"

"Those two girls are you and me." Ishika said with a smile.

Vanita put her cup on the table and went to study the photo again. As she looked closely, she could recognise Ishika, but the other girl, the one standing next to Ishika, looked lost and vulnerable. Vanita put her hand on her face, trying to find remnants of the face and wondered again what happened to her.

"Where are Mother and Father? Why are they not here?" Vanita asked anxiously. "They know I am coming home today, don't they?"

"Yes, they do." Ishika wondered how she was going to explain her parent's attitude to Vanita.

How could she tell Vanita that their mother was moody, stayed in her room for days on end, always complained and had expected Vanita to do all the work? How Vanita had to endure their hostility, their criticism, usually unwarranted and personal, attacking anything and everything about her?

Ishika had rung her parents after visiting Vanita in hospital and informed them that Vanita had been found and was bringing her home. Her mother, as usual, told her that she would not be able to come as she was suffering from migraine and her father had been too angry with Vanita, as if her running away from home was a personal insult.

• • • •

Chapter 54

"Where has she been all this time?" Devesh growled. "Why did she run away and where is she now?"

"She is in hospital." Ishika replied tersely. "Nobody knows what happened – but apparently she was badly beaten and has lost her memory. Dad, she looks awful, not like her old self at all."

"What about her face?"

"Badly beaten and quite disfigured, at least till the swelling dies down. But she has changed in other ways too, and I am certain something bad happened to her, I mean even before she was attacked."

"If she does not remember, how do you know?" Devesh sighed with relief.

"When I met her in hospital the nurse said she had been among other things, sexually abused, and that it had been on over a period of time. Vanita, of course, does not remember. And the change is not only in her eyes; her smile is sad, intense, and even hypnotic. Underlying all that is the sorrow in her eyes."

"Oh?" Devesh answered absent-mindedly, his mind racing ahead to his friend's visit.

"They are discharging her tomorrow and I thought you would like her to stay with you, or at least to meet her?"

"No," Devesh answered quickly. "It is better she stays with you. You will be able to look after her so she will make a speedy recovery."

"But she needs her parents at this time." Ishika protested.

"Ishika, don't argue with me. You know your mother is not well and I have to leave town on business."

As Ishika replaced the receiver she wondered how she had been able to form a lasting and warm relationship with Hetal regardless of her parent's absence of warmth and affection, for children who suffered rejection usually found it difficult to form emotional ties with anybody.

As Ishika looked at Vanita's eager face, she began to understand Hetal's contempt of her parents and why Vanita felt she had to leave home. And as she did, she believed that Vanita would not be able to tolerate their rejection in her present weak physical and mental state.

They sat in silence, and just when Ishika wished that Hetal was here to tide over the difficult moment, he walked in carrying Ekta.

"Vanita, look who's here, it is your niece." Ishika took the gurgling baby from Hetal. "Ekta, say hello to your aunt, Vanita, would you like to hold her?"

"No!" Vanita shrank from her. "I might drop her."

Hetal had seen the startled look on Vanita's face, so quickly held her tenderly and protectively sin his arms.

"Don;t worry, I'll put her to bed." Hetal said softly, "Ekta has been restless - also I would like to spend time with her." Hetal said curtly.

Vanita flinched, and there was a surprised expression on Ihaka's face as she looked at the receding figure of her husband, for his abrupt manner had hurt Vanita.

"You can play with her tomorrow." Ishika remarked reassuringly.

"Hmm…. Ishika, when can I meet them Mother and father?"

"Vanita, you do not remember, but father…."

"What about father?" Again Vanita felt a strange terror coursing through her body.

- - - -

Chapter 55

"He's out of town on business." Ishika avoided looking at Vanita.

"When will he be back?" Vanita was keener to meet him than her mother so she could explain and rationalise her fear of him.

"I do not know." Ishika tried to change the subject. "Vanita, are you hungry?"

"No, thanks, but tell me about father?" Vanita persisted.

"I'll just put the tea things back in the kitchen." Ishika quickly.

She hastily got up and left the room with tears in her eyes. How could she tell her sister that her father had not only been indifferent, but positively cruel when he heard Vanita was back?

She came back into the room after clearing up and found that Vanita was still thoughtfully staring at the photograph.

"Vanita, you must be tired. Why don't you lie down?" Ishika desperately wanted to change the topic.

"Mother seems nice." Vanita continued. "Tell me about her."

Ishika swallowed and her eyes glistened with unshed tears as she looked into Vanita's eager face. She decided that since she had to know sometime she would tell her gently.

"Vanita, there is something about them you should know." Ishika said nervously.

"Ishika, please tell me everything about our family." Vanita asked eagerly, and for the hundredth time.

"Well I don't where to begin. We are not a very close family and…" Ishika looked uncomfortable.

Vanita looked at Ishika's face then remarked

candidly.

"You mean they do not want to meet me?" Vanita said with the frankness of a child. "Have I done something wrong to offend them?"

"No, not really, they are like that even with me." Ishika said uneasily

"Ishika, don't try to justify their attitude, I'd like to go to lie down now." Vanita said abruptly.

"I'll take you to your room, do you mind sharing Ekta's nursery?"

Hetal entered the room and overhead Ishika.

"I am afraid that will not be possible." Hetal remarked.

"I thought we decided that....?"

Ishika drew in her breadth and raised her eyebrows questionably. She looked at her husband beseechingly, imploring him with her eyes to be gentle with Vanita.

"It's alright, Vanita, you can sleep in Ekta's room."

"No!" Hetal stood in the doorway his arms across his chest.

"No? What do you mean, Hetal?" Ishika asked impatiently.

"Ekta is not asleep as yet, I'll bring her downstairs." Hetal hurried from the room.

"I think I am an inconvenience." Vanita noticed her brother-in-law-'s abrupt manner.

"Of course you're not." Ishika smiled as Hetal came back into the room with Ekta.

"Let's go." Ishika turned towards Vanita.

"No, it's alright, I'll find my way." Vanita remarked as she disappeared upstairs.

Ishika looked angrily at Hetal as she took Ekta in her arms.

"Why did you have to be so rude to my sister?" she exclaimed.

"What did I say?" Hetal remarked innocently.

"I'm talking about your attitude that showed you did not want her to be in the same room as Ekta. Even I noticed it!"

"Ishika, even you are afraid of her! Don't deny it!"

The air seemed to crackle with hostility. Neither said anything for a few moments, then with great care and deliberation Ishika rose and stood with both hands on top of the chair, her fingers gripping it hard.

"I don't know what you mean." she retorted angrily.

"As soon as Vanita came, you sent me to get Ekta, and then you told me to take her upstairs."

"Hetal, what is the matter with you? You were the one who suggested that we needed some time together."

"Whatever." Hetal suddenly recalled that she was right.

"I thought that was what you wanted me to do. I took your cue. After all, you know your sister better than I do."

"That's where you're wrong. I don't know her at all."

"That's what I mean." Hetal cried triumphantly. "I don't want a stranger near my daughter, let alone sleep in her room."

"Maybe you are right, I too want to protect Ekta," she murmured. "Ekta is precious to me and you are right, there are times when I do not like the look in Vanita's eyes. They are so cold and distant sometimes that they do frighten me! But on the other hand Vanita is my sister and I do not want to hurt her any more than she has been."

She tried to change the subject.

"What would you like for dinner?" she asked in a light tone of voice.

"I'm going out." Hetal replied putting a finger under Ekta's chin, who was gurgling happily.

"Where are you going? I thought you had a day off?"

Ishika tried to hold on to Ekta who was trying to

wriggle her way out of her lap.

"I do but I have some things to do. Anyway, I'll leave you sisters for there must be a lot she wants to tell.."

"Not really, she has gone to bed, anyway her mind is blank, anyway, what time will you be back?"

"I'll be back as soon as I can, are you frightened?"

"Of course not! Why should I be scared?" Ishika answered much too quickly. "Take as long as you like." But her voice did not sound convincing enough.

Vanita was lying in bed and had heard Hetal's raised voice, and after he slammed the door behind him, knew he had left the house.

She tossed and turned on the bed but could not sleep, even though she was tired. She had sensed Hetal's unreceptive attitude and felt she would not be able to tolerate it for long.

She thought of the girl who had claimed to be her cousin and wished she asked Jane for her number and address. Maybe she could shed some light on who she was? She must have been in her life somehow, for otherwise why was she in her house?

. . . .

Chapter 56

Fanish, Gazal and Aditya were sitting in the lounge. Fanish looked worried for his contact abroad had told him that they were having problems. There had been reports on child abuse, their exploitation, which was making Fanish's work difficult. So far, for Fanish child trafficking had been deceptively simple for it merely meant the exchange of a child for a financial reward.

"Why are both of you looking so worried?" Gazal asked.

Fanish explained the problems they were facing.

"So why don't you stop what you are doing?" Gazal protested.

"And give up all the easy money?" Fanish retorted. "Anyway, more often than not the child would end up as a prostitute, a drug addict, in the drug business, be sold for organ transplant or be exploited in the industry."

"Isn't that what you do with them anyway? Exploit them?"

"Only if I can't find a client for them!" Fanish ran his hand through his hair. "And anyway, if I don't do it, somebody else will for there is a huge demand for children."

"Child exploitation only exists because of people like you. I know what you are doing is an answer to a demand, but that demand is only kept alive because it is catered to by people like you."

Aditya was listening quietly then remarked softly. "It's a vicious circle."

"And whose side are you anyway?" Fanish demanded angrily. "Are you forgetting that 'we', in the process, make a lot of money?"

"I know, but today I heard about some drug trafficker who used a baby to transport drugs. He strangled the baby to death, cut his stomach open and stuffed it with heroin! It is getting dangerous!" Gazal exclaimed.

"But you know we would not do anything like that, for to do something like that only calls attention to oneself." Fanish said softly.

"And anyway," Aditya interrupted "as Fanish said, there are a large number of children who are beggars, thieves and prostitutes all of who are exploited in one way or another. These children have no family life for they were not conceived out of love but through corruption, stupidity and ignorance of their parents."

"No that is not true, Fanish, what about the girls from good families who would have had a good life but for you?" Gazal exclaimed and looked at him in disgust.

He had a good-looking face, open and honest, and his brown eyes were usually gentle and warm. Although he had a sensitive mouth which was quick to smile, Gazal had gradually established that he had a heart of stone.

"And what about them? The so called good families you talk about, Gazal, yours being one of them, could not care less about their children, so engrossed are they in their careers. And don't forget. It is these very same children who help maintain your affluent lifestyle."

"Fanish, don't you dare make me feel guilty! You imagine you are living a charmed life and that immunity from justice is your right. You feel you can say or do anything and that these depraved acts of yours will not have repercussions?"

"Gazal, how dare you talk to me like that!? Have you forgotten what happens if you do?" Fanish grasped her wrist.

"I am sorry, Fanish." Gazal replied, biting her lip. "But it is true." She muttered under her breadth.

She was overcome with guilt and emotion as she thought again of the innocent children, but swiftly quashed them.

As soon Fanish and Aditya left, Gazal went into the bathroom and turned on the taps. She poured in the bubble-bath, as soon as the water threatened to rise to the rim of the tub and splash over the sides, she turned them off. She stripped off her clothes, slid into the warm water, lay back and closed her eyes

She scrubbed herself thoroughly, desperate to erase the guilt and shame. Why had she let things get so far? Why did she agree to go along with Fanish and his seedy business when she knew it was wrong? Was it because she craved love and affection or because she was a coward or was it because she was simply greedy for material things?

She thought about Kanan and was sure that Fanish had sent her abroad to one of his brothels. She tried to justify that her reason for accepting her present life was fear, for Fanish would not hesitate in doing the same with her if she disobeyed him.

Having finished her bath, Gazal went into the kitchen and whilst drinking her tea slowly and eating a pink iced cake, thought about Vanita, disregarding the momentary moral consciousness that had disturbed her.

She thought how calmly she was dealing with Fanish and Aditya, although she was seething inside. As she nibbled her cake, she was careful not to let the crumbs fall on the floor. She drained the last mouthful of tea and replaced the cup and saucer, then thought analytically again of her life. She had vowed, when she left home, shed her old life and embarked on a new one, that she would ask no questions.

However, her world had dropped to a darker abyss and her memories, what little there were, had merged into the blackness of the night.

There was a frown between her brows and a slight puckering around her mouth as if she were about to burst into tears.

She convinced herself that at least Fanish was concerned about her welfare. He had set her up in an apartment with generous clothes allowance and all expenses paid. He did this for all his girls, and they all agreed because it gave them a roof over their heads, warmth, kept them off the streets and allowed them a certain amount of freedom.

However, they soon came to realise that with the security of childhood gone, womanhood and freedom brought with it its own kind of responsibilities.

∎ ∎ ∎ ∎

Chapter 57

It was a couple of days later that Ishika walked into the lounge after dropping Ekta off at Anushka's place. Ekta had kept her up all night, so she stifled a yawn with her hand as she walked to the fireplace. She stretched out her hands towards the gas firelight to warm them and hummed softly.

The morning air was crisp, the clouds had shifted and through the window, Ishika could see black patches behind the round white fluffs.

"Hello Ishika, oh… please don't hum that tune!"

Vanita's face was suddenly white as chalk, her eyes glazed over and became devoid of all expression. She sat up abruptly, staring ahead and appeared to be gazing into some distant place. There was an extraordinary remoteness about her, and sat still and silent as if she had fallen into a trance

"Vanita, you scared me!" Startled, Ishika turned to see Vanita sitting quietly on the sofa. " You're up early, how are you feeling today?"

"I'm feeling fine, Ishika, sorry I did not mean to startle you. I am feeling a lot stronger, but please do not hum that tune." Vanita implored again.

"Why, Vanita, are you OK?" Ishika asked with a frown. "And why does this tune upset you so? You did protest once before. Does it jog your memory? If it does maybe I should do it more often!"

"Ishika, I cannot explain it, all I know is that I feel scared!"

"I am sorry." Ishika went up to Vanita and embraced him. "But don't feel scared, you are with me and I will protect you."

Ishika had lived with first her grandparents, then at University, so was able to escape the hostility at home and only had to endure it when she came home during her holidays.

Vanita, on the other hand had been constantly criticised and nagged. This had been damaging for Vanita for a child's first point of reference to the world is through the parent. The child learns to silently identify herslf as an individual through them, and all future learning stemmed from the security of this first relationship.

Consequently, Vanita had adjusted to this lack of emotional nurturing by becoming sullen and moody. And no wonder, for the first lesson she had learnt was that that the world was a cold, lonely and unfriendly place.

Vanita's eyes had strayed to the photograph of her family and she felt a stab of familiar sadness.

"Vanita?" Ishika asked tentatively.

"I'm going for a walk; I want to be alone." Vanita replied abruptly.

"You are not well enough or wait, I'll come with you, Vanita." Ishika said in alarm, but Vanita had already left.

As she came out in the sunlight, Vanita breathed a little easier and tried to shake off the tension that had gripped her. She felt confused, and unexpectedly the past tugged at her, enticing her, drawing her and because her body was still aching, she started walking slowly.

She did not know where she was going, but it seemed as if her feet had wings and knew where they were going. Vanita looked around her as she walked, searching, looking for - what was it, a sign, somebody? She reached a street busy and slipped through the jostling crowd, her eyes darting from one face to another, as if seeking out the perpetrator of the rough justice dealt to her. After a couple of hours, she got tired and turned backwards when she bumped into a tall man..

"Sorry," she murmured as she stumbled.

She caught his coat to steady herself and looked at Fanish's face. Suddenly a wave of recognition swept over her as she looked into the gentle brown eyes and sensitive mouth, followed by a wave of terror.

Her recent trauma had erased everything from her mind, so recounting any particular incident was difficult, but as she felt the wave of fear, the world crashed around her and she faded into blackness.

She woke to find herself back in her sister's house.

"Where is he? How did I get here?" Vanita tried to sit up, but Ishika gently pushed her back on the bed.

"Rest, Vanita, don't try and get up." Ishika looked tenderly at her sister.

"You don't understand, Ishika, I remember everything, who I am, where I've been, everything."

Vanita did not know whether to be glad or sorry, for with the awareness came shame and guilt of the life she had been made to live.

"That is very good, Vanita, but you must rest now."

Ishika was alarmed at the sudden change in Vanita yet again and wondered what had occurred to jolt her memory.

"I'd like to sleep now, Ishika." Vanita turned on her sided and curled up as Ishika rose from her chair.

"And next time you are not going anywhere without me!" Ishika said as she turned to leave the room. "It was lucky I followed you so could bring you back home."

"Thank you" Vanita whispered as she drifted off to sleep. She had barely been asleep an hour when a scream shattered Vanita's nightmare. It echoed around the bedroom and seemed to pierce her brain.

She sat up with a jerk, instantly wide awake, her face and arms bathed in sweat. She suddenly realised that hers had been a soundless scream for she had seen hands, cruel twisted hands reaching out for her....

There was no sound in the bedroom except the faint

ticking of the clock on the table and the faint rustle of leaves as they brushed against windows.

Vanita climbed out of bed and went over to the window. The shutters were open and she could see the night sky outside, pitch black, cloudless, fathomless and endless. Somewhere a loose shutter tapped gently against an outside wall.

Turning away from the window, she went back to bed, troubled by her memories that were humiliating and terrifying her. Slithering down her bed, she pulled the blanket around her and tried to sleep. But her memories raced through her brain in a kaleidoscope fashion.

Tears stung her eyes as she tossed and turned, for she now understood why she was terrified at the mention of her father, why she was terrified when she heard Ishika humming, for it was her father's favourite tune too, and one that he always hummed or whistled when he put her to bed.

She did not want to see her father now, for the child in her was too frightened to meet him whilst the adult in her wanted to murder him.

She had tried to minimise the severity of her abuse by keeping quiet, but had thus become Fanish's prey.

Sleep came again finally, but with it came images and pictures of her past. She tried to capture these images and analyse them, but before she could see them clearly, they faded and Vanita gratefully accepted the darkness of sleep.

- - - -

Chapter 58

"I think I have availed of your hospitality for long enough." Ena announced a week later. "Thank you very much, Akshita, I have decided what I should do."

"What do you mean?" Akshita was clearing the table and looked up in alarm.

"I have finally decided that it is best to leave Dilawar and begin a life on my own – and the sooner I start the better."

"Are you sure?"

"Yes, I have thinking about it the whole week and now cannot wait any longer in starting my new life – alone. I keep picturing Dilawar and Sai together, talking and laughing, nor can I forget the evil things he did to cover up the affair."

"Where will you go? What will you do?" Akshita asked. " Will you go to the police? You know Fanish has said you are welcome to stay as long as you like."

"Akshita, you have been a kind friend and I would like to thank you again. I will miss you. And no, I cannot go to the police, though a part of me thinks I should. Dilawar too is implicated and I cannot send him to prison, to be honest, I feel guilty for he only helped Fanish to protect me from the hurt of knowing about the affair."

Ena smiled tenderly for she had disclosed her innermost thoughts and feelings to Akshita like someone unravelling a ball of string that had been tangled into a tight ball.

Fanish entered the room smiling. "What are you two planning?"

His voice had a tender inflection and his smile expressed thoughtfulness.

"Ena was just saying that she will be leaving us." Akshita said uneasily.

"But why so soon, Ena? Akshita, you have not been looking after her. Ena, you are welcome to stay as long as you want."

Although Fanish's voice was soft and gentle his mind was forming another devious plan.

'What a hypocrite he is." Akshita thought, listening to him. 'I do not trust his casual attitude towards Ena's leaving and wish I could listen in on his conniving thoughts, for I am sure he is not going to get rid of her this easily."

"Have you decided where you will go?" Fanish queried.

"I do not know as yet, I thought I would go to my parents, but now that I know what I have to do, I can start looking for a place to live."

"If you need a place to stay, I have a friend who has a house a few miles out of London. He is abroad on business but am sure he would not mind allowing a friend of mine to stay, after all, the property is empty."

"That is very nice of you, and I will take you up on that, thank you."

Ena was blissfully unaware of how that one sentence was going to change her life. Ena tried to read Fanish's expression – was it amusement, joy or pity? However, the look of blandness on Akshita's face puzzled her.

"When can I move in for I am keen to start my life afresh as soon as possible?"

"Anytime you want, for Aditya has left everything to me." Fanish smiled smoothly." I can show you the house now if it is all-right with you."

"Yes that is fine; I'll just collect my things." Ena ran upstairs.

"Fanish, why don't you leave her alone? She is such a nice woman. Is there nothing that you would not stoop down to? Well, no sorry, I forgot, there isn't!"

"You call helping people in need wrong?" Fanish scoffed.

"You call exploiting, and getting paid for it, mind you, young and vulnerable children helping?" Akshita said getting more and more enraged.

"Yes, Akshita, I help them and alleviate their suffering. Why do you insist on accusing me unjustly without knowing the full facts? Do you know how many hundred million children there are living in the streets? They do not live as children but are adrift on the margins of an adult world. I have seen them, Akshita, they only survive by stealing and finding random jobs, and if by chance they do get a job they are underpaid and overworked! They either become dropouts of society, juvenile delinquents, prostitutes…do you want me to go on?" Fanish sneered narrowing his eyes, a slight smile on his lips.

Akshita looked at him, at his smug smile and suddenly, something in Akshita snapped. Grief, anguish, shame and guilt that had been lying dormant all now spiralled into an unmitigated anger.

"If that is only reason why you exploit children, to help them as you say, why do you do the same to innocent young girls from good families in this country? I'll tell you why. Because you profit by their vulnerability whilst you justify your vile acts by convincing yourself and others that you are doing it for their benefit."

There were tears of outrage in her eyes whilst her anger propelled her toward Fanish. She began to strike his chest fiercely with her clenched hands.

"I will tell Ena everything about you and your organisation, not only her but to the police." She yelled.

"Err. She already knows, you forgot Dilawar has told her." Fanish said mildly although and a small muscle twitched in his clenched jaw.

However, he was surprised at Akshita's sudden violence, staggered under her blows and flinched at the threat in her voice.

He shortly regained his balance and began to struggle with her, and at last managed to catch her hands, holding them tightly at the wrists. But he said nothing to defend himself, merely stood staring at her, eyes unblinking, his gaze perfectly steady.

"Just remember, Akshita, that I have the power to bring Urvi and even you into that same organisation. You know by now that I will not hesitate to use that power if you force me. Do you understand?"

"Fanish, you wouldn't!" Akshita cried in dismay.

Fanish's face was hard, his eyes narrowed as he looked at Akshita.

"Now you know what I am capable of and will not hesitate to do so. So don't you ever, ever, involve the police."

"Damn you to hell!" Akshita cried, running out of the room.

She ran upstairs to her bedroom crying bitterly, sobbing as if her heart would break. The tears were for the Fanish she thought she once knew, for the life he chose to live, for the girls he had corrupted, what they once had together, and for the life she thought she might have had with him had he been a decent man.

Eventually she calmed down and took control of herself as she remembered the danger to Urvi.

As the sunlight faded to a shade of tarnished brass, the room grew cold; and her gaze strayed through the window to the dusky sky.

- - - -

Chapter 59

Ena gathered her clothes, collected her cosmetics from the dressing table, threw them all into her suitcase then straightened the crumpled bed.

Her hair was tousled so she went into the dressing table to comb her hair. Looking at the reflection in the mirror, she saw that, despite her show of confidence, her face looked flushed and scared whilst her eyes were glassy with unshed tears.

She turned to collect her suitcase and as she passed the window glanced out. There was a couple walking hand in hand laughing and talking, and their laugher reminded Ena of the happy times she had shared with Dilawar.

She sighed, gathered her suitcase and went downstairs, alarmed to see Akshita alone in the room, sitting on the sofa her face flushed and distraught. Her posture was so rigid it seemed she was tied to the chair.

"Akshita, are you feeling alright?" Ena went over to Akshita

"Yes, I'm fine." Akshita gave a start and wiped her face, but her voice was barely audible.

"Where is Fanish? I thought we were supposed to go to see his friend's house?"

"Don't worry, he'll be back shortly." Akshita wiped her forehead.

She hated herself and wondered how she could sound so calm when her whole being was full of remorse, shame and guilt. Her anger was like a monster, feeding on itself and swelling in size. Her hands folded in fists and became so hot she thought they would start a fire merely by touching something flammable

"Ena I want to ….?"

"Yes? Akshita, there is something troubling you. For the past week you have been there for me and been listening to my sorrows. Is there anything I can do for you?"

"Nothing is troubling me, Ena." Akshita replied hastily.

She felt helpless and sad; however, when she regained her calm she wondered if her emotions were due to exhaustion rather than concern.

Ena placed her suitcase on the floor and sat down beside Akshita.

"You know, Fanish seems so nice and charming not at all like Dilawar described him. In fact, he does not seem to be bad at all! It must be another one of Dilawar's lies." Ena sighed.

Akshita was silent for most of Fanish's friends, even those who did not know him well, envied Fanish's charming disposition.

The answer to this, Akshita realised, was simple – for Fanish kept the dark side of his nature buried. Everybody was taken in by his charm, little knowing that politeness; humility and suppression of anger were only means that Fanish resolutely and impenetrably used to gain his end.

However, Akshita was puzzled because Ena was aware of his businesses – she herself had validated the fact, yet she was overlooking his wickedness! But then Fanish always had that effect on people. He reined them in with his charm so all else was forgotten and ignored.

She too had been deeply in love with Fanish at one time. His panther like grace had impressed her, the way he moved like a shadow and spoke softly with a quiet grace. He was always attentive and thoughtful, and treated her like a princess and it was not long before she was deeply in love with him. Her love was so strong that Akshita had reeled from the impact and felt it tangibly, as if it were a piece of fabric cloaking her in its magic.

However, all that had changed and now Fanish rarely spoke to her. The expression on his face had changed from love to calculated indifference and he was always absorbed in his sleazy and sordid businesses.

The few times that Fanish did speak to her Akshita felt as if he was looking through her, beyond her and even around her and afterwards Akshita would be left with an eerie cold feeling as though she had had a conversation with a corpse.

Ena jumped as a door slammed and Fanish walked into the room smiling as he saw her suitcase.

"Ready? Shall we leave?" he asked mildly.

"Yes, I am but I am worried about Akshita, she looks nervous." Ena said uneasily.

"Don't worry about me, I'll be fine." Akshita commented dryly.

"She'll be alright." Fanish agreed, picking up Ena's suitcase." And. Akshita, don't wait up for me for I have some business to attend to."

Ena hugged Akshita.

"Akshita, you have not only been a friend, you have been like a sister to me at a time when I needed kindness the most."

"It was nice for me too, Ena, you take care now." Akshita murmured with tears in her eyes.

On one hand she felt pleased that at least Ena was not under Fanish's roof, on the other hand, the thought of her being in Aditya's house frightened her - as did the thought that everything Fanish did had a sinister underlying motive.

Fanish was waiting patiently for Ena whilst she thanked Akshita. However, it seemed as if his waiting had the patience of a hunter, the quiet stillness of a man who has his emotions in control.

"I think we better make a move." Fanish interrupted.

Ena wondered if she was doing the right thing in

going to live alone. She had never trusted Fanish, but he was being so charming and nice and she had nowhere to go, and go she must.

Her face was flushed with apprehension as she followed Fanish.

"When is your friend coming back?" Ena asked.

"Actually Aditya should be back in another week, that will give us time to look for another flat." Fanish replied smoothly.

"Oh!" Ena gave a start for she remembered Dilawar mentioning something about a man called Aditya. "Fanish, going to his house may not be such a good idea after all. Like originally planned, I will go to my parents' house for I feel I am burdening everybody with my troubles."

"It's no bother." Fanish answered promptly. "Anyway, he has some business problems to sort out so may be abroad a bit longer."

Ena breathed a sigh of relief. Surely there was no harm in staying in an empty house whilst she decided what to do?

They drove past the sprawling suburbs of London whose houses were jammed with repetitive rows of small houses with tiny back gardens.

As they left the city its lights in the distance began to look like flies caught in webs.

- - - -

Chapter 60

Vanita opened her eyes sleepily as the faint rays of sunshine peeped through the chink in the curtains.

She turned on her side with a sigh, glad her memory had returned, physically too, the wounds on her legs and body had nearly healed. She heard the sound of traffic whooshing below on the street, for it had rained during the night and the faint murmur of Ishika and Hetal, talking in the next room followed by Ekta's crying.

And with the break of day her recollection of the past few years was becoming more and more lucid. She felt she was crossing boundaries, moving back through time, in a way passing into another age. The present paused like a video picture on a time deck, waiting for Vanita to push the button to start the present moving again. Vanita knew that everybody has a past, that everyone carried a certain amount of so called 'baggage', but as the fog in her mind cleared she was amazed at how heavy her load was and how strong were her feelings of guilt, shame and anger.

However, as Vanita unravelled her emotions, she realised her anger was not only directed at her Father, but also at Fanish who had exploited and betrayed her trust.

She had been explicitly abused by her father and resented him, but she had trusted Fanish, thought him to be her friend. She had been totally captivated by him- his voice, his kindness, charismatic personality and even to a certain extent his domineering manner, for Fanish had panache, charm and the most extraordinary nerve.

"Good-morning, Vanita?" Ishika entered the room quietly.

"Good-morning." The past shifted back and she returned to the present with a start and smiled wanly.

"How are you feeling?" Ishika asked gently." Do you remember everything now?"

"Yes, I do." Vanita replied miserably. "But wish I didn't!"

"That bad huh? So where have you been for the last couple of years." Ishika raised her eyebrows. "We've been worried about you."

"Who was worried about me, Ishika, who?" Vanita narrowed her eyes. "My parents who did not even bother to come and see me even they knew where I was?"

Ishika tried to change the subject.

"So tell me, what have you been doing in the last couple of years?" She repeated. "How did you manage, who were you staying with and…" she asked eagerly

"Ishika, hold on. All in good time." Vanita smiled at her sister's enthusiasm.

However, her eyes clouded - she did not want to reveal the seedy side of her life to her sister for she could not face Ishika's disappointment in her nor endure her criticism or reproach.

Ishika saw the various emotions and expression's surface across her sister's young and fragile face. She wanted to shield and protect her but how could she do so against an enemy she did not recognise?

She was a considerate woman and realised that Vanita needed space and time to adjust both mentally and physically. Adapt mentally to the present and past mingling together and physically to her changed appearance for even though the swelling on her face had healed, the ordeal had been traumatic and had had left behind ugly scars on her face.

"Ishika, where are you?" they heard Hetal's voice, the bedroom door opened and he poked his head in. "Ekta is crying and I have to go to office."

"Coming, Hetal." Ishika rose. "Vanita don't worry, I don't know what happened, but I can see you are frightened. You'll be safe here and you can stay here as long as you want. At the moment, just rest and we'll talk when you are ready. Do you want me to bring your breakfast?"

"Ishika, don't fuss! I'll be down in ten minutes and I do not know what has given you the impression that I am frightened."

"All right, all right, Vanita, maybe I am wrong."

Ishika hurried out of the room a trifle disconcerted at Vanita's abrupt tone, but then she had always been a very proud and sensitive girl.

As Vanita dressed she wondered why Fanish had so quietly faded from her life. Was it intentional or was he so sure that as she was suffering from Amnesia she could not implicate him? Or was it simply because he had no use for her anymore? More likely all three, she concluded, combing her hair.

When she entered the kitchen Ekta was gurgling happily in her high chair and Ishika was darting around the kitchen briskly fixing a breakfast of eggs bacon and coffee.

She was wearing jeans t-shirt and sneakers and smiled warmly as she saw Vanita.

"Vanita, come and sit down. Breakfast will be ready in a minute."

"Huh? Oh, I'm not hungry, Ishika." Vanita replied still staring at Ekta.

"At least have a cup of coffee. You'll feel better." Ishika placed a steaming mug before Vanita.

"Oh, all-right, thanks." Vanita pulled up a chair and sat down.

She cradled the cup in her hands and sipped the coffee slowly; letting the warmth of the cup seep through her fingers, but after sometime felt nauseous so pushed the cup away.

"Vanita, what is the matter? You look dreadful!"

217

"What do you expect, Ishika, of course I feel dreadful!" Vanita snapped.

"I am sorry if I sounded insensitive but I thought you said you were feeling better. The only reason I wanted you to talk to me about what happened was because I can sense that you have suffered and would like to share your troubles."

"Ishika, not now please! I do not want to talk about where I have been, at least not now, now I am going out for a walk." Vanita abruptly pushed her chair and stood.

"Vanita, no, but if you must, let me come with you, I am worried after yesterday's incident."

"Don't worry, I'll be careful." Vanita rose and almost ran out the house.

Impulsively and with no clear and immediate reason or a clear understanding of where she was going, Vanita started walking.

She felt a need to go down a friendly street, to see old landmarks of her childhood, to feel like a little girl again. Unexpectedly the past was tugging at Vanita, enticing her, drawing her out again, maybe to the place she had been yesterday where she had seen Fanish?

▪ ▪ ▪ ▪

Chapter 61

"Gazal, guess who I saw yesterday." Fanish asked a frown of perplexity on his brow.

"Who?" Gazal answered absent-mindedly.

Although she had resented Vanita at times she missed her and Kanan. To add to her boredom, the days were dull with rain threatening all the time so she could not go out.

"I saw Vanita; she was walking aimlessly on the streets and…. Gazal?"

Fanish lit a cigarette and held the match in front of her face before throwing it down.

Gazal was lost in her thoughts, for she still hoped and lived in dreams so the people around her sometimes seemed unreal.

"Huh? You said something?"

It was as if she saw Fanish through a mist of frosted glass. When he spoke to her, he seemed remote, as if from a long way off and the responses Gazal made came from another agency. Gazal had almost come to enjoy it, this total dissociation from life. She was becoming detached from the real world where people like Fanish made demands on her. She now had a way of isolating herself and retreating into her thoughts.

"Yes I did, Gazal, did you hear what I just said?" Fanish asked angrily.

His face was sweating and his lips were white and trembling. But it was his bewildered eyes that frightened Gazal for she had never seen him like this before.

"Sorry, Fanish, I didn't quite catch….?"

"Vanita – I saw Vanita." Fanish started pacing the room. He turned his fists into balls and spoke fast. "My God, I saw Vanita! What is she doing in London? I told Aditya to take her from her sister's house and take her abroad with him."

"Are you sure it was Vanita?" Gazal asked perturbed. "It may have been somebody who looked like her and…"

So that is what Fanish's solution had been and why he was so calm about Vanita.

"Shut up, woman!" Fanish hissed. "Don't you think I would not recognise her?"

"That is what I meant, Fanish, her looks have changed and…"

Fanish ignored Gazal and started talking to himself.

"Her memory must have returned for she recognised me. I should have dragged her here."

Fanish slapped one hand on the other. And as always, when he tried to control his anger, the small blue veins in his temple throbbed.

Gazal detected cracks in Fanish's otherwise well-polished façade and sensed his desperation.

"Do you know what this means? That Aditya did not do what I told him, that she could go to the police and bust our operations."

Never had Gazal seen Fanish's face so twisted in anger, his characteristic stoical expression gone. He looked determined to do somebody harm and as Gazal was the only one present she trembled with fear.

At the moment the doorbell rang and Gazal jumped up, glad of the diversion. She flung open the door and her mouth fell open.

"Vanita!"

"Hello, Gazal" Vanita was standing stiffly upright wearing a self-conscious expression. "Surprised to see me?"

Gazal stood speechless and her hands were dry.

"Gazal, who is it?" Fanish had come up quietly behind her and gave a start as he saw Vanita.

"Vanita, nice to see you! How are you? Your memory

must have returned for you have found us."

Fanish smiled charmingly, caught her by the hand, and tried to drag her in the house.

All the old loathing crept and crawled through Vanita as she saw Fanish's deadly smile and felt his cold hand.

"You know how I've been!" Vanita spat at Fanish." You left me in hospital not caring whether I lived or died."

Her face, which had had an expression of nervous sensitive uncertainty, suddenly darkened with an expression of maniacally intense hatred and fear which leant a wild unnatural force to every feature of her face, especially her eyes.

"Of course I cared whether you lived or died, in fact I had instructed Aditya to look after you. I don't know what happened."

Fanish voice cracked, which was unusual for he was rarely on the defensive.

"Vanita, he is not to blame, have you forgotten, I came to visit you in hospital." Gazal interrupted indignantly.

"And as soon as you discovered I had amnesia and was no danger to you, you disappeared." Vanita retorted angrily.

"You told me you were going to fake it so what was I to think?" Gazal said angrily.

"Vanita, are you alright?" a soft voice asked.

Vanita was still standing at the doorway and swung around to see Ishika standing behind her with Ekta in a pram.

"Ishika, what in heaven's name are you doing here?" Vanita asked, taken aback.

"Vanita, I told you not to wander away, especially after yesterday. Aren't you going to introduce me to your friends?"

"They are not my friends! I think we better go back

home." Vanita replied fearfully.

Vanita's eyes looked enormous in her thin face and her finger's felt cold.

Ishika thought Vanita looked tired but she could not quite recognise the expression in her eyes. Was it shame, fear or both?

Vanita looked uncomfortable and tried to grab Ishika's arm.

"You must be Ishika, Vanita's sister."

Fanish stepped forward and stretched his hand. His eyes were bright and his voice was smooth.

"That's right, but how did you know for we have not been introduced. You are…?"

"I rang up the hospital and they informed me that Vanita left with her sister, oh, my name is Fanish." Fanish's eyes were twinkling.

He spoke easily and with a familiarity that were accompanied by an unaffected naturalness.

Although Fanish's meeting was hearty and unaffected and his reception of Ishika both easy and pleasant, Ishika found that there was something unpleasant hidden, beyond a doubt, under his cool manner.

His eyes had been coldly vigilant, his voice and manner all suspicious. However, at the moment Ishika did not want to question Vanita as to the role he played during the two years Vanita had been missing, for she had seen the look of fear on Vanita's face.

Ekta started crying and Ishika picked her up cradling her in her arms.

"Ishika let us go!" Vanita said urgently.

"Alright, Vanita, but Ekta needs her feed and …" Ishika said trying to sooth Ekta.

"Here let me hold her." Vanita held out her arms.

"No, it is all-right, maybe you are right Vanita we should leave." She muttered

"No, please, you must stay and at least have a cup of tea with us, and you can feed the baby too." Fanish said persuasively.

"No, we must go, come on Vanita." Ishika took hold of Vanita's hand and they quickly walked away.

As Fanish saw Vanita leave he felt powerless for Vanita was escaping from his clutches again.

But he was aware that a show of temper or force would only undermine control, for his method of getting his own way was by manipulation and manoeuvring, therefore he made his plans carefully and unemotionally with an absolute clear and ruthless mind.

– – – –

Chapter 62

As they walked home, Ishika decided to try and get Vanita to open up and confide in her.

"Vanita, now will you tell me about those people? I did not like Fanish at all." she exclaimed

"I told you, Ishika, I still haven't recalled everything that happened, especially concerning them." Vanita snapped.

Vanita hoped that by keeping silent about Fanish, she would be able to keep Ishika away from him and his gang, thereby protecting her and her family. She was already worried for Fanish had met Ishika.

However, as her memory had stirred in its lair, so had its serpent hatred for Fanish. Similar to a leaping reptile, the feeling of hatred had leapt out, and like a lurking reptile dragged out of sight again.

"I am not a fool, Vanita. I know that you are holding something back and that somehow Fanish is involved for I saw the momentary look of fear cross your face when you looked at him."

Ishika's eyes were strained, but her movements were quiet and measured as she opened the door to her house.

"Ishika, please stop interrogating me. I am tired and going to my room to lie down." Vanita said exasperatedly.

She went straight to her room and sank on the bed tired and frightened. For the past two weeks Vanita was hoping her amnesia would lift - However now that it had and she was confronted with the reality of it all, she was terrified, not only for herself but for Ishika and Ekta.

She thought Fanish's heart to be as dry and barren as a desert, where nothing was allowed to grow for the dry heat and sand showered everything that dared live.

Vanita trembled at the thought and gradually went to

sleep.

"Vanita, are you awake?" Ishika whispered the following morning as she stood beside the bed, a tray in her hand.

"Yes," Vanita replied as she sat up in bed, rubbing her eyes. "Ishika, you have been so kind, I think we need to talk."

Vanita could hear bouts of rain on falling on the window panes and heard the wind howling. The wind thrust together the dark and angry clouds in the sky, creating a dark and gloomy atmosphere.

"First, Vanita, eat something, then we'll talk. I have got you a cup of tea and some hot buttered toast." Ishika smiled as she put the tray on Vanita's lap.

Vanita ate hungrily and Ishika watched her affectionately. Although there was the usual silence between them, Ishika felt that there was a change in Vanita and saw that her sister's loneliness was looking for ways and means to break through the barriers that she had set up around herself.

There had been a lot of animosity that existed between Vanita and her parents, but Ishika had somehow detached herself away from them all – and now felt guilty because of it.

Vanita wiped the last bit of crumb from her lips with a tissue and finished her tea.

"Thanks, Ishika, I needed that. Now about the people you met…"

Vanita felt she not only had to find the right words but also the strength that would serve as an armour against Ishika's disappointment and rejection, for she was sure of the outcome her revelation would have on Ishika. However, in the short space of few weeks, with Ishika's support, her feelings had changed from terror of the unknown to being strong.

Consequently, with a calmness she did not feel, she

related the events and the circumstances that had led her to take the drastic step of leaving her home and its consequences. She spoke in a dull voice and there was an expression of loathing on her face when she spoke first of her father then of Fanish.

Ishika did not know whether she found the dead remote quality in her sister's voice or the circumstances more disturbing. She let her talk uninterrupted so she could anesthetise herself against her sister's pain.

She embraced herself tightly and a chill ran down her spine as Vanita told her about her father's abuse. She felt guilty as she realised she was partly to blame and a moan escaped her lips.

As Vanita recounted her father's abuse she looked at her sister with resentment for she had made her go back to a time she would have preferred not to have gone to.

After she finished talking, Vanita buried her head in her hands and started crying.

Ishika sat down beside her, holding her hand while Vanita's shuddering sobs reverberated round the house.

"Ishika, what shall I do?

"Sssh, you are safe whilst you are with me." Ishika enveloped Vanita in a hug.

"You don't know Fanish, Ishika, he never allows any girl to leave him and now he has seen you! Oh god! I am so frightened!" Vanita held her sister tightly.

"But why did you go to see him if you knew what he was like?" Ishika asked. "Maybe if he did not know where you were, but now...."

"I don't know why, Ishika, I think I wanted to confirm what I felt. And as for his not finding me it was only a question of time... remember he said he phoned the hospital and knew where I was? I was only safe from him until the time my memory returned and now..." Vanita's voice trailed off as she tried to control her shaking body.

"I'll talk to Hetal maybe we should go to the police."

"No!" Vanita protested vehemently.

"Why not?" Ishika raised her brows in surprise.

"Because even the police are under Fanish's control, I think his father in law is a commissioner or something. And the matter will end by my going to prison."

"Vanita, now you are being childish. Fanish may know a few people but overall I am sure somebody will listen to you." Ishika said in a firm voice.

"What you are forgetting, dear sister, is that I was a part of Fanish's syndicate and could have left at any time."

"You just told me that Fanish would never let you go, and I have seen the look of terror on your face. Vanita, people like him should not be allowed to roam the streets." Ishika was outraged.

"That is putting it mildly and I agree with you." Vanita remarked dryly. "And you can rest assured all those things will happen to him, but not your way."

"What are you talking about? Only the police have the authority to keep us safe from people like Fanish."

"No not them, I will." Vanita voice had the remote quality again that was disturbing to Ishika.

"You!" Ishika exclaimed. "Good Lord, Vanita, you are only a girl of fifteen. How can you hurt a man like Fanish, with all his experience and cunning?"

"I am young, but not that young. Not after what I have been through."

"I still think that you should not do anything foolish and let the authorities handle him." She heard Ekta crying and left the room in a hurry.

Vanita lay back on her bed and the expression of melancholy deepened on her face. She wished she could run away and hide in a small space, which would be just small enough to contain her grief, yet big enough for her to think and plan what she was going to do next. And the more she thought about it, it seemed there was only one way to handle the problem.

· · · ·

Chapter 63

So before the morning began to overshadow the night, Vanita crept downstairs, leaving a note for Ishika.

She quietly walked to the front door, opened it and for a few minutes stood looking out into the darkness, afraid and uncertain. Then she took a deep breath, pulled the door slowly behind her and ran until she reached the corner of the road.

The streets were silent and lonely and the lights from the sodium lamps cast a greenish haze over the streets. Vanita walked slowly from one gloomy street to another, and gave a start when she saw a car drive slowly in the street.

The night was quiet and the foliage of the trees hung silently in the dark air, motionless, and Vanita saw the star's shine brightly like diamonds in a jewel velvet case. She saw that the flowers in the gardens were only an outlined shape and had no colours until one peered closely.

There were a few lights in the houses, and as the leaves of the trees stirred in the gentle breeze, Vanita wished the foliage would give her the protection she craved from the cruelty around her.

With a trembling hand, Vanita rang the bell to Gazal's house. There was no response and after waiting for some Vanita was turning away when a light appeared in the landing and a sleepy voice asked.

"Who is it?"

"Gazal, it's Vanita."

Suddenly the door was flung open. "Vanita, what are you doing here at this time of night?"

"And I am glad to see you too." Vanita entered the house and threw her suitcase on the floor.

"I'm sorry, I didn't mean...It's just that I am a bit

surprised for when you left with your sister, we thought we had seen the last of you."

"Do you think that Fanish would have let me?" she asked.

"You are right there, Vanita, all the same, I am glad you are ok now." Gazal blurted guiltily.

As soon as Vanita was seated on the sofa, she tersely replied.

"Let's not go into that, Gazal. I am well aware that even though you took me to hospital, you left me there. Do you realise how frightening it is to wake up and not know who you are?"

"Vanita, it was you who told me that you were going to pretend you did not remember anything about your past. How was I to know that you really had Amnesia? Anyway, you also know that I could not disobey Fanish, for it was his idea to leave you alone. He told me he had instructed Aditya what to do and that everything was under control. Everything would have worked out fine if you had stayed with your sister. So anyway, why have you come back?"

Vanita remembered the listening devices that Fanish had placed around the house.

"Put it this way, I could not stay away once I remembered the freedom, my independence, and most of all the money."

Neither spoke for some time for it was Gazal's way of evading her guilt. She had hoped that Vanita would stay away from them, and thus she would not know of Gazal's participation in what Fanish had planned for her.

Gazal pulled her knees up to her chest and clutched her arms around them, envying Vanita's strength that helped her overcome all obstacles.

She glanced at Vanita and saw the change in her. The ordeal of the last few weeks had left their mark on her fragile childish beauty, now scarred, and darkness now cloaked her once bright eyes. Despair had washed the radiant colours from her face and even her voice had changed. It was now deeper, with a tone of detachment and loneliness in her voice, and an expression of loneliness etched on her face.

'So this is what despair is." Gazal thought dispassionately. "It's cold and lonely, whereas I had always thought of it as something hot-blooded; it is only an outer darkness of coldness. I think it is not only a shame but a sin to cut oneself away from all warm and human contact.'

For a moment there was an expression of tenderness as she glanced at Vanita.

"Vanita, you look tired. Fanish will come by tomorrow."

"Yes, I am tired, but I am not looking forward to meeting Fanish."

"I realise that, Vanita, but you will have to sometime, and do you realise that we are better off than say the girls of some third world countries who become victims of corruption cruelty and ignorance? All because they are vulnerable, poor and..."

"I know, I know, that I am supposed to feel grateful, that I should be thankful for there the poor children, if they come into the hands of somebody like Fanish would have their arms and legs cut and twisted – how they are organised by crooks who exploit and train them to a lifetime of beggary and even going to the extent of mutilating their limbs to make them seem more pathetic and pitiable... So what's new?" Vanita remarked sarcastically.

"I only tell you all this to point out that things could be much worse for us." Gazal said dryly.

"And they could be much better. Gazal, do I still use my old bedroom?"

"Yes." Gazal sighed as they went upstairs.

It was nice to have Vanita back, but she was so changed, it seemed she was a different person, and Gazal was not sure she liked the new Vanita.

Vanita hugged her pillow in solace and fell into a tortured sleep. Demons in the guise of nightmares haunted her dreams, so that she never slept for more than a few minutes. As s wiped her eyes with the back of her hand, she felt lost and defeated.

Fanish had won - again!

• • • •

Chapter 64

"Here, let me help you." Fanish removed his jacket and rolled up the sleeves of his shirt.

Ena laughed. "There is nothing to do, nothing to unpack. I just took a few clothes with me and they'll have to do till I find work. You did say you will help me find a job?"

"Of course I will." Fanish replied. "Will you go back to Dilawar any time in the future?"

Fanish had a way of getting people to be themselves and let their inhibitions fall away

"No, I don't think so, Fanish. Dilawar is a weak man who will never face up to his shortcomings. He has not even been faithful to me. Now in retrospect, I see how his eyes always steered to other women. And he is a needy man, far too needy of attention and in constant need of having his ego comforted - when more often than not he is in the wrong." Ena sighed. "Life now with him would be now unbearable. Thank you again, Fanish, I do not know what I would have done without Akshita and you." She had tears in her eyes.

Ena looked beautiful, with her long black hair falling in soft folds on her shoulders, and there was an expression of helplessness in her eyes. Fanish longed to caress her, stroke her glossy black hair and comfort her.

She looked at Fanish from behind thick eyelashes that could not hide the distress in her brown eyes. Both stared at each other until Ena finally blinked and lowered her gaze, scepticism creasing her fine eyebrows. Resisting the impulse to gnaw her lower lip, Ena determined not make a fool of herself, but tears gathered in her eyes again and trickled down her cheeks.

Fanish wiped them gently from her face and Ena was pleasantly distracted by Fanish's gentle touch and captivated by the unexpected kindness in his brown eyes, for it felt nice to see such genuine concern.

"Ena…" His heart was beating too fast and Fanish scowled inwardly at the emotion for it was new to him.

Ena raised her hand to him in a stop motion, halting anything he was about to say. She was sure that Dilawar had been exaggerating when he told her about the business he was involved in –she had never liked him but in the last few days he had shown nothing but kindness.

She was at the point in her life when she was past caring, for what she had thought true was false and what was false was turning out to be true. Also, evil has a powerful fascination on the human psyche and immorality, to Ena, had a formidable morality because it was generating excitement in her otherwise dull life.

Fanish could not contain himself any longer so he gripped Ena's shoulder and turned her face towards him.

"Ena, what are you doing to me?" he reprimanded softly.

His breadth was warm against her face and his grip remained firm against her tender flesh.

From the distant window, Fanish could see small dark figures of girls drifting in twos and threes towards the converging street and thought they would be going to experience the usual night life, crowded traffic of shops, cinemas and bright lights.

Ena tilted her head to look at Fanish, surprised again at the gentleness in his voice, but quickly disengaged herself from Fanish's arms.

"I'm sorry, Ena." Fanish's voice was soft and gentle. "Would you like a cup of coffee?"

"Yes, please." Ena gasped with relief as Fanish went into the kitchen.

He came back a few minutes later with a tray.

"Ena, have some coffee, I have to go for some work,

but I will come back later to see how you have settled in."

Ena heard Fanish closing the door softly behind him as she took the cup of steamy coffee. She savoured its fresh aroma before sipping slowly of the rich, creamy brew and sighed as the warmth of the coffee spread through her.

She finished the coffee and replaced the mug on the table, feeling sleepy, vaguely thinking that she still had to undress, but felt too tired and exhausted to do so.

'I do not want to move, only to rest and sleep.' Ena thought drowsily as she laid her head against the sofa, allowing her eyes to close as sleep overcame her.

She woke to find Fanish on top of her. Fear and uncertainty clouded her face, but muscular arms were rolling her onto the sofa. Half asleep, Ena fought Fanish as he tried to roll her body over. Ena hissed, striking at Fanish weakly in a fit of hysteria, trying to shove his powerful frame off her, but Fanish was too strong.

With an outraged scream at Fanish's brutish treatment, Ena lifter her feet to kick Fanish in the groin, but the movement caused her to slip and fall backward on the floor. Ena screamed and within seconds her wrists were caught and pinned above her head and her body pressed on the carpet.

"I thought you were my friend who was going to help me." Ena screamed. "Let me go, you brute!"

"I am your friend, Ena, but you are so beautiful, my god, you are beautiful!"

Fanish leered at the natural fullness of Ena's dark eyelashes, almond shaped innocent brown eyes set in an oval face. His eyes had grown small and his gaze had become intense and although he had prepared himself to seduce Ena, his face softened and he got up with an apology.

"I'm sorry, I should not have taken advantage of you,

but you are very beautiful."

"What will Akshita think?" Ena's drowsy but calm voice belied her inner panic. "Get out! Get out of here, I don't want to see you again!"

As Fanish started the engine and drove off, he thought of Ena, and when he did - he felt a pattern of intermingled emotions that had a strange design with dark threads of indifference and desire running through them.

The thought of Ena's lovely almond innocent eyes and black hair falling in folds over her shoulder and the image haunted Fanish on the drive to his house. He had always thought her attractive, but being alone with her and holding her soft body against his had awakened dormant feelings and he was suddenly jealous of Dilawar.

'A weak man like him does not deserve her. For a woman like her I would give up anything." he thought as he parked his car. "I would even be willing to give up what I do now.'

However, his greed, his need to be on top, to be the one in charge was too strong, so thought it best that he forget Ena, for what Fanish feared the most was to be poor,

He always justified his greed and desire for money originated from his childhood for he was born and brought up in an estate and his family had been hard-up and poor. His childhood memories were of his mother standing at the kitchen sink washing dirty dishes and of his father, if he was not drunk, sitting in his vest in the kitchen, either reading a news-paper or shouting at him. Therefore, Fanish had spent a great deal of time hanging about the stairs, and the one source of life that he understood perfectly lay in the crowded high streets where he was born and brought up.

The estate where he lived was an area where

lawbreaking was a part of life. Near their estate was a row of warehouses, untidy street markets and sleazy lodging houses where girls and boys met.

At that time, it had seemed exciting for Fanish just to sit in a café where the conversation amongst the older lads ran on who was the best boy with a knife, the latest case of burglary, girls and prostitution.

The atmosphere of gaiety and warm coffee had become for Fanish and many of his friends, an antidote against the emptiness and boredom of their life, and adolescence, was a time of their life when they felt uncertain and driven by urges they did not understand.

They had felt a need for an amicable place where they could be together informally, to drift and experiment, feel their own way toward an adult life without supervision.

Being a shrewd boy, Fanish united the spirit of the adolescent rebellion with the criminal traditions and gave it a glamorous lifestyle. He spread his criminal outlook far beyond its usual confines, which girls were glad to join because Fanish made it appear romantic.

Fanish had realised that the teenage state of mind was such that it simply did not occur to them that an impulse, a desire which seized them, should not at once be gratified. And this freedom to follow their impulse was what Fanish strove to endorse.

In this freedom to follow their impulse, Fanish found a solution for them – he offered the girls security – especially the ones that were emotionally deprived at home. Fanish was astute enough to realise that the raising of material standards meant an increase in selfishness, he hinted to them that they could live fabulously, but for that to happen, only one thing was needed – money.

He told them there were ways of getting it – he got the young boys involved in drugs and burglary whilst the girls were implicated in what they thought to be harmless and temporary prostitution.

- - - -

Chapter 65

Nonetheless, Fanish was surprised at the affect Ena had on him, but then she had class whereas he was used to dumb, passive girls who were crudely painted. However, he tried to convince himself that he could not possibly be emotionally involved with Ena.

Although Akshita, too, was different from other women, and he had loved her at the start of their relationship, he had started to distance himself emotionally from her.

He opened the door of his house and was surprised to see the light was on. He heard the rustle of a newspaper before he saw Akshita's head appear round the side of the chair. She pushed herself to her feet, folded the paper and dropped it on the floor with the other magazines that were piled up near the fender.

She pushed back her dark brown hair which was brushed straight down, over her shoulders.

"What took you so long?" Akshita asked angrily, her heart was pumping with an effort of self-control.

"I told you I had some business to attend to, do I have to remind you again that you don't get to question me? Ever!"

Fanish's lips trembled with asperity and his eyes glowed like hot coals, brightening as the fire them raged. The veins in his temples stood out against his skin as he clenched his jaw.

The love he had had for Akshita was not only forgotten but dead and he now only treated her with disgust, disdain and a rudeness that bordered on cruelty.

"Rest assured, Fanish I do not care about your business so don't want to know about it. But Ena phoned me and told me what you did - what kind of monster are you?" Akshita said angrily.

"Unlike you, Akshita, she is a beautiful woman, anyway, now are you telling me how to behave?"

"I…I hope you rot in hell!"

Akshita tossed her hair over her shoulder in a haughty manner then sat down in the chair again.

"You can't do anything, Akshita, remember Urvi?" Fanish sneered.

He stood in the doorway, lounging insolently against the frame, eyes flashing, looking scathingly at Akshita.

As soon as Fanish mentioned Urvi Akshita, conceded defeat, she felt she could not tolerate anymore, at the same time had no other option.

Her life with Fanish was unbearable for not only was she enduring his taunts, but had started having nightmares where children and babies cried and appealed to her for help.

"And Ena asked me to give you a message that she has gone back to Dilawar."

"What do you mean?" Fanish narrowed his eyes suspiciously. "How can she go back? I just left her at the house and she was settling in. In fact, she is quite looking forward to her independence. Did you have anything to do with it? Because if you have, you know Urvi…."

"I did not say anything to her, but it was you who helped her make her mind up, and I am glad she has gone back for now you have no hold over Dilawar and he will go to the police." Akshita said triumphantly"

"But she can't go back to Dilawar, he is not a man"

But the feeble attempt at sarcasm and the tone in Fanish's voice told of his despair. Suddenly Fanish wanted to hold Ena's soft body and he felt an overwhelming loss. He looked at Akshita with cold fury as if it was her fault, then looked mollified and gave a rueful half-smile as he ashamed he if was letting a woman control his emotions.

"Oh, well if she's gone, she's gone. I'm going to bed." Fanish's voice was light and sounded artificial.

Fanish was already asleep when Akshita finally went up. She stood looking down at him, his arm dangling over the side, studying the exposed part of his face. Fanish looked dead to the world, but even in sleep he appeared ominous to Akshita, and she wished she could somehow slip in mentally behind his sleeping visage to see what he was planning next.

Fanish did not wake, but his eyelids fluttered and Akshita wondered if he sensed her presence? Akshita trembled in fear, for she did not trust him – even in repose.

- - - -

Chapter 66

Ena had taken a taxi to Dilawar's house, rung the bell and stood shivering on the doorstep.

Her face looked pale and her brown eyes, that were usually alert and clear, looked sluggish and drowsy. Her fine brown hair lay in disarray about her face and shoulders and her blouse was torn at the shoulder

"Oh my God Ena!" Dilawar exclaimed in astonishment as he opened the door. "What happened? Who did this to you, I'll kill him!" Dilawar placed his hands on her shoulders and drew her shivering body close to him.

Ena freed herself and trembling, tried to cover her torn blouse with her sari.

Ena, tell me what happened?" Dilawar repeated as he took her hand and ushered her into the house. "Here sit, tell me all about it, no first let me get you a glass of water."

"I need to have a bath and change out of these clothes first, Dilawar." Ena whispered.

"Ok, I will make some tea in the meantime and you can tell me what happened."

Ena ran upstairs with a sob. She went to the bathroom and splashed her face with cold water. Looking at her reflection in the mirror, Ena wrinkled her nose in disdain at her appearance, brushed her hair, changed her torn blouse then went downstairs. She flopped into a chair and stared straight ahead.

When Dilawar entered the room later with two steaming mugs of tea, he found Ena curled on the sofa.

"Thank you, Dilawar." Ena took the mug with trembling hands for she was still in shock.

"Now Ena, tell me what happened, I only love you." Dilawar murmured in a strained voice, holding out his hands imploringly.

"Ena, please believe me I love you." Dilawar repeated, shifting his feet uncomfortably under Ena's appraisal." Please talk to me, tell me what happened, who did this to you?"

"I am sorry I cannot, not now, Dilawar, I do not want to talk, I can't." she whispered.

"Please Ena…!"

There was something desperate in Dilawar's grovelling that made Ena wince.

The struggle with Fanish had left her emotionally exhausted and Ena wiped her brow with the palm of her hand.

"Shall I make you something to eat?" Dilawar looked at Ena beseechingly, as if he did not want to let her out of his sight for a moment.

"Alright Dilawar, I would like a sandwich." Ena reluctantly agreed." I have had nothing to eat since…."

As Dilawar went to the kitchen she remembered the cup of coffee that Fanish had made for her, and which she was now sure, had been drugged.

"Here you are." Dilawar re-entered after some time carrying a tray. There was a slight grin on his face as he sat down beside Ena. "Ena, is everything alright? You looked terrible when you came. And I missed you so…" he smiled ruefully.

He raised his hand and gently curled a long strand of Ena's hair about his finger.

"Dilawar, please don't." Ena pushed him away and sipped the tea. "But I would like to make sure that what you told me about Fanish was all true …I mean, how can anybody be so….?."

"Of course, Ena, but why do you ask? Anyway about Sai, I…"

"I don't want to talk about her!" Ena retorted sharply.

"So we won't." Dilawar answered hurriedly, "Fanish

told me you were staying with Akshita?"

"I need to tell you something about Fanish, Dilawar, but...." She bit her lower lip then shook her head.

"Yes? But you said you were going to stay with your parents? Why didn't you?"

"That was my original plan but I did not know where they lived for since our marriage they have not kept in touch, and Akshita was so nice and understanding."

Ena took a deep breath, wiped the tears from her cheeks then put her hands over her face.

"Ena, please don't..." Dilawar looked distraught and gently removed Ena's hands from her face. "I am sorry I caused you unhappiness. Please let me make it up to you."

Ena was silent as she weighed the sincerity of Dilawar's words. She looked deep into his eyes and found them shining bright with love and honesty.

However, her self-respect had been so bruised that she felt she needed some kind of reassurance. For Dilawar's affair with Sai had planted a demon seed from which suspicion would easily grow and ruin her marriage once again.

"Is the affair with Sai really over, Dilawar? Because if it isn't, there just isn't room for the three of us."

Ena forgot that she had asked Dilawar not to mention Ena's name, but sat very still staring at the carpet, then raised her head and looked at Dilawar steadily.

"Yes it has, Ena, it is you I love you and spend the rest of my life with." Dilawar whispered.

He shut his eyes feeling relieved. He wanted to shout with joy but choked on the words and turned them into a cough as he placed his arm around her shoulders.

Ena sighed as she took another sip of tea, and the anguish men and women caused each other in the name of love and the terrible things they did to each other never failed to amaze her.

She drank down the hot strong liquid then sprawled back on the sofa feeling safe and secure in Dilawar's love, the ordeal with Fanish now a faint memory. Warmth crept to her cheeks and a quick lifting of her heart made her spirits soar.

After some time, she got up, fluffed and smoothed the wrinkles from the downy soft cushions. She picked up the magazines that Dilawar had read and carelessly thrown on the floor then arranged them in neat piles.

It had taken a man like Fanish to make her recognize the fact that she too loved Dilawar – weaknesses and all. She realised she too had missed Dilawar, the look of worry around his eyes, the way his eyebrows turned in toward each other, the way his forehead creased in perplexity at any small problem.

Ena realised she loved him even though she was certain he would not know what to do or how to protect her any more than a child could.

• • • •

Chapter 67

Vanita woke to the sunlight filtering through the window. She lay quietly, watching the sun catch the tiny particles of dust and turn them into tiny jewels.

She rolled over to the side of the bed and sat up, running her hand through her dishevelled hair. She heard faint voices, sighed quickly dressed and went down.

The kitchen door was ajar and Fanish was sitting idly at the table, a steaming mug of tea in front of him. Gazal was standing looking out of the window, but turned around with a smile as she heard Vanita enter the kitchen.

"Morning, Vanita, how are you feeling? I'll get you some tea."

"Fine." Vanita replied tersely, looking warily at Fanish who was quietly scrutinising Vanita.

Gazal set another mug of hot and steaming tea and sat down beside Fanish.

She glanced at Vanita who was drinking the hot tea calmly as if nothing out of the ordinary had occurred. Although Gazal was fond of Vanita, there were times when Vanita's self-possession and reserve irritated her. However, she had come to accept Vanita as an odd mixture of childishness and maturity.

"Nice to see you again, Vanita, we missed you." Fanish smiled genially

Fanish sat smiling amicably, his voice as usual contrary to the animosity in his eyes. He waved his hand backward, a characteristic gesture that looked more as if he was chasing away flies than anything else and the huge diamond ring on his hand caught the sunlight, gleaming expensively.

He was wearing his customary white suit with matching shoes and his black hair was oiled and smooth.

Vanita looked at him in disgust and loathing and looked at Fanish as if he were an annoying insect that would not go away.

"Fanish, you don't seem to understand, I have nothing to say to you."

"Really? Tell me how is Ishika and her daughter?"

Vanita felt there was an under-current of warning in his voice and gave a start for Fanish was looking at her with an expression of scorn.

"Fanish, I am here, so leave them alone." Vanita cried fervently.

She quickly got up from the table and stood facing Fanish, her fists tightly clenched at her side.

"Why are you getting so upset, Vanita? I have not said a word; how can you even think...?"

Fanish pretended to look dumbstruck, his bulging eyes and gaping lips showing his indignation.

"You didn't have to, I know you." Vanita stamped her foot.

"Tut, tut, my dear you know all I think about is the welfare of my girls." Fanish said meekly.

"Ha! Fanish, you are the kind of person who never gives anything to charity, and even if you did, it would only be if it were profitable to you. You abuse everyone's trust." Vanita glared at him.

Fanish fixed Vanita with a diamond hard intense glare as he bit out.

"You can leave anytime; you are no good to me anyway with that face of yours!"

Fanish head snapped around as his fiery gaze raked over Vanita, who had started trembling under his gaze.

Fanish pushed back his chair and rose.

"Gazal. I'll talk to you later." he retorted sharply.

He slammed the door behind him in his usual show of anger.

"Well, well, what's got into Fanish?" Gazal remarked

as she picked up the empty mugs and took them to the sink. "Ever since I have known him, I have never seen him so angry, he is usually quite controlled." She chuckled.

"Gazal, it's not funny." Vanita sat on a chair. " What if he decides to hurt Ishika or my niece? I can't even bear to think about it."

"No, it's not funny, and I am sorry. But I think you don't have to worry about Ishika. Fanish seems to have a lot on his plate at the moment, for the business abroad is not doing well." Gazal walked over to the sink.

"Good, that is the best piece of news I have heard in a long time."

Vanita got up restlessly and went into the balcony, looking at the park and the street below, her elbows propped on the rail, realising that although she was caught in Fanish's web, she would somehow try and protect Ishika and Ekta from him.

- - - -

Chapter 68

"Fanish, what is the matter with you?" Aditya asked. "I have been talking to you for the last five minutes, but am sure you have not heard a word I said."

Aditya had flown in from Brazil and they were sitting in his house where he was trying to update Fanish on the business problems they were having

"Huh? Sorry Aditya." Fanish replied vaguely.

His determination that he would try and keep Ena out of his mind was not succeeding and he had not slept the whole night.

"Fanish, we have to do something. I feel the net abroad is closing around us. Things are not as easy as before and I am finding that there are obstacles deliberately put in my way, as if somebody is anticipating my next step."

"Don't be silly, Aditya, you are exaggerating. Corruption, especially of officials, is widespread and increases crime, and as long as that is the situation, we should be fine."

"I'm telling you, Fanish, it is not easy now, laws are tightening, for example, before, it was easy to take the children from their rural poverty to the city, but not now."

"Than maybe you are not promising them work?"

"Of course I am, and I do manage to get some children, but in the city too there are obstacles and there is difficulty in getting through the system."

"I thought we paid the officers a fee?" Fanish raised his eyebrows.

"We do, and most of them are glad to supplement their low incomes so help us through the red tape of beaurocracy."

"Aditya, I still do not see why you are so worried, for

that is not our only business, we have other businesses, don't we? We can concentrate on them."

"You mean selling babies and then there is our paedophile ring?" Aditya smacked his thick lips.

"That is your department." Fanish ran fingers through his hair.

Yes, it is for I like young girls, I like to feel loved by a young girl who is gentle and kind. I need a young girl to show me that not all women are not all dirty, violent and spoilt like my mother."

"Hah! So what about acquiring children for childless couples? They at least pay a large amount of money. And I still think you are exaggerating our problems, for as long as there is poverty, a demand for pornography and sex, we should be ok."

"You make it sound so easy, and I see you did not mention drugs?" Aditya asked dryly.

"No, I did not; reason being that even if there is no demand for them, which is not possible, our girls will need them because some of their clients can be too demanding. Oh, by the way, Vanita is back with us." Fanish looked closely at Aditya.

"Oh?" Aditya said, the expression on his face was blank.

"I thought we had agreed that she should be taken abroad like Kanan? Why didn't you take her from sister's place like we agreed?" Fanish asked sharply

"Yes, I know, but when I saw her she was beaten so badly that I thought she could not possibly survive. Later I found out she was suffering from Amnesia so she could not possibly have harmed our operations."

"You should have at least told me that you had not taken her abroad. It was a shock coming across her in the street and then again when she turned up at Gazal's house. You are so concerned with the problems abroad, and your other distractions, that you don't seem to realise there are other problems that should be concerning you."

"What do you mean?" Aditya looked disconcerted.

"Vanita is threatening to go to the police; Dilawar is threatening to go to the police...." Fanish rose from the sofa and started pacing the room.

"I thought Vanita was suffering from amnesia and you were holding Ena hostage?"

"Vanita has now regained her memory and Ena is back with Dilawar, but there is no need to worry about Dilawar. I have something else to keep him in line. But we are lucky they do not know of our work abroad or ...Aditya, what is the matter?" Fanish asked for Aditya had turned pale. "So there is something you are not telling me?"

"Yes." Aditya whispered as he wrung his hands.

Fanish sat down again. "You better tell me everything."

"Well, I don't know if it means anything, but when I took her to that monster he ..."

"I know that, but who is he and what is his name?" Fanish had a feeling of foreboding.

"I don't know! Even you don't."

"Oh yes, I tried to find out anyway, Shubi is the only one who takes the girls but I thought that you would know as you are the first point of contact?"

"None of us do. Every time he needs a young girl, he lets me know through the Internet and we arrange a time and place, and I let you know of course, and like you, I am known by another code name."

"There is nobody else involved, is there?" Fanish asked nervously

"Apart from you and Shubi, no, and...." Aditya replied uneasily.

"Yes I know but there is something else on your mind, Aditya."

"Look here, Fanish, I am trying to explain, please don't get angry. Anyway, the thing is that Vanita told me that she fought and managed to pull his mask off."

"Yes, I know, she mentioned it to Gazal

"And you did not pursue the matter? We want to find out who he is don't we?" Aditya ran his fingers through his hair." But thinking back, maybe she was delirious?"

"She mentioned it to Gaza and at that time we thought she was, but now I don't think so. On the other hand, if 'The Ravager' wants his identity to remain a secret, and if Vanita knows, would it not be dangerous for her?" Fanish's asked.

"Vanita told me if she said anything, he had threatened to kill her. Fanish, he might be a pervert but a killer he is not otherwise Vanita would not have survived so long."

All the pieces were fitting into place for Fanish.

"What? What are we going to do now?"

Aditya looked frightened for his guilty past and now uncertain future were combining to create a selfish terror, which should have shamed him, but did not.

"Aditya, I have to go, but I need to talk to you soon." Fanish got up and walked to the door.

But as soon as he opened it, found it was raining heavily, so closed it quickly.

"Aditya, do you have an umbrella I can borrow?"

As Aditya handed him his umbrella, he thought how calm Fanish looked.

'It is alright for him to look so smug, but I am the one abroad in the forefront, me who everybody knows.'

With a sinking feeling Aditya realised that if anything were to happen it was going to be Aditya who would ultimately have to take responsibility.

- - - -

Chapter 69

It was drizzling when a few days later Fanish decided to visit Ena and Dilawar. The spring evening was chilly as Fanish parked his car outside their house and rang the bell.

He put his hand on his chest for his heart was beating fast at the prospect of seeing Ena.

The door was opened by Dilawar who gave an exclamation of surprise.

"Fanish! What are you doing here? I was expecting Parul...."

"Hello Dilawar, can I come in?" Fanish asked politely, trying to peer over Dilawar's shoulder.

"Dilawar, who is it? Are you leaving?"

Ena was coming down the stairs plaiting her long hair. She gave a start as soon as she saw Fanish.

"Fanish! What are you doing here?" Ena clutched Dilawar's arm weakly.

"Are you feeling alright?" There was a frown on his Dilawar's face as he put his arm around her.

At that moment Parul walked up with a smile.

"Hello, Ena Bhabhi.... ready Dilawar? We mustn't be late for the meeting."

"Hi Parul, I am but Ena are you feeling alright?" Dilawar said anxiously.

"Yes, I am fine, just a little dizzy, you carry on." Ena replied in a feeble voice wishing she had told Dilawar that Fanish had drugged and nearly raped her.

"Hello sorry, Fanish, I have to go. We will meet some other time and..." Dilawar tightened his arm and pulled Ena closer to him.

"No it was nothing urgent, but I will stay with Ena for a few minutes till she feels better." Fanish said smoothly.

"N.nno…I am fine really." Ena looked alarmed.

"I think I will stay with her too, Ena. Parul I will see you later." Dilawar spoke hurriedly for he had not forgotten Fanish's attempt to kidnap Ena.

Parul interrupted him. "All right, if you are sure, I will go on ahead."

He was turning to leave when Fanish accosted him.

"We haven't been introduced." Fanish extended his hand. "My name is Fanish."

"Dr Parul. Nice to meet you, now I really must get going…"

Unruffled, Fanish continued speaking.

"Do you work with Dilawar?" he asked in a straightforward manner. "Oh, I am sorry; I think I am keeping you from your meeting, I will leave too for Ena seems to be better now."

"Ena, if you are feeling ok I will go with Parul as originally planned. We better hurry, Parul, I don't want to be late. Are you sure you will be all right, Ena?" Dilawar said again as he disengaged his arm.

"Of course I will, Dilawar, I don't know what came over me, but you carry on." Ena smiled affectionately.

"If you're sure…. see you later. Come on Fanish."

"I'm right behind you." Fanish said smoothly.

Dilawar gave her a quick peck on the cheek and both of them ran to escape the rain that was starting to pour down. Dilawar hurriedly opened the door of Parul's car and climbed in. As he tied the seat belt he first saw to it that Fanish had got into his car.

However, although Fanish drove off, he parked round the corner waited till Dilawar and Parul had driven of then ran back and rang the bell again.

"Dilawar, have you forgotten…. Oh it is you." Ena gave a start.

"Yes, it is me and I have been dying to hold you in my arms since the day you left." Fanish smiled as he held out his arms.

"Fanish, how dare you talk to me about that day? You bastard, you drugged my coffee! Now please leave for I have to meet my friend ..."

"I had to, Ena; otherwise I would not have been able to feel your soft and curvaceous body against mine." Fanish ran his eyes down her body and smacked his lips.

"No Fanish, please no I love Dilawar." Ena looked at Fanish beseechingly.

As she looked into his brown eyes, she felt the ground would slide from under feet. She faltered and nearly fell when she was ushered to the sofa by Fanish. Ena tried to push him away, the expression in her eyes showing her revulsion

As she felt light headed, she closed her eyes, and when opened them saw Fanish looking at her and as soon as he saw her eyelashes flutter, was on his knees.

"How are you, feeling my darling?"

"Fanish, leave me alone."Tears of fear and frustration rolled down her cheeks.

Fanish suddenly gripped her shoulder so hard that Ena winced.

"I don't want to leave you, Ena, aren't you flattered that I desire you?"

He stood up and with his hands on his hips and bent forward towards Ena, his eyes suspicious. Suddenly Fanish's smile became crooked and mean as he raised his eyebrows.

Ena made a gesture of defiance.

"No I am not, and you can be clear on one other thing, I am going to ensure that Dilawar is not involved in your so called 'operations'."

"He said that before you know." Fanish said meekly.

"I did not know the full story then and you were blackmailing him, but now he has my support, and as soon as he comes home we are going to the police and..." Ena spoke fast and angrily.

Fanish laughed, unperturbed at Ena's rage. In fact, he found her even more beautiful with her tousled black hair that framed her flushed face.

"Ena, when will you realise you are completely under my control? You know the time you stayed with us? Well, I had sort of kidnapped you!" There was a glitter in Fanish's eyes. "And you are alone with me now."

Fanish felt Ena was assessing her odds of escape.

"I know what you are thinking, Ena, and I don't think that escaping would be advisable, or for you to go to the police." Fanish said softly.

He caught hold of Ena's waist as she tried to run to the door.

"Fanish, don't you dare touch me. Even if I give you my word now what guarantee do you have that I will keep it?"

"Because, my little beauty, you know how deeply Dilawar is implicated. Why did you come back to him anyway, for I remember you said you were going to leave him?"

"You left me no choice, did you? I think I am a very lucky woman to be married to him. Unlike you, he is a good decent man who loves me." Ena looked with disgust at Fanish.

"I presume you are talking about that evening in Aditya's house?" Fanish laughed heartily. "I enjoyed myself very much. So much so that that I would like a repeat .... What do you think?" Fanish winked.

He moved his tongue over his full lips then dropped his head slightly to the side.

"Over my dead body! I love Dilawar, now please can you leave?" Ena felt sick as she recalled that evening.

"Not as yet, my sweet, I am marvelling at how certain you were about your decision to break up with Dilawar, and I don't think you love him although you say you do and cannot live without him. But if you love him so much, why do you want him sent to jail for say at least Twenty yrs.? That is unless you want him out of the way? And what will you do in the meantime —alone? You must remember that I will always be available for you." Fanish winked again and a faint smile began to curl his mouth.

"Oh no you won't! You will be in prison too!" Ena stamped her foot.

"I don't think so, you forget my father-in-law is a police commissioner and will ensure that I stay with his daughter. And even if I do go to jail, do you think that will stop me? I will leave instructions with Aditya and his friends who will be very accommodating…"

"I hate you Fanish! You do not know how glad I, and I am sure a lot of other people, will be to see you rot in prison and…"

Fanish put his hands on her shoulders impatiently and snarled with displeasure as his fingers firmly squeezed them.

"Ena be careful you do not cross me for I am a very ruthless and cruel man and always get what I want."

He pushed her away in disgust and turned towards the door, the expression on his face no longer gentle but one of anger as he grabbed the doorknob.

But before opening the door, he spun around to face Ena with narrowed eyes. The look in his eyes was cold and his voice was full of malice as he repeated.

"In fact I would strongly advise you to think about doing anything rash, for my liking for you will not prevent me from implicating you as well."

Ena jumped up, eyes flashing and threw herself at Fanish. "No you cannot implicate me; I have nothing to do with your businesses so have any proof of involvement." Ena was sputtering in anger.

Fanish calmly disengaged himself.

"Ena my dear, I shall remind you again - you stayed one week at my house – which you did because we had some business to discuss as Dilawar was too busy. Akshita will support me on this, in fact it on my instruction that she invited you to come and stay with her. Oh, and I also taped the evening at Aditya's house. Nobody can see that you were drugged; in fact, it looks as if you were enjoying yourself. I wonder what Dilawar will think when he sees the tape and if he will still profess to love you?" he sneered.

He was confident now that it was Akshita and Ena who were going to get him out of his predicament; in fact, he was ruthlessly looking forward to holding them as hostages to his fate.

"I don't believe that of Akshita, and as for taping us, how low can you get? You wouldn't dare show the video to Dilawar, for he will know it to be another one of your tricks."

"If you do not believe me ask Akshita yourself. And as for taping you, I set up everything whilst you were sleeping. I told you I am capable of anything and here's the proof, you can show it to Dilawar when he comes or burn it– but remember the original is safe with me."

Fanish gave a triumphant laugh as he took out a video from his inner jacket and placed it on the table.

"You bastard!" Suddenly Ena was pulled into a whirling mass of confusion and terror.

"I'm sorry, darling, I must go."

A knowing smirk curved Fanish's full lips as he left Ena in wild-eyed fear.

■ ■ ■ ■

Chapter 70

"Thank God that is over!" Parul remarked.

Parul and Dilawar were sitting in the hospital canteen after the meeting.

" Dilawar, is everything alright?"

"I'm just worried about Ena." He rose from his chair. "Excuse me, Parul, I'll just ring and find out how she is."

"Yes, she was looking pale ......" Dilawar hurried off before Parul could finish his sentence.

However, seeing Dilawar love and devotion for Ena reminded him of Sai. She had finally, after a great of persuasion, agreed to marry him and he wanted Dilawar to be the first to know and share his happiness.

After a few moments, Dilawar came back, a smile on his face.

"I take everything is alright?" Parul asked.

"Everything's fine." Dilawar replied, pulling out a chair.

"Dilawar, there is something I need to tell you. As you are my best friend, I would like you to be the first person to know that I am engaged and…" Parul could not keep the excitement out of his voice.

"Congratulations!" Dilawar was genuinely delighted. "Who is the lucky girl? Anyone I know?"

"Yes it is actually. Her name is Sai and I believe she worked for you for…. Dilawar, are you feeling alright?" Parul asked in alarm for the cup in Dilawar's hand had dropped and smashed on the table.

"Waiter, can you please clear this mess?" Dilawar spoke to the waiter who was hovering nearby.

Dilawar was flustered and could not look Parul straight in the eye - Parul and his Sai. He shook himself, how could he think like this? Sai was not his, never had been, and he did not want her to be.

She was too good for him and each time they met he had feared would be the last. He had always expected Sai to lose patience with the scruffy rooms, the secretiveness, and the fact that Dilawar loved Ena and would never leave her.

Although he was happy for Sai and glad that she had moved on, Dilawar dreaded the embarrassment that would arise for both Sai and himself. And if ever Ena and Parul found out, he would not only lose Ena but a dear friend too.

Parul watched with fascination the changing emotions on Dilawar's face and was curious why the news of his engagement was affecting him so much.

The waiter finished wiping the table with a cloth, carefully putting the broken glass on a tray.

" Would you like another cup of coffee, sir?"

"No, thank you." Dilawar said, looking sheepish." I am so clumsy."

"Dilawar, I am meeting Sai for lunch. Would you like to come with me to meet her?"

"Err, I don' think so, much as I would like to, I think I better get back to Ena." Dilawar replied, as politely as he could as they left the canteen.

"Some other time, then. Give my regards to Ena, I hope she feels better."

Parul got into his car and drove off, puzzled by Dilawar's attitude, finally putting it down to his anxiety for Ena.

● ● ● ●

Chapter 71

The sun had collapsed into the sky, leaving the air cool and thin

Aditya sat in his chair, swirling the brown liquid and gazing pensively at his glass. He took a sip and liked the warm feeling that coursed through his body.

"You should try it, Fanish." He remarked to Fanish who was drinking a glass of juice.

"No, thank you, you know I hate it." Fanish replied vehemently.

To Fanish, alcohol was a reminder of his drunkard father, who had usually come home late at night having spent all the money at the pub. His mother had been usually beaten and if any of his brothers or sisters were awake he would shout and beat them also with his belt.

As the warm liquid coursed through his body, Aditya thought of getting his thick hands on a young and sweet body.

"Fanish, I need a …" Aditya said hoarsely.

He was feeling restless, and at the bottom of the turmoil he felt the writhing of desire. He sighed and leaned back in his chair.

"You know Gazal is available anytime, and now that Vanita is back…" Fanish snapped as he refilled Aditya's glass.

"No, not them, I need a new girl, Fanish, a young girl."

"Tell me something, Aditya; I have never understood why you like them so young." Fanish asked enquired, his brows raised.

"Because at that age they are pure an innocent and it is only later that they cover their innocence with pink gauze, so to speak. After that discovery, they weave their life with the pink gauze, that is, thoughts of romance, poetry and music, all of which I hate."

"Gazal and Vanita are not old anyway."

"No." Aditya sat up in his chair. "Not for me! Fanish, to me adults avoid reality, whereas a child, a child will look at life fully and candidly. They are not repulsed by criminal acts or spitefulness, for they have no moral conscience to confuse them. All aspects of life are interesting to them, even those we call the dirtiest! But that is not the only thing on my mind."

"That is very selfish of you Aditya, for you are only thinking of yourself. With their innocence and purity, they are also very easily frightened by things they don't understand. Anyway I feel there must be something else bothering you for I have never seen you so agitated before. Would you like to tell me about it?"

"It is my niece, Sanjula." Aditya groaned."She phoned and…"

"I didn't know you had one!" Fanish interrupted. "You have never talked about your family."

"The reason I don't or haven't is because my family disowned me a long time ago."

"I don't mean to pry, but why on earth?"

"It's a long story and one I don't think you would like to hear." Aditya exclaimed dryly.

"Actually you don't have to explain, I think I can guess. But to get back to your niece, how come she phoned? I would have imagined you would be pleased."

"Yes and no. She is London and would like to stay with me, says it would give her an opportunity to know me."

"What did you say to that? If your sister is willing to forgive you for whatever you did it must be a good thing. I would have thought you would like to get to know your niece."

"What do you think?" Aditya retorted impatiently. "I

could hardly say no, could I? And my sister does not know Sanjula is coming here, for she would have talked her out of it somehow. And nor does my niece know the reason my family renounced me, as for getting to know Sanjula, why, I would hardly know what to say."

"No, I suppose not. When is she coming?"

"She said she would be here in an hour's time. I offered to pick her from the airport, but she said she would take a cab." As Aditya looked at his watch, the door-bell rang.

"Expecting company?" Fanish asked, raising his eyebrows.

Aditya shook his head in bewilderment and went over to the window then exclaimed.

"Good heavens! A woman with some luggage....it looks like Sanjula's here."

Aditya hurried to open the door and Fanish heard his voice faintly.

"Hello, Sanjula, I am your Uncle Aditya, I am surprised to see you for I thought it would take you an hour to get here. You are early I..."

"I am sorry uncle; I hope I it is not inconvenient. Everything went smoothly, I got through customs quickly, there was a cab waiting and as there was no traffic, here I am." She hugged Aditya and smiled.

"Hello, Sanjula glad to meet you, do come in."

"Oh and uncle this is Shaila, my daughter and your grand-niece."

Aditya's heart gave a leap as he saw a six year old dark eyed little girl wearing a white frock with a white ribbon in her hair, clutching Sanjula's hand.

Sanjula was an attractive woman and was wearing black jeans, a blue shirt with a flawless complexion. Her black hair was tied in a knot at the nape of her neck whilst her eyebrows looked like taut bows. Underneath her eyebrows her eyes were large with heavy full eyelids and long beautiful lashes, and although she was smiling, her eyes looked sad, as if they were hiding countless secrets.

As they entered, Fanish saw with surprise that she was not alone for she was followed by a young girl.

"Sanjula, you look tired." Aditya gestured towards the sofa.

"No, actually I am not." Sanjula looked around her sceptically.

She sat on the sofa and pulled her daughter towards her comfortingly, as Shaila looked watchful and hostile.

"Shaila, say hello to your uncle."

"Hello, uncle. But he is not my uncle!" Shaila whispered in her mother's ear.

Aditya's heart beat like a drum as Shaila left her mother's side, sat on the sofa and played with her doll.

"Would you like some tea coffee or cold drink...?"

"Uncle, please we'd just like to freshen up first." Sanjula got up patting her hair.

"Of course what am I thinking of! This way..." Aditya led Sanjula and Shaila out of the room.

He was still looking bewildered when he came back into the room, sat down and put his head in his hands.

"Now, why are you looking so worried?" Fanish asked rising from the sofa. "She seemed nice enough."

"No, I am not worried.... hey where are you going?" Aditya looked up in alarm. "I need you to stay with me for at least some time."

Fanish sat down again and looked at Aditya sympathetically.

"I think I know how you feel."

"I don't think so." Aditya whispered as Shaila and Sanjula came back into the room later.

"We haven't been introduced." Fanish extended his hand. "I'm Fanish and your uncle here is a dear friend of mine. Aditya, maybe Sanjula, especially little Shaila, would like something to drink now?"

"Yes, yes, of course." Aditya rose, looking perplexed as he went into the kitchen." I have lived alone for so long I have forgotten how to be hospitable."

As he put on the kettle and watched it boil, he thought it was nice to have his niece stay with him –and as soon as the kettle boiled, he poured it into a teapot, took down a tin of biscuits and laid them on the tray with the cups and saucers. He put some cold milk for Shaila in a glass and took the tray back into the lounge to see Fanish laughing heartily at something Shaila had said.

He gave the glass of milk to Shaila who took it shyly. She was tall for her age and her skin was fair. Her chin sported a devil's cleft and she had a dimple in her cheek, which was peeping in and out at something Fanish was saying.

There was a look of perplexity on Aditya's face as he placed the tray on the coffee table.

Sanjula looked at him curiously for she had only recently found out that her mother had a brother - she guessed that he was the black sheep of the family - so had only decided to contact him secretly for she needed a place to stay.

Sanjula had come to London to find her husband, Manas, who had left her suddenly, after three very happy years. Shaila had at that time been only two years of age and she had had no communication from him as to why he had left. That was until recently when a mutual friend had let slip that he was living in London.

"I cannot live like this anymore - I need to find him."

After a lot of persuasion Sanjula had convinced him to give her his address.

She gave a start as she heard her uncle's voice

"Sanjula, I have a small house, I hope you will be comfortable here."

"Uncle, don't worry about us. I have a friend here and

we will be spending most of my time with them so you won't even know I'm here. But thank you for letting us stay, Uncle."

As soon as she finished her milk and biscuits, Shaila yawned and rubbed her eyes.

"I better take Shaila upstairs." When she saw Aditya rise from the sofa, she quickly added. "Don't worry, Uncle, I will find my way, thank you."

As soon as Sanjula left the room with Shaila, Aditya wiped his forehead with hand.

"Whew!" he exclaimed.

Fanish was sitting idly, legs crossed and looking at his fingernails when he abruptly rose from the chair.

"You have a beautiful niece and even more delightful grand-niece! Veeeery young, sweet and cute!" He remarked and a slow deliberate smile curved his lips as he left.

As he got into his car he noticed a colourful rainbow was being smudged and obliterated from the sky.

■ ■ ■ ■

Chapter 72

As Shaila closed her eyes, the usual lively expression on her face gradually disappeared as she slept - and as her breadth steadied in repose, her hands lay quietly on the quilt. Sanjula looked at her daughter's sleeping innocent face and thought how much she looked like her father.

She had been angry with him for abandoning them and had always felt her life to be lacking. Consequently, she felt she was always searching for a 'something' to complete it and was irritable, because, as she did not know what it was, would be unable to recognize and hold it when she did find it.

She came to the conclusion that it was Manas she missed, and as soon as she found out where he was, decided that she needed to see him, wanted Shaila to know her father and also get closure as to why he had so abruptly abandoned them.

She lay awake in the darkness, and after some time switched on the lamp by her bed, and looked at the clock at its side. She was feeling restless so switched of the lamp again when she saw the time, fluffed up the pillows, then lay with burning eyelids and a dry aching misery.

She decided that she would meet Manas alone, although she had promised Shaila they were going to meet her father. However, given the circumstance, Sanjula did not want to stay in London a moment longer than necessary. Although he was her uncle, Sanjula was uneasy in Aditya's company even though he was going out of his way to be kind and hospitable. Nor did she like his friend Fanish, with his sly furtive eyes.

After a sleepless night Sanjula finally drifted off to sleep and suddenly woke to find Shaila shaking her.

"Mum wake up!"

"Why, what's the matter? Are you alright?" Sanjula sat up in bed quickly, rubbing her eyes.

Her hair was tousled and she looked drowsily at her daughter.

"Nothing is the matter, Mum. You always tell me that it is not good to sleep late and you have been asleep for so long! I am hungry and you promised you would take me to see father."

"Did I? Honey, not today!" Sanjula yawned and threw back her quilt.

"Mum, but you said… I want to meet my father!" Shaila wailed.

Her mouth grew tight with agitation and her eyes were defiant as she looked at her mother, and when she got no reaction, started crying.

"Shaila, I said not today, I have something to do first." Sanjula said angrily.

As Shaila continued to cry she wanted to shake her by the scruff of her neck.

"Shaila stop crying! You won't meet your father if you behave this way!"

Shaila's face crumpled with disappointment and she clenched her hands into little fists. She then wiped the tears on her cheeks childishly with the back of her fist, leaving smudges on her skin.

"Oookay…" she hiccupped.

"Now wait here while I have a bath." Sanjula said firmly.

She collected her clothes and went into the bathroom. She quickly showered and slipped into her favourite black jeans with a Polo-neck red jumper.

"Come on, Shaila let's go down and get you something to eat. Now I see you have been a good girl and have got dressed by yourself today." Sanjula held out her hand for Shaila was sulking.

"Don't wantto!" Shaila was wearing her favourite her white shorts and a cap with a white peak.

"I thought you said you were hungry? That's all right, if you don't want to come, I'll go downstairs and have breakfast. Gosh, I am hungry! I'll enjoy the hot toast with butter and tea or cocoa."

"Can I have cocoa?" Shaila's pout turned into a smile of anticipation as she quickly grasped Sanjula's hand.

Aditya was setting the table and as Sanjula and Shaila walked in, he smiled faintly although his eyes were puffed and red.

He looked at Shaila with bloodshot eyes, for her shorts showed her slender waist and tiny midriff. A white scarf encircled her neck, leaving her young shoulder blades bare. As he looked at what he thought to be her lovely bones and the smooth curving of her adolescent back, he felt he had loved her from the moment he saw her, and because of the sudden intensity of his emotions, looked uneasily at Sanjula.

"What is your programme today?" he asked huskily as they sat round the table.

"Oh, I have to meet a friend I have not seen for some time. I spoke to her from the airport yesterday and she said she would be willing to look after Shaila whilst I had some business that needs looking into. Anyway… we have not yet arranged a time. I have to phone and confirm."

"Have some breakfast before you do anything."

"I am a bit impatient to get that sorted out. Will you excuse me whilst I make that phone call?"

Sanjula received no reply from her friend and walked back to the kitchen looking dejected.

"She must be happy to hear from you" Aditya commented. "you will have a lot of catching up to do.".

"No, unfortunately that won't be possible. I spoke to her husband who told me that she had to leave urgently to see her mother who has been taken ill suddenly. And that poses a dilemma for me." Sanjula wiped her forehead.

"Anything I can do to help?" Aditya smiled faintly.

"Not really." Sanjula replied. "I had to visit somebody and my friend promised to look after Shaila."

"Don't worry, Sanjula, I am at home today and Shaila can stay with me."

Shaila gave a yelp of joy at the thought of spending the day with her uncle. Although Sanjula was not keen on the idea, however, it seemed a perfect solution.

"Oh, thank you, Uncle! if you wouldn't mind? She is no trouble and you would not even know she is here." Sanjula said, relieved." I'm going to meet your father, Shaila." She whispered in her daughter's ear

"Yeehhh…" Shaila jumped up and down with happiness

"Of course not, we will have some fun Shaila won't we?" Aditya beamed.

Sanjula quickly put on her coat and gloves and patted Shaila on the head before leaving.

"Oh, uncle can you tell me how to get to this address?"

"Of course….it is not far and if you have any problem, give a call." Aditya said as he looked at the piece of paper Sanjula handed him.

He wrote down the instructions on a piece of paper.

"Thank your uncle now be a good girl, Shaila, don't trouble uncle!"

Shaila ran around the house gleefully as soon her mother left.

"I am going to meet my father soon; I am going to meet my father!"

"Shaila, what did you say about your father? Oh never mind, I will ask you mother, now come and sit down with me and I will teach you a game. You'd like that, won't you?"

"Of course, I will, silly billy uncle." Shaila laughed as she ran past Aditya

Her hair touched his temple and her childish wrist brushed his cheek. Shaila's knees rubbed against his legs as she went to sit in the corner of the sofa. Then suddenly, with the simplicity of a child, she first stretched her legs on Aditya's lap, then sat on his lap and gradually, Aditya began to sweep his hands slowly over her young agile legs.

As his body strained to accommodate her young weight on his lap he ran his hands over her young round bottom as she sat in his lap.

" I am going to tell you a secret, uncle." She put her mouth to Aditya's ear.

But Aditya could not separate the words from the hot thunder of her breath. After some time, she grew restless and tried to free herself, but Aditya pulled her back.

"Give your uncle a kiss, my little one."

Shaila writhed as Aditya put his arms around her, and her innocent mouth melted under the ferocious pressure of his heavy male jaws before she broke loose from his embrace, not with personal distaste, but with a child demanding her need. "I want something to drink!"

As Aditya got her a coke, he watched fascinated as she opened the can and drank thirstily.

■ ■ ■ ■

Chapter 73

After taking the piece of paper with the instructions from her Uncle, Sanjula left hurriedly.

It had been raining in the morning, but in the far horizon the thunder had been swept away by a raw wind and the sky was being swept of all clouds. In the west, a small ray of light was beginning to appear and Sanjula saw the sun begin to fight its way through, growing brighter and brighter.

After having lost her way a few times, Sanjula finally found first the street, then the house she was looking for. However, her heart was thudding so painfully that Sanjula stood for some time outside the house, debating whether she was doing the right thing and hoping Manas would come out so she could talk to him alone.

She waited for what seemed an hour, before she finally found the courage to ring the doorbell.

The door was opened after sometime by a young woman holding a baby.

"Yes, can I help you?" she asked, cradling the baby in her arms.

"I am looking for a gentleman by the name of Manas who…"

"I think you have the wrong address. There is nobody here by that name."

Sanjula consulted her address and read it aloud. "This is the right address, isn't it?"

"Yes, the address is right, but I am afraid as I said before, there is nobody of that name." She was going to shut the door when a voice called.

"Ishika, who is it?" Hetal came up behind Ishika and gave a start when he saw Sanjula.

"Manas!" Sanjula exclaimed her eyes bright with joy. "This is who I am looking for…"

Hetal looked at Sanjula in surprise then began to close the door.

"I think you have mistaken me for somebody else. Ishika, why don't you put Ekta to bed? She is sound asleep now."

"But I. we…. Shaila…" Sanjula looked confused and bewildered.

I don't know what you are talking about." Hetal said angrily.

He closed the door abruptly and Sanjula realised with a pang that Manas had changed his identity and was married. Ishika was his wife and he did not want her to know about her.

She stood on the doorstep dumbfounded, with tears running down her cheeks. How could he do this to her, for only did she still love him but they were still legally married.

Sanjula wiped the tears with the palm of her hand as she turned and began to walk back. She walked aimlessly for an hour or so before she headed back to Aditya's house. How was she going to explain to Shaila that her father did not want to know her? She wished now that she had never come, so decided that she would leave as soon as possible.

- - - -

Chapter 74

Sanjula found Shaila sitting with her knees under her chin, howling with laughter, tears streaming down her eyes. As soon as she saw Sanjula, she gave a squeal of delight and ran over to her.

"Mum, we are having such a good time. Aditya Uncle is so nice and he knows so many games."

"Thank you for looking after her uncle. I hope Shaila has not been her usual naughty self?"

Sanjula noticed that Aditya looked relaxed and happy, not tense and uncomfortable as he had in the morning.

"She has been a very good girl." Aditya replied. "Did you find the place? Were my directions helpful?"

When Sanjula nodded her head Aditya asked. "So you managed to meet your friend."

"It's a long story, uncle, and one that is too complicated to explain. Anyway, I think we will be leaving to go back as soon as possible."

"But you just arrived! Something has happened, hasn't it? Shaila was saying something about her father."

"Yes it is…" Sanjula whispered. "That is why we came here."

She decided to explain the situation to her Uncle for he was being so kind.

"Shaila, why don't you go up to your room? I'll be up shortly to give you a bath. I want to talk to Aditya uncle.

"No, no, let her stay." Aditya pleaded. "She is a good girl."

"It's time for her bath anyway." Sanjula said firmly.

"Mum, can I stay? We are on holiday!" Shaila tilted her piquant face at Sanjula.

"Shaila! Do as I say!" Sanjula said sharply.

Shaila reluctantly left the room muttering. "I don't wannto!!"

Sanjula turned towards Aditya.

"Uncle I will explain, but first I would like to make myself some tea. Would you like some?"

"No, thank you." Aditya replied in a forlorn voice as he watched Shaila leave the room.

As soon as Sanjula had made herself some tea, she brought it to the sofa. Whilst she drank the hot liquid she told him about Manas.

"And so I have decided it is time I went back. Now you see why I don't want to stay here any longer than I have to."

"Sanjula, did you say you are not divorced?" Aditya asked

Sanjula shook her head. "No, we are still married. He left without a word."

"And so you are going back without fighting for what is rightfully yours?"

"Uncle, I have no choice. He made it clear he does not want to know me. He seemed quite happy and has even got a family."

"But legally you are his wife, not the other woman. Do you want me to talk to him?"

"I don't think that would be of any use, Uncle."

"But Sanjula, I would advise you to think carefully before you make any decision. Remember Shaila is involved too. You should relax, look around, try and forget Manas. Don't forget Shaila at least deserves that much."

"And that is another thing. What am I going to tell her? She expects to meet her father, who she thinks will meet her with open arms and..."

Sanjula looked out of the window at the trees. The wind was wafting through them and the falling leaves, that were not gold any more but a dull brown.

Aditya rose from the couch abruptly. "Look, Sanjula, I am sorry to leave you when you are so worried, but I have to meet a friend for dinner. Will you be alright on your own? There is food in the kitchen. And since I am going out, do you want me to get something for Shaila? Is there anything she needs?"

"I am not hungry but I'll make a sandwich for Shaila, and no, thank you she does not need anything." Sanjula replied, pleasantly surprised at Aditya's thoughtfulness.

As Sanjula fed and put Shaila to bed, she thought of Manas, for meeting him had brought all the memories flooding back, days when they had been young, carefree and so much in love. But she now realised that his love had only been pretence, made of cardboard, a kind of stage landscape, which sometimes portrayed scenery but was not and could never be the real thing.

■ ■ ■ ■

Chapter 75

"Hetal, who was that woman?" Ishika asked as soon as the door had closed.

"I don't know, Ishika. I have never seen her before." Hetal replied uneasily

"She seemed to recognise you, though." Ishika said dubiously

"Like I said, Ishika, most probably she mistook me for somebody else." Hetal replied impatiently." Has Ekta gone to sleep?"

"Yes, she has." Ishika noticed the look of perplexity on Hetal's face. "But the address…"

"But nothing," Hetal said sharply.

However, Hetal was worried for the last thing he had expected was for Sanjula to turn up on his doorstep, just when he had his life in order again, convinced that no-one from Australia knew where he was. He looked up and saw the tears in Ishika's eyes.

"I'm sorry, Ishika, don't you trust me?" he said in a much gentler tone. "Have you heard anything from Vanita?"

"No, I haven't, and of course I trust you." Ishika's eyes were glistening.

"Good. You're not thinking of involving the police, are you?"

"No, of course not. Should I?"

"No, of course not, I just thought that as she was a minor you might think…"

"But she is in danger, and I cannot do anything. If I involve the police, she said in her note that I and Ekta are in danger, and Ekta is too precious for me to take any kind of risk."

Ishika smiled wearily and wiped her eyes with the back of her hand.

Hetal let out a sigh of relief. "Did she say from whom?"

"No, and I have no clue. No that is not entirely true, for one day I followed her when she went out for a walk to meet a friend of hers. I am sure he is the one who is behind whatever she is involved in, for I heard him threatening Vanita."

"Why didn't you tell me this before? Ekta is my daughter and if your sister is endangering you or her in any way I need to know." Hetal said angrily.

"That is precisely why I did not tell you for I don't want you to do anything irrational. And before you blame Vanita; her intentions are good, I am sure she does not want any harm to come to either Ekta or myself."

"I don't know about that." Hetal replied. "I do not like the look in her eyes."

"Hetal, don't forget, it is my sister here who is the victim."

"Victim of what?"

"She told me…she did not want to but at last she told me everything. Where she had been, what she was made to do, everything!" Ishika murmured in a forlorn voice.

Quietly she told Hetal what Vanita had told her, where she had been etc.

"Now you see, she is a victim. If I am in danger from the people she is involved in, what do you think they will do to her? Don't forget, I heard him threatening Vanita, and in her letter she mentioned she was leaving us because she thought me and Ekta would be in danger if she stayed."

"Oh my God!" Hetal muttered his mind on Sanjula and Shaila.

"nooo…. a penny for your thoughts?" Ishika noticed the faraway look in Hetal's eyes and wondered if it had anything to do with the woman.

"Nothing." Hetal replied quickly. "Just trying to

think of a way to ensure you and Ekta are safe."

"I think we are safe now, thanks to Vanita." Ishika smiled gently.

"How can you be so sure? If Vanita has not contacted you, how can you be sure?"

"Her letter emphasised that as soon as she went back, there would be nothing to worry about."

"You know where this bloke lives, don't you?"

"I do, but if you are thinking we should confront him, then no! I am not going! I don't like that man! I know his name for Vanita called him Fanish." Ishika trembled.

"We won't, Ishika," Hetal put his arms around Sanjula. "Just show me the house so that if anything does happen to you, I will know where to look."

"That is a good idea. Anushka is coming over later. I can always ask her to look after Ekta whilst I show you the house."

"She won't mind? She is a nice enough woman but…"

"Oh, she won't mind at all. She loves Ekta and is always glad to look after her."

As soon as Anushka arrived, Ishika explained that an emergency had arisen.

"Anushka, would you mind if we leave Ekta with you for a while?"

"Of course not, Ishika, now you go and take care of what it is that has come up. I will look after her, you know I love to!!"

"Thank you, Anushka, I owe you one!" Ishika hugged her.

As they drove past Gazal's house, the rain started pouring down and not only did the wind blow the dead leaves around, but also drove the late blooming flowers into the soil.

■ - ■ ■

Chapter 76

"Aditya, what is the matter with you? I have been talking to you for the last five minutes, but I do not think you have heard a word!" Fanish uttered in annoyance.

"I am sorry, Fanish, what were you saying?" Aditya looked absently at a painting in Fanish's lounge.

"Just that you need to go to Brazil as soon as possible."

"You want me to drop everything and leave? Now?" Aditya ran his hand through his hair. "I have just come!"

"Of course, now. What is the matter with you? What urgent business can't you 'drop'? You know I depend on you to look after our business abroad."

"What is the urgency? I have just been and will be going next month anyway." Aditya replied indignantly.

"You're asking me what the urgency is?! Have you forgotten it was you who alerted me to the problems there? I rang up John in Brazil, and it seems you were right, we are in a predicament."

"But can't he sort out the problem? He looks after that zone and..."

"Aditya, you are the one who is supposed to keep an eye on him. What has got into you? You never made a fuss before and you know John looks to you for advice and does not make any decisions himself."

"Fanish, why don't you go and sort everything out? I have tried and failed."

"You know I cannot do that. Everybody knows you and they are used to taking orders from you."

"Fanish, Sanjula is here and she has some domestic problem which needs sorting out. She is thinking of going back to Australia and, oh, I just can't just leave them suddenly."

"Since when have you been so close to your family?

Aditya you know that if there is any problem, I will do my best to help. I will talk to her and…"

"No!" Aditya replied vehemently.

Fanish raised his eyebrows and looked at Aditya quizzically.

"If she is going back Australia, there is no need for you to get so involved. Aditya, you are acting very strangely, I must say."

How could Aditya explain to Fanish that he had fallen in love with Shaila passionately and obsessively? Her bony, young fragile face, innocent eyes, high cheekbones, and perfect childish figure were all haunting Aditya. Shaila seemed to him some shimmering cloud image, veiled in sheaths of innocence. Every time he looked at her, his heart would beat fast, and he would search for some way to express his love.

His heart had leapt out toward her like a tiger toward a young doe. Aditya knew exactly what he had to do and how to do it without violating a child's purity. Fanish was right, he was a selfish man and regarded himself as the pivotal point of all that was important to him. He only looked at Shaila in context of his own pleasure and was going to try and squeeze all bliss from her that he could, even if it lasted for a little while.

He rubbed the palm his hand for he could still feel the lingering fullness of Shaila's fleshy hand, savour the smoothness of her childish back and the smooth sliding sensation of her skin through the thin frock that Aditya's hand had worked up and down whilst he held her.

Never before had he felt this way about any girl before, and never before had he felt that he needed love so strongly from a girl who was young and pure. He liked young girls because he felt they were innocent and pure, too young to have played around or used foul language; their short lives had not had the time to learn filth and violence of the world. It did not occur to him that he was confusing love with lust or that she was family.

"Anyway, Fanish, Sanjula will confirm her plans by tomorrow, and I in turn will then let you know."

Aditya was sprawled on the chair; his legs stretched in front, his hands dangling over the arms of the chair.

Fanish's expression became hard; his lips thinned and whitened for he did not like to have his orders challenged. There was tightness around his eyes and forehead.

"Tomorrow you leave." He said firmly, through clenched teeth. I will deal with Sanjula. You can play the perfect uncle when you come back."

"But I cannot leave ..." Aditya bit his lips. "They'll be gone by then, Fanish."

Although he thought he would love her forever, Aditya realised that Shaila would one day cease to be a child and grow into a young girl, then to a woman. So for him, forever only meant as long as she remained a child.

Aditya was hoping that the precious moments with Shaila could be not be brought to a standstill, for they were like rare moments - like stopping a train or car just to pluck a wild exotic rare flower from the wayside. He felt that he could miss the transport, but not the exotic beauty of a rare flower, for if he did not pluck it there and then, its magnificence would be wasted.

- - - -

Chapter 77

Aditya drove home slowly; deep in thought and was surprised to find the light on and Sanjula sitting in the lounge in her night-gown, a mug in her hand.

"Hi, could not sleep?" Aditya asked throwing himself into a chair. "Is Shaila asleep?"

"No, she is being difficult, you have spoilt her uncle! I thought maybe a hot drink would help me sleep, but you look tired."

"I am!" Aditya ran his hand through his hair. "Shall I go up and read her a story? She likes that."

"That would be nice of you, but is something bothering you, uncle?"

"I am afraid I have to go away to Brazil for business."

"That's a bit sudden isn't it? When do you have to leave?" Sanjula's eyes opened wide.

"I have to leave tomorrow, day after at the latest." Aditya replied in an aggrieved tone.

"Tomorrow?!" Sanjula exclaimed." So soon?"

"Yes, my flight is tomorrow evening, Fanish will be following. But have you decided what you are going to do?"

"Well, I still think the sooner I go back the better. More so now that you will not be here…but tomorrow."

"How long did you come here for?"

"Three weeks. One week I spent with this friend of mine who lives just outside London, so two weeks of my holiday left still."

"But this is perfect!" Aditya slapped his forehead as a thought struck him." Sanjula, how would you and Shaila like to come with me?"

"Uncle, what are you saying? Anyway, I don't have any money for the ticket. And I am sure we won't get tickets this late in the day."

"Don't worry about the ticket, we travel often so

know people in the airline. And that will also give you more time to decide as what you would like to do."

"It does sound like fun for I haven't been to Brazil." The idea interested Sanjula.

"Please say yes." Aditya was excited and suddenly looked forward to the trip.

"Are you sure we will not be any trouble?"

"No, Not at all. In fact, I will be happy for you to accompany me for it gets quite dull and boring on my own. So that's settled then, we leave tomorrow evening. I'll fill you in on the details later."

"I must ring Mother and let her know." Sanjula had cheered up considerably.

"No need for that either, Sanjula. I'll take care of it." Aditya replied hurriedly "I will be talking to her anyway tomorrow, just make sure that Shaila has everything she needs. Oh, and I will go up and see that she goes to sleep."

"Thank you Uncle, but I thought Mum and you weren't on talking terms?"

"Well we weren't, till you came; now we have something in common." Aditya smiled faintly. "We intend to keep communication open now, and we have you to thank."

"I am glad, and thank you, uncle, for looking after us so well." Sanjula got up from her chair and kissed Aditya on the forehead. "Oh, I nearly forgot, I have a call to make!"

"Fanish said he would come by with the flight details. I will tell him that you will be accompanying me."Aditya said over his shoulder as he left the room.

• – • •

Chapter 78

Vanita missed Ishika and walked dejectedly about the room feeling suffocated. She inhaled deeply as the long lace curtains fluttered in the early spring evening breeze through the half-open window.

"Vanita, would you like some tea?" Gazal's face peered from behind her door.

Vanita shook her head and smiled sadly. "No thanks."

"Why don't you come down? I am bored and I think you need cheering up too."

"In a minute, Gazal, I have a few things to clear up first."

"Well, hurry up!" Gazal's face disappeared and Vanita sat on the bed. "Tea will be ready."

The voices and images of the recent past swirled in Vanita's mind and she tried to dismiss them from her mind. Maybe forgetting them would make all the unfairness, ugliness and injustice go away and keep Ishika and Ekta safe?

She went downstairs to find Gazal in the kitchen moving with agility around the kitchen, putting the kettle to boil and getting the mugs from the units.

"Finished your work?" Gazal asked

"Yes." Vanita's voice was cold and distant as she answered tersely.

"Fanish phoned a couple of minutes ago." Gazal looked down at her hands.

"Oh?" Vanita looked out of the window.

"He told me that Aditya is flying to Brazil tomorrow and has asked you to accompany him."

"What! Why?" There was blank amazement on Vanita's face. "And why Brazil?"

"Aditya has some kind of business there and he thought you needed a holiday after all you have been through."

"I do need to get away from this place but how come Fanish is being so considerate?" Vanita asked.

There was a mixture of suspicion and doubt on her face, for Fanish, Aditya and Gazal were still the enemy, only in a friendly guise.

"You know he can sometimes be quite kind and…"

"Okay, okay, don't start lecturing me on the good he does, I have heard it a dozen times before, but what if I don't want to go?"

"You know that is not an option." Gazal bit her lip in alarm.

"Gazal, have you been abroad with Aditya?"

"No I haven't." Gazal's voice was a mixture of fear and satisfaction in her voice.

"There is more to this then you are telling me, isn't there?" Vanita asked her voice trembling.

"Vanita, don't worry., Aditya will be with you, he is not bad…."

"Isn't he just?" Vanita asked bitterly, her lips set together tightly. "Gazal, how can you defend their conduct?"

"I am not." Gazal drummed her fingers absently on the table. "Oh, and he said to take the minimum clothes, you can do all the shopping there. Lucky you, I wish I was going."

"You can go in my place." Vanita replied quickly.

"Vanita I don't understand you! How can you pass up a chance like this?" Gazal asked.

"Because Fanish is involved and I don't trust him. I don't how you can, for not only has he stolen our innocence and childhood, but he has manipulated our every action since then. But I suppose you are right, I have no choice. And it might be turn out to be quite enjoyable, I'll go and pack. What time is the flight?"

"Tomorrow evening, I think. Fanish will give you the details in the morning." Gazal replied as Vanita left the room. "And don't forget, pack light."

As soon Vanita left the room Gazal phoned Fanish.

"Vanita has agreed to go with Aditya." She spoke softly in the receiver.

"Good girl, thank you Gazal. Vanita does not suspect why she is going abroad, does she?"

"No, she does not, though she suspects something is up." Gazal remarked.

"As long as she does not know...."

After she hung up, Gazal sat back and thought how deceptively cruel she was, then shrugged off the feeling. She could not afford to be kind and sensitive, for it was either her or Vanita.

All her life Gazal had been waiting, sure that something wonderful was going to happen She had grown up with parents who had given her an abundance of material possessions but no affection. And from the moment Fanish entered her life, she thought the moment had finally arrived – and that whatever happened, he was her future.

However, sometimes there was a stirring of her conscience that told her that what Fanish did was wrong - then there would be a battle raging within her.

She thought of herself as an adult, but there was something still of the romancing child in Gazal, a child who liked to believe that all was wonderful, and if it was not, her imagination would make it so.

Consequently, the dream in Gazal won, for weren't her dreams better than the truths she had found?

■ ■ ■ ■

287

Chapter 79

The sky was being blanketed by dark angry black clouds that looked furious and threatening, ready for a spring storm.

Akshita had overhead Fanish's conversation with Gazal, and she twisted her long tapering fingers in anguish.

She found there was something odd and ominous in Fanish's manner, and Akshita was suddenly filled with a sudden premonition of danger.

She moved swiftly and determinedly towards him.

"Fanish, I heard you on the phone to Gazal about sending some girl abroad."

Fanish gave a start, for he was absorbed in trying to find a solution to his predicament. He had begun to ignore Akshita, and whenever he did pay attention, he had this strong surprised look which infuriated Akshita, even more than his indifference.

"Yes, I am sending a girl abroad." Fanish confirmed. "But I thought you were not interested in my business. Did my answers last time not scare you enough?" there was a malicious gleam in his eyes.

"I am not! I was just wondering if I knew her, that is all." Akshita replied, flustered.

"In fact you do. Her name is Urvi, but how did you guess?" Fanish looked at Akshita with exaggerated surprise.

The colour drained from her face and Akshita looked white and frozen. Suddenly, she jerked her head back, struggling for some hope to lean against, and tried not to allow herself the luxury of fear. But how could she not be afraid, for Fanish liked to ruin the lives of young girls.

"Don't worry, Akshita. I was not talking about

Urvi.'"' Fanish's eyes were twinkling and his face twitched with laughter.

Akshita could feel relief flooding through her body but was piqued nonetheless. Fanish was watching her, and she made an effort not to let her emotions show for that is what Fanish was playing on. However, try as she would, she could not control herself and she glowered visibly. She bit her lips to keep from passing a comment that would upset Fanish.

"Why, nothing to say, Akshita?" Fanish asked meekly.

"No, just that I pity the girl you were talking about and wish I could help her." Akshita muttered through clenched teeth.

"You can't, but you can rest assured that whatever happens she will be well looked after, by all of us." Fanish laughed cruelly.

Akshita willed herself to be calm. "Fanish, father phoned whilst you were away."

"Oh? What did he want?" Fanish's cold eyes studied her intently.

"Mother is not well, so he has asked me to go and look after her."

"What do you take me for?" Fanish snarled as his eyes glittered. "You are not going anywhere!"

He spoke angrily, as if a daughter wanting to look after her mother was somehow improper and was not a matter he wanted to get involved in.

"But Fanish, Mother is seriously ill." Akshita protested.

"I don't care!" Fanish replied indifferently. "Urvi can look after her."

"But she is only a little girl."

"She won't stay little if you carry on nagging!" Fanish replied impatiently, tired of Akshita's whining.

"Alright, alright, Fanish, I won't go. But can she

come and stay here, then?" Akshita asked and her lips grew thin with tension.

"That idea I like, veeeery much." Fanish's voice dropped low in his throat as he looked at her suggestively.

"You bastard!" Akshita sputtered as her eyes widened and face filled with anger. "She is not coming here."

"Changed your mind, have you?" Fanish chuckled as he rose from his chair and picked up some documents. "You should know me better by now." he reprimanded softly as he walked out of the room.

After the front door closed, Akshita's thoughts were a mixture of frustration, disgust and helplessness.

· · · ·

Chapter 80

Fanish drove to Aditya's house to give him last minute instructions, for when he had spoken to John in Brazil; he had been told that some of the obstacles they were encountering could be due to Aditya's miss-management. Fanish also believed Aditya too be too engrossed in finding ways to gratify his perverse needs to be of any real use to him anymore.

He was surprised when Sanjula opened the door, phone in hand.

"Hello, Sanjula, is Aditya at home?" Fanish asked as his cold eyes studied her.

Sanjula cupped her hand over the receiver.

"He is putting Shaila to bed. Sorry come in." she continued talking and went to an adjacent room as Fanish walked into the lounge.

After a few minutes Aditya walked in, flushed, eyes glossy a smile on his face.

Fanish's eyebrows rose quizzically as he saw Aditya's flushed face.

"Aditya, I thought I'd come personally to give you the flight details and a little guidance about the business. What do you think about expanding? I also wanted to talk to you about a personal matter."

"Expanding? What do you mean expanding? At the rate we are going it will be a miracle if we escape detection!" Aditya frowned as he sat on the sofa.

"Aditya, you worry too much, you have to learn to deal with people with an iron hand." Fanish smiled as he lit a cigarette.

"I don't think so, Fanish. I have been thinking why you are so calm about the problems abroad. Could it be because nobody knows you and were there any trouble it will be my neck on the line?"

"Oh, don't be silly, Aditya." Fanish retorted angrily.

At the moment Sanjula walked back into the room and placed the receiver in its stand.

"Uncle, is Shaila asleep?"

Aditya frowned but nodded his head.

"And can I have the flight details now? I'd like to go shopping if I have the time." Sanjula yawned and put her hand over her mouth. "I am going to bed now, if you can leave them on the table for me?"

Fanish glanced at Sanjula's receding figure in amazement.

"Aditya, is she leaving too?" he enquired. "You know she does not have to; I will look after her."

"Eh, she is not going to Australia but has decided to come with me." Aditya replied, looking at Fanish's wooden face.

"Aditya, you are not going for a holiday!" Fanish retorted through tight lips." And I have not booked her ticket!"

"I will make book the tickets for them, there is no need for you to worry."

"But she seems to think I have made their booking!""

Aditya looked at Fanish with confusion. He had always a passionate man, but the intensity of his feelings for Shaila had plunged him into a deep abyss. He felt he was caught between heaven, hell and purgatory, consequently had to endure continual torment and heartache.

"If you think you can cope and they will not be a distraction. Now, I need to give your instructions before you leave. I depend on you for the business abroad, but now you need to concentrate on children, not drug trafficking. Just concentrate only on 'scouting' young children for adoption, and follow the chain of events of young children, the ones who run away from home with no money, nowhere to go etc. I want you to pick them up. That cannot be too difficult?" Fanish taunted.

"I explained everything before, Fanish, it is not as easy as you think, and some children have started going to the police for protection."

Aditya's eyes narrowed and he clenched his fists in frustration.

"I think you are reading too much into the problems." Fanish retorted, crossing his legs. "We actually offer a solution for children who are born to women prostitutes, junkies etc., a way out of their life of poverty, unemployment and broken family life. Keeping all this in mind, I would have thought it to be easy to migrate them from the countryside to the city."

"Why don't you come and see for yourself?"

"Aditya, you know I can't do that. And that reminds me, Vanita will be travelling with you."

"What! Why? I don't want her tagging along! And you said yourself that I do not need distractions." Aditya exclaimed angrily.

"What about Sanjula and Shaila? Won't they be a diversion? But I understand why you don't want her with you." Fanish remarked dryly. "Anyway, you know what you have to do and this time, please do it correctly for Vanita saw more than she should have."

"Okay, if that is what you want." Aditya yawned. "What was the other matter you wanted to talk to me about?"

"I just wanted to let you know that our drugs shipment route should now cover three areas."

Fanish saw that Aditya was looking sceptical.

"Aditya, if you are thinking that you do not want to work for me anymore, let me just remind you that this is a perfect cover-up for your desires and needs."

For a moment shame flushed Aditya's face, but then he felt a sizzling rage, almost as strong as his passion, and there was bitterness in his eyes.

"Tell John and the others what I have said, and I will

see you when I come back." Fanish said.

••••

Chapter 81

The following day, Sanjula woke to a bright sunny day.

As she looked out of the window sleepily, she wondered if she had made the right decision to go to with her uncle.

"Mother, get up! We will be late!" Shaila jumped around the room.

Sanjula smiled tenderly. "We have enough time."

When she saw Shaila excited face, Sanjula knew she had made the right decision, for her daughter's happiness was all that mattered to her now.

"Sanjula, I am going shopping, as usual I left things too late, anyway, would Shaila like to come with me? Aditya's voice boomed from the landing

"Yes, please mum!" Shaila pranced around the room

Sanjula wanted to have some time on her own, so was only too glad to have Shaila out of the way.

"Yes, uncle, she will be down shortly."

"Oh, and Sanjula, can you confirm Shaila's booking with the airline? I have left the details on the table. And don't worry, your ticket is with Fanish, he forgot to bring it, so will meet us at the airport."

"Will do, uncle." Sanjula said as she heard the door closing. She confirmed Shaila's booking and had just finished her packing when the doorbell rang. As Aditya was out with Shaila, she went down to answer it.

When she opened the door, she was astonished to see Manas standing outside, looking sheepish.

"Manas! How did you find me?"

She stood transfixed although she wanted to run to Manas and throw her arms around him.

"I phoned Bashi. I could not let you go without explaining. Can I come in?"

Of course, come in." Sanjula's heart sank as she opened the door wide. "But Bashi did not know where I am staying!"

Manas sat down and looked around him.

"No, but he rang your Mum, and she told him that you might be staying with her brother. Anyway, here I am."

"…Manas, how can you sit there and make small talk after the way you treated me? I am still your wife, we have a child and I think I deserve an explanation, but I don't understand, how can you have a second wife and child?!"

Sanjula eyes were glistening, as she looked at Manas, her pent up rage suddenly exploded and she glared at Manas.

"I know and I am sorry, Sanjula, but I had to leave Australia."

"Why? What was so urgent that you could not even leave a note or phone me since? I thought we had a good marriage and were friends - is that all I meant to you? I came here with such expectations, only to find that you have not only changed your name, but that you are married, well not really for you do realise that you are still married to me, don't you?"

"I know but I am sorry, Sanjula. However, did you find me?" Manas asked.

"I met Bashir one day, your dear friend."

"Bashi! Dear Bashi! Of course he is the only one who knew where I was. But he had promised that he would not tell you or anyone else."

"He did not want to, I had to persuade him. And he saw the state I was in, trying to cope as a single mother with no money and no job. I guess when he saw you living in luxury; he did not need much convincing to give me your address."

"I am sorry I left without a word, but I had to leave

my past and everyone in it behind me for both your sakes."

"Even your own daughter?" Sanjula cried bitterly. "I don't understand, you were a good father and loved her. What has she done to deserve to grow up without a father?"

"I am sorry." Manas repeated.

"You're sorry? That word means nothing, nothing at all. We loved each other since childhood and you rejected us? Forgot everything we had meant to each other? Shaila, your daughter, thinks she has come to meet her father, a father who loves her."

Manas groaned and put his head in hands.

"Stop, Sanjula, it has not been easy for me either and I have missed her too."

"Not easy, did you say not easy for you?" Sanjula laughed and there was contempt in her eyes. "Let me see, you are happily, I presume, married, have a child, have no financial problems and you say it has not been easy? You have not even asked to see your daughter, let alone find out how she has been."

"I thought it best, it would only confuse her and whatever you think, Sanjula, it is not easy to live a charade."

"What charade, do you love that, that woman?"

"Yes, I think so." Manas hesitated. "She is a very good woman."

"Then you never loved me, but Manas, I still don't understand your deception and lies. You must have really wanted to escape from me." There were tears in her eyes.

Manas peered at Sanjula from under thick dark lashes that could not hide the brown eyes that Sanjula had once thought beautiful, but now seemed deceitful, sad and secretive.

"No! That was not the reason for I loved you, still do,

but I cannot tell you the reason, I am sorry, but much as I would like to, I cannot tell you why I left." Manas replied sadly.

Sanjula sat down beside Manas with tears of frustration in her eyes, but when she saw the torment in his eyes, her eyes softened.

"Manas, I think you are in trouble. You know we have always been friends and even though I don't approve of your behaviour, it seems there is a lot you are not telling me. You know you can count on me if you are in any trouble?" she whispered as she moved closer.

Manas's heart broke at her words. He was amazed at what she saw in him, and felt she deserved better. However, when he saw her goodness and selfless love, he felt he owed it to her to tell her the truth.

Sanjula saw the despair in Manas's eyes took both his hands and put them on either side of her face.

Her love for him was unconditional and she expected nothing in return. She did not want to be the ruler and judge of his actions, nor did she want to believe that his nature hid a secret cruel dark side

"If you are happy here and my being here is a problem, we will go back. In fact, I have already decided to."

Manas was silent, running his fingers through his hair.

Sanjula was disappointed, for she had hoped that Manas would persuade her to stay, if not stay at least postpone her departure.

She was prepared to forgive him, because not only was he her first love, the father of her child, but because being with him chased away the dark shadows that had haunted her since he left.so he decided to tell her everything. He owed her that much at least.

■ ■ ■ ■

Chapter 82

"Sanjula, do you remember Raka?" Manas's eyes darted around the room.

"Raka? Of course I remember him, he was your friend. I don't know if you know this, but he was found dead a couple of days after you left." To Sanjula's surprise, Manas did not look shocked.

"It is because if him I am here." Manas said bitterly.

"Really? I thought you two were inseparable?"

"We were, but what I did not know was that he was involved with a very bad crowd, and gradually he got me implicated in all their shady deals."

"Raka, involved with a bad crowd, No.!?!" Sanjula exclaimed. "I thought him to be polite, his manners to be impeccable and a man of integrity and of honour."

"That was all a show Sanjula; I am only ashamed to admit that he was my friend. Anyway, to cut a long story short." Manas continued. "He owed some people some money who came to his house whilst I was there. There was a row, which escalated into violence and Raka was killed. I ran from the place as fast as I could, but one of the men followed me and threatened that if I ever go to the police, you and Shaila would be in danger. I am surprised they did not kill me there and then!"

"Oh my God! But didn't you promise them that you would not go to the police?"

"Oh, I did, and they in turn assured me they would not harm me. I thought I was safe, for they did not know where I lived, or so I thought. It seems I underestimated them for they contacted me a few days later, asking me to do something for them."

"Which I am sure you didn't because if they were not nice people it must have been something illegal."

"I had no choice, for they threatened me saying that if I did not, they would tell the police that it was me who killed Raka."

"Why didn't you tell me all this then?" Sanjula asked. "I might have helped, or at least I would have known that you loved me."

"And got you involved as well? They said they would kill you - they were ruthless people so I thought the best thing to do was to leave the country." Hetal ran his fingers through his hair.

"And do you think you are safe now?" Sanjula asked a frown on her face.

"No, I don't. I am frightened for their crime ring spreads throughout the world, and I believe it is only a matter of time before they catch up with me. So now you know that I only left to protect you and Shaila, not because I did not love you."

Sanjula had tears in her eyes as she put her head on Manas's shoulder.

"Didn't you know that I don't care about myself? If you had talked to me then we could have sorted something out." she whispered softly.

"I do love you and I would never have put you and Shaila through any danger." Manas kissed the top of her head gently as he stroked her hair.

"But why did you marry that woman?" Sanjula asked quietly.

However, there was not a trace of emotion in Sanjula's voice, nor was there any reproach. It was not sacrifice, nor devotion; it was simply the heart of a woman with strange complex feelings, tinged with love and jealousy.

"Marrying her seemed to be a perfect front for I had to change my identity. Her name is Ishika, she is a nice girl, and ohhhh; I am sorry, please don't cry, Sanjula you know I hate to see you cry."

Manas took her in his arms when a door slammed and he heard voices.

"Mummy, where are you?"

"I am here, darling," Sanjula replied wiping her eyes.

Shaila ran into the room; laughing and carrying parcels in her hands, followed by Aditya, a dark desperate look in his eyes.

Sanjula smiled reassuringly as Shaila drew back seeing a stranger and cowered behind Aditya, peeping at them with her huge eyes.

Manas smiled tenderly. "Hello Shaila!"

"Hello, I am Aditya, Sanjula's uncle. You must be Manas." Aditya came forward and extended his hand.

Manas gave a start when he heard Aditya calling him by name, for he had not expected Sanjula to confide in anyone.

"Shaila, why don't you go upstairs with all your shopping...Shaila, did you hear what I said? Honestly, uncle, you spoil her for she does not need anything..."

Sanjula turned to her uncle who was looking at Shaila's receding figure tenderly.

Aditya sat on the sofa and looked angrily at Manas.

"As Sanjula's uncle, I think I have a right to ask you why you are treating my niece in this way. How can you get married to someone else when you are married to her?"

"Uncle, it is alright." Sanjula hurriedly interrupted.

At that moment the doorbell rang and Aditya went to answer it.

"Ah, that must be..." Aditya muttered.

He rose to answer the door and came back a couple of minutes later followed by a young girl carrying a suitcase.

"Sanjula, this is Vanita, she is coming with us"

"Hetal!" Vanita exclaimed in surprise. "What are you doing here? How is Ishika? How did you know where to

find me? Hetal please, please don't tell her where I am."
Vanita pleaded.

Hetal looked surprised, then slightly embarrassed.

"No, of course I won't, not if you don't want me to…
anyway I must go, I have to meet your sister…."

He rose hurriedly from his chair and left the room
followed by Sanjula.

"What was all that about? Who is that girl?" she
inquired a frown on her face.

"Sanjula that is Ishika's younger sister. But how does
she know your uncle? Ishika told me that she is involved
with some very bad people, a man called Fanish, I
believe,"

"So that is it! Uncle and Fanish are very good friends,
partners, actually. Manas, are you afraid that she will tell
her sister about your visit here? I can see you do not want
her to know."

"No, I am not afraid of that, for she will not be seeing
Ishika anymore." Manas answered. "She told her that,
but Sanjula, you should not have told your uncle about
me." Manas turned Sanjula's face towards him.

"I needn't someone to talk to and…" Love shone
from Sanjula's eyes as she looked at Manas.

"I am sorry; I have no right to ask anything of you. It
is just that I am frightened that the more people know
about me, the news will somehow get to those guys will
come to find me or you and……Oh gosh anyway I guess
this is good-bye for the moment, Sanjula, and for what it
is worth I am sorry for the grief I am putting you
through." Manas put a hand under Sanjula's chin. "But
what did Aditya mean when he said Vanita is coming
with you?"

"I am going away this evening with my uncle."

"You are leaving today! Are you going back to
Australia?" Manas exclaimed.

"No, we are leaving today for a holiday before I

302

return to Australia. My uncle is going abroad for some time and asked us to go with him. I was feeling so depressed that I accepted."

"Don't go!" Manas whispered urgently. "Things have changed now. I want you to stay and you can tell your uncle that…"

"Do you really think that it is such a good idea? After all, you are now married to Ishika and have a daughter…" Sanjula's voice trembled and her eyes filled with tears. "And Manas, is it really fair on Ishika not to tell her that you are already married?"

Manas groaned. "Things have gone too far for that. She will only get hurt if I tell her."

"Manas, I think you do not want to tell her for that will bring your cosy world crashing, wouldn't it?" Sanjula said bitterly. "I would be willing to stay here and give Shaila a father that she needs, but only if you leave Ishika."

Manas shifted his feet and did not look Sanjula in the eyes.

"I think you better leave." Sanjula said with a sob. She closed the door, leant against it and started sobbing for she thought she had accepted Manas's new life and even been happy for him. She forgot momentarily that he was only leading a double life in order to protect them.

When she finally felt she could cry no more she took a deep breath and returned to the lounge to find Shaila laughing with Aditya.

She pulled herself together - the only way now was to forget the past and move on. She began to look forward to her trip and joined Vanita, who was sitting quietly, her hands on her lap, but looking strangely at Aditya and Shaila.

Sanjula was vaguely disturbed at the sudden tension in the atmosphere and saw Vanita looking at her strangely.

"Hello, I am Sanjula, Aditya's niece" she said, introducing herself.

"Hello," Vanita replied vaguely after some time.

Her eyes stared at Shaila then after some time she gazed into Sanjula's face, her yes clouded and aloof.

"Are you looking forward to your holiday? I was surprised to learn from Uncle that you would be travelling with us, but I will be glad of your company, for Aditya and Shaila are so busy having fun they are completely ignoring me." Sanjula smiled tenderly.

However, she was puzzled by the expression on Vanita's face as she looked at Shaila and Aditya.

"Yes, I am," Vanita replied shortly. She got up to see a photograph of Aditya, Fanish his wife and.......Suddenly she trembled with fear and gave a start as Sanjula spoke.

"How do you know my uncle?" she asked

"Oh, we met in…. I don't remember, it seems such a long time ago."

The palest shadow of despair ran like a ripple over Vanita's face.

Sanjula laughed. "I don't think it could be that long ago. Why, you are little more than a child, only a couple of years older than my Shaila, I would say."

Aditya came and joined them, his face flushed.

"Uncle, I think you need to exercise." Sanjula joked, as Aditya looked at his watch.

"Ha, ha. Sanjula, I think we better leave for the airport. If you could, bring your baggage whilst I ring for a cab, it would save time. Vanita, are you feeling alright?"

"Yes, I am fine." Vanita closed her eyes wearily.

Aditya quickly made a phone call whilst Sanjula got her suitcases.

Vanita relaxed and closed her eyes, wondering how

Hetal had found her and hoping that he would not tell Ishika.

As soon as the cab arrived, Sanjula picked her suitcase.

"Here, let me help you, that appears to be heavy." Aditya said.

As Vanita walked to the cab, the dry autumn leaves blew on her face and their familiar smell enveloped and mingled with her tears.

• • • •

Chapter 83

Fanish was waiting for them at the airport, and looking at him in his white three –piece suit with his oily hair slicked back, Sanjula felt a momentary feeling of repulsion. Although he had been nothing but kind to her, she began to believe in the saying that sometimes generosity was a sin rather a virtue.

He advanced towards them, using his panther like walk that signified a ruthless and cruel trait.

Fanish too, although he found Sanjula attractive, did not like her and thought her to be a woman who set out looking for trouble. He wondered idly what had brought her to London.

"Here you are at last." he exclaimed. "And Vanita, how are you?"

"Fine." Vanita snapped in a dry and unemotional voice, whist the expression in her eyes was defiant.

"Fanish uncle, where are we going?" A young girl who Sanjula had never seen before came up to them.

"Ah, Urvi, here you are." Fanish turned to Vanita, a faint mocking gleam in his eyes. "Urvi, there has been a change of plan. Akshita has just phoned to say that she has been suddenly been taken ill and is in hospital."

"I want to go my sister now," Urvi stamped her foot.

"Let me finish my sentence, Urvi," Fanish manner was firm. "However, her illness is only temporary and the doctor has advised her not to travel for now. But she has suggested that you go ahead, and she will join us later."

"I don't want to go anywhere on my own, father said that…"

Urvi looked around in panic from Fanish to the strange people around him and her eyes were wide with fright.

"You won't be on your own. You will be travelling with Sanjula, Aditya, who you know, girls of your age., and I am sure you will have fun."

"But I don't want to! And anyway why don't you come as well?"

"Urvi, I will come with Akshita, you don't want me to leave your sister behind, do you? She told me to tell you that she will meet you as soon as she is better."

"Urvi, you don't have anything to fear. We'll be with you and take care of you till your sister joins us." Sanjula said gently.

She put her arms around Urvi, thinking she was just another young girl, kicking her heels, apprehensive of any kind of control.

"She'll be alright." She reassured Fanish. "Every child feels like this, but will eventually come to terms with it."

Aditya took Fanish aside, a frown on his face.

"Fanish, what do you think you are doing?" he snapped. "Urvi is Akshita's sister, isn't she? Not only that, it would look suspicious, all young girls travelling with me.

"Really?. What about Shaila?"

"She is my niece! Anyway, why are you sending her with me? Does Akshita really know about this?"

"What do you think?" Fanish smiled evilly.

"B.. But…"

Fanish's dark and sinister appeal was strong and overwhelming and Aditya felt there emanated from him a strong animal magnetism that almost frightened him.

"I thought you would like another young girl with you. Or is Shaila enough now?"

Fanish looked at Aditya shrewdly and a mocking smile curved his lips.

Aditya flushed as he met Fanish's eye, hating the fact that Fanish read his thoughts like a book. He knew and resented the fact that he was a weak man and wished he were a stronger one.

He looked at Shaila, who was talking to Urvi in the crowded foyer of the airport with a vague kind of pain. However, he suddenly glared at Fanish, his full sensuous lips open, and his expression furious.

"Fanish, I thought we had agreed that you are not going to interfere with my personal life!"

"And the same goes for you too." Fanish fired back in an icy voice. "Don't forget I know all about your debaucheries with young girls, very young girls who you use like paper napkins and then casually throw away when soiled."

"Alright, alright, Fanish you have made your point." Aditya replied in an aggrieved voice. "However, I would like to point out that whilst my personal life does not affect you, yours affects me."

"And how do you work that one out? Any one of these girls might report you to the police, and that would implicate me as well."

"No they would not." Aditya objected strongly.

"How can you be so sure?" Fanish raised his eyebrows.

"How can you be sure of your girls?" Aditya quickly retaliated.

Fanish scowled and flashed Aditya a burning hard look.

"You know that I demonstrate in every possible way to the girls that they belong to me and me alone! Anyway, we were talking about you and..."

Easy as a mask to take off, Fanish controlled his anger and masked it with an innocent look. And it was this innocent and guileless look that made him irresistible to women.

"I can always tell Sanjula, what you have been up to you know. I am sure she will only be too glad to know what is happening with her daughter!"

"No, please don't!" Aditya's sensuous lips hung low.

His upper lip had a slight shadow and tiny beads of sweat glistened on his lips. His dark narrowed eyes held Fanish's like a fly caught in a web of its own making, waiting to be pounced upon.

"Don't worry, Aditya, I won't say anything. Your personal life is no concern of mine, Urvi is going with you, no questions asked."

"And then what?" Aditya asked.

"Now that is a silly question. You know what you have to do."

Fanish's eyes were dark, opaque and told Aditya nothing.

"Alright, but I still don't understand why first Kanan then Vanita." Aditya murmured.

"Because, my friend, you said are not getting local girls and we need girls there. Anyway, I consider them to be seeds of weaknesses that were brought and then kept under my control, but I don't know when, under stress, these seeds might bear flower, and then, my friend, is the time we will really be in trouble."

Aditya knew that whatever Fanish said or did was never a natural outpouring of action but a calculated one, motivated simply and solely by greed and selfishness.

Sanjula joined them whilst Urvi and Shaila were whispering and Vanita looked at them sadly.

"Uncle, we have another girl who will be travelling with us?"

"We do, indeed." Aditya replied.

"But uncle, who is this girl, Vanita, she looks ever so young and sad." Sanjula asked.

Vanita's deep eyes had dark shadows around them and there was a disoriented look on her face, as if she was afraid of going to a strange place.

Her youthful mournful beauty touched Sanjula's

heart and her over-stimulated imagination thought Vanita was Tragedy itself and wondered what kind tragedy had befallen her?

Sanjula came out of her reverie to see Fanish's eyes fixed on her with a mocking gleam in them.

- - - -

Chapter 84

"Vanita is the daughter of a friend of mine." Aditya replied hurriedly. "He was to come with us too, but unfortunately something came up at work so I offered she could travel with us. Anyway, her relations will be meeting her there, so we only have to look after her during the flight."

Sanjula heard Aditya's explanations with a slight frown as Shaila came running up to them. She held Aditya's hand and looked up at him adoringly.

"When is the plane leaving, uncle? I don't like this place. It is too hot and there are too many people, and I am hungry!"

Shaila glared at Sanjula, her fists clenched, as she prepared her feet for kicking and readying her vocal cords for screaming.

"Shaila, behave yourself!" Sanjula said firmly. " If you don't I'll leave you here and take the first flight to Australia."

"Won't!" Shaila started screaming.

Her screams became deafening and she began to beat Sanjula with her small fists, then kicked her legs, determined to inflict on her mother some of the hunger and pain she felt.

"Shaila, don't cry, here, come with me. We'll have some ice-cream and play some more games."

Aditya looked down at Shaila tenderly as he offered his hand. He did not see her as a spoiled brat, but only as a thin earnest child with guileless tear-filled bright eyes set in the face of a cherub. As Aditya looked at her, he instantly thought 'innocence' and wanted to put his arms around her and protect her from 'time' itself, a ticking clock that would soon rob her of her purity and simplicity.

As Shaila put her small hand innocently in his and skipped alongside Aditya, Fanish looked at their receding backs with a queer smile.

"I don't know what I am going to do with her!" Sanjula exclaimed twisting her hands in a dramatic fashion. "She needs a father and Aditya is so good to her. She adores him!"

"Hmm. And I think I realise how difficult it must be for you too, all alone." Fanish took both her hands in his and smiled.

Sanjula's expression wavered then she smiled, unable to resist his charm.

"It's just that I do not know what and how to…"

Fanish leant forward, trying his utmost to dispel her reluctance, to soothe her, to make her feel the full force of his sympathy.

Sanjula was suddenly overcome with an unbearable feeling of sadness. Her deep brown eyes were liquid and swimming with unshed tears, so she was not aware when Fanish put his arms around her.

As soon as she felt his arms, she gave a shudder and pushed away from him. She hand came up quickly, on the verge of slapping Fanish. She was not quick enough, for Fanish caught her hand in mid-air.

"I am sorry." Fanish said with a voice that was soft, cultivated gentle and kind. "You looked so unhappy. Look, I know there is still some time before your plane takes off. Shall we quickly grab a cup of coffee? I think you could do with something hot to drink."

Sanjula had recovered her composure somewhat, though still confused and dazzled with the different aspects of Fanish's different personality.

"I would love that, but shouldn't we wait till Aditya uncle comes back?" Sanjula replied, clearing her throat.

"No, don't worry; I'll let Vanita know where we are."

He went to where Vanita was sitting desolately, had

a short conversation with her and made his way back, a look of amazement on his face. However, he smiled when he saw Sanjula and they edged their way through the crowd of people, and finally just when Sanjula thought it was impossible, reached the cafeteria.

"Why don't you get a table whilst I bring the coffee? Would you like something to eat?"

"No, thank you, Fanish, a hot cup of coffee is all I need!"

Sanjula found a vacant table and sat down, looking around her whilst Fanish got the coffee, headed towards her and placed the hot cups of coffee on the table.

"Thank you, that is exactly what I need."

"You know, Sanjula, I think of you as my niece too." Fanish smiled.

When Sanjula's eyes filled with tears he asked gently.

"Do you want to talk about it? I heard Aditya mention that you were having problems with your husband, is that why you came to London?"

"He is not my husband anymore; at least he has told me plainly that he does not want to be with me." Sanjula said miserably.

"What do you mean?" Fanish asked in dumbfounded amazement." Correct me if I am wrong, but Aditya told me you were married?"

Fanish leant against the gaudy plastic covered chair and took out a silver cigarette case with his name monogrammed in diamonds. He tapped loose tobacco from one end, then lit the other with silver lighter also monogrammed with his name in diamonds.

Sanjula slumped in her chair with a queer kind of angular grace that touched Fanish because of its complete abandonment. As he looked into her eyes, they seemed hypnotic and reached Sanjula's innermost soul.

"I... I..." Sanjula's misting liquid brown eyes spoke

what her tongue could not.

"Take your time., Sanjula." Fanish said gently.

Fanish handed her his handkerchief, which Sanjula idly noticed also, was monogrammed with his initials. She admitted to herself that he was a man with flair and style.

Sanjula took a deep breath and took a sip from her coffee.

"Thank you, Fanish, I am feeling better now."

"Would you like to tell me now what is troubling you?"

Mesmerised by his hypnotic charm, she explained to Fanish her conversation with Hetal, and briefly recounted the events leading up to it - as Manas had explained to her.

- - - -

Chapter 85

After she had finished put Fanish in the picture, she leant back with a sigh whilst Fanish sat silently.

Fanish was quiet for so long that Sanjula thought he had not paid attention to her as she poured out her heart – so, feeling disappointed at his indifference she began idly to notice the people in the cafeteria. They were people from all nationalities, some going abroad, some coming from abroad and some in transit.

Outside the cafeteria, she saw a crowd of people moving in all directions, all speaking in different languages. From over and above the airport, she could hear the roaring of the planes, either arriving or departing, and Sanjula felt the atmosphere at hand to be one of incessant noise and movement.

Sanjula glanced again at Fanish, and something in his expression puzzled and at the same time frightened her.

As soon as Fanish saw Sanjula looking at him, his expression changed and he moved slightly in his chair. He watched Sanjula with a quiet appraising glance, but still said nothing.

However, Sanjula felt his unspoken criticism and she sighed, suddenly feeling tired.

"Oh I see…so that is where…. I need another cup of coffee." Fanish said finally, pushing his chair back, a smug look on his face. "Can I get you a cup?"

Sanjula smiled, puzzled by Fanish's unfinished remark, and then shook her head slightly, for she had expected bewilderment, incomprehension or questions.

She sat looking across the room sat staring at the carpet, neither seeing nor hearing the stir of activity around her.

When Fanish came and sat beside her Sanjula looked worried.

"We have been here a long time." She said, looking at her watch. "I better go and check on the children." She rose from the chair.

"No need for that." Fanish waved his arm. "Relax, sit down. I glanced out of the window on the way here and happened to see Aditya with them. He gave me a wave indicating that when the plane was due to leave he would come fetch you."

The stiffness slid from Sanjula's face and her shoulders slumped with relief as her lips moved in a gentle smile.

Fanish looked at her and marvelled at her beauty. There were no hollows under her eyes and her eyelashes curled on her eyelids like fringes. In the stuffy atmosphere her cheekbones had become pink.

"Sanjula, you think I am heartless, don't you? I would love to help you though. Did you say his name was Manas but calls himself Hetal and is originally from Australia? I have contacts, as you know, and if you give me his address, I will see to it that he is safe and keep you happy."

Sanjula swallowed a number of times and wet her lips before she said softly.

"Yes that is right - but Fanish, what exactly is happiness? I think that it is like a sun that is seen through a blurred window and is a pale fuzzy- faced gnome who is only an illusion and, for me at least, happiness has always been accompanied by a shadow. No -one can put a finger on happiness or contentment. For me at least, it is can never exist in the present but only in the recollection of the past I shared with Manas. Ever since he left me I have been wondering what I can ever hope to get from a life that is so loaded against me. You know what I think? That maybe happiness is just the acceptance of the lack of unhappiness?"

"You are too young to be so cynical, Sanjula, you

have your whole life ahead of you."

"Somehow, I don't think so, I think it will always elude me, Fanish, anyway, I will give you Manas's, no Hetal's address, if you could keep an eye on him please? But please, please do not give it to anybody else., Oh, I don't have a piece of paper on me. "She said, rummaging in her bag.

"That is all-right, I have some." Fanish grinned smoothly.

He took out his diary and a pen and handed it to Sanjula.

"Thanks, Fanish."

There was a catch in her throat as she scribbled Manas's address and handed the diary back to Fanish.

"You are very cynical Sanjula. I am sure things will work out eventually." Fanish took the piece of paper with a faint smile.

Sanjula sighed.

"No, Fanish, I somehow don't think they will, there is finality about it all. However, my only compensation in all this mess is Shaila."

She looked at her watch and gave a cry of alarm.

"Fanish, I think we better go. Aditya has not given us a sign - I must go to Shaila."

Sanjula rose slowly to her feet, her legs trembling and feeling weak. She brushed her hand over her aching forehead as she tried to hold back her tears.

After some time, she calmed down somewhat and was wondering why and how Fanish managed to persuade her to confide in him. But she had been feeling vulnerable and did not realise that to Fanish she was only another woman to study, for he was keenly observant of the differences and realities of human personality.

"My dear, I admire you for what you have been through, all alone." Fanish said as he too rose from his chair.

317

He took Sanjula's hand and lifted it to his lips, flashing his eyes upward and smiling with the easy charm of a man who knows that he is a ladies' man.

Fanish had changed his opinion of Sanjula, and thought that her years belied her wisdom. There was a light of understanding shining from her eyes, which to him appeared more vulnerable and sadder than before, and the combination to him was appealing.

They walked back in silence where they had left Aditya and the others, but to their surprise the seats were empty.

• • • •

Chapter 86

Sanjula looked around her in alarm. She stood stiffly in the centre of the foyer, her hands clenched in fists at her side.

"Where are they? I have told Shaila time and time again not to move from place to place."

"Sanjula, don't worry. Aditya must have taken them for ice-cream or something. You know how he likes to spoil the girls. We'll wait here for them."

Sanjula sat quietly listening to the indistinct voices around her. After they had been waiting some time, she turned to Fanish, palms of her hands sweaty as she asked.

"Fanish, we have been waiting for over ten minutes. It would never take that long for an ice cream, and, you know, I cannot see our flight details of the computer screen."

"Sanjula, wait here whilst I go and check, but I am sure everything is alright."

He quickly up and disappeared, leaving Sanjula agitated and nervous. At last, when she felt she could not bear the tension any longer she turned to the elderly couple sitting next to her.

"Excuse me, but have you by any chance noticed a man with three young girls with him?"

"Of course we did. Such nice girls they were. Have you come to see them off? I am afraid you are a little late because…."

The lady with the white hair smiled at her, her eyes twinkling. …

Sanjula hastily interrupted her. "What do you mean too late? What has happened to them?"

"Nothing has happened to them, my dear. They have just done what they came here to do. I saw the gentleman disappear with the three lovely girls into the duty free. That's right David, isn't it?" She turned to her husband who nodded his head.

"But that is not possible!" Sanjula gave a wild cry. "That was my daughter! No, you must be mistaken, for I was supposed to go with them! No, madam, you must be mistaken."

"I think not." The lady with the white hair replied gently, seeing the distressed look on Sanjula's face. "I remember because one of the girls was crying, no, screaming for her mother, and I had to give her a sweet to keep her quiet."

"How long ago was that?" Sanjula whispered.

"It must have been about 15 minutes ago. The plane must have taken off because…my dear, are you alright?"

Sanjula had gone pale. She was confused and bewildered, for how could her uncle leave without her, and to take Shaila with him? No, she thought, looking around dismally for Fanish. There must be another explanation for he had seen them about 15 minutes ago, maybe they both were mistaken, but by now her internal mother's instincts were screaming, telling her that something was terribly wrong and somehow Fanish was responsible.

Sanjula did not know for how long she sat there, unblinking and unfocused, her hands lying loosely on her lap, when she heard Fanish's voice.

"Sanjula, I have not been able to locate them. Maybe they have gone to a shop outside or …"

"Of course you could not find them because they have left, left without me! My Shaila is gone!" Sanjula began to cry hysterically.

The lady sitting beside Sanjula had been listening and she turned to Fanish and repeated what she had seen.

"Oh no!" Fanish's lips tightened in anger.

When he looked at Sanjula, he was reminded of a

flickering flame under the cover of his hand when he tried to keep it aflame against the wind – its flare would first be nearly crushed and would shrink to the point of going out, and then just as suddenly would spring to life again. The expression on Sanjula's face was similar, for it wavered between hope and fear.

"I shall go and confirm from the lady at the air-line counter." he said hastily.

Fanish disappeared again and re-appeared after ten minutes, his face grim, and saw that Sanjula was sitting in exactly the same position as he had left her.

"You are right, Sanjula, the flight has left." he confirmed as he ran his hand through his hair.

"Oh no, Fanish! That means Shaila has gone without me!" Sanjula cried in anguish.

"But don't worry; I'll see what I can do. That......"

Sanjula had not heard the tone in Fanish's voice before. It was not arrogance or temperament; it was something far beyond that, a deep controlled rage. However, what was even more frightening and grotesque to Sanjula was the fact that it emanated from a face that looked even more genial than ever.

"But Fanish, how did this happen? How can Aditya uncle take Shaila without me? You told me he knew where we were?" Suddenly she had an idea. "Fanish, can you book me on the next available flight? Yes, that is what I will do. "

Sanjula quickly got up, her mind now focused only on one thing – she had to be with Shaila for Shaila was her sun - and if that sun ever went out or away from her, Sanjula felt her shadow would die. She could not, and would not under any circumstances allow that to happen.

"Yes that is the best course of action - and that should not be a problem since you have not only missed your flight but your daughter has gone without you. They will put you on the next available flight."

Fanish led the way back through the crowds to the counter as Sanjula followed.

There was a queue at the airline counter and they had to wait a few minutes before Sanjula faced the receptionist.

"I have missed my flight to Brazil and would like to be booked on the next flight. My uncle and daughter have left on Flight 606 it was…how long ago did it leave?" Sanjula spoke in a rush.

"Please calm down, madam." the receptionist's hands flew across the keyboard of the computer. " Flight 606 took off about half an hour ago."

"Can you tell me if my Uncle, Aditya, and my daughter, Shaila were on the plane?"

"May I see your identification, please?"

"I don't have anything on me!" Sanjula shouted. " My baggage is on the plane!"

"Can I see your passport?"

"No my uncle had it with all the other documents. Fanish, tell her, I must to be on the next flight to Brazil."

"I am afraid without your passport that would not be possible."

"Can we see the manager?" Fanish demanded in his authoritative tone.

The airline receptionist disappeared and came back a few minutes later followed by a tall gentleman wearing a dark suit.

"Now what is the problem here?" the manager asked as he took them aside.

Sanjula explained again, feeling more and more frustrated.

"And you have no identification whatsoever with you?"

"I have not!" Sanjula snapped. "Look, I have explained everything to you before – all I want is to be booked on the next flight to Brazil and confirm whether my daughter was on flight 606. In fact, when you bring up all the flight details, it will show that I was booked on it."

"Just a moment, maybe under the circumstances...."

Sanjula waited impatiently whilst the manager fiddled around with the computer.

"Did you say your name was Sanjula?" he asked after some time. "I am afraid, madam, there is nobody of that name booked on the flight you mentioned."

"But that is not possible! What about the name of my daughter? Her name is Shaila. I confirmed her booking this morning.!

"Yes, her name is on the list."

"But I do not understand - Fanish, Aditya uncle told me you booked my tickets."

"No, there has been some misunderstanding he told me he was going to book yours himself. Something about the details...." Fanish lied easily, watching Sanjula with interest. "We can discuss this when we are at home and..."

Sanjula gasped frenziedly as she fought with Fanish, whilst he tried to hold her, but Sanjula was beside herself.

"I want my daughter...." Sanjula screamed.

Fanish put his arm around her whilst he covered his bleeding lip and said indistinctly.

"Sanjula, my dear, let us go home and..."

Sanjula came to wild life at the touch of his arm and her hand pushed it with a force that amazed Fanish.

"I am not going anywhere!" she cried vehemently. "I am not going anywhere, especially with you. I want my daughter. I don't believe that it possible that uncle did not book my ticket. Why, he was always so nice and he adores Shaila."

Fanish looked at her with a queer smile on his face. "Maybe that is why he took Shaila."

"What do you mean oh I want to go to the police." Sanjula said abruptly. "Why can't I take the next available flight?"

"The next flight is tomorrow, but calm down Sanjula, I think there has been a misunderstanding on Aditya's part. He thought you were coming with me in tomorrow's flight, and the only stupid thing he has done is take your passport. Even that was not intentional I think and you have no passport, no, I will not let you do anything without first thinking of the alternatives." Fanish took Sanjula's arm firmly and propelled her towards the exit.

"Fanish, leave me alone! I do not want to leave here without Shaila!"

"Calm down, Sanjula and listen to me. I know where Aditya will be staying. I will phone him as soon as he arrives and I will arrange for an emergency travel document to be issued to you."

"B..but…"

Tears again flooded Sanjula's eyes and smeared her mascara and she furtively tried to blot them away.

■ ■ ■ ■

Chapter 87

Fanish took his place behind the wheel silently. He switched on the ignition and backed the car out steering the car with his strong, well - cared for hands and easy and casual grace.

Sanjula sat on the seat next to him with red eyes. She was crying uncontrollably and the handkerchief that she used to wipe the tears was damp.

As she gazed out of the window, everything appeared silvery bluish and unreal. The moon was big and bright, and to Sanjula it seemed as if it was smiling mockingly and teasing her, for dark long clouds would flash briefly across its silvery globe, appearing cheerful one minute and sinister the next.

"Ah, here we are." remarked Fanish, parking the car outside his terraced house. "Now, Sanjula, do not worry. I know it is not easy, but we have to wait patiently till I talk to Aditya."

"Okay, Fanish, I will try, but it is not easy. I keep seeing Shaila's laughing face...I wonder what she is thinking at the moment, if she had had something to eat?"

She walked with Fanish up the path leading to his house.

"Akshita, we are home!" He called, depositing his keys on the landing table. "Akshita is my wife." He explained as they went into the lounge. "It appears she is not at home so I will make you a nice cup of hot coffee."

Fanish disappeared into the kitchen whilst Sanjula threw herself into an armchair, sobbing. After some time, she stood up and started to pace the room restlessly.

The wind that was howling outside came in through the crack in a window and blew a vase of crystal roses from the table. Sanjula stared at the crystal pieces and the scattered petals in horror, as if the wind was trying to convey something to her, a sinister suggestion that Sanjula would rather not think about.

"Here drink this." Fanish handed her a mug. "I guarantee it will make you feel better."

"I don't think anything could, not till I know Shaila is safe."

Nevertheless, Sanjula took the mug and drank the coffee, wondering how the airline had let three girls travel unescorted, then remembered that Aditya had told her that he knew people in the airline. And she herself had booked and confirmed Shaila's ticked. Was it just a misunderstanding or was there something more sinister?

"Would you like another cup?" Fanish asked, stretching out his hand for her mug.

"No, thank you, that was nice and hot." Sanjula replied, feeling drowsy.

She rubbed her eyes like a child, for it was not her intention to go to sleep but to think of ways and means to be with her daughter.

"Why don't you go to bed Sanjula? I can only phone Aditya in the morning, the flight will arrive then, till then there is nothing we can do."

"But I want to...I suppose you are right, I can't."

Sanjula closed her eyes in weariness, but felt as if she could wait half a century patiently, if only to she could be with Shaila.... she would never again scold her; give her all the ice-cream she could eat....

Fanish led her up to the guest-room where she fell asleep instantly.

▪ ▪ ▪

Chapter 88

"Aakar, where is Urvi?" Aninditi asked as she laid the table. She looked at the clock on the wall worriedly. "She is usually home by this time."

"Aninditi, do not fuss! I have told her not to go with strangers, and that includes Fanish, though she was puzzled and confused for she likes him"

Aakar was sitting in his armchair reading his newspaper with his reading glasses on his nose. He was home early as he had not been feeling too well.

"How can I not worry, Aakar? You know, I feel that Fanish is like a time bomb waiting to explode in our lives. He has his eye on Urvi and…"

"Aninditi, don't worry, Akshita has everything under control."

Aakar flipped over a page of his newspaper as the door- bell rang.

"That must be Urvi. Aninditi, I told you there is no need to worry. You keep forgetting that everything has been explained to her and that she is not to go with Fanish under any circumstances."

Aninditi hurried to the door and Aakar heard an exclamation of surprise. He looked up as she entered the room with Akshita at her heels.

"Akshita, what are you doing here?" Aakar looked up in surprise as his reading glasses fell from his nose.

"Dad, I have left him. I have left Fanish and I am never going back." Akshita exclaimed quickly and vehemently.

"But why?" Aakar asked. "I thought you were

managing and…"

"I cannot bear to be in the same room as him. I have not and will never be able to live with his deceitful and cunning tactics."

"Akshita, what have you done?" Aninditi and Aakar both said at the same time.

"Mum, Dad, whatever is the matter? Where is Urvi?" Akshita asked in alarm.

"She has not come home as yet. Did you tell Fanish you were leaving him?"

"Yes, I left him a note." Akshita whispered, feeling nauseous.

"When? What time?" Aakar asked urgently.

"I left a note for him this morning."

"And it is nearing tea-time now!" expostulated Aakar. "He's had plenty of time to…"

Aakar groaned and put his head on his hands.

"Dad, what are you saying?" Akshita felt futile and helpless and the same time was filled with anger.

"You should have let us know immediately what you were planning to do. We would not have let Urvi out of our sights but kept her safe and protected. Now…Oh my God, Akshita how could you?"

"Fanish must have come home early and read the note." Akshita looked from one parent to the other. "I thought you had warned Urvi not to go with Fanish under any circumstances?"

"Of course we did, but she is a child after all and considers Fanish to be her brother."

Aninditi replied in a pitiful voice, wringing the corner of her sari in her hand.

"Fanish has abducted her… Aakar, do something, ring up the police or…!"

"They won't do anything, Aninditi."

"What do you mean they can't do anything?"

"The person has to be missing for 48 hrs before they

take any action."

"Anything can happen in the meantime to my baby. Akshita, ring up Fanish."

At the same time the telephone rang and Aakar hurriedly picked up the receiver.

He shouted into the mouthpiece, then put the palm of his hand on it and spoke to Akshita.

"Akshita, it is Fanish, and he wants to speak to you. Now don't mention Urvi unless he does."

Akshita shook her head.

"You must." Aakar handed her the phone.

"Okay" Akshita said tearfully taking the phone "Hello Fanish."

"Akshita?"

Fanish's voice dropped to a husky whisper, and Akshita's heart began to pound in her chest, for by now she knew that whenever it did, he would have something particularly bitter and hateful to say.

"Just thought I would let you know that you and your parents need not look for Urvi."

Fanish's voice was hard and cold and fully in control of any anger he was feeling.

"What do you mean? Fanish, don't hang up one me. I'm sorry about the note, I was angry. I will come back and not say a word to anyone, but please tell me where Urvi is…Fanish?"

Akshita looked down at the silent receiver in her hand then threw it against the wall.

"What did Fanish say?" Aniniditi asked fearfully.

"Just that there is no need for us to look for Urvi. Mum, I think he has done something dreadful to her."

"Now will you do something?" Aniniditi faced her husband.

"You are right…." Aakar went to the wall to recover the receiver and started dialling.

"Mother, I am so sorry, please don't cry."

Akshita went over to her mother and put her arms around her, but started sobbing too. How could she explain that her action to leave had been the culmination of a long train of repressed rebellion?

"Don't blame yourself." Aninditi replied sniffing. "He would have taken her at one time or another."

Akshita began to pace the room restlessly and her eyes were glistening as she crossed the room.

"I have spoken to everybody I know."

Aakar sat wearily in the chair, and as he looked out of the window, saw some of the twilight filtering through the grey clouds.

"Akshita, what is the matter?" Aakar raised his eyebrows for he had seen Akshita open her mouth as if to speak.

"I don't want mother to know but…"

"Akshita, if it has something to do with Urvi's disappearance, or if there is anything can shed light on, I don't think she will be not being worried, only grateful for it would help us to speed matters."

"I think she will, Father, for I heard Fanish on the phone yesterday evening. He was booking flight tickets for his business partner, his niece and two other girls."

Aninditi had entered the room and overheard Akshita.

"No, you must be wrong, Akshita! Even Fanish could not be that cruel. And if he knew only today that you had left him, he could not book the ticket in advance unless….no there has to be a mistake." She started to scream

"Akshita, look after your mother. I am going to talk to Fanish."

Aakar drove fast and only stopped once he was outside Fanish's house. He opened the car door and quickly ran up the path, but before he could ring the bell, Fanish had opened the door and was standing in the doorway, a mocking smile on his lips.

"You bastard!" Aakar yelled.

"Come in, do." Fanish held the door open for Aakar to enter. "I am sure I only owe the pleasure of your visit because you want to find out about Urvi, my pretty young sister in law?"

"How dare you!" Aakar hissed through clenched teeth. "What have you done with her? Tell me where she is or else…"

"Or else what, father-in-law?" Fanish threw back his head and laughed unpleasantly. "It is alright when it is some other young girl, but nothing must happen to your own, is it? How come you are not wearing your mask today?" Fanish eyes gleamed maliciously.

■ ■ ■ ■

Chapter 89

"Fanish, what in the devil's name are you talking about?" Aakar swung around and faced Fanish, his face pale.

"I think you better sit down, father-in-law; I think you know what I am talking about."

"No, I do not." Nevertheless, when Aakar sat down, his face was pale and his hands were trembling.

"Oh, how come you are not wearing your mask today?" Fanish repeated his eyes gleaming.

"How do you know?" Aakar repeated softly.

He heaved his shoulders and glared at Fanish, his sensitive face showing the play of emotion on it.

"Vanita, of course, she saw the photo we had taken early in the year, with me Akshita, Aditya and of course you and Aninditi and she went beserk with fear. So before she left, Vanita told me, and boy was I surprised! How can you call yourself a man of the law?" Fanish said contemptuously. "My dear father-in-law, you do not serve justice, nor do you help to bring conviction to the guilty. You most certainly do not in any way deliver an innocent man from the shadow of guilt, like you portray. Rather, you only make sure he stays there."

"Do what you have to with me, Fanish; just tell me where my daughter is." Aakar pleaded. "Why bring Urvi into this?"

"And this from a man who...?" Fanish raised his eyebrows.

"What have you done with Urvi?"

"Father our business abroad was failing. We had some very good clients, like yourself, who needed a girl just like your Urvi...so!"

Aakar put his head in his hands and groaned.

"You have sent her abroad?"

"I have, with Aditya.... oh...and Vanita as well. You should not have let her live."

"I asked Shubi to send her abroad for I am not a murderer."

"Oh, I told Aditya too, but you know Aditya, he is so weak and can be manipulated oh so easily by a young girl. Anyway, your secret is now safe with me." Fanish sat with his arms folded, a faint sneer on his face.

"Fanish you cannot get away by sending Urvi abroad, what do you have to gain by it?" Aakar said as he wiped the sweat from his forehead.

"What else was I supposed to do, Akshita left me no choice. And this way I have gained your silence."

"No, it had nothing to do with Akshita leaving; you had already booked the flights for the girls."

"You are right, I had already planned to take her before Akshita left, but I had to ensure you silence."

"But you said Vanita only told you before she left, so you were planning on taking Urvi? But why? I had made a promise to you that I would not take any action." Aakar replied. "Akshita is married to you, and in spite of everything, I do love my daughters."

"How do I know you would not have changed your mind? And you say you love your daughters? Hah! I think you will have a difficult time in trying to convince them of that if they know the truth, don't you think? Even I am not as depraved as you, for at least I not a hypocrite, and I do not flay the skin of innocent young girls just for sheer pleasure, amusement and the gratification of my lust." Fanish looked at Aakar with loathing.

"But tell me one thing how could you spend so much on a police salary? Or have you been stealing too?"

"I inherited a lot of money from my uncle...."

"Which, I presume Akshita and your wife know nothing about?" Fanish said nastily. "My you are a piece of work"!

Aakar got up and took a step towards him and seemed on the verge of hitting him, then stopped. The control it took to keep his hands at his side made them clench them into fists, and a white line etched around his tightened lips.

It seemed Fanish had, as usual, everything under control, even fate. It had often dared it to stop him but had always felt he was free to run his own course and had nothing to fear,

• • • •

Chapter 90

"Fanish, listen to me, I want Urvi back here one way or the other."

"Oh, really? Don't forget that what I did with Urvi I can do with Akshita as well and your wife, she is young enough still. And you don't want to lose both of them, well three counting Urvi, do you?"

"Fanish, I am not joking, I will inform the police...!"

"If anything, and I mean anything, happens to me, father-in-law, I will not hesitate to implicate you. No, I don't mean implicate, I will tell them the truth."

"And what is the truth, Fanish?" Slowly Aakar smiled in a way that sent chills down Fanish's spine.

Aakar turned his head slightly and gave Fanish an unpleasant grin.

"That you, Aakar, not only do you encase and enslave girls, but insult and degrade their childish innocence for your selfish gratification."

"And so what if I do? Anyway who do you think they will believe, a respected commissioner or a child/drug trafficker?"

A dark ugly look glittered in Aakar's eyes for a moment then the expression was covered by one of bland benignity again.

Aakar had two sides to his nature; on one hand he was a loving family man, and the other, a pervert who could not control his warped desires. How could Aakar explain to Fanish that he loved all the girls he chose as preys to his depravities? He would look at their sweet innocent bodies and just when Aakar was filled with selfless tenderness, all at once and ironically, lust would swell again and at that moment Aakar thought the girls to be immortalised demons who were only disguised as female children, or who were sent by the devil to seduce him. They would tempt him, then haunt him with a terrible pain in the very root of his being. He thought the girls to be an intriguing combination of part child, part seductress and part devil.

But, after the moment of tenderness, he wanted to punish the girl who aroused such feelings in him, and it was then that he felt that he; the prey, met the captivated hunter.

Mountains of longing always accompanied the mists of tenderness that enfolded Aakar. However, with the ebb of lust, a sense of despair would sweep over Aakar and his passion would turn to shame and despair.

Although he did not like to admit it, he knew himself to be like Aditya; no he was much worse for Aditya was not a hypocrite and did not harm the girls. But both of them, he felt, were held together outside the web of law, yet bound together by their sick perversion.

He was sure that each had their own tragedy and meaning to their life story and that somewhere in the interplay of characters and emotions lay the truth as to why they were slaves to their perversion.

"Who do you think the police will believe you or me, a respected judge?" Aakar repeated laughing unpleasantly.

"Oh it will be your word against mine, oh, I forgot and Vanita's and Aditya..." Fanish answered viciously.

"I thought Vanita left the country?" Aakar's trembling hand wiped his forehead.

However, he looked at Fanish thoughtfully and had a sudden insight into how a general felt when faced with an opposing army who outnumbered his, was equipped with better arms or had a better strategy to attack with.

Fanish waved the interruption aside.

"Ah, but I know where they are, and I can call them back at any time."

"Okay Fanish, you win, now tell me how are you

getting Urvi back!" Aakar demanded.

At the same time a feeling of sheer cold panic crawled down his spine.

"No, I think you already know that I will never happen. And that is all I have to say to you, I have to go now to meet some friends."

Aakar got up slowly from his chair, looking haggard. He had always felt ashamed of his needs, and had taken considerable care not to be recognised. He was only glad that Fanish was not aware of how deviant and perverse his appetite really was.

If a young girl was not available, he could always indulge himself by obtaining a slender, supple- waisted, good looking young boy with firm thighs and a see through shirt whose room, food and tuition costs he could support, if need be.

"Oh, and tell Akshita to come back. I haven't had a proper meal since she left."

"You bastard! No, Akshita is not returning so you can hold her hostage too. You have one of my daughters and..."

"So I have." Fanish said meekly. "Maybe you are right; I do not need her, anyway. Good-bye, father-in-law, no I am ashamed to call you that."

He escorted him forcibly towards the door and opened it.

"Good-bye!" he repeated. Although the words were brief they were loaded with meaning.

As Fanish closed the door behind him he felt he had accomplished what he had sought out to do, which was humiliating and blackmailing a representative of the law. He had never quite got over the humiliation and pain the law had brought him as a child, when his father, his only living parent, had been jailed.

He had seen the law as Power, someone against whom he in his puny strength was helpless against. He had vowed that when he was an adult he would get his revenge, and had felt better once he made that resolution.

• • • •

Chapter 91

Aakar drove slowly feeling helpless and powerless - caught tightly within the web Fanish had built around him.

He felt that even the dripping of the rain and the howling of the wind were wailing his defeat. How on earth was he going to explain to Aninditi about Urvi? He knew he would have to tell his wife; the least he could do was to soften the blow.

He found Aninditi and Akshita sitting exactly where he had left them. Or maybe so much had transpired and changed for him that he expected everything to be different too.

"Aakar, where is Urvi?" Aninditi rose from the chair. "What did Fanish say? What does he want? And did you agree to everything he asks? Aakar say something!"

"Aninditi, what can I say? You better prepare yourself for some bad news."

"What has he done to her?" Aninditi whispered and suddenly sat down again.

Aakar ran his fingers through his hair and turned towards Akshita.

"Akshita, can I have a glass of water?"

"Of course, Dad." Akshita hurried into the kitchen a frown on her face as Aakar sat down beside his wife.

"Aakar, please tell me. I can't bear it any longer."

Aninditi tugged at Aakar's shirtsleeves and looked hopefully at him as Akshita returned and handed him the glass.

Aakar gulped the water and set the glass on the table.

"Urvi was kidnapped by Fanish, as you know, but not only was she kidnapped but she was raped and…."

Aakar was surprised at the ease with which he was lying about his daughter, but felt the truth would be much harder to bear, for his wife loved Urvi dearly.

Aninditi screamed and she flew at Aakar, her fingers reaching for his face.

"It is all your fault!" she screamed. "We should have got the police involved, no they are involved for you're the inspector - surely you could have done something …."

Abruptly Aninditi was quite, too quite. She threw back her head, stared at the ceiling and moaned. She reached covered her face with her hands then spoke from behind them.

"Where is she now? When can she come home so that I can look after her?"

Akshita was silent as she stood with her hands clenched on the arms of her chair. She had allowed the beauty of her love for Fanish to become shadows of grief, remorse, shame and guilt.

"I am afraid she will not be coming home."

There was finality in Aakar's tone that frightened both Akshita and Aninditi.

"What do you mean?" They most asked in unison.

"Fanish said that Urvi committed suicide and ……."

"You are lying, Fanish is lying. How can you believe what he says?"

Aninditi eyes were full of anguish and she started crying.

Aakar quickly went over to her and held her tenderly while she sobbed.

"There is no mistake, Aninditi. In this instance he is not lying for I met his friend who found her."

How….?" Aninditi whispered. "At least let me see her body, let me see my baby for the last time."

"She jumped into the river. This friend of Fanish's, he jumped in after her to save her, but unfortunately could not recover her body."

Although this was stretching the lie, Aakar thought it

to be far better than telling her that although their Urvi was alive, she was in a brothel abroad. He hoped, too that that would prevent more questions on the subject.

"It's all my fault! If it had not been for me, Urvi would be alive." Akshita was pacing the room. "If only I had not met him, if only I had not married him, if only I had not left this morning....!"

"Don't blame yourself, Akshita, he was planning to take Urvi regardless of whether you stayed with him."

Suddenly Aninditi came to wild life. Her eyes were a furious blaze of hatred through her tears.

"I told you, why are you sitting there? Why don't you arrest him or at least tell them about his activities? I am sure they are illegal."

"Calm down, Aninditi I have already done that. But I know it won't go far for we only have a verbal confession. Do you really think that either Fanish or his friends are going to acknowledge what they did? Or that they drove Urvi to suicide? And as there is no body so..."

"Stop talking of Urvi of a body." Aninditi snapped. "I don't know how you can take all this so calmly."

"It is because I know how the law works that I am telling you all this."

Akshita sat quietly, listening to her father. She felt a blend of painful guilt and remorse again as she thought how her young sister, someone as sweet and lovely as Urvi, had left life without once experiencing all the wonderful and beautiful things it had to offer.

Her eyes were the first to break from the frozen stare that had stilled her limbs. Akshita did not know what tormented thoughts passed through her head. One minute she felt she was in the room of her parents' house, the next she felt she was only visible in the manner of a chameleon which, sensing danger, makes itself invisible by merging into its background of leaves and grass.

341

Then she got up slowly from her chair.

"I am going to see Fanish." She said calmly and proceeded to leave the room.

"No, Akshita, you are not to go anywhere. Your mother needs you at this time." Aakar said desperately fearing his secret would be revealed.

"I need to be with her too, but I need to speak to Fanish." Akshita snapped. "Dad, please try and understand, I feel terribly guilty and I need to see Fanish. Don't worry, nothing will happen to me."

But however hard he tried; Aakar could not persuade Akshita to stay. She was so angry she wanted to scream at Fanish, to shock and terrify him. But above all, her tempestuous emotions were submerged in a tidal wave of striking back somehow.

■ ■ ■ ■

Chapter 92

A soft breeze was blowing lightly and caressed her gently as she went out in the night. It was a clear night and as Akshita looked up at the stars resting against the black velvet of the night she cursed the star which had written and sealed Urvi's fate.

Akshita drove recklessly and as soon as she had parked the car outside Fanish's house, ran up the path and knocked the door loudly.

"Fanish, come out, you coward! I know you are in there!"

Suddenly the door was opened and Fanish stood scowling in the doorway.

"Akshita, I told your father that I did not want you back here."

"I do not care what you told him." Akshita pushed past him.

"You too want to know about little Urvi? Your father did not tell you what happened to her?"

Fanish taunted and his eyes were gleaming with malice.

"He did - how dare you touch my sister with your filthy hands!"

Akshita flung herself at Fanish and her nails caught his cheeks and ripped deep gashed down the side. Fanish swung his arm and hit her hard across her face and Akshita fell to her knees screaming in agony.

"Akshita, will you stop shouting? I have not touched her, but I have a guest here who is sleeping. Why did you come back? Do you want me to ship you away like Urvi?" Fanish snarled.

Akshita looked up at Fanish.

"What do you mean send me away like Urvi? You have killed her - Fanish, your days of threatening and lying to me are over."

"She got to her feet and started pounding Fanish's chest.

"Is that what your father told you? And, no, I do not think so." Fanish remarked smugly. "You cannot touch me now."

His voice was suddenly gentle, but something in his soft voice warned Akshita that he was about to say something hateful and bitter.

"Did you father tell you what role he played in the scenario?"

"Why are you bringing my father into it? Isn't it enough that you ruined my parent's life by taking my sister's life?"

"I see he has not told you the full story. Of course he wouldn't, the coward that he is."

"What are you talking about, Fanish?"

Akshita massaged her throbbing forehead with the palm of her hand and closed her eyes.

"Sure you want to hear about it?" Fanish said calmly.

The wind had started blowing and when she opened her eyes, the room was dark. The darkness of the twilight turned everything into shadows and the atmosphere in the room was tense - was there a storm brewing, Akshita thought?

"I think there is something you should know; I am not the only bad person here."

Fanish's voice was hypnotising, soft and melodious as he told Akshita about Aakar and his depravities.

"You are lying, Fanish!" she stormed "You are two-faced, conniving and evil, you think everybody is depraved, even my father."

Akshita's face exhibited shock and disbelief, and then felt dizzy and disorientated as she felt a wave of hatred for Fanish course through her body.

She stiffened and lunged at him with her hands raised

and her fingers curled into claws as she boiled with rage.

"You are lying, Fanish; you are a two-faced and deceitful man who wouldn't the truth if it stared him in the face!"

"If you do not believe me, listen to this tape. What he did not know was that this house is wired and whatever goes on inside is taped. Actually, they were to keep you in order!"

Fanish caught her hands and with the other switched on a tape. Akshita's face paled as she listened to her father admitting to his depravities and the money he had spent.

" Now this is no longer your home so I suggest you go back from where you came from." Fanish said nastily as he opened the door.

Akshita was in a trance, her mouth dry with fright, but she hesitated only for a second before she let herself out in the fresh clean air. She drove with her mind in turmoil.

Her father was standing by the mantelpiece when she entered.

"Father, you.... Fanish said that you..."

"Sshh, you are upset." Aakar cautioned, propelling her to the sofa. "Your mother finally agreed to take a sleeping tablet and has gone to sleep. You spoke to Fanish?"

"I have, and you know, Father he accused you of..of of being a pervert who ...Those girls were sent to you to be whipped."

"I have no doubt he told you that. And a whole pack of other lies as well." Aakar said grimly.

"Dad, he said that..." Akshita looked at Aakar with eyes that pleaded reassurance.

"I don't want to hear what he told you!" Aakar snapped. "And I strongly advice you forget what he said also."

"I would not have believed him, Father, had I not heard with my own ears your conversation with him in which you admitted it! I heard the tape, for he has his house wired!"

Aakar grew pale and cursed himself for he had underestimated Fanish. He groaned and put his head in his hands.

"So it is true." Akshita whispered as a few tears trickled down her cheeks.

Akshita had thought that it was Fanish who was the one with a dark ugly past and present. She had never dreamt that someone as fine and noble as her father could have ugliness in his character - so much so that Fanish's vices dimmed in comparison.

She began to laugh hysterically at fate and its cruel deception. It showed her love whilst veiling ugliness and then vice versa. Her hurt and disappointment fluttered around the room like a trapped animal.

▬ ▬ ▬ ▬

Chapter 93

"Hetal, I am home." Ishika called out as she entered the house, Ekta in her arms. "Hetal, where are you?"

She saw Hetal sitting in an armchair, but he was lying very still.

"Hetal, wake up, this is no time to sleep!"

When he did not reply Ishika touched his shoulder to wake him and gave a scream.

For suddenly Hetal's head dropped forward in a twisted curious attitude. At the base of his skull, Ishika saw something that looked like a bright red lozenge that was staining the whiteness of his collar.

She screamed then stood in shock for a minute before she raised Hetal's hand and felt the wrist for a pulse that was not there. She went to phone the ambulance - and everything after that happened in quick confused kaleidoscope of motion.

"Is there someone who you would like to contact for you?" A policeman asked kindly.

In a voice devoid of all emotion, Ishika gave Anushka's number and within a few minutes she arrived.

Anushka was an attractive woman, though not very young, with dark hair and eyes and a general air of vitality which gave the impression of being both competent as well as intelligent, and Ishika was relieved to have her with her at this time of crisis.

"Ishika, what happened?" she asked, taking Ekta from Ishika.

"I do not know! I came home and found Hetal, I thought he was asleep and oh…it was awful. Who would do this to him? He has never harmed anyone in his life and…" Ishika gulped and started crying.

"Shhh...Here calm down. I'll make you a hot cup of tea.."

Ishika looked so disoriented that it frightened Anushka. She got up quickly with a cry as the police removed Hetal's body on a stretcher and pushed back the damp hair on her forehead.

"Ishika, drink this…do yu want me to inform your parents? I am sure your mother will come and stay with you. You should not be alone at this time.""

"What about Ekta? I have to look after her and…"

Ishika's eyes were transfixed as if she was sleep-walking and her voice was barely audible.

"You don't have anything to worry, Ishika; you know I will look after her." Anushka's voice was as gentle as her grip was strong.

"Abnushka, what will I do? I have no one, my parents will not come here, my sister has gone and ohhhhhh!""

"Here, take these tablets, Ishika, they will calm you somewhat."

How was she going to confront the lonely sofas, the empty chairs, the lonely furniture, the glittering windows which would reflect nothing but a lonely woman's face? She felt remote and colourless, as though the loss of the robust energy and zest for life that was Hetal had left her limp and exhausted, needing, oh, so badly his warmth and love.

She lay in bed staring at the ceiling and the pain of her loss engulfed her again. She started sobbing till gradually the tablets took effect and she dozed off into a dreamless sleep.

She woke in the morning and lay in bed, thinking of nothing, thinking of everything, remembering, feeling, and letting the past wash over her. She heard Ekta crying and got up from bed and opened the door when she heard Anushka's soothing voice.

Ishika relaxed, closed the door and went over to the window and watched the swaying tree that screened her back garden. It was a tall tree that looked as if it was wearing a brown and green skirt, waving arms that danced in the wind.

After some time, she went downstairs slowly and Anushka noticed about her an air of desperate tragedy. She slipped her hand in Ishika's, and saw a glimmer of her old smile for a moment before her face settled into its sobriety.

"Thank you very much, Anushka, I do not know what I would have done without you."

Ishika sat on the table and took a sip from her tea.

"I am glad you are feeling better, Ishika. The police phoned and want to see you. Do you have any idea who could have done this?"

"I can't understand it, Anushka, he had no enemies."

"Do you want me to inform your parents?" Anushka asked again. You need moral support at this very difficult time."

"No, I don't! Hetal's gone and my parents have and never will be of any support to me. And anyway, the only answer you will get is that my mother is very ill and my father is away on business. No, the only person I would like to be here with me is Vanita."

"I thought you told me that you did not know where she was?"

"I don't" Ishika pushed the hair from her forehead wearily. "However, I do know the place of one of her friends. I am sure she will tell me about her whereabouts."

Suddenly Ekta started crying and Ishika gave a start as she remembered she could not contact Vanita for Ekta's life depended on it.

She went over and picked her up, placed her fingers beneath Ekta's chin and smiled weakly and thought she would do anything for her daughter to protect her from harm.

"Anushka, I am fine now, I know you'll want to get home."

"Are you sure you will be alright?" Anushka asked gently

"I'm fine, Anushka, thank you again." Ishika smiled weakly.

Although Ishika was bitter and cynical about her parents, she missed them. However, she had come to realise by now that their parental duties were always mismanaged, as were any emotional points of contact between them.

She went about the rest of the day like a robot, doing the things that needed doing. With Hetal Ishika's life had had quality and clarity about it, and now that he was no longer here, everything to Ishika seemed unreal.

However, she felt that even in this separateness, there was a power that bound them closely.

■ ■ ■ ■

Chapter 94

"I see; do you mean to tell me that no-one by the name of Aditya is staying with you?"

Fanish clapped his hand over the receiver and narrowed his eyes as he spoke to Sanjula.

"Sanjula, it seems Aditya is not staying there." he spoke into the receiver again. "Yes, yes, thank you for your help."

Sanjula was sitting on cushions and she hugged herself with one of them. She was crying silently, great noiseless sobs that shook her body. Sadness was familiar to her, but it was now compounded with grief, despair and utter loneliness.

She wiped her eyes with the back of her hand and looked through the watery mist at the back of Fanish's head.

"Sanjula, are you feeling alright?" Fanish turned

"What do you think, Fanish?" Sanjula opened her eyes wide and replied with asperity. "I do not know where my Shaila is…!" There was a catch in her throat.

"Don't worry, Sanjula, maybe it would be a good idea if you joined Shaila, she will need you and…."

"Of course she needs me! But that is an odd thing for you to say, Fanish. Is there something you are not telling me?"

"It' about your uncle…. he…."

"He what? What is wrong, please, Fanish. I knew there was something you are not telling me."

"Sanjula, actually it is your fault. for you should not have left Aditya alone with Shaila."

There was a malicious gleam in Fanish's eyes as he saw the pain in Sanjula's eyes. He went over to the window and stood looking out.

"Why? Why shouldn't I have her alone with my

uncle?" Sanjula looked with alarm at Fanish.

He was standing with his hands in his pocket. "Why do you think your mother did not want anything to do with him?"

When Sanjula shook her head, he spoke in a jerky awkward voice as he told Sanjula about Aditya's weakness.

He dropped each word as if it were a cold hard stone that battered and hurt Sanjula. When he had finished she opened her mouth and the room was suddenly filled with an unearthly sound, like an animal in pain.

Fanish was handy with his malice and was glad to see Sanjula's torment. Fanish loved to make anyone miserable for it was only then that he was in his element.

"Oh no! Oh noo no!!! Has he been harming Shaila? I remember how he always wanted to be with her, bought her new toys, was always playing with her……ohhh I think he has harmed my Shaila…. But why didn't you tell me before?"

"I did not know for sure and after all he is your uncle.. But I did not think he would stoop so low as to include his family in his perversions – so much so as to kidnap his niece. Believe me, I am sorry and would like to help you. So whilst you were resting, I took the liberty, in case I could not get in touch with Aditya, of booking your flight to Brazil, for I presume you would like to carry out your search? I will give you all the information addresses etc. that are in my possession."

"Thank you, of course I would, but what about my passport? You are aware that I do not have one with me."

"Don't worry about that, for an emergency document can be issued to you by the embassy…. however, we will have to hurry for they close. I have something to take care of so will come back as soon as I can."

Fanish withdrew from the room, closing the door behind him and stood outside for a moment to listen with a smile at the cry from within.

Sanjula sat huddled on the sofa, her knees pulled up to her chest, grieving and not making an effort to get up to collect her things. She was grieving not only for herself, but also for Shaila's lost childhood and innocence. She cursed the decision she had made in coming to London, but most all getting in touch with Aditya.

Sanjula had wanted so much for her, but it seemed that all the magical dreams she had woven for her daughter had been trampled on by Aditya. She sat there for a few moments; unseeing, numbed by a defeat that was beyond comprehension, before she made an effort to get up to wash her face.

As she waited for Fanish she thought she would ring Manas and tell him what had happened to his daughter...she was sure he would have a solution to her dilemma for she believed that theirs was a true love, and true love to her was like a frail flower which even if it grew under solid rock would not be stopped from bursting through and blooming.

When she rang somebody called Anushka answered and told her that Hetal had been murdered and Ishika was sleeping.

Sanjula was stunned.... with one cruel sweep of her hand fate had taken one love and cloaked the other from her. However, she could not grieve for Hetal, for her love for her daughter and her safety were paramount to her.

"Are you ready, Sanjula?"

She was wiping her eyes as Fanish entered the room an hour later. He brought with him a certain liveliness that endeared him to most women. Sanjula, however, wondered if it was the light-heartedness of the true scoundrel, then shrugged away the thought.

They did not have to wait long in being issued with an emergency passport, so they were soon driving through the town towards the airport in silence.

The streets seemed full and Sanjula could hear the faint sounds of laughter. There was a constant noise about her yet Sanjula felt herself to be unseen, unheard and unknown as if she was an apparition, alone and silent.

It was autumn and the trees were a brilliant blaze of colours, which to Sanjula seemed like the years' last passionate love affair which would soon grow old and die from the cold bite of the winter.

They arrived at the airport and Sanjula handed her ticket to the woman behind the check-in and waited impatiently whilst the woman tapped expertly on her computer terminal.

"You have a one-way ticket ma'am and…"

"What do you mean one-way ticket?" Sanjula exclaimed then turned towards Fanish. "Fanish, I have to come back I thought …!"

"Now don't worry, Sanjula, I was not sure whether you wanted to come here or fly straight to Australia. Don't worry; Aditya will get you either one when you decide what you want to do."

"But how can I depend on Aditya after what he's done."

Fanish said softly. "You leave him to me. Sanjula, I think we should not read too much into his actions. Maybe it was all a misunderstanding? You do trust me don't you? And I also have other people there who can be of assistance."

"I have no choice…. I have to be with Shaila…. and oh …. sorry you were saying?" Sanjula turned towards the lady behind the counter.

"Smoking or non-smoking?"

"Definitely non-smoking! Actually I don't mind, but please could you hurry up?"

"Would you like the window seat or the centre?" The

clerk ignored her impatience and continued typing slowly.

"Err, window...but please...hurry!"

There was more tapping and finally a boarding card emerged.

"Seat 15 – Gate 29, have a pleasant flight, ma'am." The check-in clerk smiled politely.

"Thank you!!"

Sanjula grabbed the boarding pass and walked with Fanish along the long line of check-in counters.

Fanish ushered her to the departure lounge where Sanjula stood gazing at Fanish with gratitude.

"Fanish, how can I ever thank you for your help?"

"There is no need to thank me; in fact, you have been of help to me, and don't worry, there will be someone at the other end who will help you find Shaila."

Sanjula showed her boarding pass to the security guard who nodded his head, then turned to wave to Fanish and disappeared.

As Fanish watched Sanjula disappear, there was a happy complacency on his face as his troubles had been solved.

He had been trying to find Manas for a long time and Sanjula had unwittingly given him his address and Vanita was out of the country. Ena would make sure that Dilawar did not go to the police as he held that incriminating video, as for Akshita and Aakar, why they would be putty in his hands now that Urvi had been disposed of and Fanish knew Aakar's sordid secret.

There was no more sweetness or affection on his face, and his eyes narrowed into slits as he stood sombre and silent.

- - - - -

Chapter 95

Akshita could not sleep but lay in bed, thinking she was contaminated, a shoot that had grown from a wrong seed and then planted in the wrong soil. Her disgust of her father and guilt regarding Urvi were strong, and Akshita did not know which she felt stronger, the shame, guilt or revulsion. She wanted to kick, punch, shout scream or even cry, yet she was numb and moved about like a robot, neither feeling or showing any emotion.

Suddenly she sat up with a jerk as she heard a bang followed by a heavy thud. She ran out of her room to see her mother standing in the corridor.

"Mother, what is the matter?"

"It is your father…he went into the study and I heard a bang and crash…."

"Did you try to open the door?"

"I did but it's locked."

Akshita banged on the door, her heard thudding painfully. "Father, are you alright?"

When there was no answer, Aninditi cried,

"Call the police, Akshita; I know something has happened to him."

Akshita quickly dialled 999 and the police arrived within minutes and broke down the door.

A police officer tried to keep Akshita and Aninditi from entering but they pushed past him into the room.

"Where is my husband?" Aninditi cried.

When she looked at the gruesome sight, half headless corpse of Aakar behind the desk, she let go of a terrifying scream.

"Oh my God!" Akshita looked at what was left of her father, then took Aninditi arm and steered her out of the room.

She sat her in a chair, muttering quiet soothing

sounds and Aninditi put her hand in her daughter's silently. When the officer came into the room, both of them had their arms around each other in a fashion that made it hard to say which was the comforter and which the comforted.

"Officer, is he dead.... what happened?" Akshita asked tremulously.

"I am sorry; ma'am looks like suicide from the position of the gun." The officer saw that Aninditi was about to faint and said kindly. "I think you mother needs a glass of water."

Akshita nodded quietly, left the room and returned with a glass and a bottle of tablets in her hand.

"Here, Mother, drink this and have these tablets. They will help calm you."

"I don't want them, I want my husband, and I want my daughter."

"Ma'am, I think it would be good idea to do what your daughter says."

Aninditi looked at Akshita and the police officer pleadingly then took the tablets and gulped the water.

"But why did Aakar kill himself, Akshita. He must be mourning the loss of Urvi. If only he had spoken to me about it, we could have got through it together."

Akshita was silent; glad her father had done what he had done, for she knew that the truth always has a way of coming out...at the most unexpected moments. And her mother did not deserve to know the truth for it would have broken her, and innocent girls would be safe.

"Mother, come I will take you upstairs to your room."

"Maybe, Akshita, you are right, but I want to be, I have to learn now that...." Aninditi muttered as she climbed the stairs wearily.

After her mother had reluctantly gone to her bedroom, and the police officers had left the house, Akshita sat alone in the house till the early hours of the morning, her mind in turmoil.

In her mind there was only one person responsible for Urvi and her father's deaths. She was filled with an all-consuming hatred for Fanish and the web of reprisal wove its net tighter and tighter around her.

The woman that Akshita had once been, a kind girl with a passionate devotion and interest in all that was gentle, beautiful and harmless, had died. The Akshita that could once speak gently in her sweet young voice, could even laugh a little even when she was sad had become cold, hard and remote.

'I am going to see Fanish and make him see how he has destroyed our family'

Having made her decision Akshita quickly wore her coat and gloves and ran to her car.

The leaves from the trees were soaked in the aftermath of the storm that had raged the night before, and Akshita could see batches of grey clouds with dark streaks and the clear drops of rain on the flowers of the lawn garden sparkled in the weak morning sun.

Akshita started the ignition and reversed the car on the road, but later had no recollection of her drive to Fanish's house. She could only recall two things that were on her mind – one was an abiding inert sadness which was weighing her down - so much so that she sat behind the wheel of the car with her shoulders hunched and head tilted slightly.

The other was that she knew with clarity what she had to do. Perhaps her mind, which had been functioning on automatic since the time Fanish had told her about her father, had sighted it before but she had any conscious awareness of what she was going to do.

The thin rays of the early morning finally surrendered to the oppressive cover of the storm of the clouds. Akshita trembled as she heard a loud clap of thunder in the distance and then saw a jagged bright sword of lightening flit across the sky.

She saw the dim light in the window of Fanish's house, the house that had once been her home, where many of her dreams had been born then killed.

She silently let herself in with her key and crept to a small cupboard between the hall and the kitchen, where she knew Fanish kept his collection of guns. She unlocked the cupboard with a key that Fanish kept on top of the cupboard and selected a gun she knew Fanish kept loaded. She put the gun in her bag and opened the door to the lounge, grateful to her father for his insistence that she know how to use a gun for protection.

■ ■ ■ ■

Chapter 96

Fanish was sitting in a chair, smoking his cigarette, the glow of the lamp casting a shadow over his eyes, whilst his mind went round and round like a squirrel in a cage. As he flicked his cigarette ash in the ashtray, he wondered why he dragged his past with him all the time, why he remembered his cold room in London's slum, the casual but exciting atmosphere and the fun he had when he ganged up on the other boys.

He turned his head and his eyes widened in surprise when he saw Akshita standing in the doorway. He sat up in alarm for there was something lawless, wild and desperate about her.

"You! Akshita, I thought I told you to stay away from here? Ah, by the look on your face I see you have spoken to your father."

The words were uttered from a mouth that was a cruel line and his voice was thick and full of anger. His eyebrows dropped over his eyes as he studied Akshita slyly.

Akshita shuddered as she saw the expression in Fanish's eyes – a look that was cold, indifferent, and yet cunning – a look that was as far removed from warm humanity as polar ice.

Suddenly Fanish's eyes veiled and he shrugged.

"Akshita, you are not wanted here! Shut the door on your way out, thank you."

Fanish put the cigarette between his lips and inhaled deeply and after he exhaled, looked at her through the smoke.

Akshita felt disturbed, confused, bewildered and angry at Fanish's sudden nonchalance which further infuriated her. She was silent, but felt so nervous that she clenched and unclenched her hands. The windowpanes reflected her pale face; eyes opened wide and sharp with a wary fear.

She clutched at her bag and her tongue darted to wet her lips. Suddenly she gave a gasp as inch by inch she moved towards Fanish.

"Fanish, because of Urvi, Vanita and in the name of the other girls you corrupted, defiled and exploited, I am going to kill you."

Akshita took out the gun with a trembling hand and pointed it at Fanish. She had been speaking quickly and vehemently but her hands were shaking. Her eyes were wide, almost unfocused and she shrugged her shoulders as though to ease them of a burden

There was a flash of lightening and Akshita could see Fanish's face, and what she saw frightened her for his face was wild eyed and distorted in fear.

"You bitch! How dare you come to my house to threaten me, hey, be careful, that gun is loaded."

" Yes, I know." Akshita smiled as she pointed the gun and moved closer to Fanish.

Fanish got up from the chair and stared at Akshita with a kind of incredulity that further enraged Akshita.

"Don't shoot, you fool, I'll... I'll...."

Fanish's fear had abated, but even though he was furious, he now looked in complete control. He was hoping to shock Akshita into some kind of semblance of comprehension and intelligence.

"Don't threaten me, Fanish." Akshita replied coolly, even though she felt a terrible pounding of panic.

"You don't have the guts to shoot, Akshita." Fanish walked towards her then moved to grab the gun from her.

Akshita squeezed the trigger and Fanish slumped forward on his chin. His face was covered in blood, and as he fell his body knocked down a vase of fresh roses.

He was bleeding profusely, for the bullet had gone through his neck and the blood had splattered on

Akshita. Fanish made a terrifying gurgling noise as he looked at Akshita, then his limbs were still and his eyes were wide open.

"Oh, my God, what have I done?"

Akshita clutched her throat and backed into a corner as she looked at Fanish's body. She was trembling violently as she walked to the phone.

"I need an ambulance; I have shot my husband, quickly please!"

Akshita was gasping for air as she gave them the address.

As she waited, she looked at the fallen roses and recalled how lovingly she had picked out each one, some with their creamy petals ready to unfurl and others that were already in full bloom.

Akshita had always been a sensitive girl and every nuance, every rustle, even the faintest faraway whispers made an impression on her. However, now she felt cold and numb.

She smiled a slightly twisted smile as she picked the fallen petals of the flowers carefully, some of which had become stained with Fanish's blood.

- - - -

Chapter 97

The gun was still in her hand, whilst with the other she held on to the petals. Her face was pale and she was trembling when the police arrived.

"Ma'am, did you kill you husband?"

"Yes, I did, but don't you see I had to because he..."

Akshita's chin trembled, her head moved backwards and forwards in small movements and she had to force herself to swallow before she could speak.

The officer who had questioned her gave a hopeless shrug for Akshita was not making any sense. He took the gun from her hand and wrapped her in a blanket, then said gently.

"We have to arrest you for the murder of your husband. Do you understand? Officer, read her her rights."

Akshita was shaking violently as her hands were cuffed behind her back and she was led from the room. She looked at the body of Fanish lying a few feet away, but there was no sign of grief or remorse on her face as she thought of Urvi.

As she was led from the room Akshita felt like she was fluid, a flowing and sweeping fluid that never takes on a predetermined silhouette for a prolonged term.

She had killed simply and passionately, murdered without artifice or complexity, wholly driven by a bitter anguish that can only stem from a deep and loving nature.

However, Akshita did not think of it as murder but of emotional defiance, of rebellion, of vengeance, of a longing to be free and to set others free. It had come from the conviction that she never would have been at peace until Fanish was no longer alive to manipulate and control not only her, but young innocent victims.

She had ensured that Fanish would no longer make false promises of happiness that never materialised, of freedom whilst imprisoning young girls. Nor would he ever show understanding when there was no hope, show refinement with only animal enjoyment in mind.

For Fanish, and men like him, were like smooth pebbles that sparkled in dirty shallow water. However, she had boldly plunged her hand in it to bring out at least one such pebble to justice, and she was comforted by the thought that at least she had saved a few innocent children. She had killed the thriving weed, but not before it had tarnished a few flowering buds before they had a chance to flower.

As Akshita was led to the police van, wet dead leaves rustled under her feet like brown dried up ducklings. Autumn had set in, and the dahlias, which had been kept warm and alive in the late evening, would die in the night, so that by morning, they would have nothing but brown bulbs of rottenness to show.

As she got in the police van, she wiped her forehead and thought it was the innocent and pure that had to be protected so that they were not enfolded by wickedness.

■ ■ ■ ■

Lightning Source UK Ltd.
Milton Keynes UK
UKOW02f1816121215

264612UK00004B/44/P